I0716594

OFFSHOOT

Iris Kain

This book is a work of fiction. Characters, incidents, and dialogue are drawn from the author's imagination and are not to be construed as real. Any resemblance to actual events or persons, living or dead, is entirely coincidental.

Copyright © 2024 Iris Kain & Pirate Farm Books

All rights reserved.

ISBN-13: 978-1-957244-28-0

Also by Iris Kain:
Shadow Hunter
Eternal Spring

The Murphy Blackwell Chronicles
Sour (Book 1)
Sweet (Book 2)

The Blood Tribe Trilogy:
Blood Tribe (Book 1)
Blood Trials (Book 2)
Blood Treason (Book 3)

To the worlds that almost were.

OFFSHOOT

Chapter One

The haunting strains of Chopin's Nocturne No. 20 in C-sharp Minor poured through the window screens as August Webb stepped from his trailer into the steamy, thick Alabama air. The strains of classical music masked the soft hum of the machinery hidden in the shed behind his house. His eyes scanned the tree line—a movement born from months of habit—as he stretched under the meager canopy of wood and shingles sheltering his cinder block steps and pulled in a fragrant lungful of Appalachian air. He stepped out from under the shadows of his trailer into the golden Alabama sunset, which cast long shadows that danced eerily over the mountains.

August took one last scan of his surroundings before crossing the yard with calloused bare feet. Thankful for the canopy of leaves that sheltered him from the setting sun, he opened the door to the still and proudly eyed the dimly lit shelves in the small shed. Shelf after dusty wooden shelf displayed jars with lids, each labeled with heads, hearts, or feints, depending on which part of the distilling process they contained. The heads and feints he'd use again later to capture the remaining ethanol in the next batch of moonshine. The hearts… the hearts were where the money was.

Thanks to his father, August developed a knack for blending fruits and botanicals into the hearts, a skill that won the admiration—and dollars—of many back home in West Virginia. Only the trustworthy folks, of course. He wasn't a licensed brewer, and moonshine was still illegal for home brew, even in this post-prohibition era. August's father had no love lost for his own father, Earl Jefferson Jackson, and their relationship was strained. Despite his feelings, he respected the man's moonshining legacy enough to pass it on to his son.

August supposed other men might have taken pride in their children the way he prided himself on his booze. Children weren't an option for Ida and August, though. Not anymore.

The strains of Chopin abruptly ceased as he closed the door to the still. The sudden silence hung in the air, and August's gaze panned the mountains, ever watchful. A rustle in a nearby bush raised the hairs on the back of his neck up, but it turned out to be nothing more harmful than an opossum, its eyes glowing gold in the motion lights on the side of his trailer. The little fella waddled out and into the yard briefly before taking shelter in the shrubs where it was cooler.

Mountains in Alabama. August had known they existed, but had never imagined them to be this pretty. They weren't as high as they had been in West Virginia, but the emerald greens of the leaves and the peaks' smoky blues were just as beautiful. The dirt was redder here. And he and Ida were safer here than they were back home.

Far safer.

His grandfather, Earl Jefferson Jackson, had been born and raised in the hills southeast of Huntsville. Apparently, the man had owned a vast stretch of property between Huntsville and Scottsboro, and when he'd passed two years ago, he'd bestowed a chunk of his property to the grandson he barely knew.

The timing was fortuitous. August and Ida were looking for a way to leave town quickly, and Grandfather Earl had provided their salvation. August learned about the inheritance from a lawyer with an Alabama accent so substantial that he could barely understand him. The property had to pass through probate, which apparently was some doing since the man's kids—including August's father—had a problem with the land going to a grandson who barely knew the man. But Earl Jefferson Jackson's lawyer was as mean as a hornet trapped in a Mason jar and had helped the old-timer to build an indisputable estate plan. And that plan included ten acres of Appalachian Mountain property going to his middle grandson.

August and Ida said nothing to their families about leaving. August did one last shine run, scraped together every bit of the money he'd amassed distributing his hooch, and they'd loaded up their Ford pickup and a U-Haul trailer with all of their worldly possessions.

Now, they had their own house on a chunk of property in the Appalachian foothills. Their only neighbor for miles was a sweet hippie lady and her husband, who lived about a quarter mile away. She'd rapped on their door early one morning with a loaf of fresh, fragrant herb bread, still warm from her oven, when he and Ida had first arrived. Her bohemian dress and raspy voice reminded August pleasantly of Stevie Nicks. Her husband, who stood behind her the whole time with a proud, content smile, was the same height as she and sturdily built with a shock of dark hair and a firm, confident handshake. August could not recall their names, but he was terrible about that. The only thing coming to mind were Luke and Laura, but that didn't sound right.

It doesn't matter. You'll have plenty of time to get to know them later.

Plenty of time. It hardly seemed believable. The ghost of his grandfather and the legacy of moonshine had made all of this possible. August Shane Webb was a distiller of clandestine elixirs and bearer of a legacy despite his father's dispute. Who'd have guessed the money he'd saved would allow them to build a small house in the mountains? It might be a tiny cottage amidst the pricier properties nearby, but it'd be new, paid for, and theirs.

In the meantime, he'd reestablish his shine business in a new state—and this time, he could stay put. Hopefully, he'd have to get a lay of the land, meet some folks, and maybe get a feel for the local brew pubs. It'd take time, but he was good with people. People he could deal with. The Alabama weather, however, was another story.

The temperatures had grown so scorching lately that he'd pulled one of the air conditioning units from the window of their trailer and installed it on the shine shed. Ida had complained at first, but he left the one that cooled the kitchen and living room. They'd closed off the rooms down the hall and took cool showers at night to keep the heat from climbing too high. Most nights, they made love on the pull-out couch and took a second shower before finally climbing under the sheets together and going to sleep. Regardless of the heat, Ida curled up to his chest, her hair smelling of fruity shampoo and her body of that lily-of-the-valley soap she loved, a small smile on her heart-shaped face.

Ida hadn't been this happy since… well, for as long as he'd known her. Her home life had always had a pall over it—a fear that trailed her like an ever-present shadow. Now that they were over seven hundred miles away from her overbearing, God-forsaken family, maybe they stood a chance at happiness together.

August's gaze shifted to the wilting herbs in his elevated planter box, their once vibrant hues now muted in the fading light. The plants stood wilting, the strength in their stalks sapped by the unrelenting sun and lack of rain. August had planned on making his next batch of shine with a blend of juniper and rosemary, but the rosemary bush at the foot of the planter box was turning an unhealthy shade of brown. Watering plants with spigot water wasn't enough; they needed a break from the ungodly heat. August wondered if maybe something in the water supply was bad for them, too. He'd need to get that tested.

Buying bags of citrus fruit from the local health food store was an option; they sold oranges, lemons, and grapefruit in enormous bags for people who enjoyed juicing. His shoulders drooped like his tired plants. Yes, it was the best time of year for a batch of citrus shine; the fruit was at its peak, and prices were at their best, but he always found that the shine he made with local ingredients—especially those he harvested himself—did best. And he'd really had his heart set on a batch of juniper-rosemary. He could do both if he had the rosemary. He still had dried juniper berries from last season. The rosemary, though…

The herb bread the neighbor lady had brought with her had fresh rosemary. If it was from a bush of her own, maybe she had some she'd be willing to part with. Sure, she might have bought a pack from the store, and he could do that, but—*LaDonna. Her name was LaDonna. You spent the rest of the day singing Richie Valens'* Oh, Donna *after she left.* She seemed like a person who might enjoy growing her own herbs. Maybe it was just a suspicion that hand-harvested stuff tasted and sold better, but August always believed in a person's ability to imbue their crafts with a certain… influence.

The slapping of the screen door on its frame drew his attention to the steps where Ida stood, rubbing sleep from her eyes. Her corkscrew blond curls were in adorably wild disarray, and pillow creases still lined her face. It must have been some nap.

"Augie?"

"Mornin', Idabelle."

Ida smiled. Her parents had given her the name Dahlia upon her at birth, but she hated it and much preferred the moniker August had offered her.

"S'not morning," she mumbled sleepily.

"I was thinking of heading to the neighbor's house and seeing if they had some rosemary they could share. I figure they might have some, since they brought that bread over the other day. Want to come with me?"

Concern shrouded her face. Solitude left Ida wary. He knew she was not a fan of being separated from August, regardless of how quickly he'd return, but he always wanted to offer her the opportunity. One day, she'd be ready to stand on her own. Today was clearly not that day.

03   80

Marina's eyes were killing him. A deep, cloudy thicket of forest green, those eyes tracked his hasty movements around the foyer from under her pale lids. Those worried eyes pleaded with him to pause a moment, to give her some sense of assurance that he hadn't the power to give her. Standing on the bottom step of their staircase so she nearly reached his height, her blatant anxiety pierced his heart like a thorny vine.

"You know I hate this," she said. Her tone was scolding, but Wade Beringer knew his wife well enough to determine that the caustic tenor of her voice was all for show. Inside, her heart was full of concern. After seven years of life as a cop's wife, she knew this happened now and then. Because her husband's post stood in a small town like Gryphon, that tax didn't come too often.

"One more night," he said, shoving his flashlight under his armpit, feeling her stern scrutiny, and reaching blindly for where his jacket hung on the coat rack. Although it was not raining at the moment, the humid night threatened a long-awaited shower later. "Tonight's the bust. Then, it'll all be over for another few months. I promise." He found the jacket, went to put it on, and nearly lost his grip on his flashlight.

"That's what makes me so nervous," Marina said, her sharp tongue gone, replaced by one so concerned it wrenched his heart further. "Tonight's the bust, and only minutes before the big event, you come home for a *flashlight?* What—nobody had a spare? There wasn't one in a drawer or locker at the station you could use? That's a sign if I've ever seen one."

Wade paused and set the flashlight and his jacket down on the... well, he wasn't sure what it was. He'd call it an entrance table since it sat just inside the front door, past the coat rack. Marina would probably call it a "hand-carved console table," but to him, it was a relic from some old family estate. Sometimes, her eloquent ability to label things he'd never seen (or knew the words for) until he met her reminded him of the vast difference in their upbringing; it might as well have been a chasm between two worlds. While Wade's adoptive parents had done alright, they'd never become wealthy; ten years ago, he'd never imagined having a home with this much furniture. With his marriage to Marina, he'd gained a house full of it—and the house, too. He felt like he didn't deserve all the trappings of this life, and at times the house felt like a haunted mansion filled with echoes from the previous owners of the... stuff. Whatever it was called.

He had also gained a wife who foresaw portents in everyday occurrences. Raised in an overly superstitious, deeply Germanic home, she saw signs and omens everywhere, despite her belief in God— sometimes because of it. From tipped saltshakers to black cats, her urge to prognosticate the future was irrepressible, especially if the outcome was cursed. For a woman who had spent her entire life sheltered under her parents' golden wings, she harbored a strange tendency to expect the worst.

He stopped rushing long enough to look at her beautiful face straight on. Her wispy, light blond hair. Her oval face. Her lips, usually so pink and kissable, had disappeared as she pressed them into a straight, anxious line.

He stepped forward and embraced her, not sure if the pounding heart he felt against his jacket was hers or his. "Honey, if the Lord wants me to come home tonight, you know I'll still be alright."

"Don't say that!"

"But it's true." He let her go and gripped her arms firmly, dropping his head slightly to peer into her lowered eyes. "Marina, you know I will do my best to keep Zeke and myself safe. I'm not going to do anything stupid. I *want* to come home to you and Derek more than anything on earth—you know I do. More than *anything*. But this guy's been dealing drugs in Leland County for as long as I've been on the force. We've *known* it. We just haven't been able to bust him. He's even been hauled in for questioning on a couple of murders. He's a smart guy—too smart, sometimes. But he messed up, and tonight we'll get him."

Marina seemed to have found something on his shoes worth studying. After a long moment, she lifted her chin. "I know you won't do anything dumb, but even if you do everything perfectly, there are still accidents—"

He pulled her close, but she kept speaking, her voice muffled into a ghostly whisper by the material of his light cotton shirt. "And if this damn dealer is smart like you say, he still might—"

"Shh. It's okay. I'll be okay." He stroked her hair.

Her arms crept around his barrel-like middle and held him. He laid one hand between her slender shoulder blades and tapped her with the slightest comfort. Eventually, her body loosened as she resigned herself, accepting their fate. He let her go, and she took his hand where it lay there, pale and dwarfed inside his larger palm. "I just can't help but think that maybe the Lord brought you home to say good-bye." The last few words came out mangled by her clenching throat.

"Marina, you know that if I go, God will take care of all of us. He always does, even in our darkest times."

Marina rolled her eyes around their spacious home. "I'm not worried about money. You know that. I just..." she squeezed his hand so tight it hurt. "Just do me one favor."

"Anything."

"Come upstairs and look at Derek."

Wade's eyes shot to the front door, still swinging on the hinges where he'd left it, as he rushed inside for what was supposed to be a quick retrieval. His partner, Ezekiel Weidenseld, waited outside in the unmarked car with the motor running. Wade had said he'd only be a second. That second now hovered around two long minutes. In a make-or-break case like this, two minutes could make a difference between the planned outcome or the unexpected turn.

"Please?"

He wanted to say he didn't have time. He knew it'd save him several minutes of harassment from Zeke if he pecked her on the cheek and dashed out the door.

But what if she was right? What if the Lord had led him home minutes before the drug bust so he could have one last look at his family? He didn't believe that regret was possible in the afterlife, but if it comforted Marina...

"Alright. One quick look. Then I've got to go."

She smiled. Wade loved her smile, straight with that one crooked front tooth. Even now, as strained as it was, it was the realization of consummate beauty to him. "Thank you," she said.

Together, they ascended the carpeted staircase hand in hand. Once at the top, they followed the balustrade along the hall, which overhung the living area and the baby grand piano below. Turning left, they reached the portion of the hall that held the bedrooms (what Marina called the "recessed hall"). She let go of his hand and tiptoed to the second white door, which led to Derek's room. She always tiptoed near Derek's room, which Wade found highly amusing. Their carpets were so thick a battalion of soldiers could parade past the bedrooms, and no one would know. When Wade asked Marina about it, she blamed it on habit, which made sense. Nearly every room in her parents' mansion had parquet flooring—beautiful, but an acoustic nightmare.

Marina turned the handle slowly—another overly prudent measure, as the hinges and the knob were only a few months old. Easing the door open, they stepped into the rhombus of hallway light.

Derek lay sprawled out on his twin bed, his eyes closed, his breath even and quiet. Harry Potter decorations covered virtually every surface of his room: the duvet, the trim along the wall, the bookends, and the figurines. Derek, pale with his dark hair and his mother's green eyes, had taken a tremendous liking to the boy whose depiction was like the boy he saw in the mirror. Only six, he hadn't read all the books himself. However, with his mother's dedication and an agreement to help him read two chapters a night, Derek managed through the entire series. Marina insisted Derek hold up his end of the bargain, and now he could read words like "dragon," the names of the houses, and even some of the more complicated student names.

He rolled over and thrust his arm forward forcefully.

"Probably slaying dragons," Wade observed.

Marina gave him a wry look and whispered, "You really should read the books, Wade."

"Why? Between the two of you, I've got 'em down pat."

They backed their way out, Marina on her toes until she shut the door quietly but firmly.

"I feel better," she said.

"Good."

"I mean—not better. Not that everything's going to be alright, but... I'm glad you didn't rush out the door without seeing Derek." From the way her mouth stopped short, he deduced her need to bite back the words "one last time."

Wade glanced at his watch. Eleven sixteen. Only fourteen minutes to meet up with the rest of the team.

"Listen, I've—"

"Gotta go," Marina said, nodding, "I know. Go." She rose on her toes and gave him a kiss on the cheek. Wade took her in his arms and kissed her like a honeymooner.

Just in case, he thought.

☪ ☫

Sergio Vega checked his imitation Rolex with a flick of a thick wrist and a sigh. Eleven sixteen. Orchid's text said she'd meet him in the parking lot of the abandoned video store at a quarter after. Sure enough, his customer pulled into the parking lot only five short minutes after he had. Orchid eased her white Chevy Cavalier next to his Honda Accord so that their driver's doors faced each other. She was right on time, as usual.

Judging from his experience, people often were with their addictions.

He rolled down his window, letting in the humid Alabama air. A warm breeze stirred in the tree branches overhead, followed by a haunting stillness and the loud, irregular, droning song of the cicadas. Sergio wished Orchid had a less noticeable car. Hopefully, the frantically buzzing insects in the trees would be the only witnesses tonight. If he'd been thinking properly, he'd have asked her to meet him in the parking lot behind the bowling alley instead. It would've been a little out of the way for both of them, but the location was a better fit for her bright car. Less eye-catching. Bowling alleys were good places to meet, especially on the weekend; plenty of folks left their automobiles there after a few frames accompanied by pitchers of beer. Cops rarely drove by to see if anyone occupied vehicles abandoned for the night. It was the drunks who left the parking lot behind the wheel that concerned them.

The tall blonde who danced under the stage name Orchid — real name, Joan Nickel — stepped out of her car and stretched. Under the orange glow of the streetlights, her tanned skin looked like burnished copper. Judging from her outfit — plastic heels, a short mint-green skirt, and a lacy white tank top sheer enough to show off the bra underneath — she'd just gotten off work. She usually wore tight jeans, cropped shirts, and sneakers.

A Calvin Klein perfume he knew from a girl he'd dated in high school crept in through the window on the breeze. He extended a tiny, blue plastic bag of cocaine out the window of his Honda. Orchid palmed it discreetly, squeezing the bag into a hidden pocket inside her tight skirt.

Without a word, Sergio made to turn the ignition switch. She hadn't handed him any cash, hadn't spoken, but that was alright. They had an arrangement. He got to call her whenever he needed his fix, and she called him when she needed hers. Lately, hers were coming around almost nightly, whereas his need for her entertainment in the bedroom arose only a few times a month. Just before this trip, he'd considered that it might be time for him to renegotiate his fee — he needed the money more than the sex. Now was not the time to talk about it, though. Soon. Someday, when she really needed a fix. Then he'd renegotiate.

Cocking a long, tanned leg to the side and twisting her crane-like neck that made his head hurt, Orchid asked, "Don't you want to know if it's any good?"

"It damn well better be," Sergio growled. "If it's not, I'm going to take it out of his —"

"Yeah, I know," Orchid said, pulling the bag back out of the tiny hidden pocket. She pried the edges of the little bag apart and dipped a long, manicured finger inside. "He's already bunked you—what?—three times?"

Sergio cocked his jaw to the side and eyed Orchid angrily as she resumed her taste test. They might not be in the best neighborhood, but it was reckless to sample the product on the street. Desdemona Drive, the road along the front of the defunct movie rental store, was at the less-used end of one of Gryphon's main drags. Still, he waited.

Ignatius Irizarry, one of Gryphon's few dealers of illegal substances, was not in Sergio's best standing. Twice, he'd recently cut his product with what Sergio believed to be baking soda, and the last time, he'd added a substance that made his clients' noses burn. Anyone who knew their coke knew that the good stuff didn't burn. And Sergio's customers—the few he had—knew their coke.

Orchid wasn't the brightest woman he'd ever met, but there were two things she excelled at: her talent in the bedroom and her ability to discern the quality of her powder. Sergio never touched the stuff. Developing a taste for the product he relied on for side income was a bad idea.

Orchid scratched the surface of the rock and brought it to her tongue. She licked the substance off with care, her eyes rolled to the side as she judged the quality of her product. After a moment, her upper lip curled in distaste.

"Oh, Serge," she said, "This stuff is nasty."

Sergio hit the steering wheel with such force the Honda rocked. His frustration with Orchid was supplanted with rage toward Irizarry. *That son of a bitch!* "Tell me you're joking."

Orchid clicked her tongue on the roof of her mouth as if attempting to dislodge the flavor. "No, I'm not. I'm not getting any numbness at all, and it tastes…" She considered the next word as if she was at a wine tasting instead of on a darkened street parking lot describing a drug. "Minty."

"*Minty?*"

"Yeah. Like dried toothpaste."

Sergio's eyes closed. "Dried toothpaste," he murmured, thumping the steering wheel methodically. "I'm going to kill him. Does he think I don't know what I'm doing? Does he think my people won't know the difference?"

Orchid plucked another crumb from her tiny rock and popped it in her mouth, rolling her tongue around. "There's coke in there; I can tell because my tongue's finally getting a little numb. But if you want my opinion, it's probably cut with dried toothpaste."

Sergio stopped hitting the steering wheel and glared at Orchid.

"Don't look at me like that!" she cried. "It's not my fault. You'd save yourself a hell of a lot of trouble if you'd taste your bags first instead of coming to me to be your little lab rat. Why does he cut your bags, anyway?"

Sergio's mind was already traveling the distance to Irizarry's home, pulling into the driveway, shoving the short, skinny dealer onto the floor in front of his wife and kid, and demanding better eight-balls from him at gunpoint. He would not tolerate this kind of humiliation anymore. Not anymore.

"Sergio?"

Sergio leaned forward. His Glock 17 was where he'd hidden it before his evening's journey, delivering his wares like a pizza delivery driver.

"Why does he do this to you, Sergio?"

"He says I don't deal in large enough volume for him to bother with me anymore," he said. "He told me to either up my quantity or settle for dregs."

Orchid popped another crumb into her mouth. "This is dregs alright."

"Then why do you keep sucking on it?"

Orchid frowned. "No need to get snippy. If it was any good, I'd put it up my nose, not use it to fluoridate my teeth."

Surprised that Orchid knew a word with as many syllables as "fluoridate," Sergio cranked the Honda's engine and shoved the stick into first gear. Orchid's jaw stuck out with indignation.

"Don't go off all angry," she advised, pulling her toes out from where they risked tread marks. "You'll get yourself shot or something stupid, and then where will I get my—"

"You can always call Izzy," Sergio said. With a squeal of low-profile tires, he pulled the Honda out of the parking lot in search of Ignatius Irizarry.

Chapter Two

August had to give her credit: Ida never dawdled. In less than ten minutes, she showered off the heat of the day, filling the small, hot bedroom with the smell of her floral soap but no steam. He figured she kept the water cool in deference to the weather and the relocated air conditioning unit. He could have stayed in the living room where it was cooler, but he preferred to watch as she pulled on a pair of cutoff shorts and a flowing cotton top. She situated her curls into a bright headscarf tied in a topknot—an act she called "taming the beast." When she went to grab her sandals, August handed her a pair of brown leather boots instead.

"It's still too hot to walk, but I thought the motorcycle would be fun."

Ida eyed her clothing concernedly and bit the corner of her lip. "Maybe I should change."

"We won't be on the road but a minute. You should be fine."

"I've seen deer out there. And it's getting dark. And there are curves."

"True. I'll drive slow, OK?"

"Mmm… OK." She wasn't convinced, but she slipped on the boots while August grabbed their helmets and reflective jackets from their tiny closet. Her nose wrinkled in adorable distaste when he handed her the helmet—a matte black covering with Bell printed at the top in glossy black.

"Ugh. My hair," Ida fretted. She tugged the scarf from her head, and her curls sprang loose. Rather than discard her silk head square, Ida tucked it into a back pocket before using her fingers to encourage her blond coils in the preferred direction. "I can retie it when I get there, I guess."

They left the bedroom and shut the door to trap the summer heat inside, and he gave her a reassuring kiss.

"It'll be fine," he assured her. He'd gotten so used to saying those words to her over the past few months. Now, it was a matter of habit.

The sun was sinking below the treetops, and the heat hit them like a sauna as soon as they opened the thin metal door. Ida paused a moment to lock both the flimsy interior door and the screen door—a habit August knew would not stop the sort of people who once pursued them. But he wasn't about to deny her some small semblance of comfort.

Once seated on August's bright green Kawasaki Ninja, they navigated down their long dirt driveway before turning up the hill to their neighbor's home. True to his word, August kept the speed on the slower side to ease Ida's fears as they cruised through the deep woods. His slow pace served two purposes. In the handful of weeks following their move, August had noticed the peak of what appeared to be an ancient Victorian roof emerging behind a dense wall of kudzu and briers. He had never found the courage or the time to confront the overgrowth to uncover what lay beyond. The house was on their property, though, and now that he and Ida had settled into their trailer, he was curious to see what stood at the end of the lane. In the dusky evening light, August noted what he assumed was the drive to the old home. Years of disuse had narrowed it to nearly a footpath, and vines and tree branches obscured the view of what lay at the end. August made a mental note to record the path's location and put a little more speed on ascending the coming slope.

Ida's body tensed when they eased from the asphalt onto the neighbor's gravel driveway, but he handled it with experienced ease and navigated the bike to the large, gray house nearly hidden among a forest of mature trees at the crest of the hill.

After the engine died and Ida pulled the helmet from her head, she set to work retying her hair.

"I should have brought something. A gift," she said with a frown. "That would have been neighborly."

"Like what?"

"I don't know… some cookies, maybe? I could have made those molasses ones you like so much."

August chuckled. "If you'd made those, they probably wouldn't have made it out of the house because I would have eaten them all."

Ida smacked him playfully on the chest. "You are better behaved than that, Augie."

"Am I?" He gave her a wicked grin, and she blushed adorably.

Ida fell silent, her gaze drifting past August's shoulder. August turned to see their neighbor — the woman — stepping down a short stone staircase to meet them.

"Hello!" her friendly, gravelly voice called in greeting. "It's August, right? And Ida?"

"Yes, ma'am," August replied, taking Ida's hand. Ida held August's hand firmly but trailed slightly behind him. Their feet crunched on the dry gravel.

The woman chuckled, and her long skirt swayed around her feet. She pulled her long brown hair back. "No need for ma'am, August. LaDonna is fine."

"Yes, ma — OK. LaDonna. OK, LaDonna."

"Ida, nice to see you. Come on in," she said with a wave to motion them inside. "Luke and I were just having some sweet tea. Would you like some?"

"Um… sure," Ida said. Her eyes briefly met their neighbor's green ones before settling on the wooden floors inside the house.

The interior of LaDonna's home — *Whelen, they'd said their last name was Whelen last time* — was arctic compared to the meager air conditioning the window units provided for their poorly insulated trailer. August almost made a comment to that effect, but bit it back. No sense announcing right off the bat that they were poor. Ida was used to such simple luxuries and had left all that behind for a life with him. The Kightlinger family, from whom Ida descended, was steeped in coal money, lived among the wealthiest social circles in Morgantown, and had even more affluent relatives in Charleston. She never complained about leaving it behind; she spoke effusively about her love for their charming home and their life together. August wondered, though, how much of it was for his benefit and how much was genuine. Did she really not miss the grand homes, expensive clothes, and lavish meals? Was she truly happy riding on the back of his motorcycle when she once drove her own Tesla?

One day, he'd pay her back for her sacrifice. She might be safer now, but it had come at a cost.

☗   ☘

Fletcher and Amelia Kightlinger found it intolerable enough that Dahlia, their only child, had allowed that scoundrel, August Webb, to impregnate her, forcing them to whisk their daughter off to a rather questionable clinic far from the prying eyes of their churchgoing peers. No congregation member could discover what they'd done — they'd be scandalized. They were an integral part of the esteemed Presbyterian Church of America congregation, for goodness' sake.

Oh, how Dahlia had wailed! Amelia was uncertain if her daughter's tears during the procedure stemmed from physical pain or the sadness of her parents forcing her to terminate the unlucky result of her liaison with that damned bootlegger. It didn't matter. The transient discomfort of an abortion paled compared to the lifelong burden of being tethered to a criminal for the rest of her life. Dahlia was too naïve to appreciate their involvement now, but she would one day thank her parents for their wisdom.

Dahlia insisted in the car on the way home after the procedure was over that something was wrong, but Amelia dismissed her behavior as a melodramatic attempt at retribution. Unfortunately, the pain Dahlia expressed was followed by persistent bleeding. When Amelia reached into the back seat to check Dahlia's pulse, she found only a thready, racing beat. It was then Amelia noticed Dahlia had broken into a fever-induced sweat and chills, and her teeth rattled like dice. When Dahlia grew disoriented, even Fletcher agreed it was time to redirect their route; hospital care was necessary.

The symptoms swelled alarmingly fast as Fletcher drove them the distance to the hospital. As Dahlia's cries fell from an earsplitting pitch to a whimper, Amelia wondered if perhaps calling an ambulance might have been prudent. But she moved to the back seat, placed her daughter's head in her lap, and stroked her curly head as Dahlia howled and cried with a blood-soaked towel tucked between her legs.

In hushed tones, they discreetly conveyed the situation to the staff at the triage desk. Amelia bristled at the barely concealed judgment in the admissions nurse's expression as she assessed Dahlia's condition. They promptly ushered Dahlia into a room for immediate attention, a room in which Amelia and Fletcher were not permitted. However, they were relieved that their precious Dahlia was in capable hands, secure in the knowledge that the doctors were bound by HIPAA laws to maintain the utmost confidentiality.

Their daughter was septic, the doctor told them later, and her ovaries damaged. It was likely Dahlia could never bear children.

Amelia would never forgive August for that. If he had kept his redneck pecker in his pants, Dahlia would never have had the procedure that left her barren. To whom would she and Fletcher pass on their legacy now?

Then, to make matters worse, Dahlia promptly packed her things and moved in with that miscreant as soon as she was able after returning from the hospital. It was unthinkable! After all they had done for her. She even left the keys to her new Tesla on the kitchen island.

And then she vanished.

Not that August—criminal that he was—had kidnapped her. Dahlia had left a long, rambling message on her mother's voice mail in the middle of the night when she was sure Amelia was asleep, her phone on silent, as usual. Dahlia was leaving West Virginia, she said, and please respect her choice to go "no-contact." Amelia had never heard the phrase, but it didn't take a Phi Beta Kappa to gather what she meant. Please never contact her.

They gave her time, hoping the luster of this romance might fade after several days of constant contact with the man she believed to be her True Love. When Dahlia didn't return within a few weeks, they asked acquaintances at the club for references for a quality private investigator. Within a few days, the man they hired, Cedric Coleman, had located their erstwhile obedient child. Now, Cedric sat on the leather couch in their living room, perched on the edge as if afraid to lean back for fear he might appear at leisure. A manila folder pulled from a briefcase on their coffee table held records he leafed through with agile fingers as he explained in his stuttering cadence what he had uncovered.

"It appears this man, this Ear—Earl Jackson Jefferson, left some land in Alabama to his—his grandson, this August you said she was—was with. And recently, this la—land has had a—a manufactured home recently placed on—on the property."

"A trailer?" Amelia exclaimed. "Do I understand that she's living in a *trailer*?"

Coleman's wide eyes blinked. "Uh… y-yes, yes, m-ma'am. That's—yes—"

"She's living in a trailer, Fletcher!" Amelia's anger boiled over, her hands thrown up in frustration. Cedric waited until he was sure she was done protesting before he continued, his eyes an ocean of serenity.

"Yes, ma'am. Um, outside of H-Huntsville by about an—an hour? In the mount—mountains."

"A trailer in the mountains," Amelia muttered, shaking her head.

"Yes, uh, y-yes ma'am. They have had u-utilities in—in-stalled, and the truck he dr—drives appears to be there."

"Are they surrounded by woods?" Fletcher asked. Amelia's brows knitted as much as her Botox allowed at his inquiry, but she didn't interrupt.

"Yessir. They are. The a-area is quite b-beautiful."

Amelia snorted, but said nothing while Fletcher nodded sagely. He swept a hand through his salt-and-pepper hair. The shadows under his cheekbones had deepened in the weeks since Dahlia disappeared, and the creases in his forehead had magni-fied as well.

"But they're—they're there. I have the a-address here," the detective pointed a finger at a section of the top sheet of the file, then collapsed the folder and handed it to his employers. "Did—did you need anything fur-further from me?"

"No phone number?" Fletcher asked. Cedric shook his head.

"No. They s-still have the s-same cell phones you said they did. The n-numbers are s-still active."

Amelia didn't have to remind Cedric that trying to reach Dahlia on the phone they'd given her was as useless as an ashtray on a motorcycle. She'd considered canceling the bill, but what good was cutting off the one method of reaching her daughter she knew still worked? And what if they were struggling for money? No, as much as she hated supporting Dahlia in her life outside their home, she would not cut her daughter off completely. Not the way she had them.

"Thank you, Cedric. We appreciate all your efforts." Amelia stood to signal the meeting was over, and they walked to the front door together. Her heels clicked loudly on the tile foyer floor.

"You're—you're welcome. And you h-have my n-number if you n-need anything else."

Fletcher offered a hand, and Cedric shook it firmly. "Thank you, Cedric. You've done an outstanding job."

They said their goodbyes, and after closing the door, the Kightlingers stood under the chandelier in their grand foyer, eyes blazing. They had already discussed what they would do if the P.I. located their daughter. This was their breaking point. Dahlia going no contact was not acceptable. But in order to bring her home, they had to get her away from that criminal. Amelia would *not* have her daughter living as an accessory to Webb's offenses. What if she wound up in jail? What would her future be like then? They'd offered their daughter so much in their effort to change her mind—money, trips to wherever on earth she wanted, stock in the family business, generous donations to her favorite charities, even a house! Nothing had convinced Dahlia to leave her outlaw boyfriend. It was all in vain.

Well, almost everything.

"Do you still have that other phone number the Sinclair's gave us?" she asked.

"I do."

"When do you want to call him?"

Fletcher pulled in a chest full of air, making his broad upper body even wider, before releasing the breath in a pensive sigh. "Tonight. We'll call him tonight."

慘 恃

The team tasked with Ignatius Irizarry's bust was small, but it was the best the Leland County Sheriff's Department could assemble. Gryphon, Alabama, was not a large town, and they'd had to pull in folks from the State Bureau of Investigation field office. The team consisted of two undercover officers, Wade, his partner Zeke, and Lieutenant Jeff Miller. The undercover officers were rookies, as far as Wade was concerned. Lt. Miller offered to stay in the van and monitor the recording equipment while Wade and Zeke—both detectives—took point. Zeke was in charge of the video camera, a tiny Sony that fit into the palm of his hand.

Ezekiel and Wade hid in the scraggly crepe myrtle bushes near a sliding door behind the rusting corrugated warehouse on Industry Avenue. The undercover officers, Veronica Grayzel and Michael Cooper, waited for the man they called Iggy Izzy. Fifty feet down an abandoned alley, the detectives' car lay concealed beside a towering magnolia tree next to a burned-out streetlight. The van was parked across from the undercover agents' car, an aging Crown Victoria so ancient that anyone who noticed it might easily mistake it for an abandoned vehicle.

Crouched and ready, Wade listened to the sounds of Cooper's feet as he paced back and forth on the gravel scattered in the center of the concrete warehouse floor.

Stop pacing, Cooper. You look like a nervous rookie. Even in his undercover outfit's grubby, trendy clothes, he still stuck out far too much. Cooper's work was shoddier than any inexperienced cop Wade had ever seen. Jittery, clean-cut, and collegiate-looking, with hair the color of white pine wood, Cooper's tension was palpable. The rookie was likely to shoot off his foot in his zeal to catch the most significant drug dealer Leland County had seen in years. Wade was surprised a seasoned dealer like Irizarry had agreed to sell anything to him—much less the massive quantities they had scheduled to receive tonight.

He supposed Izzy's blindness was probably because of the other cop in on the deal. Grayzel was the smoothest talker Wade had had the privilege of listening in on. It didn't hurt that she looked like a dark-skinned, young Angelina Jolie.

Wade fingered the strap on his holster. *I will wear through the enamel if I keep grinding my teeth at Cooper's flaws.* He wiggled his jaw subtly to release some of the tension gathered there.

The heavy clouds that had promised rain cleared as they waited, and the breeze left with them. Izzy wasn't known for his promptness;

he ran an hour late, on average. Half the time the undercover team had scheduled to meet him, they'd given up before he'd turned up. It'd look suspicious if they waited longer than an hour and a half. Most folks have things to do; even those waiting on drugs typically had more than one source and didn't appreciate being played. Tonight was about solidifying Iggy as Grayzel and Cooper's sole source of drugs. Or so Iggy thought.

Zeke's pale skin practically glowed under the light of the gibbous moon—a stark contrast to Wade's dark color. The lunar lighting made Wade more aware of his partner's appearance. He'd already known that Zeke was attractive—the appreciative female stares that followed his fellow detective around the precinct bore witness to that. But in the pale moonlight, Wade noticed how chiseled his features were. He had soap opera hair, short and well-styled. In fact, Zeke was almost his physical opposite: very tall, where he was just above average; lean, whereas he was brawny. Strange, he'd never thought of it before.

"You keep staring at me like that, and we're gonna have problems, pard," Zeke joked, his eyes never leaving the space between the door and the outside wall.

"I was just wondering when you were gonna notice that spider on your cheek."

Zeke's hands flew from his side to his face as he sputtered and swatted at the imaginary arachnid. Wade sniggered, and Zeke brought his flailing to a halt.

"You asshole!" he rasped.

Grayzel's voice broke through the squabble, coming through the earpieces like the voice of God. "Mellow out, you two. Iggy Izzy has arrived."

He and Zeke took their positions, hovering near well-placed holes in the warehouse's side wall. Zeke positioned the camera at the ready.

For a man who undoubtedly made more money a year than he did, Iggy Izzy drove a relatively subdued vehicle—an immaculate midnight blue four-door BMW. From running the plates on it, Wade knew the model was seven years old—plenty old enough to make it a fraction of the original dealer price.

Izzy had never fallen into the trap of many with money to burn. The car was pristine and detailed, but not pimped out. His clothes were new but not flashy. His home was only a better middle-class ranch just outside of the poorer part of town. He was a rock-star personality without the talent or high standard of living.

One day, while driving by Izzy's home, he'd seen him outside playing with a short, skinny toddler that could've been Izzy thirty years ago. For a moment, a flood of compassion for the man came over him. Who would take care of his kid while he was behind bars? Wade's compassion had shrunk much more quickly than it had inflated when he thought of Izzy's crimes. Although they'd never been able to collect enough evidence to prosecute him, Wade knew Izzy had killed at least once during his side hustle as a drug dealer.

Izzy took his time parking, backing his vehicle into the broad side door of the warehouse with only the parking lights on. *Combat parking*, Wade thought. The flashback to his time in the Army brought a smile to his lips that quickly faded. Izzy's parking had nothing to do with spending time serving his country. His parking style was more about a quick getaway, should the need arise.

Grayzel and Cooper paced back and forth eagerly, vultures eager for the carcass. Grayzel shoved her hands into the large pockets of her baggy jeans. A sky-blue flannel shirt draped over a tight-fitting white tank hid her service revolver and recording equipment. Cooper's jeans were also loose, as were his shirt and jacket.

Once parked to his satisfaction, Iggy Izzy emerged. Five foot four and skinny as a crane fly, he wore a white wife-beater over a pair of worn Levi's. Wade knew that despite his tiny physique, Izzy was no wimp; he held black belts in more than one form of martial arts. Short, spiky brown hair topped a tanned face no older than thirty that lit up when it saw Grayzel's smile.

"You ready?" he asked, his voice surprisingly soft and high for that of a multiple felon. He stepped forward, ready to embrace Grayzel, who towered over him by around four inches.

Wade's breath caught in his throat. The odds that Izzy's arm wouldn't sweep against Grayzel's .22 or mic pack were small. Minute, even. If he brushed against her service pistol, the situation would likely escalate into a firefight. Alternatively, he might drive away, making up an excuse to be elsewhere, leaving them with no concrete "probable cause" for a search, no recording.

God, please don't let this end so soon. We've been working way too hard on this. Don't let him get away from us.

Grayzel, though, handled it like a champ. Feigning awkwardness and masking it as ill-concealed infatuation, she bungled the conclusion of the hug, almost executing a curtsy, which helped her slip away from Izzy's falling arms. If he suspected anything, the twinkling in her eyes convinced his ego otherwise.

Cooper descended on him now, offering a lengthy handshake with unabashed machismo and salutations worthy of royalty. Irizarry retreated a few steps, his eyes never leaving Grayzel's, whose smile implored him not to leave on her awkward friend's account.

After disentangling himself from Cooper, Izzy turned to Grayzel. "Did you make your half?" he asked, referring to the story Grayzel had offered earlier. She had told Izzy that she hoped to secure her portion of the drug funds from others to prepare for tonight's transaction.

Grayzel nodded and walked to a small nylon bag a few steps away. She hoisted it over her shoulder and carried it to Izzy's Beemer. Motioning that she'd like to put the bag on the back of the car, Izzy waved his hand dismissively. Grayzel plopped it on the trunk, unzipping it in a manner that somehow bordered on flirting.

"She's good," Zeke whispered, his eye pressed against the video camera. "He's probably thinking the less she talks, the worse the odds are that he's being recorded." Wade nodded in agreement, afraid to speak. Even at a low volume, his deep voice carried much farther than Zeke's.

Izzy stepped up to the bag and fingered its contents. "Looks good," he said with a shrug. He took his car keys from his pocket, turned his back on them, and popped the hatch on the trunk.

Cooper went for his gun.

Not now, you dummy! Wade thought. *What are you, crazy?* He and Zeke jumped to their feet in unison and dashed for the open crack in the door just as the sound of a gunshot broke the silence of the night.

 og ಬಿ

Marina sat in the leather recliner and stared at the empty fireplace, a frustrated wrinkle across her brow. There was nothing she could do. The one person in her family she had the power to protect lay sleeping in his bed, surrounded by Harry Potter paraphernalia, his glasses on the nightstand beside him. The rest was up to Wade.

Marina turned off the evening news, set her Piers Anthony book on the glass-topped table, and leaned her recliner back. Attempting to sleep was pointless. Tonight, there would be no rest until Wade crossed the threshold of their home. Until then, petty diversions only held her attention for so long. Soon, the words blurred, or the television sounds grew muddled in her ears, drowned out by the power of her worried thoughts. Nothing helped for long, knowing her husband was putting his life on the line that night.

Part of her longed to go upstairs and climb into bed with Derek. The sound of his soothing breathing was often the last thing she heard before turning in herself. Even after Derek passed the danger of crib death, she still had to have one last peek at her baby before going to sleep. The sound of his delicate breath in the darkness of his room was more relaxing than any sedative.

She doubted Derek's steady breathing would help her unwind tonight. Her strange intuitions didn't happen often, but when they did, they hit with uncanny force, and she knew it was best to trust them. If Wade was home, he'd gently chide her until a grin crossed her lips, however insincere. She longed to talk to him, to hear his voice telling her that her feelings were unwarranted, but calling him was out of the question.

Wade's detective skills were unsurpassed—he was the best. The best cop, the best husband, the best father, and the finest man she'd ever met. When she needed his strength, he was her rock. When she needed a kind word, he provided that, too. He never failed to enfold her hand in his when she needed reassurance. And she supposed that was where part of her irrational fears came in. Nothing too good to be true was supposed to last. And yet, for them, it had.

She knew it was an incredibly negative way to live, waiting for the other shoe to drop, but her intuition overrode her logic. Too good to be true equaled impossible, despite years of proof to the contrary.

Her parents had raised her with the belief that life came with a set of invisible scales that ensured everything evened out in the end. An unseen hand ultimately rewarded good works. Charity and kind words were one way to keep life's joyous events flowing. To them, fate had dealt Wade into their charming, intelligent, generous daughter's life the way it should.

Marina never entirely bought into her parents' wholehearted be-lief that life was that simplistic. To her, life with Wade was a wild, un-expected blessing. But maybe fate waited to deal them a crushing blow, like sickness or death. A bullet, a car crash, the big "C." Or worse, a horrible fate for their son, Derek.

And her intuition had been proven right before. What about her cousin David's car crash last summer? The moment he'd shared with her he planned to drive to Pennsylvania, she'd told him she had a feel-ing he'd better be extra careful and take his time. He'd rushed to make the trip in less than ten hours, fell asleep behind the wheel just outside of Mechanicsburg, and wound up on crutches with a four-inch scar on his face and his spleen removed.

And what about their dog, Roddy? He wasn't due for another check-up for a couple of months, but Marina knew better. It started when the setter failed to keep up during their morning jog. He spent the day listless and quieter than average, not responding with his usual talkative growls when she tried to engage with him. When he acted nauseated but was incapable of vomiting, Marina rushed him to the hospital. The doctor dismissed his behavior as a stomachache, but Marina knew there was more to it. Still, she didn't press the issue; after all, Roddy had shown no symptoms other than fatigue. He died of bloat in the backyard later that day. Poor Derek had been inconsolable for weeks afterward.

So, it wasn't as if she was getting worked up over nothing—more than once, her gut had been right. Though she knew several more in-stances, this didn't seem the time to recall how often her hunches were on target.

There's a phrase that'll make you feel all kinds of good right now, Ma-rina. Let's pray that the one who's right on target tonight is Wade and not that jerk he's trying to bust!

Righting the recliner with a creak of leather and springs, she rose and paced the floor barefoot, looking for anything to distract her. The kitchen needed cleaning, but Rosie would take care of that in the morning. If Marina touched it, she'd get a scolding from the older woman for cleaning before the maid showed up to do her job.

What else is there? What else, what else, what else?

Striding to the kitchen, Marina drew the narrow green watering can out from under the sink and set it under the tap. As the water trickled into the container, she eyed the row of plants at the inside edge of the breakfast room bay window. It'd probably been days since she'd watered them, but she hesitated. Her mother had told her never to water her plants at night—something about mildewing the roots. Marina didn't know if it was true, but the thought of doing nothing while her ivy died of drought seemed as asinine as watering them at midnight.

Marina pushed the lever down, and the water slowed to a stop. She withdrew the watering can from under the sink and crossed the tiles to the breakfast nook.

During the day, sunlight flooded the many-windowed room like a greenhouse. An arch of glass covered the bay window and made its way overhead to the juncture of the kitchen roof. Pale cream and coffee-colored furniture and pillows made for a cozy area to eat and read the news. The table was round; the chairs curved and comfortable. Now, at night, it seemed too cheerful—like a pop singer at a funeral.

Marina placed her knee on one of the chair cushions and leaned forward, stretching the can toward the plants to the left of the window. An earsplitting bang made her jump, and her grip on the watering can loosened. It clattered to the floor, but she waited a moment with her hand on her chest for her heart to beat again before kneeling under the table to retrieve it.

It was a car backfiring out on the road. Or maybe a heavy board fell on a neighbor's patio.

In the middle of the night? Who are you trying to fool?

Years as a cop's wife had attuned her ears to the sound of a gunshot—nothing else had quite the same report. She'd spent too many hours beside Wade at the shooting range to convince herself otherwise.

Well then, why don't I hear Derek? He can't sleep through a fly buzzing in the next room! A noise like that, and he'd tear through the door screaming for me.

The watering can collected, Marina sat up and strained her ears, but there was no cry for help, not even a sleepy, muffled "Mom?" from the landing. Nothing. It was as if she'd imagined the whole thing.

She stood to fetch a towel and let out a slow breath as she rose, her grip on the handle of the watering can so tight her knuckles whitened. Derek might not have heard it, but Marina knew this wasn't something to brush off.

Chapter Three

LaDonna's husband, Luke, joined them at the large wooden dining room table, settling his bulk into a chair at its head. Their hostess had poured them all icy glasses of sweet tea, and the four made small talk while sipping.

"What brings you over today, August?" LaDonna asked. "Y'all need anything, or were you just in mind for a visit?"

"A little of both, actually," August admitted, his eyebrows raised. "I noticed you had some fresh herbs in the bread you brought by, and I was wondering if they were your own or store-bought. I could use some fresh herbs for a recipe I'm working on. Rosemary, especially."

Luke set down his glass and let out a booming laugh that made Ida jump, and August leaned back in surprise. LaDonna said nothing but gave Luke a small, loving smile that made her eyes sparkle.

"Take them out back, hon," Luke suggested with a knowing gleam in his eye. "Let them see your garden."

"Sure, that'd be fun," LaDonna agreed. "That is, if you don't mind stepping back out into the heat. It won't take long. I'll give you the short tour."

August shot Ida an inquiring glance. She shrugged, but her spine was straight, and she showed none of her usual signs of apprehension. August reached for Ida's hand, and as they stood, Luke and Ladonna joined them. The four of them made their way to an arched wooden door at the side of the house. LaDonna opened the door and flicked on the exterior light with a proud flourish. Under the generous outdoor lighting, August saw a sea of lush, green plants and brightly colored flowers, seemingly unaffected by days of relentless heat and drought.

"Wow," he breathed, impressed with the verdant plants that seamlessly blended with their neighbors' luxurious, yet cozy home. Ida's eyes widened, clearly enchanted with the garden's beauty.

The cool of the house vanished in the space of a few heartbeats, and then they were again at the mercy of the heat, muggy with the threat of much-needed rain. August and Ida followed LaDonna and Luke across a short flagstone walk to the small iron gate. Moths, attracted by the bright floodlights and strategically placed landscape bulbs, beat their wings frantically, mindless of the heat, their fat bodies *tick-tick-ticking* against the glass.

Gooseflesh stood up on August's arms as they passed through the gate. He scanned the surroundings, trying to identify the source of his reaction, but found nothing that could explain it. No breeze stirred. No fan blew.

Probably nothing. Just moving from the cool air back into the heat is all. August took a deep breath of flower-and-herb-scented air and willed his heartbeat to slow down. Ida's concerned gaze needed answering, and he brushed it off with a tiny shake of his head as he forced his mouth into an inscrutable expression. She frowned slightly but said nothing, trusting he'd tell her anything she needed to know later, as he always did.

LaDonna had picked up a pair of pruning shears and a small muslin drawstring bag. "Just let me know if you want anything, and I'll add it to your bag. We've got mint, basil, thyme, oregano, sage." With every herb she named, LaDonna motioned to the plants with the pointed tip of the shears.

"Ooh, mint?" Ida said, perking up. "I'd love some mint if you can spare some."

"Ida, I can more than spare some. The stuff grows like weeds. How much do you want?"

While Ida and LaDonna discussed the acceptable amount of mint to trim, Luke motioned to August to join him by the rear of the garden, where a second gate led to the deep, green woods beyond. Two enormous rosemary bushes—as tall as August's waist and wider around than he could embrace—stood sentinel on either side.

"Holy shit," August exclaimed, feeling his eyes bulge. Luke just laughed, his bushy dark hair and eyebrows reminding August of a happy dwarf from a Tolkien film. All that was missing was a long, flowing beard.

"Rosemary by the garden gate deters pesky critters and encourages pollinators," he explained. "As you can see, we've got plenty of the stuff to spare." He had picked up a set of clippers along the way and now trimmed off a handful of stems. Holding them up for August's inspection, he asked, "Will that do?"

"That's perfect. That's… wow… very generous. Thank you."

"No problem. Any time you need herbs, you're welcome to come by. You're welcome to come by anytime you like, herbs or not."

LaDonna and Ida joined them, and Luke added his rosemary trimmings to the top of the bag, now almost filled with fragrant, fresh-cut herbs. Ida had added some oregano to the bunch as well. The smell made August's mouth water.

"It's hotter than blazes. I'm going to have another glass of tea, and you're welcome to stay awhile if y'all still want some. Or is it too late for tea?"

Ida's unexpectedly full, genuine smile caught August off guard as she said, "It's never too late for tea."

CI   ∂C

Thankful for the rainless night and the absence of the town's recent ominous clouds, Sergio hurried his Honda down Gryphon's back roads beneath the feeble, yellowish streetlights. A town of less than ten thousand people, Gryphon's Industry Avenue comprised unmarked packed-dirt and gravel roads winding between abandoned riverfront warehouses and old factories that limped along to support much of the town's population and the nearby villages of even fewer people.

His short-lived call to Irizarry repeated itself in his mind on a continuous loop. With every recap, his foot grew heavier on the pedal until the Honda dipped in and out of the potholed road with a clatter and, at times, caught a few inches of air on his way out.

"Toothpaste, Iggy?"

"So, how's Orchid doing, man? Still paying you with a little action? If she is, I'm surprised you hit me up this quick — she's a wild ride."

"You son of a — "

"You know how it works, Serge. I'm not pushing top-shelf product to anyone picking up less than a dozen eight-balls at a time."

"You've sold single eight-balls to me for four years. Since when have you started regulating quantity?"

"I'm leveling up, man. Fentanyl, ice — gotta chase where the money's flowing."

"You and me both know if you were really moving up, you would've bounced to Mobile or Birmingham years ago. Don't hit me with that bullshit."

"Suit yourself. But when you're ready to take the 'bull' by the horns, you let me know. In the meantime, I've got Amp-Daddy Wayne, who's willing to buy in bulk — "

"Anthony Wayne? Man, he's gonna get popped any minute, and we both know it. That idiot brings home anyone he meets at a club in Huntsville. He's reckless, all balls and no brains. I'm surprised he ain't locked up already."

"There are others, Sergio. He's not my only connect, but he's handling the coke while I move on to where the real money's at. And let's be real, your reputation ain't exactly spotless. Anyone who trades in favors ain't counting on my cash to get by. You think Maria knows how Orchid's really paying for her stash?"

The part about him not relying on the drug money had been true recently. Sergio made decent money as a bouncer without the surplus cash he got from peddling Izzy's pharmaceutical goods. More than that, Maria, his girlfriend of seven years, had gotten a decent-sized inheritance from her parents when they died in a traffic accident. Although she and her parents hadn't spoken in years, they'd left her a chunk sizable enough to ensure she didn't have to worry about money for several years. Unfortunately, Maria's urge to live the good life outweighed her financial sense. Breast implants, a nose job, and a new car had reduced the windfall to a tiny perk in their checking account. However, his request for a few hundred dollars to go back to school had gone unheeded, as had his request for a monogamous relationship.

Sergio hit the steering wheel again. *It's not the money. It's about Izzy messing with my name. Who the hell does he think he is? What if, just once, I didn't go to Orchid first? What if I went to Ben? Ben would rip my* bicho *off if I tried to pass off toothpaste for the real thing!*

How had it come to this, anyway? Early missteps, misguided high school friendships, an extended trip to a juvenile detention center, and before long, he was peddling illicit substances to former friends. Not that he had that many customers. He kept his clients local, unlike Izzy, who didn't mind driving if it brought in some money. Now, he was losing his mind over an eight-ball?

It's just not fair. I'm just trying to make a couple of bucks. To have a nice life. Why can't I have a nice life?

The end of the row of manufacturing plants came into view quicker than he expected. Sergio slammed on the brake, causing the tail end of the Honda to fishtail in the gravel before coming to a halt. Fortunately, gravel didn't squeal and give his presence away, and it was unlikely anyone inside the warehouse would notice the sound of crunching gravel or bouncing pebbles.

Beyond the corner of the row of buildings, he could make out the bright red CR-Z driven by Anthony "Amp-Daddy" Wayne. After his chat with Izzy, Sergio had called Wayne, who'd said with a brag in his voice, after a minimum of prompting, where to find Izzy at eleven-thirty that night. He and Irizarry had scheduled a drop-off of sizable proportions. Three whole kilos. A fortune in drugs, by Gryphon standards. Enough to put Amp-Daddy away for a very long time when he recklessly hustled his stock off in a jubilant flurry typical of inexperienced pushers.

Sergio parked the car and reached under the Honda for his pistol. He had no plan. He had no witty dialog stashed in his cache, no means of knowing if Izzy was packing, and no idea what he was going to do. But he knew that his days of getting ripped off were over.

He exited the Honda, pistol poised in his sizable, dominant left hand as he swiftly moved to the side of the corrugated tin building, displaying a stealth uncommon in someone of his stature. He crept to the large sliding back door, watching the ground at his feet for sticks or other obstacles. The night was silent, save for the persistent droning of crickets, cicadas, and a nearby conversation. Izzy and Wayne were already inside making the exchange, Anthony's six-foot frame looming over the shorter dealer by over half a foot.

"Dog, I can't believe I'm doing this!" Wayne exclaimed. "I mean... *dang!* It's—it's..."

If he says it's like a dream come true, I'm gonna shoot his ass out of general principle.

Izzy shook his head at his apprentice's exuberance. "You better calm down, man," Izzy said, "especially if you plan on sampling some of the shit yourself."

"Aw yeah, yeah!" Wayne said. "Lemme check the quality."

Izzy took a four-inch butterfly knife and picked a small bag from his pocket. "Same batch," he said.

Oldest trick in the book, Sergio thought with a shake of his head, but if Wayne had a complaint about using a sample from a bag that wasn't part of his purchase, he said nothing. *Probably figures that'll leave just that much more to sell — or use.*

Irizarry dipped the blade into the bag and brought out a large bump of white cocaine on its edge that he offered to Wayne. The sight of the overzealous dealer sniffing the powder—the good powder that he should've gotten—from the edge of the knife was more than Sergio could stand. He threw his body around the corner, his Glock at eye level, and pointed at Irizarry.

"Didn't anyone ever tell you not to give free samples?" he growled in Irizarry's direction, his eyes never leaving Wayne's face. "It cuts a serious hole out of your profit margin."

Wayne's face registered shock and fear as he stared at the hole at the tip of Sergio's 9 mil pistol. Though Sergio's aim was at Irizarry, little stuttering "W-w-w" sounds issued from Wayne's lips, and Sergio had a momentary urge to shoot him and put him out of the misery of his pitiful existence.

If Izzy was fazed, he didn't show it. Instead, he licked the remnants of the coke from the knife, wiped it on his pants, and flipped the blade shut with a fancy flick of his wrist.

"So now you're a party crasher," he said. "No surprise there. The real question is, what took you so long? I've been jerking you off for months, and you finally found your balls now?"

Sergio's finger quavered on the trigger. His heart hammered loudly, and it surprised him when tears stung at the back of his eyes. He wanted nothing more than to erase Izzy's smugness and witness his agonized screams and apologies at decibels that were painful to the human ear. But his sweaty finger didn't budge.

Izzy pocketed the knife. "So, what now? You gonna shoot me?" He scoffed. "One thing I know about you, Vega—you're too smart for that. You're not gonna throw away that little setup you got with Maria over some bad product. You're doing just fine, bro. You don't need me, or this," he nodded toward the stash in his trunk. "You're not like Amp-Daddy, out here just trying to scrape by."

Give it a couple of months, Sergio thought, his mind racing over the speed with which Maria sifted through her inheritance. But Izzy was right about one thing. Sergio didn't want to kill him. Make him pay, yes. Make him cry out for hell to save him from his agony, absolutely. But going to prison over toothpaste-laced cocaine?

"You've got it too good, man," Izzy said, "I can't believe you'd—"

It turned out it didn't matter what Izzy believed. Wayne, whom they'd ignored during Izzy's monologue, had dug his cell phone from his pocket. Innocuous as this act seemed, even under the circumstances, the situation took a sudden turn when Wayne hurled the phone toward Sergio's head and bolted for the front door of the building. Sergio ducked, jumped backward, and felt his heart leap as he accidentally pulled the trigger.

Irizarry fell to the ground.

∛ ∰

It was a phone call Fletcher Kightlinger never expected to have to make. Even when Dahlia began her ridiculous love affair with the moonshiner, he'd expected it was a fire that would burn intensely, but briefly, the way most first loves do. His primary concern was that she did not get pregnant before completing college—she was woefully behind in her classes. When he'd asked Amelia if she'd ever spoken with their daughter about contraception or family planning, his wife was aghast.

"No, of course not," she breathed, stepping back from him with a hand pressed to her chest.

If she were wearing her pearls, she'd be clutching them. Fletcher drummed his fingertips on the granite countertop. "How is she supposed to know how to avoid getting pregnant?"

"Mercy, Fletcher. I imagine they teach those things in school. You were the one who insisted she go to public school. I'm sure she's gotten an earful there."

He should have pressed her then, but the glower on Amelia's well-preserved face dissuaded him. He'd meant to broach the subject again, but the days slipped away without the subject rising. It was as if, on some level, they believed that by ignoring the problem, it might fade away.

Now, they'd lost both their daughter and their chance at grandchildren. They would not let Dahlia continue to ruin the rest of her life. He discreetly inquired amongst his associates, including friends whom he sometimes had to admit to himself he didn't like, to find someone willing to do the necessary dirty work for the right price. The name he'd been given was Arturo Stone, and the phone number was an international one. He'd paid a young man, the recusant son of one of his employees, to purchase a burner phone for cash, offering him a healthy "hundo" as a tip for his service.

Now, he and Amelia sat beside one another behind his broad desk, the burner phone on speaker. Their maid, Valentina, pushed a vacuum in the neighboring room with practiced efficiency. Fletcher monitored her progress with half an ear to ensure she kept a safe distance from the door.

"You understand it must look like a hunting accident, right?" Fletcher said.

"I understand." The voice was gravelly and somewhat distorted, and Fletcher wondered if a poor international connection caused it, a voice modulator, or both. Perhaps his imagination was playing tricks on him. Since his recent foray into the world of hired thugs, he'd jumped at every shadow and grown vigilant of every unusual sound.

"Don't worry, Fletcher," Stone said. "No one will be suspicious. You and your wife have nothing to worry about."

I shouldn't have given him my real name. Well, it was too late now. And he supposed it wasn't as if Stone could turn him in to the authorities without implicating himself as well. Still, it unnerved him to hear the man referring to him by his first name as if they were golfing buddies instead of client and hired trigger man.

"How long will it take?" Amelia asked.

"As long as it takes," Stone replied casually. "I've got to learn his patterns, his movements. Find out the most likely angle for the shot to be written off as a hunting fatality. And there's the question of whether you want me to wait until hunting season officially starts."

"When is that?"

"Fall. I would have to look into Alabama hunting laws for his location to know precisely."

"No," Fletcher said. "The sooner the better. Surely, some people hunt off-season illegally. Also, it seems more plausible for someone to deny responsibility for an accidental shooting if the incident occurred during the off-season."

"Do you have a hunting rifle?" Amelia asked.

Fletcher couldn't help himself; he turned to Amelia and eyed her like she was a damned fool. Of course, a hired gunman would have a hunting rifle; that he hunted people was likely no different from hunting a deer or other large game. The corner of his lip twitched with disquiet when he thought of August as nothing more than a trophy animal.

"What?" Amelia barked. "I mean like those redneck fellows have. Not an assassin gun or whatever. They will look at bullets and confirm they come from a hunting rifle, right? We can't have him mowed down with an assault rifle. It wouldn't be believable."

Fletcher supposed she had a point. The lingering pause on the other end of the phone left his skin prickling with nerves, and he became acutely aware of the sweat growing under his armpits. He wondered if Stone was laughing at his wife or had hung up on them, giving them up as too stupid to work for. When Fletcher pulled in a breath to inquire if Stone was still on the other end, the deep, resonant voice spoke.

"I have a Winchester that should do the job nicely."

Fletcher didn't know what adjective he would use to describe killing someone, but he doubted *nicely* would be one of them.

☙ ❧

The voices on the video chat sounded confident, but many of

Harper's clients spoke with bravado. It was often a facade, and the disquiet in their voices revealed their uncertainty. This Fletcher and Amelia Kightlinger seemed like the sort of older, middle-aged adults accustomed to not having to raise their voice to assert themselves, who used money as leverage in both positive and negative ways to influence those around them. Images of bespoke suits and classic dresses accessorized with pearls and expensive (but comfortable) heels or pumps came to mind. And a name-brand handbag, no doubt. One for every outfit — or perhaps Amelia was the sort of woman with a narrow spectrum of color in her wardrobe and only required one black and one possibly beige or brown. Maybe taupe.

At any rate, they sounded like assholes. Whatever. They were paying a shit-ton of money for one little job that likely wouldn't take long. Maybe she could add on a charge once she neutralized this guy. An asshole tax. It wouldn't be the first time she'd added a surcharge for her services — although usually, it was because of the length or complexity of the task. Or the desire to rent a helicopter or chartered jet.

Harper Cross disconnected the voice modulator and hung up her phone before tossing the modulator casually onto the nearby sofa. She strolled to the window and pulled back the curtain, looking down from her room's 12th-story window onto the busy Atlanta street. Cars cruised by, nearly kissing one another's bumpers as a confident cyclist and a not-so-confident scooter driver wound their way through traffic. Thanks be to all things holy and unholy, she'd be getting out of this hellhole. The traffic here was nearly as bad as D.C. Only, this fucking city was hotter than the devil's goddamn kitchen. Fucking Hotlanta.

She asked her phone for directions to Gryphon, Alabama. The app suggested the drive would take a little over three and a half hours. She estimated it would take her between two and a half to three. She tried to pull up more information on the town, but other than a handful of stores with piss-poor, dated websites and a couple of manufacturing businesses, there wasn't much to find. A clothier. A tiny grocery store with the ever-so-clever name of Gryphon Grocery. A coffee shop that sold — of all things — metaphysical wares. *I'm sure the town loves* that *place.* It looked like the founding industry of Gryphon had once comprised small manufacturing plants. According to an article in the *Gryphon Gazette*—this town had a way with words, clearly—many of the plants had collapsed when more prominent, more competitive plants had seduced those companies to more cost-efficient locations overseas.

Whatever. It's a job. Huntsville is close enough to set up camp while I learn about this loser. August Webb. What a name. I bet he's as stuck up as they sound. Wonder what the fucker did to deserve to get a bullet to the brain?

She pulled her hair back and tied it at the nape to keep it out of the way as she dragged her suitcase from the closet. She'd need to clear out of the hotel room tonight. Given the generous rates the Kightlingers were paying her, she could go anywhere she desired after collecting the second half of her fee. Anywhere at all.

Fiji sounded nice.

ೞ   ಬ

The gunshot echoed in the vast, shadowy emptiness of the warehouse, deafening Wade as he crossed the threshold. In just five seconds, the scene had transformed dramatically. Cooper lay prone on the dusty warehouse floor, his breath ragged and eyes wide as a stranded fish on a desolate shore. Grayzel was now ensnared by Izzy's iron grip, her spine arching painfully, her wrists pinned under one of Izzy's talon-like hands, rendering her service revolver unreachable. At her temple, Izzy clutched a chrome-plated pistol.

But what unnerved Wade the most was the second man who had appeared on the scene. Standing on the far side of the BMW, nearer to Izzy and Grayzel than Zeke and him, was another young man, perhaps twenty-five years old. Not much taller than Izzy, his hair topped with a Bama ball cap, Wade suspected he had some relation to Irizarry. The semblance couldn't be ignored—even the mole on their cheek was the same.

The car's back door loomed open, an oversight neither Wade nor Zeke could fathom.

They didn't check the back seat. Oh, man. How'd they miss that?

"You'd think they were freakin' rookies," Zeke muttered under his breath, a sentiment Wade wholeheartedly shared.

Wade didn't remember drawing his pistol, but the weight rested in his hand, heavy and reassuring in its familiarity. He and Zeke lifted their service weapons into firing position in slow motion as they advanced, as if creeping their guns into place might somehow seem less intimidating.

"Don't... freaking... move," Irizarry hissed, his brown eyes locked with Wade's. He and Zeke halted their advance, though Wade knew he was good for a headshot at this distance if Izzy stood still long enough. Izzy had no way of knowing Wade's proficiency with firearms. It was the one advantage Wade had. Still, the idea of taking a shot so close to Grayzel's head made Wade's stomach churn as if he'd swallowed a cupful of vinegar.

Dragging Grayzel back with him, Izzy approached Cooper's prone body as Bama Cap kept the detectives covered with a pistol of his own. Kicking Cooper's chest and ribs with every word, he shouted, "I. Knew. You. Were. A. Freaking. Cop. You. Fucker!" He gave Cooper one last, vengeful kick as if hoping to punt his head from his shoulders. "I *knew* it!"

Grayzel screamed at him to stop and wriggled ferociously, but Izzy seemed made of tensile steel.

"Hold still, you fucking bitch, or my finger might slip, and I'll blow your fucking head off!"

Grayzel ceased, her face cold and furious in her helplessness. Izzy must have had a once-in-a-lifetime stroke of luck to catch her off guard. Wade had seen Grayzel in the gym practicing tactical training. She was no wilting flower. He had little doubt she was calculating the best way out of her predicament, and Wade planned to give her that opportunity if it arose.

Wade and Zeke stood frozen in a standoff with Izzy and his unidentified accomplice, who trained Zeke and him at the end of his gun in alternating sweeps, his arm shaking with fear and agitation.

His fury abated, Izzy turned his attention to the nearby detectives.

"Don't do this, Irizarry," Wade said. "We might have you on drug charges, but that's still not as bad as murder."

"You don't have me on squat!" Izzy crowed. "You got nothing."

Wade chose not to dispute the intricacies of probable cause. Holding an officer hostage to avoid letting others see the inside of the trunk was ample justification for popping the lock. Not to mention Izzy's assault on a fellow officer.

"You're right," Wade said, concealing the truth with the ease that came from years of negotiating with criminals. "So let her go, and we'll call it quits."

Izzy's eyes darted from one corner of the warehouse to another, searching for further adversaries on whom to vent his rage.

"You're not going to let me go after this," he snarled. "I've got one of your own here and drew blood from another. You think I believe you're going to forgive me for putting a gun to her head?"

Wade knew that the more Izzy contemplated his dire predicament, the slimmer the chances of everyone escaping unscathed. He only hoped to out-talk Irizarry.

"Just let her go, Irizarry," he said. "We'll work something out."

Worry replaced anger and fear on Irizzary's face, and for a fleeting moment, Wade thought he'd convinced the man to give up. The grip on Grayzel's neck appeared to loosen ever so slightly, and Wade saw Grayzel tense, prepared to move. Whatever notion dawned on Irizarry next, though, Wade never knew. One moment, he seemed resigned to his fate; the next, his fingers clamped around Grayzel's wrists again.

"Uh-uh. I ain't going to—"

Wade never heard Izzy's last words. The desperate drug dealer wrenched his pistol from Grayzel's temple, turned it toward Zeke, and unleashed a bullet that drowned out his reply. Thankfully, both his shot and his accomplice's missed their marks. With Grayzel's head farther from his as he steadied to take aim, his new position also left Irizarry a more open target.

Wade released his breath, perfected his focus, and fired.

og   ഇ

A bullet whizzed dangerously close to Wade's ear, momentarily jarring him. He corrected his hold to take his next shot.

I know I didn't miss. Oh, man, where'd that bullet come from? Both of them were pointing at Zeke! Is someone else hiding in the car?

Wade tried to find his target — Izzy's head — and the sight before him disoriented him further.

Before him, Irizarry's body lay sprawled on the ground, his head bleeding from a precisely placed bullet wound. Grayzel and

Cooper had vanished, as had Bama Cap. He risked a glance to his right. Zeke had disappeared, as well.

What the hell's going on? Did I die?

The thought was irrational, but so was the inexplicable scene before him. Izzy's car was still there, but it had inexplicably shifted a few feet closer. Izzy was there and appeared to be a slightly different color. And he knew *he* was still there because he stood right in front of himself. Him, but not him.

That's not me. I would never wear that stuff; Marina would kill me. And I don't... I don't stand like that.

Incredibly, his doppelgänger stood directly across from the BMW, gripping a weapon that closely resembled the pistol in his own hand. Wade suspected the expression on the man's face mirrored his own puzzled visage. It was like looking into a warped mirror—not the version of himself he was used to, but probably the one the world saw.

It was him, but it wasn't him. So, who was it?

Chapter Four

Sweet teas empty, their visit concluded, Ida and August bade their goodbyes to Luke and LaDonna and walked to the Kawasaki. The air smelled hot and green, and the dry gravel driveway crunched underfoot. They gently looped the cargo net over the fabric bag containing their herb loot and eased themselves onto the vinyl seats. August brought the engine to life, revved the engine once, twice, and steered the bike toward home.

August had seen LaDonna sneak an extra bag of something in with the rest of their goodies as they made their way to the door, and he was curious what it was she'd added to their already generous gifts. And why had she ensured only he had seen her do it? Was it something he was supposed to keep from Ida or Luke? The idea made him skeptical of his kindly neighbors. They seemed like a loving couple, but they'd only just met them. Maybe they weren't as straightforward as his first impression would lead him to believe. He hoped that wasn't the case; he liked them a lot so far, and Ida had taken to them surprisingly well. She never took to anyone.

Just check it out when you get home. No sense worrying about it now.

He paused at the end of the Whelen's driveway and flicked the visor on his helmet. Ida did the same. "Hey, you want to scope out that house by ours? See if we can see anything from a different angle?" He had to yell to make himself heard over the din of the idling motorcycle and the padding of their helmets. "I know it's dark, but…." He let his voice trail off, not wanting to say out loud that he was in no rush to return to their sauna of a trailer.

"Sure," Ida said with an exaggerated bob of her head in case he hadn't heard her. The movement made her helmet wiggle slightly, and she adjusted the chin strap more securely.

He hadn't specified, but there was only one place to which he could be referring. They'd passed the driveway to the mystery house on the way to the Whelen's.

He eased the bike onto the street and pointed it downhill, bringing it up to a slow, safe speed to keep Ida's nervousness at bay. Sweat already trickled down his back, and he knew he'd need to wash his hair and everything else when he got home. Ida, who usually clung to him during their rides, now held herself a few inches away, letting the air circulate between them. Her hands on his hips the only contact between them. The wind felt fantastic on his skin, even at the slower pace. Despite his name, August was not his favorite month—especially now that they were this far down south.

The driveway was across from a slight curve in the road; he recalled that much. He slowed as he neared the hidden driveway, afraid he might pass it by accident and be forced to loop back. The night nearly hid the narrow break in the trees, but he found it in time and steered the nose of the bike onto the disused driveway. Once they were off the street, he let the growl of the motorcycle drop to a loud purr, and August set his feet on the ground, pausing until Ida leaned forward to listen.

"Drive it or walk it?" he hollered.

Her head bobbed back and forth as she considered the options. "Let's see how far we can drive it without getting scraped up. Maybe it's not too far," Ida suggested. "And if it gets too bad, we'll walk the rest."

"Good idea," he agreed as he eased the bike down the driveway.

03 80

That's it. I know I heard it that time!

Marina's gut clenched as she waited to hear Derek's fearful call from the landing above. Even if he directed his tired voice down the hall toward the room she shared with Wade, she should be able to hear it from the kitchen.

Nothing. Her little light sleeper slept on. Unnaturally so.

She set the empty watering can down on the table and sank onto the chaise, wiping a hand across her brow as if she expected to find perspiration. The room seemed to close in around her, shadows deepening.

Maybe he's sleeping really hard tonight. Maybe he wore himself out at camp today.

It occurred to Marina then that she did not know what Derek had done at camp that day—who he'd talked to, what he'd learned, what he'd played. Ashamed that she'd been so preoccupied with Wade that she hadn't asked her son more questions about his day, Marina strode to the phone on the wall and lifted the cordless from the receiver. She punched 9-1-1 with trembling fingers and put the phone to her ear.

"Nine-one-one emergency. How can I help you?" The voice was a very Southern woman. Obviously, a native Alabamian from a long line of the same.

"Hi. My name is Marina Beringer. I live at one fifty-five Regency, and I have just heard gunshots somewhere in my neighborhood. Two of them."

"Could you give me an idea of the direction of the shots, ma'am?"

"I—" Marina's voice drew short as she struggled to recall. How had the shots sounded? And from which direction had they come? She swiftly scanned her kitchen, trying to remember the instinctive head swivel she had used to pinpoint the source of the shot. Her adrenaline had subsided, though, and now she struggled to remember her response. She hadn't turned toward the shot at all. Instead, her head had swiveled from side to side, searching for—for what? Had she felt the shot was so close she expected someone to be standing right before her with the gun?

Pull it together, and give what information you can.

"I'm sorry. I'm not sure. I'm inside. I can't say."

"That's alright, ma'am. We'll send a car out and see if we can spot anything."

"Thank you," Marina said, fighting the urge to apologize. What did she have to apologize for? Shots in a rural subdivision were a legitimate reason to call the police. It wasn't as if they lived in the countryside twenty miles west, where gunshots were not only expected, they were the norm. Folks getting drunk and taking potshots at cans and bottles were a regular weekend activity in rural Alabama.

So why did she feel she'd done something irrational by calling the police? A late-night driver passed her home, the headlights casting eerie shadows on the walls as she wondered why she could not shake her uneasiness.

⋐ ⋑

"What was that?"

Startled at the unexpected sound, Clark Sandwell broke his gaze from the dirty library window and saw Leah standing rigidly in the middle of the room, ears perked like an attentive dog's, an uncharacteristic bloom of excitement on her youthful face.

"What was what?"

Leah Zeller tilted her head toward the sitting room on the opposite side of the entrance hall. "That noise? You don't hear it?"

Clark uncrossed his arms and took a handful of steps in her direction to see if he picked up on the sound. His feet were silent on the hardwood floor, but some old boards creaked underfoot. No matter how hard he strained, he did not hear the sound that had caught Leah's attention.

"Where's Minnie?" Leah asked.

"Last I knew she was—"

"—in the kitchen," they said together.

"God, she can't even *cook* anymore," Leah said with a roll of her eyes. "Not that she needs to. What in the hell is the matter with her? Why does she waste her time there?"

Clark shrugged. "They say the kitchen is the heart of the home."

Leah snorted as a burst of faint growling noises came from the front of the house. The timing almost made it appear she had emitted the sounds from her nostrils. He fought the urge to laugh at the thought as Leah trotted to the sitting room. Clark trailed behind her, curious to see the cause of the hubbub.

Sure enough, Minnie raced to join them from the kitchen at the rear of the house, her long skirts gathered in one hand as she hastened with uncommon speed. She met them in front of the window seat, which was framed with tattered lace curtains. Her hands came to rest on the sill of the bay window, her hands and dress mercifully spared the coating of dust that rested in a thick coat there. She tipped her head back and forth, straining on tiptoe to see beyond the overgrown azalea shrubs obstructing the view. To Clark's surprise, Minnie could almost clear a small part of the window of grime, but it wasn't enough.

"Do you hear that?" she asked them, the inquiring expression on her handsome face like the one Leah had worn moments ago.

"Yeah, what is it?" Leah asked, scootching next to Minnie until they were elbow to elbow. Minnie sacrificed her prime lookout spot without complaint but still peered out the sliver of the wiped window nearest her. "Can you see anything? What do you suppose it is?"

"It sounds like a motorcycle," Clark observed.

Minnie's thin brows furrowed. "Motor...cycle?" She said, tasting the word on her tongue and finding it bitter.

"Yeah, you know. Like a bicycle, only... with a motor," Leah offered, standing on her toes and craning her neck to peer past the waist-high weeds and scraggly shrubs.

Minnie's sudden grin was the widest Clark had ever seen, save for the day he had met her and Leah. She clapped her hands together and hopped with delight, her long skirt bouncing around her ankles, stirring up a hint of dust and revealing the complicated pattern set into the parquet floor.

"Ooh! Maybe it's guests!"

"We don't *get* guests, Minnie," Leah said sardonically, dropping to her heels with a frustrated frown. Her shoes today were square at the toe and cherry red. Clark wondered how she managed to have so many options.

"Well, we *could* have guests. If we wanted," Minnie insisted.

"No, Minnie. We can't."

Minnie stopped her hopping, her face falling as her joy drained. "Well, why not?"

Leah shook her head, and her short, wavy hair shook too. "You know why not. We're fucking ghosts."

ೞ   ೝ

Harper would have to retrieve her Winchester 70 out of storage to complete this job. Typically, her SIG Sauer handgun or the AT308 sniper rifle were her weapon of choice, but the pompous Kightlinger woman was right. In this case, their daughter needed to believe her boyfriend's death was a tragic hunting accident for the clients to be satisfied. She would prefer a silencer-equipped weapon, but she had never had reason to look into the work involved in silencing the Winchester before, and time was a luxury she could not afford.

As always, Harper conducted a meticulous inventory of her suitcase before leaving her quarters. She methodically extracted the carefully folded clothes and set them into four neat rows on the bedcover. Harper exposed her arsenal's hidden pockets with a rip of heavy-duty Velcro. One side held the tools, each slightly marred from years of use but always kept in working order. Tactical knife in its sheath. Compact camera. Cellular scanner that allowed her to infiltrate even LTE and 5G networks. Eavesdropping devices capable of hearing a whisper from afar. Emergency passports and forged IDs. Extra burner phones. Lock picks. Compact first aid kit—a necessity with her trade's hazards. And, of course, some emergency cash. Her faithful sniper rifle lay beside its barrel and scope, and she gave it an affectionate caress. The second side of her suitcase held her concealable body armor, night vision goggles, and tactical gloves.

One by one, Harper pulled each item from its pocket, scrutinizing them for completeness and integrity. She powered up the items that needed juice and determined they had an adequate supply of battery life. She located each power cable and tucked them back in with the associated tool.

The ritual comforted her, a dark ballet of her own choreography that assured her she was prepared to face her task with little fear of reprisal.

Satisfied everything was in place and in working order, she sealed the equipment behind the Velcro fabric again and replaced the clothing, strapping them in with the extra-strong elastic she'd added to help keep the equipment in place.

After a quick shower, she wiped the steam from the mirror. A deep set of coal-dark eyes framed by long, sable hair stared back. She grimaced at herself before brushing her teeth and donning a pair of sweatpants and a T-shirt.

She collapsed down onto the bed. Maybe she had no business being this tired, but here she was.

A ping from her phone informed her that the Kightlingers had sent the information she'd requested. She tapped and scrolled. First and last name. Home address. Last known phone numbers. Photo of Dahlia and her boyfriend—the one she'd be killing soon. Turned out, he looked nothing like the Kightlingers sounded—no wonder they wanted him gone. He probably didn't fit the ideal posh boyfriend mold they had in mind for their daughter. Ripped, worn denim shorts. A black T-shirt with an inscrutable band logo on the front. Muscular, tanned arms. Longish blonde hair.

Hm. He's cute. Too bad.

She set the phone back on the table and plugged it in. Chances were, she'd ditch it once she was on the highway, but she couldn't have it dying on her too soon. She set the alarm for seven. She'd head to Gryphon in the morning.

⦋   ⦌

The flash of the pistol blinded Sergio for a split second. The sound echoed in his ears, accompanied by the frantic drumbeat of adrenaline. Izzy collapsed to the ground, limp, his eyes unblinking, his body still in death.

Sergio froze.

Holy fucking shit. What was I thinking? Jesus, Mary, and Joseph, what was I thinking even pointing that fuckin' thing at him? Oh my God. Oh my God, I killed him!

He hadn't meant to pull the trigger. Scare him, yes. *Terrify* him, yes. Intimidate and humiliate him in front of his high-paying customer, absolutely.

But not kill him. He was not a killer.

Until now.

The sound of running footsteps broke into his thoughts. Sergio turned without thinking, his pistol raised at eye level as he took aim.

Amp-Daddy Wayne scurried for the exit on the opposite wall, his Nikes hustling so fast all Sergio saw was tread and flapping windbreaker. His cap flew from his head in his haste, but Wayne didn't even look to see where it fell.

"Drop it!"

The frightened voice caught him off guard. Frightened, but commanding, and deep, like his. Something wasn't going right for this guy, whoever he was, but he still felt as if he had the right to boss Sergio around.

He slowly turned around, and the sight before him hit him like a punch to the gut. He couldn't move. He couldn't even think straight.

The man who'd addressed him… was him.

Not a close resemblance. No, Sergio's physical echo was five-ten, dark-skinned, dark-eyed, heavily built, and had the same face as Sergio, right down to the mole on his left cheek. Staring at him was like peering into a terrifying, warped, funhouse reflection. It was him, only backward, the way the rest of the world would see him.

He wore more middle-class clothing, like a well-dressed father-slash-business person. Or maybe a cop. That he might be a cop wasn't what terrified Sergio. The doppelgänger stared back, just as frozen. His mouth opened, closed, then opened again, like he was trying to find words that didn't exist.

"What the f—" Sergio started, but his voice cracked. His throat was suddenly dry, his mind screaming that this wasn't possible. This wasn't real. He lowered his pistol. Several phrases crossed his mind, but it seemed ridiculous to ask who he was or what he was doing there. Still…

The other man saved him the trouble.

"Who are you?" he asked. "Where—where are…?" His voice had lost its confidence. He looked around as if expecting to see something that wasn't there, waving his arms as if expecting to see something to gesture at.

Sergio finally had something to say. "Where are what?" His heart was hammering in his chest, and he wondered if the… other him… was scared, too. Did the other guy feel like he was looking into some sort of messed-up mirror? His head was spinning.

"Not what, who," his reflection said. "My partner. My...." He motioned around. "Grayzel. Cooper. My…" He took a small device from his ear that Sergio was familiar with from police dramas. The other him held the earpiece and miniature microphone. He inspected them and reinserted the earpiece.

"Grayzel? Cooper? Do you copy?" His voice was shaking. "Where the hell are you guys?" Clearly, he got no response. He yanked the piece from his ear and rubbed his eyes like he was trying to clear his head or wash away what he saw. "This isn't happening. This isn't happening," he muttered.

Grayzel? Cooper? Sergio didn't know those names. *So, he is a cop. Or maybe a government guy from one of those places with three-letter names.*

Holstering his gun, the cop guy turned on him. "Who the hell are you?"

Sergio shook his head violently, trying to snap himself out of the haze. "No, no, no. This is bullshit! Who the hell are *you*? And how did you get here?"

"I don't know!" the other Sergio yelled, desperation creeping into his voice. He paced the concrete floor, eyes wide. "My entire team just up and vanished. How in the hell?!"

"I don't know what you're talking about, man. There wasn't anyone here except Amp-Daddy and Izzy. And Wayne is gone."

The other Sergio stopped pacing and stared at him, eyes narrowing. "Wait. What did you say?"

"Look, man, I don't know who you think you are, but—"

"You said Amp-Daddy? You mean Anthony Wayne?"

Sergio's mouth went dry again. "Yeah, Wayne. You know him?"

His double looked like he was piecing something together, like Sergio had just thrown him a lifeline. "I knew I recognized that bastard." He paused, his hands clenching and unclenching nervously. "But that doesn't explain this," he gestured at Sergio and himself.

"Are you trying to bust him? Is this some undercover cop thing?" He looked the man up and down. The clean-cut clothes, the way he held himself. His voice sounded like that of an irritated white college professor instead of a first-generation Puerto Rican American. "Are you a fed or something?" Maybe there's some drugs you've got floatin' around here, and you're making me see things? 'Cause if you are, I'm gonna sue —"

The other Sergio let out a shaky laugh. "A fed? Hell, no. I'm just as lost as you." He pulled out a badge, flashing it quickly before pocketing it. "Leland County Sheriff's office. I'm a cop. But that doesn't explain this." He motioned between them, his voice tight with disbelief. "And you're not hallucinating."

"If you're a cop, why aren't you busting me?"

"For what?"

"For shooting Izzy."

"But I shot —" The suit stopped. "You shot him too?" His voice was hollow.

Sergio nodded, wondering now if admitting to pulling the trigger was a mistake. Sergio withdrew the pistol from his jacket pocket — a Glock 17. Too big of a gun to hide on most bodies. The cop pulled a handkerchief from his pocket and extended his hand for his weapon. Sergio handed it over without a fight, his hands shaking. He felt like he'd been thrown into some alternate dimension and would wake up any second now.

Careful to preserve any fingerprint evidence, his copy pulled an evidence bag seemingly out of nowhere, bagged the pistol, and pocketed it. He then walked over to Irizarry, crouched, and peered at the bleeding body, first from one side, then the other.

"Two holes," he said, "Opposite side of his head, but right in the temple. Maybe they collided or went clean through. I don't see the rounds." He stood. "Not to belabor the obvious, but… you still haven't told me who the hell you are."

"Sergio Vega. Who the fuck are you?"

"Wade Beringer," he said. His manners said he was used to shaking hands at this point in the conversation, but was avoiding it. The man's eyes flickered away, then back to him. "Did you just say Vega?"

"Yeah, so what?"

Wade appeared nonplussed. "My mother — my birth mother — was a Vega. Isabela Vega."

Sergio blinked and guessed his features were a baffled duplicate of Beringer's. "That's my mother, man."

"Your — your mother…" Beringer's brow creased. "When were you born? What day?" His words carried an eerie weight;

he was clearly used to giving orders.

"July ninth, 1975."

"Where?"

"Mercy General, Lexington, Florida. Hey, you need to tell me some shit, too. I can tell you're a cop, but I mean..." Sergio's hands flapped back and forth between himself and Wade, conveying his need for mutual disclosure.

Wade paced. "Yeah. Yeah, alright. We have the same birthday, so the logical conclusion is that we're identical twins who've never met. Though Lord knows how we both wound up in Gryphon, Alabama."

"'Logical conclusion.' Listen to my *gringo* brother. Lemme guess. You went to college."

"But that can't be right!" Wade exclaimed, ignoring Sergio's snide remark. "I mean, we've got to be—brothers. That makes sense. But it doesn't explain how or where my partner went. Or Grayzel and Cooper. What happened to the guy who jumped out of Izzy's car with the gun? And where did Anthony Wayne come from?"

"Wayne was here to buy from Izzy. I never saw nobody but them."

Wade sighed. "The whole bust just vanished, and then you and Wayne show up like you dropped out of the sky. I don't get it. I just don't get it." He ran his hand through his dark hair in a strange mimicry of a nervous motion that Sergio himself made often.

"What I don't get is why my *mamá* obviously put you up for adoption and kept me. Now *that's* some baffling shit. If she knew her crack-addicted ass didn't have it in her to raise two kids, what made her think she could raise one?"

Wade hesitated, his mouth opening and shutting as if part of him wanted to defend his mother, whom he'd never met. Sergio had known her. Probably still knew her. His stomach roiled with confusion and dread.

He'd heard stories of twins living surprisingly comparable lives miles apart, but the way he and Wade spoke and dressed showed they lived with vast disparities. Yet they carried themselves similarly. And though only God knew how, they'd both shot the same man at precisely the same moment from opposite sides of the same warehouse.

"Come on," Wade said, "We'll go talk to my lieutenant, call in the shooting."

"No way, man," Sergio said. "One of those bullets is mine. I'll get hauled in for murder."

"You *did* murder him," Wade replied, his voice an ominous undertone, "or, at least half —." He didn't know how to finish the sentence. He knew he should have Sergio in cuffs by now. Why didn't he feel threatened by the man? Because he probably shared chromosomes with him? Was it hard for him to believe in Sergio's inability to attack him just because they looked so much alike? Did he subconsciously trust that Sergio had a justifiable reason to kill Izzy, as he had, because they might be related?

Sergio said nothing in his defense. Wade's stomach crawled for a moment as he wondered why his double remained silent. Why *had* Sergio shot Irizarry?

"Just come with me," Wade entreated. "You don't have to get close enough for the LT to see you — not right now, anyway. Not until I get some stuff sorted out."

Sergio eyed Wade with suspicion but followed him to the edge of the warehouse and behind the shelter of a hedge of gnarled azalea bushes.

A puzzled look crossed Wade's face as he cleared the leafy threshold and moved to the amber ring of light under the busted streetlamp. He studied the ground on both sides of the gravel road, searching for answers in the ominous darkness. When Sergio saw no other officers waiting for Wade, he joined him in the vacant spot at the side of the road.

"What?" Sergio asked, not liking the unsettled tone in his voice.

"The van and my car are gone, too," Wade said with a sweep of his hands. His broad shoulders drooped. "There's not even a tread mark from either of them. I must be losing my mind."

Sergio, more relieved than he wanted to let on, hooked his arm and motioned to his car. "Come on."

"Come where? I can't go with you anywhere. I've got to arrest you." He unhooked his cell phone and pushed a few buttons but still made no movement toward his cuffs. Sergio, despite his reluctance to spend time behind bars, waited, trapped emotionally, if not physically. Even though he could run, he didn't. The mystery of Wade dropping so inexplicably into his life was too intriguing to leave before the odd riddle between them was solved.

Chapter Five

Wade's face scrunched up as he pulled the phone away from his ear. He hit a sequence of keys on its face, put the phone to his ear again, and then hung up in frustration.

"Dead," he said. "Not even a signal. And I've still got a full battery."

The two stood silently under the silver moonlight for a full minute. Humid summer air blew toward them from the river running alongside the row of factories, and Wade smelled the dampened air it carried. Sergio stood patiently a few feet away, his stance lending him the appearance of a cocksure version of himself, but not in a swaggering, arrogant sort of way. More like a streetwise version, confident in ways Wade, as a cop, wished he could be. Sergio's face, however, remained as puzzled as his. Exactly as much.

"So, what do we do?" Sergio asked. His voice was an odd mix of Puerto Rican and Alabama accents—heavy on the Puerto Rican, light on the Alabamian. It struck Wade as odd that Sergio trusted his judgment, much like Wade trusted him not to run away. Although they had never formally agreed to a truce, the two had developed an unspoken sense of respect based solely on their physical similarities and a presumed mutual honesty.

He sighed. "I don't know. This whole thing is too—too—"

"Jacked up?"

"Bizarre was the word I was going to use, but yeah. It's like my entire night just fizzled up and never happened. Now you're here, and you're—you. You look just like me. I don't get it."

Sergio pulled a cigarette from his pocket and lit up. Wade craved a smoke, though it had been ten years since he'd touched one. Sergio caught his longing glance and offered the pack, shaking it until a lone cigarette extended invitingly past the soft pack edge. Wade shook his head.

"Don't smoke?"

"Used to," he said, "but I quit when Marina and I were trying to get pregnant." He gave his wedding ring a reflexive twist with his thumb.

"I keep a pack handy, but I'm trying to quit." Sergio regarded the lit end of his cancer stick with a squint before turning his attention to Wade. "You're married. And her name is Marina?" He chuckled and inhaled deeply from his cigarette.

"What's so funny?"

He exhaled a puff of blue-gray smoke that drifted lazily in the summer air. "My girl's name is Maria. Maria Guzman."

Wade chuckled and shook his head.

"So'd you do it? Have a kid?"

Wade nodded and kicked at the gravel at their feet. The soil was pretty well packed. Maybe it'd never taken the tire tracks very well. "We had a boy. Derek. Looks like a little Harry Potter."

Sergio chuckled again, took a long drag, and then crushed the cigarette under the heel of an engineer boot. "So, you've never said what we're going to do? You're stuck out here with a cell phone that doesn't work. My car's the only ride for a couple of miles. You could walk; a big, dark-skinned dude like you isn't likely to be messed with in this neighborhood, but who knows? Or I could give you a ride where you want to go, drop you off."

"Drive me to the station?" Wade suggested.

"And drop you off? Sure."

Wade snorted. "I can't just let you drive off."

"Look, it's not like they don't know where I live, man. They have my plates, my make and model, my address, and…" He looked off into the woods across the creek, his jaw angrily poking out. "They know me. I'm a regular."

"I doubt that."

"Why?"

"Because I've never seen you."

Sergio's flashing black eyes met Wade's. "Then you must

not've worked there long."

"My entire career. Fourteen years."

Dead silence descended once more. Sergio looked up. "Look, you got your little notebook? Cops always have those, right? And a pen?"

Wade checked his front breast pocket, found a pen and paper (*Finally, something is where it belongs.*), and showed them to Sergio.

"Take down my information. I'll give you everything from my plates and VIN to my driver's license and social security number. You can call and verify that I was still at that address the last time I got picked up about three months ago, right?"

"If my cell phone worked, sure."

Sergio pulled a shiny silver flip phone and presented it to Wade. Moonlight glinted off its smooth surface.

Part of him wanted to cuff Sergio and force him to walk the three miles to the station. He knew it was the right thing to do. Even so, the entire night had been overwhelmingly surreal. As if none of it from the moment of Cooper's profound stupidity had really happened. He half expected that he'd wake up on the cold warehouse floor as an EMT bandaged an enormous goose egg — or maybe a gushing bullet wound — on his head.

Without a word, he accepted the phone and dialed the number for information, hanging up after the first ring. Unlike his, Sergio's phone had service.

Sergio deftly dug a fat leather wallet from his pocket and handed over his Alabama driver's license and social security card. Wade copied the information quickly and legibly, followed Sergio to his Accord, and took down the plates, vehicle identification number, and registration information.

"I can't believe I'm doing this," he muttered from the driver's seat as he jotted down the last of Sergio's info. "I can't believe I'm even *considering* it."

"Thanks. You're doing the right thing, man," Sergio said. "You arrest me —"

"I have to at least send a car for you. You've got to know that. One of your bullets went through the man's head!"

"It was an *accident*," Sergio insisted. He rolled his eyes when the unlikelihood of that story sank in. "Okay, it was an accident that shouldn't have happened. It was stupid — *I* was stupid. I had my gun drawn. I was trying to scare him for—for punking me out."

Besides his service revolver (which he requested because of his large hand size), Wade had a Glock-17 like Sergio's in his personal collection, a cache kept under lock and key high in his bedroom closet, well out of Derek's reach. He knew the gun well. Although it didn't have a hair trigger, if Sergio had jumped or jerked, an accidental shooting was possible. The same thing had happened to him.

"Iggy sold you some bunk stuff?"

Sergio's eyes sought the heavens again. "Yeah. Something like that. Anyway, I tracked him down, and I pulled the gun, but it wasn't as if I stuck it in his face. I wanted to scare him, that's all, man. Then Wayne goes and throws his phone at me. I didn't know what he threw, so I jumped, man. The trigger went off. I—it's—it does that easy. It's got a hair trigger. I didn't mean to kill him."

There it was. An accident. And Wade believed him; he heard the same fervent honesty he used when explaining the incredible. Wade paused, then placed his pad and pen on the passenger seat. It was possible that a knee-jerk reaction could've caused Izzy's death. But if that was the case, how'd Sergio hit Izzy squarely in the head?

"I was aiming for center mass, dude," Sergio said, as if reading Wade's mind. "The gun jumped when I moved back."

"A fluke headshot?" Wade said skeptically.

Sergio shrugged. "Weirder things have happened." Wade couldn't argue with that. Especially not tonight. "And to be fair, you shot him too."

"In the line of duty. He was firing at us."

Sergio's mouth opened, then shut without saying a word. His brow took on a puzzled furrow, but he withheld his thoughts.

His lips pursed, Wade touched the extra pistol in his pocket. Sergio waited for his next move, strange behavior for a man who'd been arrested more than once and knew that Wade planned to arrest him again.

"So, what've you been hauled in for?" Wade asked.

"Mostly assault, aggravated assault, and battery. I'm a bouncer at the Pretty in Pink club over on Malvolio. Sometimes things get out of hand, guys get pissed off that I've knocked 'em around, kicked 'em out. They decide in their drunken wisdom to drag the cops in, try to have me arrested. It always gets cleared up before the night's out, but they've still gotta bring me in, you know? And I've been in a few other fights. A couple of B and E's and trespassing as a kid." His gaze was steady, unblinking, but not embarrassed. Not the face of a liar. "I've never done hard time, man. Never."

It sounded honest enough, and judging from his body language—which, up to this point, mirrored his own—Wade had no reason to doubt it.

"Alright," he said. "I'll have to come by later and pick you up for questioning. You'll probably be brought up on voluntary manslaughter, maybe second-degree murder, and I can't promise what's going to happen from there, but I'll see what I can do."

The look of relief on Sergio's face was evident. Murder two and manslaughter weren't much better than murder one. Maybe it was the concern on Wade's face that promised Sergio fair treatment for whatever he'd done that night to contribute to Irizarry's death.

"Ready?" Sergio asked.

"Hmm? Oh, yeah. Let's go." Wade rose and held out his hand. "But I'm driving."

⋘　⋙

The motorcycle trekked as steadily as a war horse over the dusty dirt driveway and through the tall weeds and slim tree branches framing their path. A few times, the overgrowth drew close enough that August was tempted to ensure that Ida's arms and legs, more exposed than his in her denim-clad shorts, weren't getting too scraped up. At one particularly narrow pass along the drive, he turned to check on her, but as he did, she leaned closer, positioning herself for a better view over his shoulder. He couldn't see her expression through the tinted visor, but he didn't need to. She was as eager as he to see what lay on the other side of the drive.

Once past the last of the crowded, mature trees that shielded the house from view, the mysterious structure finally came into sight. It took his breath away, and once more, goosebumps rose across his skin, this time from head to foot. This was no ordinary house.

The old Victorian was as hidden from the street as their own trailer. All August had seen from their yard was a hint of a steep green tile roof and a fancy decorative spire at the pinnacle. Now, under the bright light of a barley moon breaking through the clouds, he saw three stories of what had once been an architectural beauty. Ivy and trumpet flower vines, likely ornamental when planted, now twined around the building in a tight embrace. Azalea bushes that concealed most of the front windows were interwoven with spiderwebs of Virginia creeper and kudzu vying for the narrow chimney peak. The roof of the wrap-around porch below the second-story turret was heavily weighed down with greenery. The paint on the siding and trim was faded, chipped, and peeled. It was impossible to tell the original color in the dark, but August guessed it had once been earthy greens and browns.

August drew the bike to a halt and kicked down the stand, waiting until Ida dismounted before swinging his leg across. She removed her helmet and shook her hair loose, but her focus never wavered. She stood, mouth slightly agape, her chest rising and falling with each shallow breath. The home had riveted her attention even more than it had his.

"Augie… it's *beautiful*."

He smiled. Leave it to Ida to see the loveliness in the derelict home. It was one of the many reasons he adored her.

"It is," he agreed. "I reckon it has a lot of potential if the structure is still sound."

"Do you think it's safe to go inside? I'd love to see what it looks like in there."

August shrugged. "We'll have to clear some of the overgrowth away from the door, it looks like, but we can try. We'll have to test the wood inside—there's a chance it's rotted. I'll check to see if there's a back door that looks any better. Hopefully, the door isn't stuck."

"Oh my God… I just realized… that's *ours*," Ida breathed. "You inherited the property it's on."

He nodded. "Yeah, remember the lawyer said there was a

run-down house we'd probably have to bulldoze if we wanted to use—"

"I don't want to knock it down! I want to fix it! It's freaking gorgeous!"

He chuckled. "Let's see what the inside looks like first. It may be a disaster."

She snapped the chinstrap and slung her helmet onto the bike handle, and he did the same on the other side. "OK. Let's go."

"Just be careful in this long grass. Watch for snakes."

Heedless of any reptilian danger, Ida marched across the yard to the wraparound porch. She trooped up the faded concrete steps and started yanking at the vegetation blocking the door. August took a quick trip around the home's perimeter and verified the back door was no less obstructed than the front before joining her.

"Careful," he cautioned. "There might be prickers. Or spiders."

She paused only for a moment to shoot him a *look.*

"Are you going to help me, or what?" she chided. August grinned and started pulling from the other side. It was easier than he expected. Despite the thickness of some stalks, most of the foliage was desiccated from the lack of rain. As they exposed inch by inch of the front door, August had the crazy impression they were unwrapping a three-story Christmas gift.

☙ ❧

Marina spent the next several minutes in a nervous blur. She paced, checked on Derek, made some raspberry tea with honey, and struggled through two more pages of her novel. Her eyes passed over the words, the plot slipping through her fingers like Tennessee river water. Thirty-two minutes after her frazzled call to the nine-one-one operator, Marina heard a light rap on her front door.

At least they didn't ring the bell and wake Derek. She set down her book and exited the library, her hands shaking as she crossed the foyer. *They probably want to talk to me about what I heard.*

She punched the alarm code, unlocked the bolt, and pulled open the door. A stout man in police blues stood on the other side. His round face held deep-set, tiny blue eyes, and his mustache was so luxuriant

Marina wanted to scratch his nose for him.

"Mrs. Beringer?" he said. "I'm Officer Brody." His drawl made him sound like the male equivalent of the operator she'd spoken with earlier. He didn't offer to shake her hand or look to see if she tried to shake his. She knew from her conversations with Wade that officers skipped protocol like that only when they were uneasy, especially when addressing the families of victims.

"Yes? Is this about the gunshots I reported?"

He shuffled uncomfortably. "Yes, ma'am. I'm the officer they sent out to check on those shots, but I haven't found anything unusual or heard anything since I've been out here."

Marina nodded. "I haven't heard any new shots, either."

His head bobbed as well, a mimicry of her motion. "I just got a call from the station house asking me to drop in for another reason. They knew I was in the area and needed someone to speak with you."

The words sent ice through Marina's stomach, and she drew in a shuddering breath. Her body and mind braced to hear the words she'd always dreaded would come. Part of her mind sank like Alice, falling down the deep hole to Wonderland while her body stood, weak-kneed, clutching the threshold of her doorway.

Brody's feet did a nervous shuffle on her step, and his breath came out in a gruff murmur. "Ma'am, I don't quite know what to tell you—"

Her heart sank to her feet. "Is he dead?"

"Dead? Well, no, I don't—Let me tell you what I understand, and then we'll take it from there, alright?"

He's been shot. Injured. He's in the hospital dying, and I have this hackneyed country bumpkin trying to clarify what happened while I could be at his bedside holding his hand! I knew something was going to happen! A sickening sensation swept over her, and she fought back a swoon.

"Ma'am? You alright?"

Marina nodded, bracing herself again with the doorway until her knuckles turned white with the effort. The pain of clenching the wood in her hands kept her anchored. "Go on."

"There was a hostage situation. Detectives Beringer and Weidenseld had to enter the scene. Shots were fired. And Detective Beringer... disappeared."

Marina waited to hear the rest of the explanation. When none proved forthcoming, she said, "What do you mean he disappeared?"

Brody looked painfully embarrassed as his feet took on a small, self-conscious dance. "That's all they told me, ma'am. They asked me to bring you into the station."

Disappeared. Thank goodness he's not dead. Part of her was relieved, but the more significant portion had grown confused and concerned. Her free hand pulled her hair away from her face and now rested on her forehead, but she had no memory of performing the motion.

"Do you mean he fled the scene? Was he chasing someone down, and now they can't find him? Do you mean the others lost contact with him?"

"I don't know, ma'am. I'm not sure I understand, either. They didn't go into it over the radio. Please, come with me." He motioned to the black-and-white at the curb.

"I have to get our son," she said, backing up. "Please, come inside."

Officer Brody nodded and stepped into the foyer. His dusty feet finished their uneasy dance, but he conscientiously remained on the welcome mat.

Marina backed a few steps away, allowing the officer to trail her into the house. He did so, and closed the door behind him as she rushed up the stairs to gather Derek. A hundred thousand questions tumbled through her mind, each begging to be asked first. But she turned around and ascended the stairs to where Derek lay in unsuspecting slumber.

☘ ☙

Leah, Clark, and Minnie stood inside the vestibule, their eyes shooting back and forth, each studying the other's countenance for reassurance, for a comforting nod to dispel the growing unease. The sound of foliage scraping and rustling against the thick wood of the front door, soft and unfamiliar, had set all of them on edge. The voices of strangers—living strangers—unsettled them. They hadn't had a living visitor in years.

"Do you… feel anything from them?" Minnie whispered, her voice barely audible over the sound of leaves brushing from the porch. Clark nearly laughed. It wasn't as if the people on the other side of the door could hear them. He wondered why, if he didn't have a physical body, it felt like his knees and hands were shaking? Why, if he was only a spirit, was he capable of moving through walls (though he hated to—it felt so *odd*), and yet he stood on the floor without fading through the planks? Why was he in *clothes*?

"Nothing," Leah said, her voice only slightly louder than Minnie's. "I don't feel anything. They aren't inside yet, though."

"They're on the porch. We should feel something bad if they were up to something, right?" Minnie pressed. "I mean the house… it kind of has its… way."

"It'll be alright," Clark assured them. He wasn't any surer than the ladies, but his time speaking with conviction at the ambo and at his anxious parishioners' sides in hospitals, homes, and the confessional had instilled in him the ability to convey a strength he lacked. Perhaps, after forty years of sharing the mysterious home as their spiritual prison, they'd learned to see through his facade. If they did, they did not show it.

Forty years. Four decades together under this roof, thousands of days and nights. Trapped in their dusty detention as if washed up on the same deserted island, they had learned everything there was to know about one another: fears, joys, sorrows. They'd spent hours poring over the mystery of the house itself, a vain attempt to unravel its secrets. To find an escape.

And now, they would face this together. Whatever it was. At least it would not kill them.

The brushing sound subsided, and then a knock. Not the sort of knock to see if someone would come to the door. It was more like a test, as if a person on the porch wished to estimate the door's strength. The murmur of a brief conversation between a man and a woman, probably in their late twenties or early thirties. A metallic rattling indicated a person on the other side was trying the knob. All three watched as the handle jiggled, but the door remained shut.

Maybe that will deter them.

Silence. Then came a loud *crack*, and they flinched as someone from outside pushed against wood wedged into the doorframe by time and disuse. Another *crack*, and then a beam of silvery moonlight shone onto the dusty floor.

"They're heeeere," he said, half joking. Neither Leah nor Minnie understood the allusion. Neither had been alive when the cultural reference became popular.

The door eased open on creaking hinges, and with apprehensive steps, their guests entered.

Chapter Six

As Wade made the short drive behind the wheel of Sergio's unfamiliar Honda Accord to the police station, the oppressive Southern humidity clung to him like a heavy shroud. The crickets sang a mournful song in the background. Wade borrowed Sergio's phone again and called Yolanda Haitsen, the desk sergeant, to verify Sergio's story about his multiple arrests that had mysteriously escaped his attention. He hated to talk and drive; it was one of his biggest pet peeves, but he didn't see where he had a choice.

"Leland County Sheriff's Department, Sergeant Haitsen speaking. How may I help you?"

"Yolanda? It's Wade."

"Uh-uh." Yolanda's distracted voice registered no recognition.

"I need to know if we have a file on a Sergio Vega. I need to know his last arrest date and the home of record."

The pause was so long that Wade took the phone away from his ear and glanced at it to make sure he hadn't lost the connection. His patience was wearing thin, and he wiped his brow with the back of his hand and replaced the phone to his ear. Finally, Yolanda's voice crackled through the line.

"...ry, sir, but I can't give that information to a civilian, especially over the phone. You're going to have to bring in a—"

"Yolanda, it's Wade. Detective Beringer."

Another wait. Wade could almost hear the gears turning in Yolanda's head. "Are you a transfer?"

The phone floated from his ear on an arm seemingly detached

from his body; he was barely aware of it. *Yolanda doesn't know me? Why is she acting as if she doesn't know me? Is this some kind of joke?* After driving for nearly a quarter mile, he noticed her voice faintly asking if anyone was still there. He hung up the phone, his mind so stunned that his thumb missed the button and he had to jab at it twice.

Single-story clapboard houses hovering near the cracked sidewalk flew by as he drove, his eyes and hands working robotically. The bust that had vanished. The twin who appeared out of nowhere. Now, his coworker — a woman who'd told him only a month ago that if Marina wasn't doing her job in the bedroom, she'd be happy to fill in for certain marital duties — was acting like she'd never heard of him. *What in the hell is going on?*

Sergio remained silent, his expression unreadable. In the quiet of the car, he most likely had heard both sides of the conversation, but if he had, he chose not to question it.

Ten minutes later, Wade pulled Sergio's car up to the curb of the Leland County Sheriff's Department, Gryphon, Alabama. The weathered sign tacked to the red brick exterior was barely readable. He parked and killed the engine, and within seconds, the heat in the car began to climb despite the late hour. The station itself was an old, weathered building, its paint peeling and its posture strangely slumped against the backdrop of aged trees.

Wade removed Sergio's phone from his pocket and scrolled down the list of names until he found the one he sought. *Home/Maria.* He opened the door and waggled the phone at Sergio as they exited the car. Sergio slid behind the wheel and caressed it like a long-lost friend.

"I'm keeping this," Wade said, indicating the phone.

Sergio shrugged. "If it'll help, man," he replied. If his twin was put out, he hid it well. Sergio's eyes studied the road ahead, undoubtedly aching to drive away.

"I may need it," Wade mumbled, not bothering to explain further.

Sergio nodded. "OK. We good?"

"For now."

Sergio tore his attention from the road and gave Wade a curt nod, which Wade returned before Sergio sped off.

Knowing he'd made a potentially career-breaking mistake

and wondering how he'd cover it, Wade pocketed the phone and climbed the steps to the station house. He pulled open the front door and blinked in the light of the dirty fluorescent bulbs that cast a sickly pallor over the place. He focused as best he could on the cheap wood paneling, the darkest thing in the room, until they adjusted.

Behind the night counter sat Yolanda Haitsen, her blonde hair pulled tightly back into a bun that made her appear older, which was good. With her petite body and juvenile features, Yolanda was often used by a local internet crime unit to bait men into soliciting underage females.

She looked up, and although her face registered recognition, it wasn't a good association.

"Evening, Mr. Vega," she said, her voice conveying a businesslike authority. "Haven't seen you around in a while. Staying out of trouble?"

Wade's jaw flapped. *Mr. Vega? She knows Sergio, but not me? She wasn't just having a brain cloud on the phone a second ago. God, this is getting weirder by the minute.*

His eyes rolled from her unfriendly face to the row of twelve eight-by-ten photos in cheap wooden Walmart frames displaying the Chief Deputy's idea of a moral booster: Officer of the Month. Wade had won just last month, somehow edging out another detective who'd caught a murderer, Noah Halabrin. Now, over the strip of white tape that read "August" was a picture of Ezekiel "Ez" Weidenseld.

Ez? Zeke is… Ez?

It was as if not only his night, but his whole life had been erased. Wade's sense of unease deepened, and he felt trapped in a nightmarish world where everything he knew was unraveling.

He realized his keys were in his pocket, a weighty anchor weighing against his thigh. *I could use my key. Get down the hall and check out my office.* The urge was strong. His leg muscles tensed, ready to propel him to the door and down the hall to his office. *And I'd get arrested before I looked for the first clue to my existence. All they'd have to do is find my service revolver.*

He thought of his malfunctioning phone, the vanished automobiles, and the lack of recognition on Haitsen's face. *Hell, I'd bet even my office is gone or handed to someone else. What the hell is going on?*

"Is there a problem, Mr. Vega? Can I help you with anything?" Officer Haitsen asked, her tone laced with a hint of suspicion.

"Sergio!" a familiar voice boomed. "Hey, nice suit. You come from a wedding?"

Wade turned and saw his partner heading toward him, a friendly but guarded smile on his face. Zeke offered his hand, and Wade shook it; it felt weird. He'd seen the man less than an hour ago. Zeke took a brief look at his knuckles before letting his hand go.

"Ahh, you haven't had to manhandle anyone tonight. That's good. Oh, wait. I almost forgot. You're a lefty." He checked out the other hand with comic exaggeration. A curious look crossed his face, but vanished as soon as it appeared. "No blood. Good." He chuckled. "What can we do for you tonight?"

"I, uh," Wade hesitated, his mind a whirlwind of confusion. He had been so sure that the precinct held the answers he needed, but now his irrational thoughts bobbed in a sea of indecision. "I, uh," he stammered, struggling to find his bearings. *Where do I go from here?*

He wanted to tell Zeke about Irizarry's body lying in a warehouse only a few miles away, but that guaranteed a trip to jail—possibly for years. Unlike him, his partner would never shirk his duty to arrest someone for murder, especially if that someone walked, talked, and looked exactly like a man known to him for brawling. It didn't matter that he knew the names of the precinct chain of command, showed him his earpiece, or gave any other clues that he was telling the truth. To Zeke, Wade was Sergio Vega, a local man with repeat offenses. Behind bars, he'd never figure out what the hell was going on.

His mind reeled, wondering how much evidence he'd left at the scene, how long it'd take the crime scene analysts to figure out it was him. Had Zeke already noticed the weight of the guns he carried? *What will happen if they run my prints, seeing as I don't seem to exist anymore?* He tried briefly to recall if the similarities between twins extended to their fingerprints. He didn't think so, but saw no reason to push his luck.

As strange as it sounded, Wade knew his best course of action lay in the hands of the man who, along with him, had inadvertently murdered Izzy. No matter what, Sergio knew Wade spoke the truth, even if no one else did.

The weight of the situation was taking its toll, and Wade found himself trembling. Had Zeke noticed? "I… need a ride home," he murmured.

"Call a cab," Yolanda suggested, her voice dripping with indifference.

Zeke shook his head. "Been drinking?" he asked, eyeing Wade with concern and suspicion. Wade noticed his eyes lingering on the pocket hiding Sergio's gun.

Wade, unable to come up with a better excuse, nodded. "Bar Stools and Pool Cues had a tequila shooter special," he fibbed. He slurred his words slightly, trying to sound convincing. "I shouldn't drive. And I'm too broke to call for a car."

Zeke chuckled and checked his watch. "Well, I've got a free minute. Let's go."

As Zeke grabbed his jacket from his office behind the steel gray door, Wade pulled Sergio's information sheet from his jacket pocket and memorized the address—twenty-two Cornwall Drive—praying it was accurate.

Zeke returned, and together they walked to the unmarked. It felt weird sinking into the passenger seat.

"Still over in the Shoalbrook subdivision?" Zeke asked as he cranked the engine.

Wade took a moment to place Cornwall Drive in his mind and nodded. "How did you—"

"Domestic dispute about a year ago, remember? I came out to make sure Maria hadn't done too much damage." He eased the nose onto the road that, at this hour, was empty except for cars parked at curbs before their respective homes. As usual, Zeke's back was straight, his body poised as if ready to eject from the vehicle at any moment.

"Right," Wade said, thinking it strange that Sergio hadn't brought up this episode with the police. Unless, of course, Zeke wasn't joking, and the fault had lain with Maria.

The tires rolled quietly over the smooth asphalt. The moon had risen several degrees since the failed bust, and Wade wondered how long until dawn broke. He glanced at his watch and saw that the hands were frozen at 12:44 — the moment when he had turned a corner into a world in which his life had become an existential puzzle.

"Sergio, can I ask you something?"

Wade blinked. *How well does Zeke know Sergio? And how am I supposed to answer a question the way Vega would?* He swallowed hard and tried to imagine that he was Sergio. It wasn't too hard. He had the costume, but the dialogue might be tricky.

"Sure, man," he said, trying to inject a bit of slurred speech, street slang, and a hint of an accent into his words. It wasn't perfect, but it would have to do.

"You come into the station house dressed nicer than normal. You don't smell anything like tequila or any other booze. Then you ask for a ride home from a cop. What's really going on? Are you in trouble?"

You have no idea.

Wade's mind reeled. Having dealt with a motley crew of criminal minds, he'd heard quite a few stories — most implausible. He hated the idea of lying to Zeke. Still, there wasn't much to tell yet. What did he know? Nothing that didn't confuse the hell out of him. And even with a quantum scientist for a father, Zeke lacked the talent to think flexibly.

Think. Come up with a good, sound, logical story, and say it like you mean it.

Wade looked at his shoes. He loathed lying. "I, uh… I met Marin--Maria at the Oyster Factory, next door to Bar Stools. It's our, um, anniversary." *Stop with the ums. He'll know you're lying.*

His mind envisioned a scenario, ruled it out, came up with another, more plausible one, and he continued. "She wanted me to call a… friend. Wanted to party. I asked her to leave the partying for another night, but she got pissed off and left. She took the car."

Zeke, ever the cautious detective, chuckled at Wade's explanation. "So why not call a cab?"

"I was pissed off, too. Wanted to walk it off before I got home, give her and me a chance to cool off. Then, some guy started following me. Guess it's the suit." Now that he had started, the lies were coming easier.

Zeke chuckled.

"Anyway," Wade continued, "I didn't want any trouble

tonight. If I get hauled in on our anniversary…" He spread his hands as if at a loss for words. "Well, I didn't want no trouble."

Zeke signaled with a bob of his head that he understood, but never took his eyes from the road. His overcautious driving had always driven Wade crazy — it was part of the reason he kept the keys to the unmarked. He absently wondered if the keys in his pocket would work on this vehicle, too. The number on the back had been the same, he'd noted.

"Smart thing to do," Zeke said. "But you've always stayed just one step ahead of serious trouble. One day, I hope you decide to go the distance and get away for good." He broke his stare to give Wade a penetrating look that Wade returned as he suspected Sergio would — part appreciation, part glare. Then, as if panicked that his brief glance away from the pavement was a sure death sentence, Zeke returned his focus to the street.

The Shoalbrook subdivision was only two miles from the station house, a small cluster of houses on a dozen streets, each a single-story combination of brick and siding with a driveway just large enough to hold two vehicles side-by-side. It was a place time seemed to have forgotten. Most homes were old enough to start deteriorating, and nearly all the owners or renters were too poor or careless to do the upkeep. A few homes sported patched roofs and manicured lawns, but their efforts were overshadowed by the slapdash general upkeep of the neighborhood.

Number twenty-two, Cornwall, was an L-shaped ranch with a fresh-cut lawn and trimmed shrubs. Wade sighed in relief at the sight of Sergio's dark Honda in the drive. The gold-rimmed license plate with a Puerto Rican flag on it and the "Puerto Rican Pride" bumper sticker were a dead giveaway. He'd been honest about where he lived, at least.

Zeke laughed as he coasted to the curb. "That bad, huh?" Wade didn't understand at first, but then he recalled his large exhalation moments ago. Safely arriving at a stop, Zeke tore his eyes from the pavement. "If it gets bad again, Sergio, just remember, you can walk away."

"And she'll throw all my shit on the sidewalk," Wade said. *Hey, my ad-lib skills are improving.*

"Better to relocate than risk us having to come back out here," Zeke said. "Or getting pelted by a lamp again."

Wade raised an eyebrow and said nothing. *So it was Maria.*

Zeke put his hand inside his jacket and pulled out a brown leather wallet, from which he extracted a business card. "I know you're probably sick of these," he said, "but here's another. Just in case."

Wade swallowed an enormous lump in his throat and accepted the card, which read *Leland County Police Department, Ez Weidenseld, Detective.* He put it into the pocket beside Sergio's cell phone. His inability to explain the circumstances barely overshadowed his guilt at not telling his friend the truth. *Buddy, I wish I had it in me to tell you everything, but I don't. Not right now, when I have so few answers.* "Thanks," he said, reluctantly getting out of the unmarked. "I, uh… you're cool for a cop."

Zeke grinned and put the car in gear. "Don't you forget it."

Wade looked up at Sergio's home, hoping for some sign of welcome. Instead, he saw a dark-skinned woman standing under the overhanging roof by the front door whose wide, brown eyes glared at him from under dark brown bangs. Terribly thin, with arms crossed against a narrow chest covered with a striped halter top, she looked anything but welcoming. She did, however, look a hell of a lot like a darker, undernourished version of Marina.

Wade's shock must have appeared to Zeke as if he was dragging his feet. "You want me to wait?" Zeke offered. Wade shook his head. "Good luck," Zeke said in parting as Wade shut the door.

α β

It took August and Ida longer than he'd first guessed to clear the thick vines from blocking the door. Dry leaves fell like fat green snowflakes as they worked. More than once, spiders sent Ida skittering across the porch, brushing her arms and legs off frantically and squealing with a startled dance. She only paused for a moment before rubbing her hands on her denim shorts and diving right back in. With zeal, she yanked the trumpet vines from the tendrils anchoring them to the building and pulled apart the Virginia creeper. Both of their arms were scratched from swinging branches, and their hands were red from effort. August suspected he had a bit of an allergy to the creeper, but he wouldn't let that keep him from making it inside. Ida's joy and exhilaration were catching.

They paused to catch their breath after clearing the last obstruction. August put his hands on his hips, and Ida unconsciously did the same as they studied their unwrapped gift. The exposed door was either a dark walnut or stained to look like it. When August rapped on the center, the wood emitted only a thick *thump, thump*.

"Sturdy door," he observed. "It's crazy. It barely shows any sign of wear at all." Ida nodded, her attention glued to the knob.

He gave the handle a jiggle, but there was no give; the knob refused to turn.

"Locked?" Ida guessed.

"Maybe," August said. He gripped the knob in one hand and butted his hip and shoulder forcefully against the door. There was a fraction of an inch of give at the frame—enough to show that it was likely unlocked but stuck in place.

"Stand back, I'm gonna kick it, and there might be some wood or doorknob flying in a sec," he said, motioning her to the side with a flat hand. Ida nodded and stepped back a bit, biting a corner of her lip in anticipation.

In high school, August became friends with a kid called Wizard, whose real name was Jace Pinkerton. August never asked Jace how he earned the nickname, but he and Wizard had palled around for a chunk of his sophomore and junior years. Over the summer, they'd taken jobs as dishwashers at a downtown restaurant known for greasy food and friendly service. During their downtime, Wiz had taught August a few moves he'd learned in martial arts classes he'd taken over the years while earning his black belt. One thing about those lessons that always stayed with August was that you don't kick the board. You kick *through* the board.

August hated the idea of ruining the door, but regardless, he gave it the best kick he could right by the knob. The aging metal of the knob cracked, and part of it fell to his feet with a *clunk*.

The heavy door opened with a protesting squeak.

ʘ ʘ

Marina woke and dressed Derek, grabbed his ever-ready bag of diversions, and held him close while Officer Brody moved his booster seat into the patrol car. Instead of sitting in the front seat, she climbed into the back next to Derek to prevent her son from feeling distanced from her by the heavy barrier between the front and back seats of the patrol car. Nearly ten minutes had passed, during which she caught portions of a conversation between Officer Brody and Officer Haitsen's disembodied radio voice that was meant to be discreet but held a somber weight. It didn't take a detective's intuition to deduce that Wade had not returned.

As they drove to the station house, Derek took her hand with his frail one and dozed, his pale, oval head to the side, his lips slightly parted. She was surprised he'd fallen asleep, but he'd always had Wade's ability to adapt to the unexpected. Derek had matured quickly, yet he clung to a childlike belief in magic and wonder, like tales of dragons, wizards, and heroic superpowers.

They reached the station house, and Brody helped her ease Derek from the car without waking him.

"Do you have children, Officer?" she whispered once Derek's head leaned against her collarbone.

Brody nodded. "Three and one on the way," he said. "Two girls and two boys. Well, one and a half boys."

She took the steps to the station house slowly. As she looked up, the glare of the fluorescent bulbs inside made her wince. She wished Derek still used a baby blanket, something she could lay gently over his head to keep the light off his face. As if reading her mind, Brody appeared with a wool blanket, one he must have kept in the trunk of his cruiser to treat shock. Marina gave him an appreciative, meager smile as he laid it across Derek's slim form.

Brody opened the door to the station, and Marina was surprised at the silence that greeted her. The Leland County troopers' outpost, nestled in rural isolation, was never a bustling hub of activity, but tonight, it felt more like a ghost town.

"This way," Brody said, heading with slow, deliberate steps for the gray door to the rear offices. He withdrew a key to unlock it, but the door flew open before he used it.

"Marina!" a voice called. She barely registered the curly red hair and tall, lean body before being enveloped in a hug.

"Zeke? What are you doing here? Why aren't you at the bust?"

Zeke let her go and looked her over, scanning her body and expression for clues to her state of mind. *Ever the detective.*

"Lieutenant Miller is handling the details with Grayzel and Cooper. They sent me back to talk to you."

"Did you get him? The dealer?"

Zeke nodded, a distracted look on his handsome face. "Yeah, we got the asshole, in a manner of speaking. And his cousin. Irizarry died in the crossfire."

Marina's concern shifted immediately. "Well, if you've got him, where's Wade? What's all the confusion about?"

Zeke hesitated, arms crossed. His fingers tapped on his muscular biceps, and his mouth pressed thin for a moment before opening long enough for him to take a deep breath and let it out with a sigh. With every second he stalled, Marina wanted to hand Derek over to Officer Brody so she could shake it out of him.

He extended his arm toward a room on her right. "Come in here, Marina. I need to try to explain."

Marina wanted to argue but accepted when she saw the folding chairs in the room. Not only was Derek, at nearly forty pounds, getting heavier by the moment, but she sensed she'd need a chair once she heard Zeke's account of the evening.

They settled in on opposite sides, Marina near the door, Zeke with his back against the wall, his chair tilted back on its hind legs as he fidgeted. He eyed the coffeepot longingly and tapped his fingers on the table as he searched for words.

"Just spit it out," she pressed.

"Okay," he said, relieved at her readiness to deal with brevity. He dropped the chair legs to the ground and leaned in, elbows on the table, his hands ready to convey the intensity of his tale. "Without going into too much detail, here's what I know. Things got hairy tonight at the bust. Irizarry took Grayzel hostage and put a gun on her. Wade started talking him down, which was working at first, but..." Zeke stopped when he realized he was getting sidetracked. "We fired shots. Wade's shot hit Izzy right in the temple," he motioned to the side of his head with an index finger, "and Izzy went down. Then Wade was gone."

"Was he hit? Is he alright? Where'd he go?" Marina asked, not sure which question she wanted answered first.

Zeke's palms flew skyward. "That's the thing, Marina. There wasn't time for him to *go* anywhere. He was there one second, and the next... he was gone."

"Maybe he has an invisibility cloak," said a small voice from under the blanket. Derek pulled down the wool cover and grinned at Detective Weidenseld.

"Hey, Derek," Zeke said with a weak smile toward Derek. "Maybe you're right. It's the only thing that'd make sense."

"You're saying he didn't run off after someone?"

Zeke put his hands flat on the table. "Are you sure you want me to go into this now?" he said with a meaningful look toward her son.

"I've already heard everything," Derek said. "Daddy disappeared."

Zeke frowned, his eyes apologizing to Marina. Her shoulder performed a microscopic shrug that she hoped he caught.

"Go on," she said.

"I'm saying he vanished. I only took my eyes off him for a second."

It was Marina's turn to frown. "Zeke, this makes no sense. People don't vanish."

"I know. My dad's a quantum physicist, and I'll bet even he couldn't explain this shi—uh, stuff."

Tears of disbelief burned behind her eyes. This was impossible. She had to make sense of this. "Zeke, tell me something."

"Anything."

"Did Wade go CIA or something? NSA, FBI, TSA, or anything else with initials that I haven't covered? Is there something you can't tell me?

Zeke held up his hands. His face revealed his genuine earnestness. "Marina, no. I'm telling you everything I know. Really. I swear on the Torah, my mother's grave, and everything else I hold holy."

Marina's surety that Zeke had kept an element of his tale hidden from her faltered. Zeke held his faith in high regard, second only to his mother. *He wouldn't say that unless he meant it. Would he?*

"I'm telling you, Mom," Derek said, "he's got a cloak."

"That must be it, honey," she murmured, stroking his head and pressing it close to her shoulder. "You're right, that must be it."

Marina felt her certainty waver as the unsettling mystery of Wade's disappearance unraveled everything she thought she knew about reality.

Chapter Seven

If Clark ever doubted that emotions came from the spirit more than the mind while alive, that doubt vanished when his soul left his body. Perhaps the reason he still experienced emotions was part of the punishment meted out to him for taking his own life. Maybe souls who transitioned via a natural death the way God intended did not have to spend eternity trapped in the homes where they died. Minnie and Leah did not know any better than he the reason for their imprisonment. Minnie had died at fifty-eight of pneumonia. She and her husband had been the home's original builders in the early 19th century—he could never recall what year. Leah had died as an unfortunate result of trying to self-induce an abortion. She had never gone in depth with him about her methods. He assumed she would rather not discuss the subject with a man she knew had been a priest, even though she knew he had also died committing what the church considered a cardinal sin at the time.

Regardless of the reason, here he stood (by what means, he did not know), watching a beam of moonlight stretch across the floor for the first time in decades. On the other side stood a young couple in their late twenties—almost his age when he passed. They pulled slim rectangular objects from their rear pockets and pressed their fingers on the surfaces of these items. In moments, lights shone from the corners of their tools. Tiny flashlights, which they used to pan the rooms from floor to ceiling, although he guessed they were more than mere flashlights from the way the objects also made their palms glow.

The woman made her way to the doorway and paused. Her enormous eyes took in everything from the entryway and its parquet floor to the hall and stairs beyond with the hand-carved railing, from the sitting room and the bay window on her right to the library with its elaborately engraved built-in floor-to-ceiling bookshelves on her left. Minnie stood tall with pride as the curly-haired woman, clearly impressed with the home's appearance, caressed the door frame with her free hand as if it were a work of art.

"Oh my god, Augie," she breathed, crossing the threshold. "It's perfect."

Augie, Clark guessed, was this woman's significant other. He saw no wedding rings on either of their hands, and they did not appear similar enough to be blood-related. The tanned young man with tousled blond hair entered after her and shuddered before brushing his arms as if feeling an icy breeze. He searched his surroundings with a curious, penetrating gaze, and he appeared to be actively listening as if searching for something he could not find but knew without a doubt was nearby.

"He senses us," Leah whispered. Clark agreed.

"It appears so."

Clark, like most ghosts, had gained insight into a portion of universal knowledge when he passed. When he first crossed over, this insight showed him the depth of occultist weaving that had gone into the fine details of the home that he had never seen in life. Now, it showed him certain qualities about the newcomers. More than love, their guests' bond was borne of hardship and protectiveness. Their love ran deeper than most, and the trench had been dug more quickly. And while they trusted and relied on one another implicitly, that trust didn't extend beyond them. They knew people to be cruel, and their faith in others was hard won.

"I like them," Leah said, and Clark chuckled. Leah, who had been a rebellious woman at the forefront of the Women's Liberation Movement of the 1960s, had similar feelings about the outside world. It made sense that she would find the newcomers relatable.

"I hope they come to stay with us," Minnie said. "It would be wonderful if the house was lived in again." Clark agreed, but kept his thoughts to himself. He did not miss the doubtful expression on Leah's face.

Augie crossed the room, swooping the tiny ray of light from right to left, his eyes following the beam. A hint of a smile lifted the corner of his mouth; he was pleased with what he saw. The smile did not light up his entire face, however. Like a wild animal on an open plain, he was cautious, keenly watching for predators.

Their human visitors did not see the dark network of hidden symbols and the true nature of the bespoke engraving on the wooden decor. Nor did he see the gray-blue amorphous cloud emerging from the wall behind him that coalesced into an entity dressed in clothes from Minnie's era.

"Passerby," Leah muttered. "Shit."

"I see it," Clark hissed, keeping his voice down needlessly.

The three apparitions watched, frozen, as the new entity gained its ghostly footing inches from where Augie stood. The phantom hesitated to take in its surroundings, as they often did after extricating themselves from whatever realm they had emerged. The movement reminded Clark of a cat who had fallen suddenly only to land on its feet in an unexpected place. Clark felt a surprising amount of frustration at the thought of this new-comer scaring off their human guests.

"Maybe it'll pass through," Minnie said, her voice shaky. "They usually do."

"I hope so," said Leah. "It would suck if it scared the new cats off forever."

The three of them stood rooted to the spot. If the Passerby took too much notice of them, it might try to interact the way previous ones had—with wild, gesticulating hands and mouths exaggeratedly moving as it strove in vain to express its thoughts. Frustrated at its inability to communicate, previous specters often devolved into poltergeists until finally moving on to whatever realm came next for them.

This phantom, however, tipped its hat, favoring Minnie in particular with a broad, friendly smile full of crooked teeth before strolling through the adjacent wall and vanishing.

"Thank heavens," Minnie said, her hand on her chest. "That was a close one."

"Do you ever wonder where they go?" Leah asked. "The

Passerbys?"

"Passersby," Minnie corrected as if for the thousandth time. "And as long as they don't stay and wreck the house, I don't much care."

Clark said nothing but joined the other two, trailing Ida and Augie through the house. He, too, wondered where the passersby went. And where they came from. He wondered often.

按 按

Once Zeke—*Not Zeke. Ez*—had made it a block down the shadowy road. The woman on the stoop yelled, "You Wade?" Her Latina accent was thick, even in those two brief syllables.

Wade nodded wordlessly in response, his tongue paralyzed by the strangeness of it all.

Maria scoffed. "*Ven pa' acá.* Can't have you standing in the streets *como un tonto.*"

Wade recalled a few words from his high school Spanish class—enough to know when he was on the verge of being insulted.

That's the least of my problems. Wade picked up his feet and trudged to the porch where Maria stood, her crossed arms unwavering, her gaze unwelcoming.

As Wade reached the last stretch of the driveway, Sergio poked his head out from the front door. Speaking to Maria in heated Spanish, which she retaliated freely, he motioned to her, the stoop, and the house's interior. Maria motioned to Wade, Sergio, and the house, demonstrating her displeasure at their unexpected guest each time. Finally, she threw up her hands and stormed inside, throwing words over her shoulder as she disappeared down the hall. The few words Wade picked up weren't flattering, but if she intended them for him or Sergio, he didn't know.

"Sorry about that, *hermano,*" Sergio said. "She forgets, sometimes, what it's like to need help."

The inside of Sergio's home displayed an odd juxtaposition of a humble existence and a sense of quiet comfort. He stood in a large living room with a new-looking sofa and loveseat in a deep honey-gold hue flanked by flattering square walnut tables. A matching entertainment center held a plasma television and several old bolero CDs mixed with what looked to Wade's untrained eye to be dance music, rap, or both. Along the far-right wall stood a wide desk and a gaming computer with two large flat-screen monitors and a Nikon digital camera plugged into a CPU emitting a soft, otherworldly blue glow.

"Come in, *ven sientate*," Sergio said, motioning to the couch. Wade sat, noticing that despite the crowded surroundings, the house had a very homey feel. Tidy, but not sterile; lived in, but comfortable.

"Nice place," he said, and he meant it.

Sergio shrugged and collapsed into the loveseat. "It's too small."

"Looks like you're just outgrowing it."

"We are." Sergio leaned forward, put his elbows on his knees, flexed his fingers, straightened them, then meshed them together. "I figure that since I'm not in cuffs, you're not here to arrest me. What's up?"

Wade put his hands up. "I don't know. To be honest, I'm not sure why I'm here other than that you were there when everything went… pear-shaped. I went to the station, but…" he trailed off. Why, when he had such a hard time telling Zeke (*Ez*), did he feel Sergio would understand better than anyone? Because he was there when it happened? Because they looked alike? "I saw a woman at the station I've known for five years. She called me Sergio. My own partner offered me a ride to *your* house. It was like…"

"Like you'd never existed?"

Wade blinked in astonishment. "Yeah."

Sergio nodded as if this was what he'd expected. Sergio's nonchalant acceptance of the situation unnerved Wade, and he wondered how unruffled the man would be if their roles were reversed.

Sergio moved his attention from his hands to Wade's face. "You read any sci-fi? Watch sci-fi-movies? Or maybe those Marvel movies?"

"Science-fiction stories? No," Wade admitted. "I'm more of a history/biography kind of guy. I caught the more recent Spider-Man flick, though. Why?"

Sergio smiled. "I read a lot of books. Heinlein, Zelazny, Love-craft, Philip K. Dick, you know. The stuff that they made Star Trek out of. And I know that even though I don't understand quantum mechanics, lots of people believe in things like parallel universes and alternate realities."

"You think—you think I've slipped into some other reality? *Your* reality?" Wade's mind recoiled at the notion. Slipping through a crack in some universal fabric was a lot less likely than a blow to the head, or maybe a stroke, or amnesia, or discovering that he had a twin. Perhaps he'd had a neurological episode and would wake up in a hospital, and none of this was more than a dream. Anything was more likely than living the plot of a science fiction novel.

Sergio's response, however, carried a conviction that un-nerved Wade. "Bro, think about it. Go back over this whole night and everything that's happened. Can you come up with a better reason for all that shit to've happened?"

"That it isn't happening at all," Wade said. "I'm dreaming, in a coma, or brain damaged."

Sergio spoke sternly as he leaned forward, his gaze piercing through Wade's. "Look around you, man. It's *happening*. And you'd better get that soon, or you might miss your chance to get home. If you can't believe that you're really here, in my world, in my time, then you won't even try to get back to yours. You—we—don't want that. Think about it. Your wife. Your kid. Who knows what'll happen to them if you're stuck here? I don't know how this multi-dimension stuff works. I'm not sure if time's passing the same way here as it is there, or if the window you passed through is going to last, or—"

"Wait, wait, wait," Wade interjected, waving his hand back and forth, a chill scraping his spine at the thought of never return-ing home. The room, which had moments before felt so homey, now seemed to close in on him. "If this is a… an alternate uni-verse, then who are we? How'd I come to meet you? Why here? Why now?"

Sergio licked his lips, and it looked like he was assembling the best way to express his thoughts. "Why here and now… I don't know. If I guessed, I'd say it was because somehow, on both planes, we shot the same guy at the same exact time. Somehow, that seems to have triggered a crack between dimensions that let you slip through. As to who we are…" Sergio paused, reluctant to say what he had in mind.

"What?"

Sergio met his eyes. "Dude, don't you get it? *I'm you.*"

೮೪   ೮೦

The black clouds obscuring the night sky had passed without offering a drop of the rain they had threatened, leaving the sky full of stars and a moon that helped light August and Ida's way through each musty room. The old home had once been a polished, stunning work of art, and most of that craftsmanship had survived decades of neglect. Some items that immediately caught August's interest were a hand-carved fireplace mantel in the parlor, the unique spiderweb patterned stained-glass windows, the tall baseboard trim, crown molding and corner blocks, and the transoms over the doors. Everything within the house held a personal touch from floor to ceiling. Every aspect of the home was a labor of love, now coated with a thick dust layer obscuring the finer details. The faded paints and wallpapers, no doubt once bright jewel tones of greens, reds, and oranges, had faded like fall flowers into dimmer, more earthy shades.

Earthy. That was what made the house so stunning. The owner had taken great pains to bring the feeling of nature into each of the home's handmade creations. As he and Ida took in room after room, August noted how the designer had meticulously incorporated aspects of the outdoors into each room. The fireplace mantel appeared like twisted wood grain. The railings with delicate leaves sculpted into the sturdy posts. A snowflake-shaped ceiling medallion decorated the ceiling above the chandelier in one room, a second medallion in another room was modeled after flower petals, and yet a third room had one engraved with a crescent moons and stars.

The place was exquisite. So why had it been abandoned? He'd half expected to see faded brown blood splatters on the walls of a room or an enormous gaping hole in the center of a floor. Maybe collapsing interior walls or telltale bullet holes. But no. Besides the heavy dust, hundreds of cobwebs, and signs that mice and probably squirrels had taken up residence, there was no sign of foul play or poor construction. On the contrary, they could turn it into a castle with some elbow grease, time, and a lot of money. It'd need to be retrofitted with some high-velocity air conditioning. Electricity would need to be checked—there's no telling what time had done to the wiring. And the plumbing, too. *Didn't they used to use cast iron plumbing back in the day? How long does something like that last?*

As he watched Ida study the wallpaper, he calculated the cost and time needed to make the place habitable. When he imagined the two of them changing the home to make it their own, a sense of unease washed over him. As if to do so would trigger a sequence of events between him and a grisly fate. He cast his thin flashlight beam around the room, searching for a logical reason for his concern, but of course, found nothing. Other than the sense of heebie-jeebies the place gave him, the house was perfect.

The floor creaked behind him, and he spun around, his nerves shooting off like fireworks as he braced himself for… nothing. Again. Nothing but a few dust motes danced through the flashlight beam. He turned to rejoin Ida, who pranced light-footedly up the next staircase and had not noticed his irrational moment of panic.

Relax. Breathe. It's an old house. Old houses creak.

By the time they reached the third floor, the temperature had to be at least a hundred and ten. August wondered how high the temperatures had climbed during the heat of the day. A thin sheen of sweat made Ida's skin glassy, and her hair had grown into a frizzy mess, but she danced from room to room with glee.

The parquet floor in the stuffy third-floor tower room had been set into a compass. Based on the direction of the sunset earlier that night, August deduced the cardinal arrows pointed in the right directions. He could imagine how the sun would light up the room during the day through its many windows. Once they had installed climate control, the room had the potential to be downright gorgeous. He tried to envision the room's purpose; unlike the others, this space held no furniture to provide clues about its former use.

Ida spun around in the center of the compass, her arms outstretched, making the light from her phone flashlight cast morphing shadows on the ceiling and dust-hampered sparkles on the surrounding windows as she turned.

"I can't believe anyone would walk away from this house!" she crowed. "I—August, is this really ours?"

"Maybe it's haunted," he joked, his voice flat.

She stopped spinning. "Maybe they're friendly ghosts," she laughed.

"Maybe it's dangerous. Like full of radiation or something."

Ida made a frustrated sound and frowned at him before petulantly crossing her arms over her chest. "Are you *trying* to take away my joy?"

"No, Ida. No. I just… we've got to not get our hopes up. Not yet. Let's do some looking into the place, OK? Maybe we can ask around. I'll bet LaDonna and Luke might know something about why the place was abandoned. We can search the internet and see if there's something we need to learn about this place before we set our hearts and money and work on fixing it up, OK?" He chose his words carefully, but despite his disquiet, he already envisioned Ida filling the room with plants and the house with cats and dogs. This room would be perfect for a snake to sun itself in—Ida loved snakes (much to her parents' dismay). He wanted to love this house as much as she did, but…

I just need to figure out what's setting me off. Maybe the place will look less creepy in the daylight.

Ida fanned herself with a hand and let out a frustrated sigh. "Fine. OK. I guess you have a point. But we'll start asking right away, right? Because if we can live here…" She spun around in another circle, arms outstretched, head back. She froze, and her enormous eyes grew more prominent than he thought possible. She shone the beam of her light onto the ceiling.

"Look, Augie! The ceiling has stars painted on it! I'll want to keep that part when we paint it."

"*If* we paint it," August said, the feeling of unease pestering him again at the thought of modifying the home.

"*If* we paint it," she agreed. She shot him a delighted grin. "We'll paint it, Augie. I have a good feeling about this."

He offered her a small smile, and as he looked at where a chandelier once hung, goosebumps rose on his skin again. *That makes one of us.*

Wade choked on nothing and sat up, his eyes so wide they felt ready to bulge out of his skull. The air hung heavy and thick with tension and uncertainty.

"You're what?" Wade's voice quavered.

"Think about it." Sergio spread his hand out and ticked off each point as he went. "We were born on the same day, to the same woman, in the same place. What else could it be?"

"Twins," Wade snapped, his voice taut with disbelief. It didn't explain the weirdness at the police department, but his head refused to wrap around Sergio's suggestion.

Sergio let out a frustrated scoff. "Is it so unbelievable that you're me, and I'm you in different realities? Dude, I thought you were a detective."

Wade said nothing, taking in his counterpart's hip-hop clothing and his cocksure manner. Unbelievable didn't cover it. *This is me? I could've turned out like that? No way.* "This whole thing is unbelievable!" Wade said, throwing his hands up and slumping back onto the couch.

Sergio scowled in irritation at Wade's stubbornness. He checked his watch. "Look. It's three in the morning. Let's try to get some sleep, and tomorrow we'll talk to Mom, see if she can help. If she says she had twins, we can check out your theory, see about getting you to a doctor for your brain damage."

Wade struggled against the urge to glare at Sergio. "Thanks. I think."

"Don't thank me yet, *amigo*," Sergio said. He stood and then crouched at the opposite end of the boxy coffee table. He withdrew a thick comforter from a set of doors, which he handed to Wade.

"The couch is comfortable. We don't have any pets or kids to wake you up in the morning, and Maria doesn't work until ten when she works doubles, like tomorrow. We should be able to get a little sleep before we head to Mom's."

"When does she work?" Wade inquired, his voice laced with curiosity regarding his unknown mother.

Sergio scoffed and subconsciously eyed his watch again.

"She's probably working now."

"Now? What, does she work in a factory or something? Night shift?"

"Dude, she spends her nights… making men happy."

"What?"

He rolled his eyes. "Wade, man, she's a hooker."

Chapter Eight

In the following hours, Wade never knew if he'd drifted off or if his sleep-starved mind wandered into surreal thoughts loosely based on what had inexplicably become his reality. Friends becoming strangers. Solid objects vanishing without a trace. Men with his face leading entirely different lives. If there was a logic-based answer that didn't involve head trauma and a wild, coma-induced fantasy or science-fiction, he didn't know what it was. His life had morphed into a bleak scene from Edgar Allan Poe's tales, where reality and the macabre blended in ways that rarely benefited the protagonist.

At eight-fifteen, he gave up on sleep, roused by a gurgling coffeepot in the kitchen. He padded his way into the next room to discover an automatic coffee pot timed to percolate at a quarter past the hour. The dim light filtering through the slats in the blinds cast elongated shadows across the room. Wade searched for a mug, creamer, and sugar, which he discovered in the cupboard above the machine. He helped himself to the closest mug at hand (which read *I Prefer the Term Drug Hobby*), sugar, and powdered cream, careful to sniff the powder from a distance before adding it.

"It's safe, man," Sergio said, trudging into the kitchen and flipping on the overhead lights. "I don't do powder." He scratched his stomach, lifting his shirt as he did so. Wade noted Sergio's muscular abs with an envious glance.

Wade tried to erase the guilty look he knew painted his

features. "And Maria?"

"Prefers pills." Sergio reached for the cupboard, grabbed a mug (100% Boricua), and added matching condiments. They met at the round, glass-topped kitchen table and sat opposite one another in the leatherette and chrome chairs. Wade noticed a few superficial, straight scratches in the glass and tried not to ponder the cause.

"What's your plan for today?" Wade said. *Funny. Yesterday, I was the cop, and he did what I said. Today, he's the man with the life, theory, house, and mother, and I have nothing.*

"You said you wanted to meet my — our — mother. Still want to do that?"

Within the hour, the two of them — Wade now dressed in one of Sergio's warm-up suits and feeling more than ever like a poorly rendered carbon copy — were buckled into the Honda.

"You sure you want to do this?" Sergio asked once he had the car pointed down his street.

Wade snorted. "What choice do I have?"

Sergio reached the end of the subdivision without coming up with a response. He turned his blinker on, indicating a turn toward the highway.

"Wait," Wade said, "I have one last request."

Sergio, anticipating a direction change, flipped the blinker off. "Name it."

"Let's drive by my house."

Wade didn't know what had taken him so long to think of this idea. Perhaps the events and exhaustion of the night before had rendered him incapable of coherent thought. Perhaps, on some level, he was terrified of the possibilities. Regardless, Marina was the most logical woman — no, the most logical person — he knew. She'd come up with a solution to their problem. His problem. *Whatever. As long as she's there. God, please let her be there!*

"Where's that?"

"Forest Dale."

Sergio let out a choked laugh. "You mean you live in Ivory Towers?" He turned the blinker on in the other direction and then turned almost immediately. "Man, I really got ripped off."

Fatigue made Wade incapable of a flippant rejoinder. He watched the changing landscape through the window, searching for any sign that this world was not the world he knew. As far as he could tell, everything was exactly the same as it had been twenty-four hours ago. *Well, what did I expect? I'm not exactly George Bailey from It's a Wonderful Life. I lived like a regular guy; I didn't change many other people's lives — unless I put them in jail.*

"You alright?" Sergio asked.

"Just thinking that maybe I should've done more with my life," Wade said.

Sergio laughed derisively. "Tell me about your life, man. Bet it's not that ordinary."

Wade gave him a skeptical look.

"No, really, man. I want to know what it's like to be you. Wade… What's your last name?"

"Beringer," Wade said with a shrug. "Not much to tell. My parents lived in Gryphon, adopted me, and had a pretty uneventful life. Graduated from Gryphon High. Went to college at the University of Alabama and got a degree in criminal justice. Joined the Leland County Sheriff's Department, and now I'm a detective. I met Marina in college, where she was pursuing her nursing degree. We got married before our college graduation—her parents didn't like that, but they forgave us once we graduated. We're both pretty driven." He gave his wedding ring a twist with his thumb.

"Yeah, I noticed you're not exactly a quitter."

"She wound up getting pregnant and having Derek right after we left college. No big deal, really. She took some time off for him and went back to nursing when he was two."

"And now you're happily married and living in Forest Dale. Where's the money come from? A detective and a nurse don't exactly rate that neighborhood."

"Her folks," Wade admitted.

Sergio's derisive scoff became contemptuous. "You got parents, school, a wife, a kid, a good job, and you wish you'd done *more* with your life?"

Wade felt as if he'd had cold water thrown on him. What had he been thinking? Compared to most, his life was pretty amazing.

From the corner of his eye, he watched Sergio steering through streets that were, undoubtedly, becoming decreasingly familiar to him. The man sat slumped in the seat like a thug. His clothing was an advertisement for a street-smart man, and his manner never lost the edge of anger that churned layers below.

"What about you?" Wade asked.

Sergio snorted. "My life? Well, that's not so easy, man. See, my mother was a whore hooked on drugs who didn't believe in responsibility for anything but her habit. She used to be a 'dancer'—a pole dancer. Then, she got hooked on heroin. My whole life, she's bringing home strange men at night—usually more than one.

"She didn't care what I did during the day since she was sleeping or high most of the time, so I played with the other kids on the block. Some of them had crack mamas, too. Mom never gave me toys, so I made 'em or stole them. Dug 'em out of dumpsters.

"Time came for me to go to school, and she didn't sign me up. Child protective services almost took me away then, but she cleaned up for a little while, straightened everything out. Then she fell in love with the Oxy the doc gave her for her back. Once I was on the bus route and everything was cool with the court, she went back to normal—which, for her, of course, meant more *hombres* and more shit.

"By the time I'd graduated high school, I had a record. Breaking and entering. Trespass. Shoplifting. Still, they never got anything bad to stick. Been busted and charged plenty of times, but none of it stuck.

"I'm a big guy. I know how to fight. Got a good job at the club where I met Maria. Amateur night. She liked how she danced, and she was cute. She asked me what I thought of her set, and I told her. I went home with her that night, and pretty soon, I moved in to get away from Mom and help Maria pay her bills. Now Maria doesn't like that I work where I do with all those women taking their clothes off, but she also says she wants an open relationship. She hates I get hauled into jail when I swing on guys who take it too far with the dancers. She's got all these—these ideas about what our life is supposed to be like. Rich—or at least doing a hell of a lot better. Upper-middle class. And we both make decent money, but she loves spending it. She has to have the right clothes, the right toys, and the right wheels. Plus, she's nearly gone through a stack of cash her *tia* left her when she died, and now I'm selling drugs to make sure we don't go into debt. It's so stupid. I've been telling her to stop, and now we always fight. She's really *loca*."

Sergio realized he was ranting, sharing the dark history he'd always hidden, and stopped. His words hung in the air, and the tension they caused made Wade feel as if the car they sat in was holding its breath.

Turning to Wade, he asked, "Still think you haven't done enough with your life?"

Wade was saddened that his impression of Sergio's life had been dead accurate. Of course, it wouldn't have taken a detective to add up the clues.

He saw the entrance to his subdivision against the glare of the morning sun. He pointed at the large, beige sign, the words "Forest Dale" written in gold against a rectangle of beige. Below the sign, a waterfall fell into a crystal-clear pool surrounded by starkly contrasting, colorful chrysanthemums. Sergio nodded and turned right, scaling the hill into the neighborhood.

The difference between Shoalbrook and Forest Dale wasn't as bad as comparing the average ghetto to Beverly Hills, but Wade guessed Sergio wouldn't quite agree. Here, homes started at two stories and went up. The neighborhood wasn't large; Gryphon didn't harbor many wealthy folks, but the few they had were enough to make up a small neighborhood—Wade's neighborhood. Landscaped lawns. Trash cans hidden out of sight. Pets kept inside or within fenced-in yards. No bright plastic toys dotting the front yards—for all Wade knew, only he and Marina had kids. The few driveways that held cars seemed to prefer German manufacturers or late-model luxury SUVs. It was, Wade realized, an ideal place to live.

"Take a left down Regency," Wade said, indicating a road toward the rear of the spider web of streets. Sergio nodded, struck dumb by the tony area. Even his car seemed somehow smaller now that they cruised its roads.

He turned, and Wade craned his neck to see the place where his home had stood. Large, white, three stories, and just beyond a slight curve, he should have easily spotted it from the corner, even through Sergio's heavily tinted windows. Instead, he saw a vast, cobalt-blue French provincial monstrosity on the lot.

"No," he whispered. Sergio shot him a quick look, unsure what brought on Wade's anxiety.

"What's the house number?"

"One fifty-seven," Wade whispered, his voice fading. His hand went to his mouth, much the way Marina did when she was distressed.

"What's wrong?" Sergio said. The numbers of the mailboxes came into view, and he coasted to the proper number. White post, black box, red flag, bright gold numbers read one, five, seven.

Not even if his house had burned to the ground, not even if there had been a vacant lot where his house once stood, could the three-story atrocity have been erected overnight. His home was gone.

"That's not my house!" Wade snapped, pointing an accusing finger at the lot. "I mean, it's where my house was, but…"

His house was gone. No, worse than gone; there was no sign it had ever been.

My God. If there's no house, where's Marina? And Derek? Can there really be a reality in which Derek doesn't exist?

Sergio slowed the Honda to a crawl but didn't stop. He studied the property in Wade's home's plot as if he debated asking if they saw the same thing.

"Go," Wade snapped, flapping his hand urgently at the windshield. "Just go."

Sergio pressed the accelerator and cruised to the end of the cul-de-sac, where he turned around.

Holy crap, he's right. Sergio's right. I'm in another reality. My house, my marriage, my son — all nonexistent here. How in the hell do I get back?

Never had Wade longed so intensely to see his wife and hold his son. The chance that he might never see them again weighed on his heart almost more than he could bear. He did not know how he'd gotten here. If he didn't know how he'd gotten here, how in the hell would he find his way back? If Sergio was right and he arrived in this dimension because they had replicated the same action at the exact moment in separate lives on different planes, how could they recreate it?

They couldn't. And unless they came up with a solution, Wade would be stuck here, away from the life he knew and loved,

for the rest of his life.

α β

Marina sat in her breakfast nook, nursing a cup of coffee that grew colder with each minute she spent ignoring it. The room felt darker than she recalled, as if stuck in perpetual twilight despite the coming dawn. Crumpled Kleenex dotted the table before her. As she hastily balled up another one and added it to the mix, she felt her shoulders slump with misery.

Gone. Just gone. Vanished. This is insane. People don't just vanish!

But after Zeke's tale, as the sky outside the sheriff's department window grew to a bruised blue, Grayzel and Cooper added their chilling accounts of the night's events. Then Lieutenant Miller. Each story echoed the other in stunning detail.

After their accounts, she heard Irizarry's cousin pleading desperately as someone forcibly hauled him to the rear of the station.

"You can't arrest me for dealing when you use drugs during your busts!" he shouted, his back arched as he hopped forward with his arms held behind him by a bulky officer, fighting against the advance toward the cell block doors. "You makin' me see shit vanish! I'm gonna call me a lawyer and sue y'all—every last one of ya! Y'all can't do that! I got my damn rights!"

Then Lieutenant Miller brought in the video camera. He hastily plugged the device into the station television and let Marina watch while Zeke kept Derek occupied with another tour of the station. It was probably the boy's third tour that night, but her tired little boy didn't argue.

She tapped her feet impatiently as Miller fidgeted with the settings on the camera. At last, the footage of the bust came on screen. Her skin grew clammy as she watched. Never had she seen so clearly the type of work Wade did and the danger he put himself in. The sight made her heart hammer as she sat on the edge of her chair, transfixed.

The first minute was a few muffled exchanges, but then the young one—Cooper?—took out his gun. Suddenly, the shot tilted, bounced with a loud clatter, and shifted sideways. Zeke had dropped the camera on the floor as he dashed into the warehouse. She still had a good view of everything from Wade's back to the corner of the warehouse.

Her breath caught as the drug dealer took Grayzel in the crook of his arm, a gun trained on her husband. Her hand pressed against her mouth, and cold sweat covered her skin. Then came the most convincing part of all. Shots fired. Her heart threatened to explode. Wade waited, took a shooter's stance, pulled the trigger, stepped forward...

And disappeared. With that sight, the last shred of Marina's disbelief faded as well.

Back in her silent home, nearly finished with her first pot of strong coffee, Marina prayed her son might sleep for hours—perhaps days. However long it took until some of this made sense.

It wasn't a game. It wasn't a fabrication, a cover-up, or a joke. Her husband vanished, a phenomenon as incredible as spontaneous combustion or a rain of frogs.

Where had he gone? Was he still alive? Was it possible to bring him back? How?

The sound of tiny feet in cotton socks turned her head. Derek stood in his flannel pajamas, his rectangular black-rimmed glasses askew as he rubbed an eye, a worried expression on his elfish face.

"Mom? What's wrong?"

"I'm worried about your daddy," she said, her voice tinged with sorrow.

Derek nodded. "I understand. He disappeared, and we don't know where he is now."

She wanted to shield him from the painful truth, to utter comforting lies. But now was not the time to start lying to her son.

"That's right," she said with a nod. She pulled another Kleenex from the box and blew her nose.

"Can we look for him?"

She crumpled the tissue into a ball with shaking hands. "I don't know, son," she said. "I want to try."

Derek stepped toward her and curled into her lap like he hadn't done since he was a preschooler, wrapping his thin arms around her and burying his pointed chin at her collarbone. Her heart, already tense, clenched tighter than she knew possible.

"I want to help," he said.

Her first instinct was to protect him. He was only six, for Pete's sake. He didn't need to see her frustration, her anger, her sadness, her fear, and the inevitable tears. Still, he deserved a chance to do what he could. If Wade, God forbid, never came back, how would he feel toward a mother who denied him his chance to help bring him home? And she had to admit that it soothed her heart having Derek within eyeshot.

She sighed. "Alright. Today is Saturday. You can help today and tomorrow, too, if it comes to that."

He picked his head up from her collarbone. "And what then? What if he isn't home by Monday?"

His bravery touched her. "Then you go to school—"

"But Mom—"

"No buts. You go to school. Anyway, maybe we'll have him back by then."

Derek smiled, his green eyes shining behind his glasses. "I think we will. If we try hard."

I hope you're right. Marina prayed her face didn't reveal her overwhelming doubt.

⊰ ⊱

As the first light of dawn crept in, a fine mountain mist hung in the air, though the local radio station claimed most folks weren't seeing a drop of it. Through the smudged kitchen window, August noted that the plants in the stand beside the moonshine still had perked up slightly, now standing only slightly dazed instead of passed out completely like they'd been on a three-day bender. The dappled golden sunrise was making quick work of the thin layer of moisture, and it wouldn't be long before the air turned into one of those thick, sticky saunas that only the mountains could cook up.

Ida slept peacefully on the pull-out couch in the nearby living room, her mouth parted slightly, and her breathing was light and regular. He watched her curl up with a pillow, peaceful as a cat in a sunbeam, and his heart swelled. He poured coffee into a large cup and added ice and a generous dollop of cream. Stirring the brew absentmindedly with a long-handled spoon, he recalled one of the morning blessings his Aunt Lyra used to say.

Thank you for another day
Please bless my steps and guide my way
Bless my tongue, make my words true

May love and joy and peace come through.

"Always stir clockwise, August. Always," she'd say with her musical voice before tapping the fancy silver spoon on the edge of her coffee cup and setting it at the edge of the sink. His family never had much in the way of fancy things, but Aunt Lyra's silver was impressive cutlery. The spoons even had little scrolls on the backs of their tiny bowls, like they were meant for royalty and not for a family who ate most of their meals off mismatched plates.

He wished Aunt Lyra was here. She was one of the few in the family who didn't roll her eyes or tell him to hush when he talked about feeling things that couldn't be seen, like that eerie prickling sensation on the back of his neck. She even encouraged it.

"We're all a little magic, August," she insisted. "Some of us are more in tune with it than others."

Most of his family scorned his Aunt Lyra's belief in magic. They joked about how she'd set out mason jars of rainwater to collect energy by the light of the full moon, her crystal necklaces, and her love of astrology. She loved going on ghost tours and visiting places reputed to be haunted and insisted she sensed ghosts in many of the sites. August thought it was fascinating. He couldn't help but wonder what Aunt Lyra would've made of the old Victorian. If she'd have picked up on something the way he had. He'd never know. Cancer had taken her from this world with fearsome speed. That spring, she'd been vital, laughing, a colorful dark sheep in the family's dull flock. By Thanksgiving, she had withered to a beautiful, balding, bravely smiling corpse.

Was the energy in the Victorian truly as dark as he'd thought? It had been late and dark. Maybe he had filled the house with the fears he'd carried with him from West Virginia. They'd been running and hiding for months. And LaDonna had already weirded him out by sneaking that extra something into their bag.

August withdrew the muslin bag from the refrigerator and brought it and his coffee to their old-fashioned, clunky dining room table. He tugged the strings loose and removed the fragrant herbs one at a time. Rosemary. Mint. Oregano. And a small lunch bag-sized package folded into a small envelope. Written in beautiful script was one word: *August.*

The sound of creaking couch springs told him that Ida was awake. He turned the package over, held it to his nose, and sniffed the brown paper.

"What is it?" Ida asked.

August shook his head. "LaDonna gave us a little something extra. Gave it to me, apparently. It has my name on it."

"Well, open it already. I want to know what it is."

The couch springs protested as Ida shifted, rolling herself off and onto her feet. Barefoot and bleary-eyed, she padded over to the kitchen, pouring herself a cup of coffee with surprising grace for someone still half-asleep. She tossed in a spoonful of sugar, stirred it with a quick flick, and then pulled out the chair next to him. She lifted a sprig of rosemary to her nose and took a deep breath. A slow, satisfied smile crept across her face.

August found a piece of tape holding a flap of the bag shut. He slid a finger underneath, popped it off, unrolled the top of the bag, and peered inside.

"What is it, Augie?" Ida asked again, leaning forward.

He tipped the bag in her direction, and she also peered in. "More mint?"

He shook his head. "I don't think so. Smell it."

She took a quick sniff and wrinkled her nose. "No, not mint. It smells like… tea? Like a funky tea." Her face softened, and she leaned back. "How can one herb smell like tea all by itself?"

"Hmm." He poked his nose back into the bag to smell the herb again and noticed a slim piece of white notepaper against the edge of the bag. The handwriting on the note matched that on the outside of the bag.

I think this might answer some of your questions. Do some research and ask me if you need help. I am more than willing to guide you.

August pulled the bundle of leaves from the bag and furrowed his brow. He knew a lot of plants—years of brewing shine had taught him the benefits of several—but this one was not familiar. The leaves looked like mint, but the fragrance was nothing like it.

Guide me with what?

"You need your phone?" Ida asked, and he nodded. She stretched backward, exposing a hint of bare stomach from underneath her tank top as she reached for August's phone on the end table. He took it from her and flipped through his phone until he found PlantPuzzle, the app he used to identify foliage with which he was unfamiliar.

He held the plant at an arm's distance, allowing the phone to focus on the leaves. In moments, it scanned its directory for similar patterns.

"Well, according to this, it's spearmint, catnip, or sage."

"But it doesn't know for sure?"

August was already searching the net for the answer, since the app didn't provide a simple explanation. After several minutes of searching, he threw up his hands. The leaves were too wide, not ridged enough, or not appropriately grouped to be anything he found on the internet. It'd be hard to research when he had no clue what the plant was.

"I say let's ask her," Ida proposed, one shoulder raising and falling in a little half-shrug.

"Yeah. There's got to be a reason LaDonna gave this to us."

"To you," Ida pointed to his name on the bag. "And I'm really curious why."

Chapter Nine

"Where to?" Sergio asked once he'd reached the exit to Forest Dale.

Wade's first impulse was to point Sergio toward Marina's parents' plantation-style manor. He wanted to track down his wife, talk to her, help her see the reality that he knew, and help her love him in an instant as strongly as she had in his world. He craved to have his wife back in his life. He wanted his son to be alive. To exist. He longed for his life back. If his will alone had been power enough, the thought of holding his family again would have sent him back to his world in a shot. Instead, an unknown future loomed ominously before him.

Going to Marina's folks' house makes no sense — they'd have no idea who in the hell I am, either. They sure as hell wouldn't tell me where she is. And all I'd do is scare the hell out of her, even if I found her. So now what?

He'd started the day intending to meet his mother. He needed no further proof to confirm Sergio's multi-universe theory, or whatever it was called. However, he believed the best way to chart his future path involved delving deeper into his past.

He shrugged. "Let's go to Mom's."

Sergio's eyebrows shot up under his shaggy bangs. "You sure, man?"

Wade couldn't help but laugh at the absurdity of it all. "Well, it can't hurt anything."

"You don't think seeing you might freak *her* out?"

He hadn't thought of that. "We'll just have to spin a tale. Tell her we met by some freak coincidence and were wondering if we could be brothers or have some other thread of kinship. You said yourself she's not exactly forthcoming."

Sergio laughed. "That's an understatement, *hermano*."

Hermano. Brother. It was strange hearing that word. His whole life, knowing he'd been adopted, he'd wondered about the possibility of siblings he'd never met. Now, he'd found the closest thing, only to discover that the man he'd met was… him.

"What do you think you're going to do there? At Mom's?"

"What do you mean?"

"What you think you're gonna get done over there? At Mom's?" Sergio seemed to have trouble saying the word when he meant the two of them.

"I don't really know," Wade said. He rubbed his sweaty hands on the track pants and only slid the fabric farther up his thighs. "I suppose a part of me believes that if I can pinpoint the moment when everything went to hell, maybe I can fix it."

Sergio regarded him skeptically. After a pregnant pause, he turned the Honda toward the highway.

"Mom's it is."

؃ ؄

Marina was up and pacing her kitchen now, each step echoing in the quiet room. Her thoughts reached out, grasping for answers beyond the limits of her understanding. Reality had shattered, leaving her stranded in a world where the unthinkable was undeniable. Wade had disappeared. Where did she go now that everything she knew had turned on its head?

"Mom?" Derek said, his spoon scooping up a bite of fruity cereal and dripping technicolor milk onto the counter. "What's wrong?"

Marina halted and faced her son, struggling to keep her expression serene. "I'm thinking. I'm trying to think of somebody who can help us find your daddy."

Derek carefully spooned up another mountain of cereal, his small, dark brows wrinkled in bafflement. "Why can't we do it?"

Marina sighed. She didn't want to be frustrated with her son, but she did not know if there was a time limit on her task, and it wasn't easy to come up with solutions when dealing with a six-year-old's curiosity.

"Because, sweetie, I don't know what made Daddy disappear. To get him back, we need to know how he got... where he is." Her hands fell limply to her sides. The whole thing was impossible. Everything she knew had vanished, replaced with a reality where even death was preferable to vanishing without a trace.

Derek nodded. "We can go where it happened," he suggested. "Maybe there are clues. We can be like those CSI people."

Marina let out a small laugh. "What do you know about CSI? You've never watched that show. Have you?"

"No," Derek admitted. "But I know from the commercials that they track down bad guys with clues, and I know what clues are. Maybe we can find some if we go where it happened."

"That's a good idea, honey," she said, not bothering to mention that it was already first on her list of things to do as soon as she had her son ready to rush out the door.

A chilling thought crossed her mind. What if the hole in the universal fabric was still there? What if Derek fell through—or she did, and left Derek behind? It was crazy to think this had happened once, but she couldn't rule out the idea that it might happen again. In this twisted reality, they could rule nothing out. The fear of losing her son, of being separated from him, clenched at her heart.

However, if she left Derek behind, she'd spend the day in constant fear of losing him, too. The thought of being separated from him frightened her. What if the same mysterious force that had taken Wade lurked around her son and others she cared about? As egocentric a viewpoint as it was, it was part of that superstitious lens through which she'd viewed her life. There was no way she'd let her son out of sight. Not if her presence might keep him from... from vanishing. Her world was unraveling, and she refused to let her son out of her sight. She didn't care if it meant clinging to a superstitious belief that her presence alone might shield him from an unthinkable fate.

She didn't know how she would find Wade, but she felt in her bones that time was short. *I need to get a shower*, she thought, and then realized Derek was speaking.

"I'm sorry, honey. What did you say?"

"I said, 'What's quantum?'"

"Quantum...." Her sleep-addled mind searched for an explanation that a six-year-old might understand. "Wow. That's a hard one. What made you think of that word?"

"I've been thinking about it since last night. Mr. Weidenseld used it before he almost said the 'S' word."

The bit of conversation Derek spoke of flashed across her mind. Zeke sat across from her at the table, his expressive hands gesturing wildly as he leaned in, emanating frustration and confusion. *I know. My dad's a quantum physicist, and I'll bet even he couldn't explain this shi— uh, stuff.*

She'd been so distracted by his censoring himself that she'd overlooked the most crucial part of the sentence.

"Derek, that's it!" Marina cried. Her hands flew to her face, then combed through her hair hastily. *To hell with a shower.* She dashed around the kitchen, shoving things into her purse; keys, her phone, a pen and notepad, a tiny flashlight from the junk drawer, anything that made her feel more like Wade on the job. "Hurry, Derek, finish eating and go get dressed. Mommy has an idea."

ଔ   ଲ

"Why would the neighbors sneak a weird, unknown plant into your bag?" Ida asked, her head shaking slowly in confusion. "Do you think it's a drug? They can't be drug dealers. Can they? They don't *seem* like drug dealers." Her voice trailed off toward the end; August doubted Ida knew drug dealers outside of television shows. As far as he knew, he was the only criminal she kept company with.

August thought back to the shadier streets of their small Appalachian town in West Virginia—streets Ida had never set foot on. The handful of homeless meth addicts with their scabby skin and rotted smiles. Opioid addicts who moved through their lives in a fog, always struggling to score their next hit. In poorer communities like his, one didn't have to look far to find folks who learned which clinics were the best pill mills and which pharmacies caught on slowest to families stocking up on ephedrine.

LaDonna and Luke didn't strike him as dealers, but it wasn't as if he had much to compare it to. And he and Ida were new to Alabama. Although August could spot the occasional user by their behavior and appearance, he imagined dealers had their shit together. He supposed most of them refrained from using their product—otherwise, how would they make money? If that was the case, maybe the Whelens were dealers.

He thought back to the plants in LaDonna's garden. He and Ida had gotten a tour of it last night, and he didn't recall seeing marijuana leaves or poppies. Marijuana he'd have known on sight, but he wouldn't have made any special connection with poppy flowers since he wasn't concerned with them using it to make opiates. A handful of poppy plants in a garden wouldn't be enough for big-time drug dealers, though, right? *What other plants are used for drugs?* August could not recall. Was marijuana legal in Alabama yet? He'd never had a reason to look into it before, but he doubted it. Southern states were slow to move toward anything that smacked of progressivism, and Alabama was one of the slowest. He remembered that from American History class.

"They don't seem like drug dealers to me, either," he agreed, his voice no more convincing than hers.

Ida took the plant from him with stormy gray eyes and turned it over in her hands as if searching for the answer imprinted on the foliage. "I say we straight up ask her," she said.

August had been thinking the same thing. They'd never exchanged phone numbers with the Whelens, so it would require another visit to their home. He checked out his phone. It was just after eight o'clock in the morning.

"Do you have anything going on this morning?" he asked.

Ida shook her head. She'd been taking cosmetology classes at a local academy—another way she would let her parents down if they knew. Her folks had foreseen the University of Michigan's Ross School of Business as Ida's future since infancy, but Ida had other dreams—ones August was happy to support. She had found a school that let her take evening classes to help her dream of being a hairstylist. Night classes suited her circadian rhythm much better than an office job would have. Like him, Ida was a night owl.

"Wonder if they're up?" he muttered. He thumbed the phone screen back to the PlantPuzzle app and eyed the herb on the screen, then the plant in his hand. It appeared to be a close match, but the tiny flowers at the top differed. Perhaps the app was wrong.

"If they're asleep, then we know they're home," Ida said, half joking.

"What did they say about what they do for work? I can't remember." August asked. They'd touched on a handful of topics as they sipped their tea the night before, but little of the conversation had stuck with him. He'd spent much of the night admiring their room, the heavy furniture, and the delicate glassware they used.

"Mmm… LaDonna said she works with plants. A greenhouse, I think. And he makes jewelry."

August snapped his fingers. "That's right. Well, if they have day jobs during the week, they sound like the type that don't start until retail hours. They're probably up now, though."

Eager for answers, they hastily got ready and loaded into the F-150, the bag of herbs folded up inside Ida's backpack purse. "No bike this morning," Ida had insisted. "I did my hair."

The heat hadn't yet reached an exhausting level, and August was grateful. The truck didn't have time for the air conditioner to kick in before they pulled up the Whelen's long gravel driveway. A classic green Mercedes sedan rested at the top of the hill, and it struck August as the sort of vehicle he would have imagined LaDonna owning. Mature, dignified, classic.

Definitely not drug dealers. Right?

He put the truck into park, but he moved sluggishly when it came time to get out. He wanted answers about the plant, and yet he didn't. Right now, the Whelens were a loving couple with steady jobs and a beautiful house and garden—ideal neighbors. If that hidden plant turned out to be anything but harmless, it'd change how he saw them. He didn't want that. He liked the idea of them growing into friends—a mature couple that he and Ida might use as mentors, the sort of couple who could guide them through the bumpy honeymoon phase the way neither of their parents could.

"You coming, or what?" Ida asked, already halfway to the door.

"I'm moving, Idabelle, I'm moving." He pushed open the squeaky truck door and trailed her to the door.

They rang the doorbell, and August heard a strumming harp chime inside the house. Luke and LaDonna greeted them at the door together, and the couples faced each other from across the threshold. There was a brief, uneasy pause.

"I need to ask you about that herb you gave me," August started.

LaDonna held up a hand to stop him from continuing. "I imagine you do. Come on in."

❧　☙

After a lavish hotel breakfast topped with three cups of coffee, Harper retrieved her Winchester featherweight rifle from temporary storage. Fully equipped, she deftly maneuvered her Audi R8 through Atlanta's traffic, indifferent to other motorists' annoyed glances and honks. Harper knew every inch of her vehicle and used her superb spatial awareness to race through the congestion as she escaped the city. She'd considered leaving the vehicle in storage, but the drive was short, and she missed the roar of the engine and the surge of g-forces as she depressed the accelerator. If she left it behind, she'd have to return to Hotlanta to reclaim it. No, thank you.

Once on Interstate 75 outside of town, she ramped up the velocity, unleashing the engine's full potential. She let her streaming service choose a randomized playlist of her favorite tunes— an eclectic blend of high-energy metal, classic rock, gangster rap, and electronic dance tunes.

Upon reaching a clear stretch of road, Harper stopped the music long enough to secure a hotel reservation in downtown Huntsville. Harper then contacted a car rental service known for delivering vehicles and arranged for a modest car to be delivered to the hotel shortly after her expected arrival time. It wouldn't do for her to drive in such a standout vehicle to do reconnaissance. Audi R8s might not be as uncommon as supercars, but they likely stood out on country roads in backwoods, Alabama. Better to cruise by in a Chevy Malibu with full coverage to avoid the rental agency's wrath when she returned it covered in scrapes from branches used for concealment. Of course, by then, "Anna Waterhouse" would have vanished, but paying the extra fee prevented the vehicle rental service from pursuing her for repairs, leaving "Anna's" ID good for at least one more use.

Harper often mused about the rental services' reactions to the returned cars, frequently scratched and damaged. Scratches were probably typical — although not too often on the hoods or roofs. Once, she had returned a car in pristine condition, but it was that or return it with a bloodstained trunk. That had been a bitch — cleaning every droplet out of the trunk in the middle of winter. Her fingers had grown numb and turned as purple as the UV light she used for evidence detection, but when she parked the Elantra in the lot, no hint of her misadventure remained. Not to the visible eye, anyway; that was all that mattered. "Veronica McNamara" had disappeared like a grain of sand in the desert.

Highway 72 to Huntsville was about as nondescript as the car she'd arranged to rent. The miles passed in endless variations of farms, cotton fields, corn, livestock, collapsing sheds, trailer homes, and lots and *lots* of signs asking her to repent and come to church.

Fat chance. Unless there's someone there with a price tag on their head. I can play the devoted Christian long enough to pull a trigger.

As Harper left the highway for Jefferson Street, she frowned. The only high-rise buildings within sight were a bank building and the hotel where she'd made a reservation.

There's no city in this city. What the hell?

In her statistical research of Huntsville, Harper learned from the Internet that Huntsville was the most populous city in Alabama, a major hub for aerospace and defense industries, and ranked as one of the top cities in the country for engineers. Where were all the towering office buildings and research facilities? The condominiums? The fast-food establishments?

The city offered few places to vanish into the shadows. And unlike Atlanta, people here looked one another in the eye and seemed… friendly. She'd have to make nice or risk standing out like a daisy in a dog food bowl.

Harper drove around the center of downtown and studied the people strolling down the sidewalks and meandering through the park. No one seemed too worried about keeping their purses close. They maintained a respectful distance, not because of caution but because space in the pedestrian areas was plentiful. To call the scattered clusters of people a 'crowd' would have been stretching the truth. Mistrustful glances were nonexistent.

This city was weird.

Death and dash it is. Harper recoiled at the notion of lingering in a city where Southern hospitality appeared so prevalent. It was unnatural. Her best path forward was to locate August Webb, make a quick plan, take out the mark, and follow it with a rapid exit.

But as her eyes flicked over the cheerful faces in the park, a knot twisted in her stomach. Something about this place—its strange quiet, its too-easy charm—made her uneasy. She wasn't just an outsider here. And in a town like this, standing out wasn't just a nuisance. It could be dangerous.

Chapter Ten

Sergio's mother's home was a squat, square, decrepit red brick building half hidden by a fringe of tall, thick weeds that nearly fooled the eye into believing they were a mass of thorny bushes. A spindly iron pole painted in chipping white held up a slumping corner of a patio roof that seemed on the verge of collapsing under the weight of its despair. Discarded thrift-store clothes and shabby yard furnishings covered the patio. Holes pockmarked the gravel driveway, which contained the only sign of occupancy: a rusted red Ford of indeterminate make, its windows reflecting the morning gloom.

The neighboring homes looked no better; they, too, seemed to have been forgotten by time. Trash lingered by the leaf-strewn curb, and weeds and grass sprouted freely, threatening to devour the sidewalk and break through every crack in the pavement. Splintered planters on porches held wilted and lifeless plants.

Sergio pulled in behind the car and killed the engine as he gazed upon the house that harbored too many haunting memories. When he left, he'd sworn he'd never come back. He'd broken that promise more than a few times, usually after hearing his mom's desperate late-night calls. She always needed something—money, food, gas for her car. Without Maria knowing, he'd handled it, skimming off his drug profits and slipping her a twenty here and there—just enough to keep her fed, keep her from sinking deeper, or buy whatever she was fiending for.

Part of him hoped she was zoned out, lost in one of her drugged-up hazes. If she was, Wade's news might go down easier, even if getting a response from her would be like talking to a wall. But if she was sober, or close enough, he wasn't sure her heart could handle the truth Wade was about to drop on her.

"You okay?" Wade's voice broke the oppressive silence.

Sergio nodded. "Just thinking," he muttered.

"About?"

Sergio let a heavy breath out through his nostrils. "She's gonna freak, you know that."

Wade paused. Blinked. "Maybe not."

Sergio scoffed. "Dude, you're like my clone. She's my mother. She, of all people, knows that there's only one of me."

"Maybe she had twins," Wade said. "Maybe she never told you about me."

"Sure," Sergio said, "and maybe a hologram is covering your house, and everyone in your life suffers from collective amnesia."

Wade's mouth remained sealed, unable to come up with a response.

"Sorry, man," Sergio said, "but I'm trying to brace myself for this. I mean, she's…" His hands gestured aimlessly, like they were searching for words he couldn't find, trying to say what his mouth couldn't. "She's a Puerto Rican mama. What else can I say?"

"That about says it all," Wade agreed. They met one another's gaze, an identical anxious expression on their faces.

"So, here's a thought," Wade said. "We ask her about maybe being twins—hold on, hold on, bear with me. If—no, when. *When* she says we aren't twins, we offer her some explanation. Tell her that maybe we were a clone experiment or something. Ask her if she remembers any peculiarities at the hospital the night we were born."

"Are you serious? You can't be serious."

"Well, we've got to say *something*. Besides, maybe this started the day we were born. Maybe she remembers something useful. We've got to draw her out, see if she knows anything that can help."

Sergio didn't have the heart to tell Wade he believed the idea was pointless.

The door to Sergio's mother's home creaked open. In the shadows just inside the door stood a scrawny woman with long, dark hair shot through with gray. Even in the dim interior of the home, Sergio saw the heavy circles under her distrustful eyes and the downturn of her mouth.

"Guess it'll have to do," Sergio conceded.

ଓ ଚ

She should have called Zeke to tell him she was on her way, but she was in a hurry, not to mention too tired to be coherent. It was enough of a risk driving at her level of fatigue to complicate things with a cell phone conversation.

The previous night had stretched on for hours, and Marina prayed that by some miracle, Zeke Weidenseld had either found the night as sleepless as she or was a very early riser. She took the brick sidewalk to his French provincial home, feigning an artificial calm. One hand held Derek's. The other stood poised to strike the door.

She needn't have worried; the wooden door flew open before she raised her arm. She blinked. Zeke stood before her with a cup of steaming coffee, his curly hair in irregularly spaced peaks that stood testament to many a manual combing-through. He wore a snug-fitting sleeveless tee with a pair of blue plaid pajama bottoms too free of wrinkles to have been slept in, and his feet were bare.

"Coffee?" he said in greeting.

"Love some."

Together, they trudged through a great room full of chunky wood and green plaid furniture to the kitchen, where Marina and Derek took seats at the island. Zeke poured Marina a cup of joe in a large, clay-colored stoneware mug that matched his rosewood cabinets. In the background, the voice of a British newscaster described a horrific battle disaster. It seemed there was tragedy everywhere.

He handed her the mug and offered her matching containers of sugar and powdered creamer with a spoon. As she added both, he directed his attention to Derek. "Milk?"

"Chocolate, if you've got it," Derek said. Marina smiled.

"I've got it, but it's soy milk."

Derek shrugged. "Soy's fine."

"One cup of chocolate soy milk, coming up." Zeke padded to the fridge and prepared Derek a tall glass.

"Did you sleep?" Marina asked.

Zeke shook his head, and his features darkened. "After that? No way. I kept going over and over it, you know? Trying to figure out what I missed. Trying to remember something—anything." He handed Derek his glass, and her son thanked him before taking an enormous sip. "You're welcome," Zeke said, leaning against the counter near the sink. "But no. I didn't sleep much."

"Zeke, tell me about your father. What does he do?"

Zeke's brow wrinkled. "Dad? Gosh... uh... I don't really know. I mean, I sort of know, but I can't say I understand. He's a physicist. He studies subatomic particles and math and probabilities and..." Dawning transformed his face. "You think he might give us some idea of what happened?"

"If he can't, maybe he knows someone who can."

Zeke's hand moved to his chin as he contemplated. "S'not a bad idea," he said. He pushed off the sink and grabbed his cell phone from the counter. Marina sipped her coffee and watched Zeke stride back and forth in his kitchen with his phone to his ear.

"Dad?" Zeke said. "Hey, what's going on?"

Marina watched him pace as he arranged for them to meet with his father. His tone carried enough gravitas to satisfy her, but she still wanted to reach for the phone and underscore the gravity of their situation.

Zeke hung up. "The earliest he could do was lunch. Hope that's okay."

"That's fine," she said. "It'll give you time to show me where it happened."

Zeke's hand hesitated where it had dropped the phone on the counter. "You sure you want to do that?"

"She's sure," Derek said. "We're going to be CSIs and look for clues."

Zeke looked at Marina with arched brows, and she nodded with grim certainty. "Okay," he said. "Lemme change my clothes, and we'll go."

ڇۖ   ۞ڃ

"Do you think they will come back?"

Minnie's soft voice from behind caught Clark off-guard, and he jumped. He had not heard her approach, but then, Minnie had been dead much longer than he or Leah, and at times, her presence seemed as insubstantial as air. Conversely, she had also learned the subtle art of stirring minor aspects of her environment and was capable of making sound when it suited her. Clark was not sure if her ability to move silently was a choice or involuntary, and he preferred not to ask for fear it might be a sign part of Minnie was fading as time wore on.

"Goodness, Minnie," he said. "You nearly scared me to death."

She giggled at his reply, covering her mouth with her hand as she often did. Her teeth were a bit crooked, and she had carried her discomfort with that feature of her appearance for decades. He wished she would not. Her smile, what he saw of it, was as delightful and charming as the rest of her.

"I am fairly certain you're beyond that, Clark." She glided into the room, her feet hidden under voluminous skirts. "We're all beyond that now." She sat in the wingback chair and smoothed her pleats down. The fabric of the chair barely creased at her presence.

"How do we do that?" Clark asked, motioning in her direction. "Sit, I mean? Or stand on the floor? Lay in a bed? We had no bodies, no substance. And yet, we don't move through walls like the Passersby do."

"We expect the furniture will hold our weight—even knowing we are incorporeal—and so it does. We expect the walls will be barriers, and, as we think, so it is."

This conversation echoed one he and Minnie had exchanged many times, yet Clark was no closer to understanding how it worked. Minnie's Cartesian logic sounded plausible, but was belief really all he needed? *There has to be more to it than that.*

"Why do you think Leah has a never-ending wardrobe while you and I remain largely in the same attire? We see no need to change what is serving us. Leah sees herself as multidimensional, and therefore, the clothes on her back are multidimensional as well."

It was true. Minnie and Clark rarely appeared in anything unusual. They each clung to the fashion of their day—Minnie choosing long dresses and wearing her hair pinned up, Clark opting for comfortable slacks and button-up shirts or the occasional polo. However, Leah saw herself with many options, though each outfit was drawn from what Clark presumed had been in her closet when she passed away in the late 1950s.

Clark moved to the couch across the room and sat, wondering as he did if the fabric behind him had creased at all.

"Are you worried about them?" Minnie asked. "Our young visitors?"

"They loved the house."

Minnie sat tall and beamed, pride showing in her closed-lipped smile. "They did, didn't they?"

"They did. It sounds like they plan to move in and fix the place up."

"That would be so wonderful."

"It would. But…" He let the words fade, unable to complete the thought.

"The Passers."

"Yes."

Her posture shrank. "Do you think they'll harm them? We've not seen them among the living often. Only LaDonna, and she never stayed long. It's been weeks since her last visit."

"More like months." Clark shrugged. "I don't know. We don't know quite what the Passersby are, do we? Only that they pass through our home as quickly as their forms allow."

"And if they know we see them, they seem frantic about reaching us. Why do you think they stop moving through the house and try to speak to us, Clark?"

"I suspect they are searching for a destination, and they believe we may have answers for them."

"But we don't! We cannot leave the house! I wish we had the means to move about like they do."

Clark thought about the confusion on many of the faces as they passed from wall to wall, from ceiling to floor, from doorway to doorway. The way they moved with determination, their focus on a destination that they appeared to believe lay behind the next wall—or hoped it did. Clark feared that their mission was a never-ending one, that perhaps this was the Passersby's hell, moving from one unknown location to another in an eternal quest for a spiritual resting place.

"Would you rather be one of them?" he asked.

Minnie cocked her head to the side as she contemplated his question, but she was not long in answering. "No. No, I suppose I would not. This is my home. The Passersby oftentimes appear quite stressed. The way they roam, never stopping. It is almost..."

"Desperate?" Clark ventured.

"Yes, desperate," she agreed. "Don't you agree?"

Clark had to admit he did. He wished he knew why these anxious beings emerged through the walls only to pass into another in what looked like a ceaseless journey. He wished he knew what drove them on this path of endless searching. "Maybe they're looking for something they lost," he mused, "or searching for an answer. Whatever it is, it seems to consume them entirely."

No sooner had he finished his thought when a diaphanous, smoky form pooled from an unseen hole in the ceiling above them and began its trek to the floor between them. Minnie and Clark drew their feet in and away from their uninvited guest, who only paused for a moment to take on a distinctive bipedal shape long enough to comprehend their horror before descending through an equally nonexistent hole in the floor.

枅枆

August and Ida trailed LaDonna and Luke into their home once more. Morning sunlight poured through the many windows. Luke and LaDonna moved side by side, a couple comfortable with one another's proximity, nearly in step as they led Ida and August to the kitchen. They didn't look back or offer conversation as they went, and August's concern rose. Ida took August's hand, and they gave each other a quick squeeze, trying to reassure one another that everything would be fine.

"Coffee?" Luke offered once Ida and August were seated across from LaDonna at the table.

"Um... sure," Ida said, her eyebrows raised at August, who nodded, but kept a sharp eye on Luke as he prepared their drinks.

"Cream? Sugar?" Luke asked.

"Black is fine," Ida said, and August agreed. Normally, they both took sugar, but he guessed she was thinking the same thing he had — they didn't want to ingest anything that might contain unexpected substances.

Luke brought them their mugs, refreshed LaDonna's cup from the carafe, and brought her a container of creamer from the refrigerator before sitting at her side. LaDonna and Luke exchanged a fleeting concerned glance, and August realized that they, too, were anxious about the conversation about to take place.

LaDonna licked her lips and placed her hands flat on the table. August noticed the nails were short but clean, the skin weathered, most likely from hours spent working with the plants she loved so much.

"August, Ida," she said, "I am going to say some things that you may find surprising. They may sound crazy, and I don't want you to feel uncomfortable, but I want you to keep an open mind, OK?"

That's it. They really are drug dealers.

"Luke and I… well, we're witches."

August didn't know what to say at that point. *Are you serious?* didn't strike him as the kindest reply.

"Is that like… like Wicca?" Ida asked with a tilt of her head. August had to give her credit for continuing the conversation with an open mind.

"Not exactly," Luke said. "The Craft doesn't follow any particular doctrine, and Wicca leans more toward paganism. They believe in the god and goddess, which isn't necessarily how witches practice — although it can be. Ethics in the Craft can also vary, and Wiccans believe in karma more than we do."

"What *do* you believe?" August asked.

"Luke and I are the high priest and priestess of the Lughaidh coven," LaDonna said. "Our coven believes in universal balance, and that everything in the universe shares an intertwining energy that we can harness through spells and rituals."

Neither August nor Ida knew how to respond to that. LaDonna only let the silence linger for a moment before continuing.

"Every once in a while, someone crosses our path that we believe has a natural aptitude for the Craft. And from the moment we met you, August, Luke and I knew you were one of those people."

"Wha — me? That's…. Why would you think that?"

We're all a little magic, August. Some of us are more in tune with it than others. His Aunt Lyra's words echoed in his mind.

"I can't say in what way you're inclined, August," LaDonna said. "All witches have gifts, but most of us have specialties. Luke is what we call an orange witch — he has the gift of prophecy. He knew when the land next to us was about to change hands, and he knew it was a young couple who would move there."

"You're from the mountains somewhere north of Alabama, right? But Appalachian?" Luke interjected. They'd never shared that detail with them. August swallowed and nodded, his eyes large as he studied the couple across from them for any sign of a joke or insanity or anything other than that they believed every word they said.

"West Virgina," August said.

"Did you know you had a gift?" Luke asked. "Any sense that you might be more… in tune with certain aspects of your surroundings? Or influence things with no logical explanation?"

"I, um," he shot Ida a look to see if she was struggling to believe the conversation happening around her. Her expression was as placid as a pond on a still day, reflecting no skepticism. "I sometimes… feel like… like I know when things are around me that I can't see."

"Ghosts?" Luke asked.

August shrugged. "Maybe. My Aunt Lyra said that was a possibility. I get goosebumps and this really strong feeling like there's someone there, but I can't see them."

Luke and LaDonna faced one another, each subtly nodding, their spines straighter than they'd been a minute before.

"Indigo witch," they said at once.

"Oh, we really could have used him when Ryan first got here," Luke chuckled.

"What's — what's that? What's an indigo witch?" August moved his attention from Luke to LaDonna and back again eagerly. Did they have the answer to his strange response to places like the Victorian?

"One in tune with otherworldly intuition. They can often see and communicate with ghosts and sense large amounts of magical energy in places like ley lines and locations where a large amount of power is focused."

"Like a nexus," LaDonna added.

August slumped. "I don't think that's it, then. I can't see or hear anything. I get a weird feeling, but there's nothing there."

"What you have now is what I call a knack," Luke said. "It's an untrained gift."

"I am what is called a green witch. I have a gift with plants and animals," LaDonna said. "Although I've always known they drew me to them, I still had to learn how to work with them. It took time, but now —"

"Now you have an amazing garden in the backyard," Ida finished, one corner of her mouth pulled up.

"I do," she agreed.

"What does this have to do with the plant you gave me?" August asked. "Is it a magical plant?"

LaDonna let out a gravelly laugh that reminded August, not unpleasantly, of a happy duck quacking. He smiled despite himself.

"We're finding out right along with you," she said. "Luke knew you were coming. I knew to trim the plant before you arrived. Once you got here, I knew — I just knew it was meant for you. And now I know why."

"Why, then?" Ida insisted.

"You're going to help the ghosts in the house next door."

Chapter Eleven

"Stay low," Sergio said, opening his door. "Lemme talk to her a minute." Wade arched an inquisitive eyebrow but complied with Sergio's request.

Sergio stood cautiously, leaving one leg poised for retreat, half prepared to climb back in the car if his mother was as caustic as usual.

"*Mamá?*" He hated the tentative tone in his voice.

Her thin arms crossed a chest covered in a threadbare T-shirt. "Why you so early?" she said, her voice clipped, accented, and cautious.

"It is too early," Sergio said. "I'm sorry. I know you usually sleep in..."

Sergio's mother's mistrustful eyes went from him to the passenger's side of the car and back. They were clearer than usual; she wasn't high, at least not noticeably. Sergio wondered if that was to his advantage.

"Who's your friend?" Her crossed arms barely lifted from her bosom in a limp gesture of direction.

Sergio cringed. He hoped he'd be able to brace her a little for the impact of what she was about to see. "*Mamá*, that's why I came to see you. I want you to meet—"

Sergio's mother's eyes bulged, and she sprang into a rapid-fire assault of Spanish, her hands waving frantically, as if she could compel his guest from leaving his car by force of will. Sergio's Spanish was fluent, but he had a hard time keeping up with his *mamá's* panic-stricken tirade. He caught enough of it to understand what concerned her, though. One word explained the reason for her distress: *"policia."*

"No, *Mamá*," he fibbed, easing his reluctant leg from the car, crossing the space between them, and waving back at her. *"El no es policia. Solo un amigo. Un amigo! Familia, Mamá, familia. Mira!"*

Finally, her curiosity won out, and she waited with her arms crossed again on her chest as Sergio signaled for Wade to emerge, which he did, grudgingly.

"Mamá, este es mi amigo Wade."

His mother's jaw fell open, revealing teeth yellowed from years of cigarettes, drugs, and poor hygiene. Her hand flew like a fluttering bird to her lips. *"Dios mio, mijo. Quien es?"*

Sergio's attention switched from studying his mother's reaction for signs of shock to seeing if Wade's expression looked in the least bit intimidating. It didn't. If anything, his burly look-alike was doing his best to look like an enormous teddy bear. *"Pienso que es mi hermano."*

A huff of air escaped her lungs as if he'd punched her in the stomach; he imagined it might feel much the same if she had.

Sergio wasn't sure how much of the conversation Wade had tracked up to that point, but his mother's next word needed no translation.

"Imposible."

ത   ണ

"I'm sorry?" August said, his voice shooting up embarrassingly high. First, they tell him they're witches. Now they want his help with *ghosts?*

LaDonna placed her hands flat on the table again, a poker player revealing that she held back nothing. Her expression was that of a woman with many emotions roiling under the surface, but none were readable.

"The herb will help you," she said, her gravelly voice soft, calm. "It will help open your spirit up to your gift."

"So it *is* a drug," Ida said, her eyes narrowing. "Is it a hallu-cinogen? Is it dangerous? Can't you teach him how to use his gift without it? You said you were a high priestess."

"I'm also a green witch without a knack for using an indigo

witch's power."

"What about Luke? Or another witch? How many colors do you have in your coven?"

"My gift is prophecy," Luke said. "Not intuition."

"Another indigo witch then, like Ida suggested," August said. "Is there another one in your... you call it a coven, you said?"

"Yes, coven is the word you're looking for. But there isn't an indigo witch in our coven."

"We could ask Murphy," LaDonna suggested to Luke in an almost-whisper, an eyebrow arched uncertainly.

Luke shook his head. "She's got her hands full right now."

LaDonna let out a sigh. "Yeah, I guess she does." She turned her attention back to August. "The herb I have given you can provide a short-lived altered state. That's one benefit to it as opposed to other psychedelics. I can guide you through it if you're willing to try it."

"This is insane," Ida said, her hands up, fingers splayed. "I can't believe you're asking this of him. He barely knows you. How can we know this is even for real?"

August wanted to tell her it was fine, that he knew the Whelens were telling the truth. From the moment LaDonna and Luke had said what his gift was, their voices had resonated within him like words whispered by a soul twin to a hidden level of his consciousness. *Indigo witch.* He wondered what his Aunt Lyra would think of Luke and LaDonna.

"I'll tell you what, August," LaDonna said. "We'll go to the house together. All four of us. I'm not an indigo witch, but I know enough about universal energy to coach you through some basics so that you have a taste of what you're capable of. We won't use the herb. If we do that and it leaves you with a bad feeling, or you decide somewhere along the way you don't feel comfortable with it, we'll leave it alone. OK?"

Ida's mouth was squashed into a frustrated line, and her flinty eyes and elfin jaw tightened with apprehension. Her gaze penetrated him to his core.

"There might be ghosts in our house," August said, his voice soft and coaxing. "We were talking about fixing it up and moving in. Maybe we should look into this before we commit too much time and effort and money into it."

Ida let out a long exhale. Her head and chin lowered slightly in resignation, and August took her hand. Without meeting his eyes, Ida turned her attention to LaDonna and Luke.

"Why do you want to help the ghosts in that house, anyway? I mean, it's not on your land. It's not your house. Is there something special about it?"

"The house? No," LaDonna said.

"Then what?"

LaDonna's large green eyes were doleful. "I think August may be the key to repairing the soul of that house. It's a personal issue for me. I have reason to believe my friend Clark is trapped there."

Ω   ℥

Wade didn't know what to call her. In this parallel world, his mother, his DNA, if not precisely his flesh and blood, stood before him.

Is this what my mother is like in my world? Scrawny? Poor? A prostitute? Or is she as different from my mother as I am from Sergio?

"Uh… *Buenos dias, Señora,*" he said, his voice growing as faded as the crumbling paint on the home's exterior.

Sergio's mother scowled and waved at him dismissively. "He don't speak Spanish," she said, switching languages for his benefit, even if her only reason was to reject him. Her accent was as thick as the humidity. "He's not family."

"*Mamá*, that's impossible," Sergio said, gesturing to Wade. "How else can we look so much alike?"

"I didn't have twins!" she said. She tapped her temple sharply. "I know. I have one baby. *Uno. Es tu.*"

Sergio paused. "*Mamá*, think back, will you? Is there no way you had two? None?"

His mother cut them off and gestured for them to go to the house. "We no speak outside. People hear us."

Wade's spirits lifted a little, a phantom hope. It sounded as if Sergio's mother had a secret she didn't want the world to hear. *This is it. She must know something!*

Wade and Sergio followed the petite woman inside the ramshackle home, floorboards creaking underfoot. In the sudden change from the bright outdoors to the dreary interior, his eyes took a moment to adjust. When they did, he wished they'd stayed outside. A worn blue mattress took up a corner of the home, propped against piles of dusty goods on wire shelves. Thick quilts covered the windows, hung from curtain rods to block out daylight. Paper food cartons littered the floor, and the air smelled of an unpleasant mélange of old takeout, mildew, cigarettes, garbage, and cat litter. Against the wall, a trash can spilled over onto the spotted carpet. From his vantage point, Wade got a clear shot into the kitchen. He wasn't sure if the appliances were white or had been once upon a time. Whatever the case, a coat of nicotine and a haze of dirt had tainted them with a brownish-yellow hue.

Sergio's mother snatched a handful of tattered clothes from a pair of worn-out armchairs and gestured for them to sit with one hand while tossing the clothes into a corner with the other. Wade resisted the urge to perch on the edge like a bird to avoid contact with the furniture, feeling like an intruder in this shadowy home.

"Ahh, *Mamá*?" Sergio said.

She turned, and Sergio continued, thankfully, in English. "*Mamá*, Wade. Wade, *Señora* Isabela Vega." Although the language was English, the accent was fluent and gave his mother's name an impressive flair. Wade offered his hand, but the woman shunned it. Sergio gave Wade an apologetic glance, as if asking for forgiveness for his mother's rudeness.

"*Mamá*, you were saying?"

"*Si. Escuche*. I had one baby. Your *abuela,* she helped me push. At home. No hospital business. She didn't want the neighbors to know you were coming. I wore big clothes. We kept you hidden, hid my pregnancy. It was a tough time, *mijo*."

"I was born in a house? You never told me—"

Isabela cut him off with a sharp wave of her birdlike hand. "After you arrived, a whole lotta blood came out. Your *abuela*, she took me to the hospital. I almost died." Isabela cleared her throat as if regretting any debt to her mother. Or was it mother-in-law? It only took moments for Wade to realize it had to be Isabela's mother. Sergio's father was probably an unknown, as was his.

"She kept you with her while doctors took care of me." Isabela's eyes glowed, manic with some perceived insight. "I bet she let them do stuff to you when they was fixing me up. Like some kinda test on you. An experiment, maybe. Like cloning. And now…" she motioned to Wade as if arriving at the solution to everyone's problem. Wade knew now that her need for secrecy was more because of her conspiracy theory than any knowledge that might help.

"*Mamá*, why would you say that? *Abuela* was a good woman."

Isabela scoffed as her shoulders shrugged in frustration, a motion that looked habitual. "*Mira, mijo*," she said, gesturing at Wade again. "What else can it be?"

Sergio turned to Wade as if looking for evidence that backed his mother's story.

Yes, indeed. What else can it be? Wade was glad that Isabela had concluded that fit his existence into her life. It was the story they'd planned on handing her if she remembered nothing unusual. He didn't believe it, but was glad they'd made the trip. His detective mind whirred with possibilities.

In one world, she gave me up for adoption, probably because of pressure from Sergio's abuela. That's where our lives diverged. In the hospital. My entire existence is because of one moment of happenstance…

Elbows on his knees, face buried in his hands, Wade wondered how to correct this wild diversion of fate.

Chapter Twelve

In the hushed pre-dawn hours, Marina drifted into a fitful slumber in the passenger seat of Zeke's car. Zeke navigated slowly through Gryphon's streets to the town's industrial district. Derek's voice kept up a patter in the backseat as he played with toys she'd packed for him in his travel bag. The sound of plastic on plastic intermittently broke through her reverie as the characters engaged one another in a duel.

Her thoughts churned unsteadily, as they often did when she had a fever. Trying to wrap her mind around these impossible events while exhausted was hard—no, impossible. She felt as if she'd discovered herself in a dream, called to the front of the classroom, and asked to answer a problem written in an alien script. How would she figure out how to bring Wade back when she did not know how he'd vanished? She wasn't some comic book superhero with extravagant powers of deduction and the strength of Atlas. She was only... Marina, BSN, wife, mother, and believer in discombobulating superstitions and far-fetched reasoning.

That might be to my advantage, for once.

She registered that the tires had exchanged blacktop for gravel, and in a few moments, the car ground to a gentle stop. Marina lifted her head, her eyelids fluttering open. She stared through the branches of a sapling pine at the side of a corrugated building identical to the one in the video she'd watched at the police station.

"This is where we set up the bust for our undercover guys to meet Izzy last night," Zeke said, sliding out of the car. Marina followed suit, and Derek clambered after, abandoning his plastic pirates on the seat.

Marina inhaled deeply, the purity of the morning air in her lungs tainted by the muddy creek water behind them. From a few buildings away came the mechanized sound of factories. What she didn't sense, however, was anything special about this place.

She'd expected more; a tingle to the air, a charge in the ozone, some lingering trace of a rift in the fabric of reality where her husband had vanished. There was nothing. As far as she could tell, it was a normal, boring part of town.

Her conviction in the story faltered despite having watched the video. *This is ridiculous! People don't just fall through holes! This must be a conspiracy. I must be out of my mind for even considering—*

"Mom! Hey, mom!" Derek's excited voice cut through her self-critical thoughts. Her heart quickened, and her feet followed suit.

Did Derek find Wade's body, maybe? Or...? He sounded excited.

She raced to where her son stood, pointing, his eyes shining, a massive grin on his face. "Look, mom! I'll just bet this is where it happened. Dad doesn't have an invisibility cloak. Look, the air is shiny! I bet it's a magic door!"

"Shiny?" Marina squinted toward where Derek's pointed finger aimed, but she saw nothing. She turned her head from side to side, aligning herself with Derek's perspective, squatted to his level. Still, whatever he saw was beyond her perception.

"Try standing here," Derek suggested, moving so her feet stood where he had. She did, but nothing changed. The air was just... air.

Zeke's rubber shoes scuffed the dusty warehouse floor behind her, notifying her that he'd arrived.

"He says he sees a shiny spot," she called back to Zeke. "I don't see it. "Do you?"

"No," Zeke replied solemnly. "But he's pointing right to the spot where Wade vanished."

C3   80

The Whelens made a few phone calls to let their employees know they would be a little late. As the older couple chatted on their cell phones, Ida and August strolled around the large sitting room and peered at the forest beyond the cathedral windows.

"This house is amazing," August observed.

"Ours is amazinger," Ida joked. "Or it will be. Eventually."

He chuckled.

"Do you really think it's haunted?" she asked, her eyes stormy as a winter sky.

He shrugged. "I think it's possible. I got one of those feelings I get sometimes when we were there."

"That goosebumpy feeling?"

"Yeah." He took a few steps to the fireplace. It looked well-used but also well-kept. The mantelpiece had two squat green candles on either end, and in the center was a statue of three women: one young, one middle-aged, and one elderly. LaDonna had decorated it with flowers interwoven with branches from one of her shrubs. He was curious about what material it was made of but refrained from touching it, afraid he might break it.

Ida sidled up to him and brushed his arm. "Hey, if you're willing to see if there's any truth to this, I'm in. I mean, I don't know if ghosts exist, but who knows? This could be pretty cool."

"Or pretty terrifying," he countered, running his fingers along the polished wood mantle.

"There you go again, being the negative one," she scolded.

"Is it weird that I feel I'm being the realist when I'm the one saying we should look into the possibility of ghosts in that old place?"

Ida cocked her head and gave him a meager smile. "Who knows? You might have a gift, like they're saying. We'll give it a shot. What's the worst that could happen? Yeah, it might wind up being... spooky. But you know if we walk away now and don't see if there's any truth to this, we'll always wonder what would have happened if we hadn't tried."

She was right. Like it or not, they had to figure out if the Whelens' story held any water. Ida was usually more doubtful than him, but he knew better — there were things beyond the veil. And what if he really was an indigo witch? What if LaDonna could help him learn how to look beyond that? He paced the room, nerves jangling, caught between wanting to dive right in and being scared to death of what he might uncover.

And what if you can't turn it off? You could be stuck seeing ghosts everywhere. He immediately scorned himself for the thought. *I don't even know if I can do this shit at all, and I'm already worried about how to turn it off.*

"Augie?"

He stopped moving. Ida took his forearms into her hands and gripped him, encouraging him to meet her gaze. He complied and found nothing but support and love there.

"It's an adventure," she said, giving him her signature half-shrug. He laughed. That was Ida. That was her answer to all things unknown. Everything to her was an adventure.

LaDonna poked her head in the room, "Y'all ready?"

August nodded, feeling nervous yet determined to learn the truth.

  գ

Damn. We went to Mamá's house for nothing. Judging from the wrinkles on Wade's brow, even the detective had found no leads in his mother's story.

Damn. Now what?

In the books, there was always an intelligent man, a scientist friend, an associate, or a crazed eccentric who invariably weaved their way into the narrative and had the answers everyone sought. He had no friends that fit that description, and he doubted Wade did. Probably the closest thing his counterpart knew were people who analyzed crime scenes. There weren't too many brainiacs in Gryphon, Alabama. Not the type of people who knew the science they were looking for. Blood spatter patterns were one thing, but Wade's blood was still in his body, and they needed to get the whole body back where it came from.

Wherever that was.

They didn't linger at his mother's, but spent only a few more minutes assuring her that the clone theory must be right. Sergio made a few futile attempts to dissuade her from connecting the puzzle to his *Abuela*, though he knew it was a lost cause. Her inexplicable grudge against his grandmother cast a long shadow over their relationship.

He pointed the nose of the car back toward Gryphon, a general course toward Highway 65. He hadn't consulted with Wade on a destination and wasn't sure where he was taking the man. Heading home crossed his mind, but doubts gnawed at him. Maria's patience was limited, and he knew she wouldn't tolerate

Wade's presence for long. But where else could they turn?

"What now?" Wade mumbled.

"I'm taking you back to my house," Sergio began. "That is…"

"What?" Wade's voice exhibited so much hope in that one syllable it pained Sergio. So much of the man's spirit rested in his ability to give him something to cling to, a shred of optimism, and he had so little to offer.

"Know any scientists?" he asked, half joking.

"What? No. I—" Wade's voice faltered, but then a glimmer of hope surfaced, and the tension in his face eased. "Wait. There is someone. My partner, Detective Weidenseld. His father is a quantum physicist in my world. I imagine it's the same here. Maybe he can help."

Sergio nodded. "Maybe. So where to?"

"We have to ask Zeke. Um, Ez. He's called Ez here. And I don't know where his father lives."

"Where do we find this Zeke-Ez guy at this hour?"

Wade licked his lips. He had the business card in his pocket, but he thought Ez would have an easier time digesting the story with both "Sergios" in front of him. "I'm not sure. Where I'm from, he has a house over in the eastern part of Gryphon, but… but… he found it because I led him there. I spotted the listing while Marina and I were scouting for places to build."

Sergio let out a breath. "Do you think he'd still be there?"

"I doubt it. He's probably somewhere else. Not where he was when I met him, though. He lived in this tiny studio apartment until he had enough money for a down payment someplace nicer."

"So you think he moved, for sure?"

"I'd be surprised if he hasn't."

Sergio's hand tapped the steering wheel. "Well, we can try the other place. Maybe fate guided him to it, even if you didn't help."

Wade thought of all the people George Bailey had affected in the Frank Capra classic. Maybe Zeke would be in the same house without a Wade in his life to lead him there. Would he have to wait until Zeke showed up at work to ask him for this father's help? He didn't think his nerves had the power to withstand that many hours of stress.

"Let's try the station first. Maybe we'll get lucky."

☃ ☠

Panicked, Marina pulled Derek away from whatever it was he pointed at. The oppressive, humid air turned icy and raised gooseflesh on her arms as she pulled her son toward her protectively. Her eyes squinted as she gazed into the gloomy space between herself and the corroded gray metal wall. She tried to let her gaze drift to a point beyond the wall. She tried emptying her mind to see if that helped. She saw nothing.

Derek stared at his "shiny" spot with a grin, his gaze transfixed. At least, she guessed that's what held his attention. His eyes never moved, fascinated with his discovery, as if a secret lay hidden just beyond the sheen.

"Here?" she asked with a quavering voice. She pointed her finger as Derek had and turned to Zeke, who had now joined them. She tried to remember from the video, but with the skewed angle, she had to make sure.

Zeke nodded solemnly. "Right there. We came in from that door," he aimed at the corner behind them, "and Izzy and his cousin had parked there... You can still see the oil from their car. Guess they've got a leak—"

"But Wade vanished, right...?" Marina's hand sliced through the air toward the unseen abyss where Derek's gaze was fixed.

"Now you see him, now you don't," Zeke said, his voice glum.

Marina sighed, trying to ease the creeping tension coiled around her muscles. It didn't work. Derek's zealous happiness set her more on edge. He looked almost manic. He pulled away from her, and her hands curled into claws that clutched him back to her side. She eased her body between Derek and the void she did not see but knew was there.

"So, what do we do?" she asked.

Brimming with enthusiasm, Derek bounced on the balls of his feet, his excitement palpable. "Isn't it obvious?" he exclaimed.

"What?" Marina asked.

Her disbelief turned to horror as her son swiftly pirouetted around her, bounded across the short distance, and vanished, instantly swallowed whole by the unseen void.

cg so

Harper parked her Chevy Malibu rental into a pull-off area designed for folks to take advantage of the scenic overlook into the valley where the sleepy town of Gryphon lay below. Harper didn't understand why — the view was more valley than town, and the town wasn't much to look at. Picnic tables in the "scenic overlook" area dotted the dusty grass a few feet away from a low stone barrier. A few yards away, she'd passed the newly constructed mailbox with the street number and the name *Webb* stenciled on the side in military-style text. How convenient for the state of Alabama to provide a parking spot so close to her target.

She planned on only reconnaissance today but saw no reason to pass up what might become an opportune moment, should it arise. The sooner she tagged this guy, the sooner she could be on a beach in French Polynesia. She popped the trunk and pulled out two canteens of water, which she strapped to the back of her belt, her lock-picking kit, a tiny but powerful pair of binoculars, rosin powder to help with the grip on her rifle, and a compass she doubted she'd need, but better safe than arrested. Using her phone, she pulled up a tiny topographical map of the area. Ears perked for traffic, she waited until the only sounds were the birds in the trees and the faint sound of the meager summer wind in the leaves. She yanked the Winchester from its hiding place under a fleece blanket and darted across the street and into the woods, ensuring she was out of sight of the road before slowing down.

Mindful of snapping branches and protruding tree roots, Harper jogged silently through the woods. She didn't have far to go for today's mission, which would likely be strictly surveillance. From his social media accounts, August Webb considered himself an "entrepreneur," which was, in her experience, guy-speak for either a crypto bro or a couch-surfing video game wanna-be "content creator." Since this place was terribly countrified, she guessed the latter.

She flashed back to the smooth diction and open wallets of her clients. No wonder the Kightlingers wanted this jackass out of their daughter's life. He sounded like a loser. Based on his picture, Dahlia likely got with him because he was cute. *Probably has a dick dipped in chocolate or something.*

The trailer Dahlia and her gold-digging boyfriend lived in came into view quickly. She squatted behind a wide fallen log, pulled her binoculars from her pocket, and surveyed the home. It looked new, probably purchased with money Dahlia had swiped from her folks. Minutes passed, but still no sign of movement from inside the house. She saw no sign of an outdoor dog, which was good.

Staying in the tree line, Harper circled to the back side of the trailer where a shed stood, a window unit of air conditioning protruding from its tiny single window. From the look of the rear side of the house, a window unit had been extracted from what was likely a bedroom.

Who pulls an a/c unit from a window in the middle of summer in this ungodly heat?

Maybe Dahlia and August were already on the outs, and he'd moved into the shed. If so, her window of opportunity for easy money was limited for another reason. If Dahlia changed her mind, left August, and headed home, there'd be no reason for Harper to fulfill her contract. She'd be out thousands of dollars.

Would he really sleep in a shed, though? Seems like a lot of trouble to go through. Maybe he's turned it into a man cave?

Curiosity pecked at her until, unable to repress her inquisitiveness, she crept up to the shed door.

It was padlocked.

A locked shed in the middle of nowhere, Alabama. Now, she *had* to know what was inside.

Harper leaned the Winchester against the side of the shed and pulled her lock-picking kit from her back pocket. Ears perked for sudden sounds from behind her, she unfastened the shackle from the body within seconds. She shot a look over her shoulder and pulled open the door, praying it didn't squeak. It didn't.

She suspected a few possibilities might await her inside, but none included Mason jars. Loads of them filled with clear liquid, some including what looked like herbs inside. Next to the jars were copper drums with gages on the outside connected with copper pipes.

Shiiit. He's not a crypto dude or a wanna-be influencer. This guy's a moonshiner. Her respect for the man slid up a few pegs. Entrepreneur, indeed.

Harper closed the door with a quiet *click,* refastened the lock with nimble fingers, and retreated to the woods. From a few yards away came the sound of voices, a couple of which sounded the right age to be Dahlia and August, accompanied by the crunch of footsteps marching through the trees. She darted behind a wide oak and slowed her breath to better listen and watch.

Four people came into view: Dahlia, August, and a middle-aged hippy couple. They were strolling out of the forest on the opposite side of the lookout and heading to an aging three-story home covered in vines and other ropey flora. Harper couldn't make out much of their conversation, but from their body language, the couples did not know one another well. Not hostile, exactly, but unfamiliar and slightly awkward.

They paused on the porch for a moment to have a verbal exchange. The older woman posed a question to Harper's target, giving him reason to contemplate before answering. The woman appeared satisfied with his answer, and the four headed inside.

There were too many risks for Harper to take her shot now, mainly because she hadn't planned her exit yet. But she could wait and watch. And learn.

Chapter Thirteen

The warehouse looked the same, except for one creepy thing—his mom and Detective Weidenseld weren't there anymore. That weird, shiny thing he jumped through was still glowing like a giant silver puddle standing up, so Derek knew he could go back if he needed to.

I went through the silver thing, and now I can't see Mom and Zeke. I must be in the place Dad went. His stomach felt funny, like when he'd eaten too many fries at his friend Liam's house. *What if the silver thing disappears? Maybe it's like a spell that only works for a little bit. Better hurry.*

But hurry where? He thought about home, but that was way too far to walk. Detective Weidenseld's house? It was closer, but still kinda far. Walking that long sounded like a bad idea. Especially alone.

He tried to remember the streets his mom and dad drove on. Even though this part of town was old, he wasn't good with street names. He knew there was a road nearby that started with a "B," though. "Blue... something." "Bluebird?" Then he remembered—Blue Heron Drive! The road that the bagel place was on that made the really good breakfast sandwiches. The police station was kind of close to that road. Cops helped with emergencies. His dad was a cop, and so was Zeke, and they were awesome.

Maybe there is a Zeke here, too. The building here looks the same as the one I left. Maybe people have doubles, too. If there is a Zeke here, he'll help me for sure.

Derek nodded to himself. "Okay," he whispered, "police

station, here I come!"

☙ ❧

Marina's voice resounded through the warehouse, echoing ominously off the walls. She hadn't realized she'd been screaming, but there she was, her throat raw, her outstretched arms flailing for the spot where her husband, and now son, had inexplicably vanished.

Zeke struggled to restrain her, his voice becoming clearer as her sheer terror subsided. "Marina! Marina, hold on. Hold on. Don't! Stop fighting me!"

His grip on her was vice-like, leaving her limbs bruised and sore. How long had she fought him off? She had lost track of time in her blind panic. Judging from the pain that lingered after he released her, she'd struggled for quite a while.

Sobs wracked her body. Her knees buckled, and she was saved from collapsing solely by Zeke's strength.

"Marina... Marina, hang in there. Hold on. I've got you."

"He's gone. He's gone." Repeated like a tuneless lyric, the phrase brought her shattered reality into place. The courage she'd mustered to rush after her son without an anchor in this world had vanished. "Dear God in heaven, they're both gone."

"We'll get them back," Zeke assured her.

"Of course we will. Hold my hand," she commanded, stepping forward once more. "I'm going in."

"Marina, no," Zeke said, restraining her by the wrist. "We don't know what's on the other side of that—that spot. We don't even know what it is. Do you know what will happen to you once you go through? You can't even see it. What if you wind up cutting yourself in half or something?"

"I don't care. I can't just stay here and do nothing!"

Zeke's grip tightened. "Marina, think about it. We don't know how this thing works. What if all it takes is for you to make it through that— that—whatever, and then, because we're connected, I'm there, too? How will we both get back when no one knows where we are right now, what we're doing, or how to get back? Don't you think that if Wade could have strolled right back, he would have?"

Marina hesitated, torn between her desperate instincts and Zeke's rational argument. All she cared about was Derek. But Wade—Zeke was right. Wherever Wade had gone, he would have returned by now if it was possible.

Reluctantly, Zeke let her go, but the tension in his frame told Marina he was prepared to restrain her again if she behaved irrationally. "Look. I want to help, really. But we need to make sure that if one of us goes in, we all come out. We don't know how to do that yet."

"Will we ever?" Her voice trembled on the brink of despair.

"We'll try. Let's go talk to my father."

"Wait," she said. Looking around, she found a piece of rebar with which she approached the spot where Derek had left. Though she couldn't see the silvery place like Derek had, the spot was engraved on her mind.

Cautiously, she tiptoed forward and scratched at the concrete. As she extended and retracted the metal stick, the tip appeared and vanished, appeared, and vanished. Her breath came in ragged gasps. Was Derek on the other side, watching the metal as it entered his... dimension? Had he gone in search of his father? Or maybe something far worse? Was he safe?

When she was done, the scratch she left on the surface of the cement stopped at the edge of the invisible barrier as if measured by a ruler.

She had felt nothing desperately gripping the bar as it crossed to the other side, and that gave her a small measure of hope. As far as she could tell, Derek wasn't desperately looking for something to pull him back to the world he'd left.

⚃ ⚂

If LaDonna and Luke could tell that August had kicked in the door to the Victorian home, they refrained from mentioning it. Ida told them on the way there that she and August had visited the home once already, and LaDonna had peppered August with questions on their walk over. What were his impressions of the house? Did he experience any odd physical sensations? Had he heard any strange sounds? August confessed the peculiar sense of disquiet, the goosebumps that broke out as he entered, and how the creaking floor had half convinced him that someone stood behind him.

"But it didn't last?" LaDonna pressed. They stood on the dilapidated porch as if waiting for someone to join them. August didn't understand why they hadn't gone in, but he guessed it had something to do with LaDonna's process of evaluating him as an indigo witch.

"No, it didn't last," he admitted. "I mean, it did, but not really. Like… I felt a little weird, but I also knew at the same time that there was nothing to worry about." He realized he'd been using his hands to convey the complex emotions he had experienced, but neither his words nor his hands explained it well. He dropped his arms to his sides.

"Weird, as in maybe you were in a house with someone you couldn't see, but also sensed they weren't there to hurt you?"

August's jaw fell. In one brief sentence, LaDonna had summarized his experience perfectly.

"Yeah," he said. "That's a good way to put it. That's exactly what it felt like."

She reached for the broken doorknob August had put back in place before leaving the night before and gave it a turn. It rattled loosely in the socket but didn't come off in her hand. "You knew on a spiritual level what your senses did not. You weren't alone, but the spirit or spirits around you were benign." She pushed the door open and motioned for August and Ida to enter first.

He followed Ida in, bolstered by the knowledge that he and Ida had shared a peaceful trek through the house on their previous visit and that LaDonna believed the spirits of the house—if there were any—were friendly ones.

This time, though, as he stepped through the doorway, the chill that enveloped him went beyond simple goosebumps. August thought for a moment that a broken, disused pipe had dripped a cold, thick fluid onto the crown of his head. His hand sought the wetness appearing there, and his heart skipped a beat when he found nothing but dry hair. Yet the sensation his body was saturated grew with every step he took deeper into the house.

Icy, thick, but invisible, it poured viscously from the crown of his head past his ears to his shoulders, yet nothing hindered his breathing except the racing of his heart and the fearful tightening of his chest. His arms tingled painfully, like frostbite setting in, while his body became colder, the icy grip wrapping tighter. It wasn't just cold—it felt personal, invasive, like something was trying to crawl into his bones and hollow him out from the inside. The cold clung to him, curling around his limbs as though it knew every inch of his arms and wanted to reclaim them. Its tendrils burrowed deeper with every breath, like it was aware of his thoughts and wanted inside. His breath hitched.

By the time he was at the foot of the staircase, he felt as if his body was encased in ice, and his breathing had become shallow. He gripped the banister with clawed hands, afraid his frozen legs would fail him.

"August?" Luke asked, "Are you alright?"

Ida, alerted to a problem with August, did an about face. Whatever she saw in his expression deeply unsettled her. She rushed to his side and gripped his biceps. The touch of her fingers burned him like flame, but he sensed the skin she touched was fine—the burning not physical, but spiritual.

"Augie? What's wrong?"

He wanted to assure her he was fine, but the words did not come. No words did. He could not speak.

og   ku

Clark swore to himself when LaDonna and Luke returned to the house, this time with the young couple who had visited earlier. That morning, the house was swarming with an unusual number of Passersby strolling, floating, and crawling from one part of the house to another. They moved through doorways and walls. They climbed the stairs only to vanish on the landing. The air crackled with the energy of their presence, leaving Clark feeling hazy as television static, as permeable as a spider web.

On days like this, the ephemeral transients rarely paid any mind to the resident ghosts who stood aside and let them pass, always cautious never to touch them. Never make eye contact. Never to let them know they sensed their presence. Clark knew if their energies touched, the there-not-there feeling would swell until he was certain that his essence might break apart, that *he* might break apart, the last of his ghostly existence sent to far-flung corners of the universe.

Today, for the first time, Clark saw what happened to a living being when a Passerby took possession of them. August had entered after Ida with little of the trepidation he'd shown before. When Clark saw LaDonna and her husband Luke had accompanied them, he understood the reason for August's confidence. LaDonna had undoubtedly picked up on August's spiritual discernment and had offered to coach him through his concerns with the house. That this visit was during daylight hours likely helped.

Unfortunately, August's discernment did not activate in time to avoid the Passerby seeping from the ceiling.

Helpless, Clark watched as the Passerby dripped like ectoplasm onto the young man's scalp and poured onto August as he passed into the entry. The Passerby grew until it trickled down over his face, ears, and shoulders. Slowly, the smoke-colored phantom oozed over the hapless August as he walked, encasing him in a viscous, invisible, unbreakable trap.

"Oh, shit," Leah breathed. "He's toast."

Clark shook his head, unable to stop watching the scene unfold before him. "I don't think so," he said. "I wonder if this thing believes one of our visitors can help it. I think the Passerby is trying to reach out or use August to communicate. They're always striving to go somewhere, haven't you noticed? Like they're on an unending quest to find someplace."

"Never bothered to talk to one long enough to find out," she drawled. "Neither have you. Neither has Minnie. Those things creep me out."

Clark scoffed. "I'm sure we'd freak those four living folks out if they knew we were here."

"True." She crossed her arms and cocked a hip.

He and Leah stood helpless and watched as their human guests strove to break whatever spell had August in its clutches.

"August? Listen to me," LaDonna said coaxingly. "I think an entity in the house is trying to communicate with you or through you. You need to let them know they aren't welcome."

August's eyes made up for what his mouth was incapable of saying. *How?*

"Your body is yours, August," LaDonna said. "Nobody and nothing else's. You need to let that spirit know it is not welcome there. Imagine your spirit, August. Not just your body, but the spirit, the energy within you that makes you *you*. That spirit within you is every bit as strong as this thing trying to take your body for a joyride."

"Maybe stronger," Luke added.

LaDonna nodded. "He's right. Maybe stronger. Envision pushing this thing out of your body like sweat from your pores. Evict it, August. It has no right to hijack you. Take rightful control of your body. You can do this."

August's chin made the tiniest micro-nod, and his eyebrows released some tension before the young man closed his eyes to turn his attention inward. Clark could practically feel the effort the young man was exerting into evicting the spirit that had hijacked him. His body trembled with the effort, and a groan emerged from deep in his throat. Ida stood before him, one hand atop his, the other on his shoulder, prepared to offer him any aid she could provide.

Emotions swept through Clark as the scene unfolded: the depth of the love between Ida and August; the frustration, fear, and determination August must be going through as he fought for control of his body; the way LaDonna and Luke stood by, likely feeling some sense of responsibility for August's predicament; and the helplessness he and Leah shared, invisible and all but nonexistent to the others.

All of them except August, that is.

"What are you thinking, Clark?" Leah asked. "You've got that look."

"I think… I think I'm going to see if I can help August."

Ϗ   ʅ

Harper's calves were cramping, and judging from the way her lower back was cramping, she was pretty sure her period was coming on. Neither was doing much for her mood. At least the woods smelled pleasant. At her last outdoor job, she'd had to bury some reeking animal scat before taking her position. The smell was so bad it had lingered in her nostrils for over an hour.

Sitting up, she brushed off the moss that had transplanted from the tree to her elbows. Her stomach growled, and she took a swig of warm water that tasted of plastic from her canteen. *I should have brought a snack.*

She set the binoculars on her eyes again and let her vision adjust. If they stayed in that dump much longer, she would have a tan line around her eyes. Before settling into a reverse position, she took a second slug of water from her canteen and replaced it on her belt. Thankfully, with weeks of range practice, she was an expert ambidextrous shooter, so it didn't matter which hand her position favored. It'd been a while since she'd practiced with the Winchester, but she was confident that August didn't stand a chance against her aim regardless of which dominant hand she used. As long as he was in the crosshairs of her scope, he was a dead man.

After ensuring that the rear door of the massive, neglected building was overgrown enough to prevent them from exiting the house that way, Harper turned her attention to the grimy front windows. She intently monitored the building's sole egress point, now alternating from watching through her binoculars and the scope of her rifle. There was only one way to get out of there, and she had her attention fixed on it.

Her efforts were damn near futile. Why did the windows have to be so filthy? She couldn't see a thing other than the occasional blurry motion through a small circular spot that, for some reason, was a hair less dirty than the rest of the windows.

On the plus side, If I can't see them very well with my optical enhancers, they sure as hell can't see me with their naked eyes.

Harper lifted the rifle, placed the butt into the crook of her shoulder, and lined up the sight with the patch of slightly cleaner window. All she needed now was a split second of August's wavy, dirty blond hair, his purple shirt, or his face to come into view. She'd pull her trigger, take him out, and be off on her way without fear of being sighted. The obstructed view, while a hindrance to getting a clear shot, would hide her from their sight while she bolted for the car. They'd be too freaked out by what happened to her target to think about finding who shot him until she was long gone. By the time the cops showed up, she'd be back at the hotel packing her bags.

Perfect. One day, in and out, and I'll get my money and run. Too easy. Come on, bootlegger. Give me just one little peek at your pretty noggin.

Chapter Fourteen

Despite her years at the university, which included several math courses and one in physics, Marina had little comprehension of what quantum physics entailed. As she and Zeke steered down the long, black asphalt drive that led to Zeke's father's house, her emotions were a mixed bag of eagerness, fear, hope, and dread.

In the few minutes since Derek had vanished, her life had lost much of its brightness, and now, as Zeke killed the engine, she realized how much of her strength of late was derived from her need to be a pillar of might for her son. As she stood, part of her wished for his slender hand to find hers. That way, she could draw from that pool of stalwartness she found whenever she took on the role of mother and mighty one. Instead, she felt pitiful and helpless, lost in a world of mysteriousness.

Everything she'd believed in was unraveling. She'd had her superstitions, what others considered her odd beliefs, and her gut feelings, but nothing had prepared her for circumstances like this. Suddenly, science fiction had entered her world through a hole that led out of it.

Were there more portals scattered throughout the earth? How many? What caused them? Did they hover in the air? Or might the very world she walked on open up and swallow her? She didn't know. Faced with the need to bring her husband and son home, her lack of knowledge seemed beyond cavernous—it seemed more extensive than the depths of space itself.

"You alright?" Zeke asked.

Marina found herself staring at the air before her as if expecting one of Derek's "shiny" spots to materialize. She blinked. "Yeah."

"You sure?"

She met his gaze. "I have to be. What choice have I got?"

He nodded. His green eyes, though pale as lamb's ears, reflected warmth and concern. Wade's absence no doubt weighed heavily on his partner, too.

Zeke's father's home was a two-story red brick colonial revival. A sloping green roof held a jutting dormer, the window to which held a view of an enormous gray-striped tabby cat that arched its back as if preparing to descend the stairs to open the door for them.

"Dad's not here yet," Zeke said, "I don't know—"

He stopped and smiled as a metallic emerald-green classic Dodge Charger pulled into the driveway. Marina didn't know the year, but she guessed it to be circa early 1970s. From a stereo inside the vehicle, she heard the riffs, a soul-felt blues melody.

"That's his baby," Zeke said, his smile revealing that he, too, felt sentimental about his father's ride.

"Nice," Marina said, her voice dull and mechanical. And it was a nice car, she supposed. But the vehicle's beauty was hard to evaluate when her soul was weighted with despair.

The Charger rolled to a stop, and Zeke's father exited. Marina had to smile at the sight of him. The man was short, his brown slacks cinched below a round stomach. In fact, his whole body seemed to be made of various-sized circles; his cheeks, the bulbous tip of his nose, his brimmed wool cap, and the swirling design on his green tie all seemed to emphasize the man's circularity. His green eyes and red hair, now turning white, appeared to be Zeke's only inherited traits.

"Marina, this is my father, Esau Weidenseld."

Marina extended her hand with a pleased smile. Marina considered his red hair and wondered if his parents had decided their son's name before or after seeing his fiery mane. "Thank you for seeing us, Mr. Weidenseld."

Esau shook her hand with one of his and waved lightheartedly with the other. "It's Esau, and I'm glad to finally have the chance, though I wish it were under different circumstances. Zeke tells me Wade's missing?"

Marina nodded, unable to think of an adequate way to reply.

"Well, come in, come in." He waddled to the door, his hips seeming to rotate from either side of his stomach. "Zeke says he wonders if I can help? I'm not sure what good I can do; I'm a scientist, not an investigator…"

"Dad," Zeke said, opening the door for them, "let's get comfortable first, and I'll explain everything."

The Weidenseld home, like Marina's own, was spacious yet homey, and smelled of citrus and freshly cleaned floors. However, this home had a few luxuries she didn't want to acquire until Derek was older and less rambunctious—leather seats, curios with glass shelves, and a few tasteful but delicate statuettes. Yet the worn magazines on the coffee table, the well-worn coasters on the end tables, and the family photos displayed in places of pride still spoke of a family who lived in their house instead of using it as a showplace.

Once seated at a large walnut dining room table with mugs of yet more coffee, Zeke shared the tale of Wade's mysterious disappearance, the "shiny" spot that Derek alone could see and then passed through, and the disappearing tip of rebar. Esau listened intently, his hand sometimes on his chin, other times on the table clasped in a chubby circle. His eyes barely blinked; he was like a man hypnotized. To Marina's surprise, Esau displayed no disbelief, only a face full of scientific curiosity. At times, he punctuated the conversation with insightful questions: Had Wade and Derek disappeared at once, or did their passage appear to be more like traveling through a curtain? Did they hear any sounds from the other side? And the one Marina felt was most confusing; what were they thinking about when all this occurred?

Zeke polished off the last of his coffee and set down his mug. "When Wade disappeared, I'm sure we were both thinking the same thing—stop Izzy, get Grayzel back safely, and don't get shot."

"Mmm," Esau said.

Marina sipped her coffee and waited to make sure that Zeke was finished. "Esau, I don't know what it is that you do, exactly, but if you have any ideas about how I can get Wade and Derek back—"

The man held up a short, pudgy finger. "Marina, I'm sorry, but what I do—it's largely based on theory. I work with quantum information processing—"

"But you were telling me something the other day about quantum teleportation," Zeke offered.

Esau frowned. "Yes, I did." He sighed. "Listen, I don't mean to upset you two, but… well, let me tell you a few things about quantum science. It's not exact. Far from it—we're not really sure how it works."

"Tell her about the other dimensions," Zeke pressed.

Esau regarded his son with an expression that hovered between frustration and pride. "You get that from your mother," he said. Turning back to Marina, he wrinkled his nose and added, "Always interrupting."

"You know about the other dimensions?" Marina said. "Why haven't we heard about this?"

"We suspect. Well, some of us do." He paused as he considered his next approach. "Ever heard of string theory?"

"Only in name," Marina admitted.

"String theory is a tricky thing. For one, it's impossible to test; no experiment has proven that 'strings' exist. Some even argue that it's not science because of this; it's philosophy. But out of it comes the potential for other dimensions. Eleven, in fact. Possibly right next to us."

"Next to us?"

Esau nodded. "All matter is largely insubstantial. Particles can jump from one spot to another without appearing to have moved through the space in between. You, me, this table, this floor, we're all largely made up of a vacuum between particles that appear and disappear, though we're unaware of it. We don't feel it."

Marina found herself staring at her hand as if waiting for it to grow dim, a ghostly appendage, as the particles within moved.

"In fact, the entire purpose of quantum mechanics is for us to attempt to get a grip on a world which, when viewed from a quantum level, is unpredictable. We even call it the principle of indeterminism."

The point of Esau's dialog sank in. "You can't help me," Marina said.

"I can offer what little I've come to learn about the possibilities of other dimensions."

Marina met his eyes. Intelligent. Compassionate. And disappointed that he didn't believe he had the power to help her bring Wade back.

"Anything. Anything at all to help me understand. I'd like to hear it."

☙ ❧

Ez despised the ceaseless bureaucracy of paperwork. He'd been forewarned during his training about the burdensome piles that built up during routine police work. Still, nothing had prepared him for the suffocating ratio of desk time versus street duty. He'd have given his left nut to pass it off to someone else. Some days, it was almost enough to put him off his job.

Some paperwork was almost worth doing. Officers found the lifeless body of Ignatius Irizarry in a run-down warehouse during the night. Weird, but, in Ez's opinion, the motive was understandable. The man was a bottom-feeder. None of the deputies were sorry to hear of Irizarry's passing. Although he wasn't the primary on the case, he'd found himself dragged in by a young, angel-faced but smug Officer Chartier. In a small department like his, it wasn't unusual for officers to help one another at a crime scene, especially a murder. Many hands made light work, and many eyes increased the chances of finding critical clues

Once the criminalists, Ron Wallace and Merl Edwards, had taken the necessary photos and secured the obvious evidence — a couple of bullet casings of the same make on opposite sides of the warehouse — Ez and Chartier were summoned to aid in the search for leads. Irizarry had been found with two bullet holes in his skull, one on each temple. That two separate people might want to shoot Izzy simultaneously was easy for Ez to believe. So was the possibility that Izzy might have inadvertently walked into the crossfire. The man was clever, but not smart enough to avoid trouble.

The oddity of Izzy's death was intriguing. What perplexed Ez most was the eerie symmetry and placement of the bullet holes on Irizarry's body. Two shooters — possible crossfire? Or had Izzy spun after the first round before catching a second? The possibilities boggled his mind. Izzy had been shot on opposite sides of the body, each bullet hole so alike it almost appeared as if a single bullet had gone right through. According to Wallace, both holes showed signs of being entry wounds. The astronomical odds against that blew his mind.

Another odd detail was the scratches on the concrete that, based on crime scene photos, hadn't been there the night before. Seventeen feet away from the victim, they were shallow, straight, and around two to three inches long. In case they might prove helpful in the investigation, Edwards snapped photos of the scarred floor, but Ez doubted their significance. Judging from the lack of evidence, he also doubted they'd catch whoever did it unless they got a hit on the casings.

"And now, the paperwork," Ez mumbled. He leaned in and tried to focus on the page, but his eyes blurred. He caught himself slumping over his desk as he craned over his work, and he righted himself with a sigh. The gray walls of his office seemed designed to sap one's spirit, which, that night, he felt intensely.

He scoffed and sat back, rubbing his eyes. "Man, if I'd wanted a career of filling out forms, I'd have gone into tax auditing." No one heard his joke. He was the only person within earshot. Where was everyone? *Probably poking their nose into this weird-ass case.* Ez noticed a fervor to the investigation he'd rarely noted in a case before. It wasn't every day Gryphon saw a death by gunshot. The sleepy Alabama town had its share of hunting accidents and pistol-wavers, but death by firearm was unusual.

He lifted his mug of coffee and stared into an empty cup. "No coffee, no workee," he quipped, pushing his chair back with a squeak of hinges. *Talking to myself. Now I know I'm tired.*

Unfortunately, the station's solitary coffeepot was near the front of the station house to make coffee convenient to witnesses, the occasional guest, and rare suspects detained for lengthy questioning. Ez's office was toward the rear of the building.

"My luck, the pot'll be empty. Again." Realizing that he'd spoken aloud again, he chuffed to himself.

As he made his way to the front of the building, he replayed the details of the warehouse scene once more, searching for a clue or a missing link in the evidentiary chain. Could the lines in the concrete have been stage marks—there for a shooter to know when Izzy was in place to be taken down—or a safe place for a decoy to stand to avoid a bullet? *But a bullet from who?*

Deep in thought, Ez nearly collided with Sergeant Haitsen as she approached.

"Detective Weidenseld?" she said, her pretty cheeks flushing.

Ez jerked to a stop and snapped to attention. "Yes? What?"

Her eyes dropped the way they always did when she talked to him. "There's a boy here to see you."

Ez felt his brow furrow. "A boy?" He flipped his wrist over and checked his watch. Days had lost meaning during the setup and resultant chaos of the Iggy Izzy case. It was Saturday, so it wasn't like the kid should be in school. *It's awfully early, though. I wonder what he wants.* "And he asked for me specifically?"

"By name," Haitsen said.

"Did he say who he was?"

"Derek Beringer."

"Derek who?"

Haitsen lifted her gaze to his, and she smiled. Her teeth were an orthodontist's dream. "He's right outside the door, and he seems stressed. Go talk to him. I've got to get back to the counter."

Ez frowned, recalling the stack of paperwork on his desk awaiting him. What did this kid want? Was he a student from one of the schools where he'd spoken? Maybe one who remembered him and sought him out when he got into trouble? Maybe the boy's family lived nearby, and he didn't have a way to call 9-1-1 for help.

He reluctantly unlocked the secured door and stepped into the station house lobby. A thin young boy, five or six years old, stood with straight dark hair and rectangular-rimmed glasses. Despite his youth, the boy looked tired but composed.

"Can I help you, son?"

"Detective Weidenseld? I need help finding my dad."

Aw, poor kid. He must be lost. Ez's heart went out to the child, and he sat down to better view the young man face to face. "Well, I can try to help you with that. When did you lose him?"

The boy's face scrunched up in a puzzled mask. He consulted a bright blue watch, which looked oversized on his wrist. The tiny tool looked like a mini version of his own smart watch. Derek raised his head to look at Ez. "I last saw my mom at eight seventeen. I don't remember what time I last saw my dad. He went to work after I went to bed, and a lot's happened since then. I really need your help, Detective Weidenseld."

"Eight seventeen, huh?" Ez peeked at the clock above the reception desk. It was almost nine a.m. "That's awfully specific, buddy."

"You don't need to call me buddy. I'm Derek. Derek Beringer."

Ez struggled to recall the name and face, but nothing came to mind. "I'm sorry, Derek, but … did I visit your school?"

The little man's hands balled into frustrated fists, and the words tumbled out of him in a rapid-fire cadence. "You don't know me here. But I know you. Sorta. Your dad—he's a quantum physicist. You like to watch the England station—the BBC. And you drink chocolate soy milk."

Before the shocking impossibility of this young man knowing all these details about him fully registered, two Sergio Vegas entered the building.

"Daddy!" Derek said. He stepped toward the men, took in the similarities and differences, and froze, mouth agape.

%♂ %♀

"Stay with us, August," Luke coaxed. Which wasn't a problem. August wasn't going anywhere. In fact, not being able to go somewhere was precisely the problem. His body stood rooted in place while his eyes, now wide open, darted around in panic, reflecting the growing alarm on his companions' faces. He'd tried desperately to evict whatever was controlling him, but had only achieved fleeting moments of bodily autonomy. As soon as he felt the slightest control of his body again, the sinister thing trying to gain ownership of him latched on once more, taking his breath away and leaving him shaking, trapped in invisible icy chains.

"Is it your friend doing this?" Ida demanded, her voice edged with accusation as she glared at LaDonna. "Make him stop!"

LaDonna blinked rapidly. "I can't believe this would be Clark," she stammered. "This is something else."

"Well, make it stop!" Ida repeated, her voice cracking.

Cautiously, LaDonna approached August from the side, placing a hand near Ida's on his shoulder. She smelled of outdoors and fresh herbs. "August, you can hear me, right?" she said, looking up into his eyes. He blinked twice, hoping she understood what he meant.

"You can hear me?" He blinked twice again, confirming.

"Is your name August?" Ida asked, apparently wanting to establish that he had answered the previous questions in the affirmative. He gave them a third double blink.

"Are you in pain?" LaDonna asked.

Other than feeling like Encino Man at the start of the movie, I feel OK. Scared and cold as hell, but OK.

He blinked once.

Ida let out a stressed-filled breath. "He's not hurting, at least. What do we do?"

No one spoke. Ida tucked a strand of blond curls behind her ear, and the creases in her brow deepened. Luke cleared his throat and opened his mouth to speak, but he never had a chance to voice his suggestion.

An electrical charge zipped through August's body from his left hand to his right, leaving him infused with warmth and the air smelling oddly of ozone. His eyes were no longer hostage, and the twitching he'd barely managed as he fought for government of his limbs had grown to perhaps an inch rather than millimeters and were gaining momentum. His previously constricted throat felt looser.

"Id—Ida," he rasped.

Ida crept closer. "I'm here, Augie. I'm here."

From the recesses of his mind came the echo of a voice, not his—deeper, more resonant. *You've been invaded by something I call a Passerby, but I'm going to help you get it out. It would help if you pushed now the way LaDonna told you to, August. Take control back. Push it out now.*

"Push—pushing," he gasped and closed his eyes. He sucked in a deep breath of dusty air and fought the urge to cough as he exerted himself physically, psychically, and spiritually. Drawing from LaDonna's suggestion, he envisioned his body as a fortress, impervious to invasion, a solid entity where every molecule was distinctly August Shane Webb with no space within for anything else.

That's it, August.

Yet there was something else, that growing heat within driving away the clinging presence inside of him. He held onto that presence, wishing only for the loosening of the spiritual chains that bound him.

Don't worry about me, August. I'm just here to help. Keep at it. You're almost there. It's nearly out.

The friendly voice left August feeling not invaded so much as inhabited—like a home with a visitor that understood the dwelling they stood in was not theirs to keep. By inches, the icy feeling poured from him, replaced by a nurturing sensation of warmth. His heart and chest swelled with the sensation of light as a luminous presence grew within.

You did it.

With your help. Thank you. How… what are you?

My name is Clark.

August let out a nervous chuckle, a mix of relief and apprehension. "LaDonna, your friend is here."

"Clark?" LaDonna breathed. She looked around for a sign of her friend's presence.

May I borrow your voice for a little while? I understand if you refuse. I will leave you now that you're safe, if that is what you want.

After your help, how can I say no?

The sense that his mouth and tongue were not his came over him once more, only the sensation did not threaten to choke him this time.

"LaDonna?" The voice had a different timbre than his own, a depth he didn't know he was capable of. "It's nice to see you again."

LaDonna's green eyes grew enormous, and a hand flew to her chest. "Cl-Clark?"

☙　❧

"Derek!" Wade's heart soared as he crouched low so his son could fly into his arms—which he did, nearly bowling Wade over despite his small stature. Wade's hand found his son's dark hair, and his arms almost crushed Derek's slender body next to his, as if verifying through maximum contact the boy was truly before him. *He's here. How did he get here? Unless…*

He broke the embrace and took Derek by the shoulders. "Where's your mother?"

"She um… she's still…" Derek shot a worried glance over his shoulder at Zeke—*Ez*—and then to Sergio. "She's still over there," he whispered with the exaggerated loudness of young children.

"Over—? Ah." Though partly overjoyed at the sight of his

son, his heart sank that Marina was not with him. He hated that his family was separated. If they were together, he would hardly care about being away from his previous life. Poor Marina was probably losing her mind. *Damn. Damn!*

"How did you get here?"

Derek shrugged. "I went through the… the thing. And then I walked here."

He walked. Wade shook his head, impressed at his son's resourcefulness. *Thank goodness he's OK, the little bugger.*

He stood and put a hand on Sergio's shoulder. "Derek, I'd like you to meet my, ah. Your…"

"Sergio Vega," Sergio said, saving Wade the trouble of trying to figure out a way to explain their obvious similarity. He offered a hand to Derek, which the boy shook somberly. Gaging by the appraising Derek was doing of Sergio's form, clothes, and demeanor, if he hadn't figured out the truth, he wasn't far from it.

A thousand questions longed to be answered. How had Derek made the jump here? Was the portal still there, ready for him to pass through? Did they merely have to travel back to the warehouse and then return to their former lives? Wade's heart was beating hard, his excitement almost overwhelming. The nightmare might nearly be over. Soon, he could return to his plane of existence with his family again.

"Is it still there?" he asked. "That place? In the warehouse?"

"Yup," Derek said. "I checked."

"You can see it?"

Zeke — *Ez, dammit, gotta try to remember that* — butted in. "Warehouse? Which warehouse? See what? What's going on? Sergio?" His face, painted with confusion and cop-like determination, swiveled between the two burly men before him. Something they'd said had set Ez off.

The body. They found Irizarry, and now Ez is putting the pieces together. He glanced at Sergio from the corner of his eye. The man was rubbing the back of his neck with arms and shoulders that appeared tight, and he looked ready to bolt.

"Ze — Detective Weidenseld, can you give my son and me a ride somewhere?" Wade asked. "It's not far. And, um, I might need your help if… Long story, but I might need your help if something I'm looking for isn't there."

Ez needed very little prompting. His detective instincts had kicked in with the intensity that Detective Weidenseld had, regardless of which universe he lived in. There was a mystery here to solve, and he was dying to see it through to the explanation — especially since it appeared there may be a link to Irizarry's murder.

"Sure, I can do that," Ez agreed. Wade knew his partner well enough to tell the man's wheels were already struggling to put the pieces in the right place.

Wade directed his attention to Sergio. "If you want, go on home. I don't think we need you there for this next part. Thanks for the ride." His suggestion was met with an audible release of pent-up air from his doppelgänger.

"I, uh… Are you sure?"

"Yeah, like I said, I appreciate the ride, but I think I may be good now. I'll, uh, touch base with you later if I need to. If I don't, I guess no news is good news."

Sergio let out a half-laugh and gave him a sly smile that Wade knew would never look natural on his own face. "Yeah, man. OK. You've got my number."

Ez turned, his mouth pressed into a stern frown as the three men and one little boy left the precinct. Unable to stand it any longer, Ez asked. "So, which one of you is Sergio?"

Chapter Fifteen

"String theory," Esau said, "like I said, is complicated. It took years for science to develop a unified premise—we had to go through five different theories only to find M theory, which explained that all five calculations were merely looking at the same thing from different angles. And we're still working to unify M theory with Einstein's theory of general relativity."

"Dad, keep it simple, please," Zeke said, rising and going around the island to the kitchen to help himself to more coffee. He held up the carafe, offering to top off Marina's cup, and she lifted her cup to signal her desire for more.

"Right," Esau said, rubbing his chin. An idea occurred to him, and he nodded. He pushed his chair back to the walnut china cabinet. He extracted a card from a drawer below the glass display shelves and lightly tossed it across the tablet to Marina, who lifted it to study it more closely. On the card was what appeared to be a trident with what appeared to be three prongs.

"How many prongs are on there?"

"Three," Marina replied.

"Are you sure?"

She wasn't. Try as she might, the more she studied the card, the harder it was to make out how the center prong attached itself to the pitchfork. Her eyes traced the lines but could not distinguish the middle prong's origin. Even when she used her finger to follow it, the puzzling prong foiled her attempts to solve how it worked.

"How in the—?" She traced the lines with her finger again and finally understood how the object worked. What appeared to be the side of the bottom trident was the entire prong, and the center "prong" wasn't a prong at all, but a ruse. The fork had been designed to deliberately be misinterpreted, a blending of 2-D and 3-D animation. "Clever."

"It's called an 'impossible object.' Like this one." Esau tossed her another card. "Do the stairs go up or down?"

Marina let out a short laugh as she tilted the image back and forth. "It's like an Escher painting."

"That's a great comparison. Escher had a great technique, making things appear the way they can't be in real life. But I often wonder... like these pictures, is it maybe that our eyes aren't trained to perceive these other dimensions?"

"What do you mean?"

His eyes met Marina's. "You took psychology in college, right?" When she nodded, he said, "Well, then you may have heard of this one. A couple of guys named Blakemore and Cooper did this rather sadistic experiment on kittens. They fitted them with goggles that only allowed them to see vertical lines, and when they didn't keep them in the dark, they stuck the poor things in a round room with only vertical lines. Over time, the kittens weren't capable of perceiving horizontal lines properly. They didn't develop the right neurons. 'Perceptual set,' it's called—when we develop a way, mentally, to see one thing and not another."

"A scotoma," Marina said.

Nodding, Esau chuckled. "It's something I have to overcome sometimes when thinking my way through a challenging problem—at work or otherwise."

"So, you think we can't see other dimensions because we're not taught to? And that's why Derek could see the spot, the portal, or whatever, and I can't? Because he has the right neurons?"

Esau shrugged. "Well, it's a possibility. Another theory was that the only thing that might be able to get through the dimensional barrier is gravity, but that's much harder to explain—not to mention that your son and husband have completely disproven it."

Marina let out a deep breath and slumped back into the chair. "You really don't know how they did it, do you?"

Esau's eyes grew weary, saddened. Palms up, he said, "I'm sorry, dear, but as far as explanations, that's all I've got."

Zeke snorted. "That's not true, Dad," he said, leaning in from his place at the head of the table, "tell her your theory."

Esau grabbed the cards and leaned back, his posture somewhat guarded. After he shut them back into the drawer, he rested his arms on his stomach. "My theory. Oh, Zeke, I don't know about that."

"Tell her," Zeke pressed.

Esau slumped. He looked at Marina, then looked away, almost ashamed of himself, it seemed. She hoped her eyes portrayed the depth of her pleading, her need to know if she dared hope. Finally, he sat up, his hands fidgeting nervously with the cards.

"It's not my theory," he said, as if offering a disclaimer. "It's... well, it's what some consider pop-science. Pseudo-science, even. Even so... I feel there are things difficult to explain."

Sounds just like what we need, Marina thought. But she didn't speak, afraid that if she interrupted, Esau might rethink his willingness to share his theory and stop talking.

"It all stems from a handful of experiments. For example, did you know that watched experiments often have different results than experiments that are not observed? And certain experiments have shown that a choice made now can influence a *past* experimental result. Another experiment by a man named Zelinger showed that one microscopic ball went through two slits at the same time."

Marina was confused. First puzzles, now observers, choices, and balls being in two places at once? "I don't understand."

Esau nodded. "I'm sorry. I'm jumping around a bit. Let me start over.

"There are things called quantum wave functions—sometimes called QWFs. Quantum mechanics is a baffling science, but several things have been observed in these QWFs. Quantum particles are the fundamental building blocks of the universe, but they act in ways that differ greatly from the objects we encounter in our everyday lives. Imagine the smallest particles you can think of, like atoms or the particles inside atoms, such as electrons, protons, and neutrons. Quantum particles are even more basic and exist in a field where the rules of classical physics don't apply. Quantum particles are very erratic, but certain particles have been shown to affect other particles—an entangled particle, so to speak—at a distance. Combine that with the idea that particles can occupy two places at once, and another possibility that with every choice a person makes, a dimension involving both choices may come about…"

"He's saying that on a subatomic level, our thoughts, our will, may be shaping reality and making new dimensions," Zeke interjected, "And that it looks like maybe your husband has found a way to move to one of those other dimensions."

Marina froze, her mind awhirl with ideas spinning like a roulette wheel. She thought of Derek in the warehouse moments before he'd vanished. Had he been the only one with the power to see the hole because he'd wanted to find his father more than she had? But how had Wade gone through? Was he stressing so much during Grayzel's capture that he'd wished himself someplace else? That didn't sound like her husband at all. "I'm sorry, Esau, but I don't understand how that explains Wade disappearing."

Zeke had to agree. "He's never been the sort of guy who's dissatisfied. We've had some pretty deep talks over the years. He's a pretty content guy. It's not as if he had a reason to leave… here. This dimension."

"But," Esau said, "what if there was something, or someone, over there, who desperately needed Wade to be in *that* dimension?"

"You mean there's someone else, in another plane, who needs my husband more than I do? More than Derek?" She fought to keep the hysteria from her voice, but it climbed higher than she intended.

Esau held his hand up. "Well, it is only a hypothesis. And we can't forget the possibility of an ultimate power behind all this."

Marina's brow furrowed.

"God," Zeke said. "He means God might have intervened."

Marina closed her eyes. *If God took them, I can't do anything to get them back but pray. Pray for the power to reach them… somehow.* She lifted her eyes skyward. *Please, God. Please bring them back to me.*

☓ ☔

"Is August OK?" Ida demanded. Her grip on his shoulder tightened painfully.

August felt the spirit within him directing his head in an up-and-down motion, and he wordlessly asked Clark for control to speak for a moment. August received an impression of Clark's understanding, and in seconds, the ability to move his mouth was his again.

"I'm here too, Ida," he assured her. "Clark helped me to push that last thing out — he called it a Passerby — and asked if he could speak to LaDonna. I told him it was fine. He's not like that first thing that took me over. He's... different. He wants to move through me but not use me. Not like that last thing."

Ida's lips drew into a tight line, her entire countenance taut and skeptical. "As long as you're OK with it," she allowed.

"I am. Don't worry, Ida." His gaze drifted away from her inquiring eyes, and he reached for the presence at the edge of his consciousness. His focus moved to a point beyond the physical world, and his expression grew introspective. "Clark?"

August shuddered as the spirit within him seamlessly resumed control and borrowed his mouth once more. His eyes sharpened with an otherworldly focus that made the real world shimmer faintly as the edges of things grew indistinct. A faint smile, not quite his own, played at the corners of his lips. "LaDonna, I am glad to see you again."

"It's been a long time," LaDonna said. Large tears broke from the corners of her eyes and rolled down her tanned cheeks. She gripped the hem of her flowing blouse in her hands and curled the fabric into a ball. Luke stepped up and placed a supportive hand on her shoulder, but remained in the background.

Clark's remorse clung to the spirit within August, and the air around him grew charged with the weight of the spirit's regret. "I wanted to tell you so long ago... I am so sorry. I never should have —"

"You were in pain, Clark. I know. So much pain."

"I always believed that ending my life would condemn my soul to hell for eternity. But I didn't care. I didn't care that my dear friend would be the one to find my earthly body. I cared about nothing but escape, and I did not believe hell could be worse than —"

"I know. I know. You lost Judith, and —"

"That's no excuse, LaDonna, and I will never forgive myself for what I did to you. What I forced you to deal with. But I didn't think things could improve for me. I was too reckless. I had no business falling in love with Judith. I can't forgive myself for allowing myself to fall for her or allowing her to fall for me."

"Judith… I wanted to tell you before, but I wanted to be sure you heard me. Clark, she, um… she is still nearby. I see her sometimes. In Huntsville. And we're friends on… social media. Do you know what that is?"

August's eyes grew large, and his heart swelled in sympathy with Clark's recognition of LaDonna's words.

"Is she… alright?"

LaDonna bit her lower lip. The tears still flowed. "Clark… she had the babies."

"Ba-babies?"

"Twins. William and Patrick."

August, with Clark, let out a choked gasp of a laugh. His eyes grew hot and glassy, and soon, tears flowed from his eyes, too. "Twins."

"She found a wonderful man when the boys were just toddlers. He married Judith and raised the boys as if they were his own. They have grown and have their own families now. One of them looks a whole lot like you."

His hands clenched into a fist at his chest. Relief, joy, and gratitude threatened to overwhelm him, and August sat on the stairs near his feet with the weakness Clark felt in his happiness. "She's alright. Oh, dear Lord, she's alright." August sobbed. It was too much. Clark needed to break away and deal with the staggering feelings that had become his entire world. "I… I will step away now. I hope I have a chance to speak to you again."

"Of course."

August pulled in a breath and peered into LaDonna's tear-stained face. "Before I go… Can you forgive me, please? For what I put you through?"

LaDonna shook her head. "Clark, there is nothing to forgive."

August's head bobbed up and down subtly, and his body grew quiet as an almost imperceptible shift passed over him. The world around him snapped into place as he regained control of his body once more.

ೞ ೲ

To Marina's dismay, Esau glanced at his watch. His eyebrows shot upward with concern. He pushed his chair back with a groan of antique wood, and her heart sank. All Esau had given her was more questions than answers, and she was no closer to finding a means to Wade's return.

"I'm afraid I have an appointment with a friend and need to be there soon." He paused and considered Marina's tired eyes and Zeke's frustration. "I'll tell you what. How about you both come with me? You may find it interesting—she believes she's found proof of paranormal activity at an abandoned house in the hills. And afterward, we can go to lunch at the posh end of town—I'll buy—and continue our discussion. Maybe between us, we can figure something out."

Marina nearly laughed at Esau's reference to the "posh end" of Gryphon, although she knew what part of town he meant. Anything north of Mercutio Crescent was on the higher end of Gryphon's price point and led into the Appalachian foothills at the village outskirts.

Zeke gave Marina the universal it's-up-to-you eyebrow raise, and Marina found herself nodding. "Sure. Sounds good." *Sounds like the only option I have.*

Esau exchanged the keys to his Charger for ones to his more practical Volvo station wagon. Once on the road that led them into the foothills outside of Gryphon, Esau turned down the classic rock station and continued expounding upon their conversation as if they'd never stopped.

"Perhaps," he said as he fussed with the air conditioning until the chilly air flowed more fully, "an event at the drug bust triggered a local disruption in the fabric of reality. Something that caused a temporary convergence or entanglement of particles that resulted in a brief, unstable connection between two parallel universes."

"Do you think Wade's entire body may be 'entangled' with someone in a parallel world?" Zeke asked.

"It's possible. Theoretically, two particles can connect in such a way that whatever happens to one particle will also affect the other, no matter how far apart they are."

"Even if they've never touched?" Marina asked.

"Certainly. There is something called spontaneous Parametric Down-Conversion. This is where, in experiments, entanglement is generated using processes where a photon passes through a nonlinear crystal and splits into two entangled photons. These photons are entangled from the moment of their creation and have never been in physical contact."

"Dad, I have no idea what you just said," Zeke laughed. "But it sounds like you're still talking particles. Wade's a whole person. That's a lot of particles."

"He had to go somewhere, son. Do you have a better explanation?"

Ruefully shaking his head, Zeke had to admit he did not.

"Could we, I don't know, use that—that entanglement to bring him back somehow?" Marina asked. "Is Wade maybe tangled with something here strong enough to pull him back?"

Esau waggled his head back and forth. "It is theoretically possible, but it would require the creation of a quantum portal using entanglement to link two different universes. A connection could be established by manipulating the entangled particles, allowing them to act as a bridge between the two universes."

"So, it's possible," Marina said.

"Marina," Zeke said, turning around to face her, "you have to remember—there are potentially countless universes. Not only are we dealing with theoretical science and the notion that your enormous husband can be equated to a particle, but we'd have to narrow down where Wade is now out of... possibly millions of worlds."

"Millions?" Marina whispered, her heart sinking.

"Ah, there she is!" Esau exclaimed, pulling his Volvo onto the parched ground behind an aging Hyundai Sonata. He eagerly slid the car into park and hefted himself out of the vehicle. Marina and Zeke followed suit.

A lovely woman with long, wavy brown hair dressed in hiking shorts and a button-up shirt with rolled sleeves was waiting for Esau with a strange-looking piece of equipment strapped around her neck. In her hands was a meter of some sort, the needle buzzing erratically but steadily.

"Rebecca, you've met Zeke, I believe," Esau said, motioning to his son. Introductions were made, and Esau cocked his head to peer over Rebecca's shoulder to investigate his friend's device.

"Your meter seems to be quite excited there," he observed.

Rebecca's joy at his interest radiated from her like sunshine. "Yes, isn't it? I've made a few adaptations to the original model. Now, I can track temperature, humidity, and vibrations, which is incredibly useful. Look at this, Esau. I've never seen anything like it. We've known there was something odd about the Wenke house for years, right? And I always suspected there would be some electromagnetic activity around it, but nothing like this. Esau, we're not even inside the house, and the meter already shows spikes. Look at it!"

"It is, indeed."

Marina found Rebecca's excitement contagious, and she managed a meager smile.

"Didn't you say you'd looked into some of the events that happened here?" Rebecca asked. "It seems right up there with something your research consortia might enjoy." Esau's eyes crinkled at the corners as he gave Rebecca an indulgent smile. Evidently, their mutual passion for unconventional sciences had earned them the scorn of their more closed-minded colleagues, but that had not dissuaded them from their passions.

"I did," Esau said. "And this seems like a splendid time to do a bit of my own investigating. Shall we investigate further, friend?"

Rebecca's eyes sparkled with delight. "We shall!"

☙ ❧

I'm going home. I'm going home. The words echoed in Wade's mind like a mantra—one laced with peril. He wasn't back yet. Far too much remained uncertain.

To Wade's surprise, on the way out of the precinct, Sergio had decided against driving home. It took little effort to deduce that Sergio knew Ez might figure out there might be a link between Derek, Wade, Sergio, and Izzy's body, and had decided he wanted to be there to help explain the bizarre story, should Wade need back-up. Wade was impressed with the man's integrity.

At first, Ez had ardently protested against driving with Derek in the backseat without a booster. His insistence on safety, usually so appreciated back in Wade's timeline, now clashed with his pressing need to return to the site where this all began. What if there was a limit to how long the thing lasted?

The humid Southern air wrapped around them, adding an oppressive heaviness to their frustrated verbal exchange. Ez's green eyes bore into him, reminding Wade of the piercing scrutiny Zeke reserved for subjects when they answered a call. The charge between them was palpable, but Wade refused to back down.

"Wade, not only is it unsafe, it's against the law. I'm a police officer. If anything happens when we're driving around, I could lose my job for doing something so stupid, for Christ's sake."

Wade bristled at the apprehensive tone in Ez's voice, and the man flinched ever-so-slightly. "So, what? I'm supposed to sit here while you drive to Walmart, pick one up, and come back?" Wade shook his head. "Sorry. Normally, I'd be the first person to insist on safety, especially when it comes to my son, but not right now. Not now."

"But—"

"We have to leave. It's important."

Ez paused, infuriated, but the conviction in Wade's eyes must have convinced him he was up against a wall. He heaved a frustrated breath and stepped away from Wade, his hands dropping to his sides.

"We'll take a response car," Ez announced, his low tone closing the discussion.

"Sure," Wade agreed, steering them all toward the parking lot at the rear of the building. "Get the keys from Yolanda, and we'll meet you out back."

"Yolan—how do you know all this stuff?"

At a pace just shy of a trot, Wade said, "I'll explain in the car."

His emotions were a toss-up between exaltation at Derek's presence and frustration with Ez's hard-headedness taking them so long. Zeke's headstrong personality had always come in handy when the man was on his side; now, it stood as an impediment to Wade's return to normalcy.

The four of them trotted to the back of the building, where Wade took a brief survey of his surroundings before opening the gate to the stable of Ford Explorer Police SUVs. He pulled the doors open, slid the gate stoppers into place with practiced ease, and waited for Ez to appear, his leg jiggling anxiously when he wasn't pacing. He caught Sergio eying him curiously and then realized it might have seemed odd that he had moved through the motions as if he'd done it hundreds of times.

After several long minutes, Ez appeared, keys in hand. The click of the unlocking vehicle doors echoed in the stillness. As Wade slid into the back with his son, Sergio took shotgun.

Ez checked his mirrors, adjusted them, and moved the seat back. He put the key in, surveyed his surroundings, and finally backed out of the parking space. Weidenselds in both universes used cautious movements, and the crawling pace grated on Wade's nerves. Before they'd even left the parking lot, Wade was ready to yank his partner—could he call the man in this dimension his partner?—from behind the wheel and take his place so he could drive to the warehouse with sirens wailing and lights blazing.

"Take it easy, Dad," Derek said. "It'll be OK."

Wade struggled to match his son's optimism. He cracked a meager smile to show Derek he had heard his son's words and prayed his face didn't reveal his doubt. Derek put his hand on top of his, a gesture of affection his son hadn't done for at least a year, perhaps more, ever since he'd grown old enough to think of himself as a "big boy." The sign of affection touched him.

"There's a lot of stuff in your car," Derek observed.

Ez chuckled. "Yes, there is."

"What does it all do?"

Ez gave Derek a quick tour of the vehicle as he drove, everything from the spotlight to the radar, spare body-cam battery, loudspeaker, radio, horn, siren controls, traffic ticket storage, the citation printer, weapons rack, and the old laptop.

"That's a lot of stuff," Derek said, impressed.

"It is. And Wade—you said you'd explain what's going on," Ez reminded him, jolting Wade, who had been watching the world pass by, back to the present.

Wade and Sergio exchanged glances, but neither seemed eager to begin their unbelievable tale.

"I know Sergio doesn't have a brother," Ez pressed. "We went to the same high school. Unless you were adopted. Were you adopted?"

Wade heaved a dry laugh. "Yes, I was. But not here. Sergio, maybe you'd better explain. This is more your territory."

Sergio's raised eyebrows conveyed an unspoken need for guidance. "Where should I start, man?" he asked, his voice calm, his face asking Wade's permission to conceal their role in Iggy's death.

Shoot. Damn. If I leave, who'll make sure that Sergio doesn't get charged with Iggy's murder? Inwardly, he cursed himself for inviting Ez along. Getting a cop involved in their drama? What had he been thinking?

"Do the best you can," he said, knowing the constraints Sergio had to navigate.

Sergio nodded. Wade watched as the man thought momentarily before running up against a mental wall. His eyes said what Wade already knew; there was no way to convey the story without divulging how they'd met in the warehouse.

"I'm sorry," Wade mouthed.

"Sorry?" Ez asked. Wade caught his partner's eyes in the rearview mirror. Of all the times for the man to take his eyes from the road. "For what? If somebody doesn't start explaining shit soon, I'm pulling this car over." Wade nearly laughed; he'd heard his partner relay stories of his father, Esau, using the same threat throughout his childhood when their family took road trips.

Sergio gritted his jaw, heaved a sigh, and began. He unspooled his theory of Wade's passage from an alternate universe, each detail weighed and laid bare, satisfying Ez's insatiable thirst for clarity as the detective fired off with question after question. Starting with accidentally shooting Iggy Izzy, Sergio revealed a knack for conveying stories that Wade envied—and wondered if he had buried within himself. When Sergio concluded, Wade filled in his side of the story, starting with the drug bust until Ez had a complete, if incredible, report.

When Sergio's account of his adventures with Wade ended, Ez asked how Derek had entered the story. Derek provided his explanation with the simplicity that only a child could muster.

"That's easy," Derek said. "Me and Mom went to go find Dad. When you—the other Ez in my world, we call him Zeke—took us to the warehouse, I saw a shiny, glowy spot in the air. When I saw that spot, I knew it musta been where Dad came through. So, I jumped in to go get him!"

"And then what?"

"When I saw this place looked kinda like my world, I just walked over to the station and found you," Derek said with a shrug and an air of nonchalance, as if the answer was obvious.

Sergio pointed to the alley they needed, but Ez needed no prodding. The man must have already known about Iggy's demise, which meant the police had canvassed the crime scene. Wade was glad Derek would not have to see his first dead body that way—spread out on a concrete floor with bullet holes in its head—but he wished for Sergio that they might have avoided this moment for his double's sake.

It was an accident! Surely, Ez won't go hard on him.

From the stern expression on his would-be partner, Ez not only didn't buy the story about the multi-world theory, but he had every intention of arresting his double—and likely him—after this was over.

Together, they entered the warehouse. Wade looked for the shiny spot that Derek spoke of but saw nothing. Derek's freckled nose crinkled as his eyes panned from wall to wall. He ran to the center of the building, his head oscillating, his body displaying an urgency that made Wade's heart beat faster. He instinctively grasped the cause of his son's distress, and his heart sank as his worst fears were confirmed.

"Dad!" Derek cried, his panicked voice cracking. "It's gone! The shiny spot—it's gone!"

Chapter Sixteen

Wade refused to give up hope. "Are you sure it's gone, Derek? Try looking around. Try other angles."

Derek paced the warehouse in parallel with his father, his face screwed up in concentration behind his wire-rimmed glasses. "I'm still not seeing it, Dad."

"Do you think the light had anything to do with it? Maybe if we played with the light some more. Or tried shining our phones at the spot in the same direction the sun shone on it?" He pulled his phone from his pocket and used it for one of the few things it was currently suitable for — a flashlight. He studied the direction of the sunbeams coming through the warehouse windows and swung his arm around, trying to position the beam to best mimic the recent rays. A few steps away, Sergio and Ez watched the two of them move over the concrete floor, Sergio not wanting to interfere, and Ez, gaging from his skeptical stare, trying to determine how much was real and how much was fake.

"Dad, I'm telling you, it's not there." Derek stopped his circling of the scratched floor. His shoulders stooped, and his arms fell to his sides dejectedly. "I'm sorry, Dad."

Tears shone in Derek's eyes, and Wade stepped to his son and lifted the frail boy into a hug. Zeke had once said Derek had bird bones because he was so light. The memory of his partner, made heavier while under the inspection of this universe's double, brought tears to his eyes as well.

"It's OK, son. We'll figure something out. We'll be alright."

The words sounded hollow to him, but he hoped that his six-year-old son bought into the lie. The portal was gone. His only hope for returning to whatever dimension he and Derek called home had apparently vanished like a mirage.

I have to get us back there to his mother, to my wife. To our lives. I have to find a way.

"It's gone?" Ez's voice, tinged with suspicion, echoed in the empty building. Wade bristled. His son was a child. Did he really think Derek would lie about something like this?

His would-be partner was still not convinced, and no doubt had questions. Wade needed friends now. Most of all, he needed his partner—the version of Ezekiel Weidenseld who believed him and would move hell and earth to help a person in need of saving. That was what made this man such a fantastic police officer. If that were to happen, Ez required convincing.

He met Ez with a stern set to his jaw and set Derek down on the concrete. "Your name is Ezekiel Benjamin Weidenseld. You were born on October nineteenth, 1992, at Huntsville Hospital to Rachel and Esau Weidenseld. If things hold true in this world the way they are in mine, you got engaged in college to a young woman named Hope, but you broke it off because she was a Gentile, and your Jewish faith is extremely important to you. How'm I doing?"

Ez's jaw, which had fallen from his upper lip as far as it could, was all the answer he needed, but he pressed on.

"You struggled in college—Athens State University, bachelor's in criminal justice—but aced the police academy like you were made for it. You're a dead shot with a handgun but hate rifles. Oh, and your parents used to have a dog they called Chance. A little Springer Spaniel. And your mother is allergic to cats."

"How—How did you—?"

"I'm telling you, Zeke—Ez, sorry. I know you. Or my world's version of you. Hell, Zeke helped me name my son."

"He did?" Derek perked up, pleased to hear he had a role in the story.

"He did," Wade confirmed. "I almost went with Elliott, but Zeke said it reminded him too much of—"

"Elliot Stabler from Law & Order SVU. Holy shit, my dude. I

love that show."

"I know."

"I would have guessed E.T.," Sergio joked. Ez was too gob-smacked to laugh, but his "I'll be damned" expression was all too familiar. Wade's heart was in his throat as he waited to hear if Ez was finally convinced that Wade had slipped through an inexplicable wormhole.

"This is for real," Ez breathed, his hand pressed to his forehead.

Sergio scoffed. "I'm glad you came around quick. You wouldn't believe how much convincing this motherfucker took. He had to see that his whole entire house wasn't there anymore."

"OK, um…" Ez kicked at the floor with his running shoe. "This parallel-dimensional thing sounds like something maybe has to do with quantum wormholes, don't you think?"

Wade and Sergio both shrugged.

"Maybe," Sergio admitted. "I never took those classes. My knowledge of parallel worlds comes from books and movies. Fiction books, though. Not like college."

"I have a thought," Ez said, his face brightening, his eyes darting around the way Zeke's did when he was on a roll processing a case. "Let's go talk to my father. He deals with quantum physics all the time and loves diving into theories like wormholes in time and space. Maybe he'll have an idea how to get you back home."

挅 樃

Minnie leaped to Clark's side once her friend had reoriented himself into his ghostly body. Leah raced to join them, curious and attentive. She laid a hand on Clark's arm to assure him he was alright.

"Clark? Do you think August would let me…?" Minnie waved a vague hand in August's direction, "do what you did?"

Clark monitored August but did not meet her gaze or turn to face her. "He must be struggling with the idea that he has been bodily invaded by two beings already," he stated. "Adding another so soon is asking too much. Wouldn't you agree?"

"I'm with Clark. The guy's been through a lot," said Leah.

"I disagree," Minnie said, her voice taking on a very un-Minnie-like stubbornness. "It is terribly important that they *learn about this house*! And as soon as possible!"

"I don't think now is a good time."

"Well, when, then?" Minnie demanded, stomping her foot and sending up a puff of dust. "After they come back and another Passerby takes hold of him? Maybe one stronger than you can rid him of? When they fetch a crew to rebuild this place and discover what happens when they touch things they oughtn't move? When they bring in their furniture and put it in a corner that plays tricks on their minds? When they *start a family*? If we don't tell them now, they'll skedaddle out of here none the wiser, without a lick of knowledge about what they're up against every time they cross the threshold of this house!'"

"Minnie, I didn't mean that. Of course we're going to tell them. I don't believe now is a good time, though."

Leah nodded in support of Clark's opinion, and Minnie's whole spirit burned with frustration. Clark's cavalier attitude and condescending tone infuriated her. She knew her friend did not mean to brush her off, but he was putting these people *in danger*, for Saint Peter's sake! It didn't help that Clark's delivery and body language at the moment reminded her so much of Frank. Frank, who insisted that all the extra touches were simply ornamental. Frank, whose love of the supernatural and unhealthy interest in the occult should have tipped her off to his motivation when he suggested they design and build their own house.

Frank, who had inadvertently trapped his wife and two strangers in their home, and had turned their unique architectural masterpiece into a highway for lost souls traveling between worlds.

Yes, she knew what the Passersby were. She may not have been the genius Frank once was, but Minnie always had good horse sense. It was time for the rest of the world to know what she did about the entities traveling through her home.

Pivoting on her heel, she marched away from Clark and approached the wall nearest August and LaDonna. Willing her hand to become more substantial, she reached out and tapped her knuckles on the wall. All four living beings turned to the sound.

"Did you know she could do that?" Leah said.

Clark's head moved back and forth, his lips pursed. "No, I did not."

Minnie had been dead for over a century before Clark joined her in the Victorian. Long enough to learn a few things. Not to mention, she was mistress of the house. Minnie rapped again.

"I know you're hearing that," Ida said, noting how they were all riveted to the spot from which the sound had emerged. Minnie's flesh-and-blood visitors nodded.

Minnie stepped back and knocked a third time.

"Does it sound farther away to you?" Ida asked. No one answered.

Minnie knocked more insistently.

"What do you think it wants?"

Minnie backed two paces and rapped yet again.

"It's definitely going away. Should we follow it?"

August shook his head. "What if it's one of those creepy Passerby things that jumped me as soon as I walked in the door, and it's trying to lure us where more of them are waiting to take you over, too? No way."

"Could be Clark," Ida countered.

"August, what does your spirit tell you?" LaDonna asked.

August sank. "I'm too exhausted right now to guess. Sorry."

Minnie rolled her eyes. How to tell them she intended them no harm? Then it came to her—the funny little ditty that Clark and Leah taught her.

Knock, knockknock knock-knock.

Ida let out a bark of laughter. "Did it just do 'Shave and a Haircut?'"

In answer, Minnie added two more knocks. Her guests let out a few cautious laughs, but no one moved in her direction.

Minnie did it again. *Knock, knockknock knock-knock.*

Ida reached to the wall and added two taps of her own to finish the tune.

Delighted, Minnie took a few steps backward and once more played the familiar percussive ditty.

Knock, knockknock knock-knock.

August picked it up this time, his gaze fixated on the spot where the sound originated. *Knock knock.*

"Think we should follow it?" August asked.

LaDonna gave them a what-the-hell shrug. "Maybe I'm being naïve, but I have a hard time believing a nefarious ghost would lure us in with 'Shave and a Haircut.' Let's see where it goes."

Dancing a few paces away, Minnie kept up the familiar rhythm until her earthly visitors followed her to the nearby library. Ida sneezed a few times in the dusty air, and Minnie wished she had a tangible handkerchief to offer her. The entire house needed airing out horribly.

Once everyone stood waiting for her next move, Minnie pushed every ounce of her will into turning her incorporeal being into a physical presence, if for only a moment, to pull on Frank's binder until the spine protruded from the shelf with a quiet rasp of old leather and paper. The binder felt dry under her fingertips.

The faint whisper of the portfolio brushing against the shelf sounded unnaturally loud, instantly capturing the attention of the others, and they turned, almost in unison, towards her. Minnie was overcome with the eerie feeling that the mortals, standing like wide-eyed statues across the room, somehow perceived her presence, though she knew, deep down, this was impossible.

Summoning the energy to exert her will upon the physical realm was exhausting. She gathered her skirts and slipped onto the floor to observe what came next, her form now incapable of stirring even the slightest dust mote. Eyes fixed, she waited, watching intently to see how the unfolding scene would play out.

From the doorway, Clark and Leah observed, curious as cats.

Luke pulled the binder from the shelf, taking care not to spill any loose pages on the floor. He made an impressed sound. "This thing is old. I wonder what's so important about it that Clark needed us to see it?"

Minnie threw up her hands in frustration — if only they knew Clark wasn't responsible for every supernatural happening within the home's walls — but watched intently as LaDonna peered over one of Luke's shoulders, August and Ida the other, and Luke leafed through the pages.

Chapter Seventeen

Sergio, Wade, Ez, and Derek piled back into the Leland County SUV, and Ez nosed the vehicle onto the road. As Ez made a phone call to see where they'd be able to meet up with his father, Wade stared out the window, appearing to search for any sign that this version of the town of Gryphon appeared any different from the one he knew. Sergio felt terrible for the guy. Here Wade was, stuck in a world he didn't ask to get pulled into, and now his kid was stuck here, too.

I hope whatever brought him here wasn't my fault.

Leaning one elbow on the center console of the squad car, the other hand on the wheel, Ez explained to Sergio about his father's work.

"Listen," Ez began, his tone serious yet tinged with a hint of uncertainty. "I might not get all the science stuff, but my dad, he's deep into quantum physics. He works mostly at the university, but sometimes heads out into the field for his research."

Sergio faced Ez, unable to hide his hope. "Quantum physics? What does he do?"

Ez scratched the back of his neck, searching for the right words. "From what I've picked up at the dinner table, quantum physics isn't just about what's happening in our world. It's about possibilities, parallel universes, and all that... stuff beyond our normal understanding. Like what you two told me about how Wade slipped over here the second you shot Iggy Izzy. My dad loves talking about the theoretical side of things, how one tiny change here could mean a different reality somewhere else."

Sergio narrowed his eyes. "Are you saying your dad might

know how to get Wade and his kid back to his universe?"

"Derek," Derek piped up. "My name's Derek. Remember?"

"Sorry, Derek," Sergio said with an apologetic glance to the kid. The shaggy-headed boy gave him a forgiving smile and sunk back into his seat.

"It's OK."

"I'm saying it's worth a shot," Ez added confidently. "Dad's always going on about the interconnectedness of everything, how particles can be entangled across distances, and…. Maybe he's run across something in his work that can help us with Wade and Derek. I mean, if anyone's got a shot at figuring out a way to bridge universes, it's someone who spends their days knee-deep in quantum theories and their nights reading and watching documentaries about it."

Sergio considered this, the gears visibly turning in his head. "Your dad works in quantum physics. What are the odds? Man, this is the weirdest week of my life."

"You?" Wade joked. "Try being sucked through a wormhole — or whatever — into a parallel universe you didn't even believe in until you landed there."

Ez let out a half-hearted chuckle, the gravity not lost on him. "Welcome to the world of theoretical physics. My dad is a professor and all, but I don't stand a chance of ever understanding it. Let's hope my old man can give us more than theoretical answers."

A black asphalt driveway led to a handsome two-story red brick home with a green 1973 Dodge Charger Rallye in the driveway. An older man was heading out of the door, a cell phone pressed between his shoulder and his ear, and a manila folder clenched between his teeth. Esau noticed them pulling into the drive and thumbed a button on his phone to hang it up. The older man finished locking the door, gave them a friendly wave, and met them in the driveway, his protuberant belly jiggling as he hurried. Ez lowered his window with a gentle press of the electronic button.

"If I'd have known this was a party, I'd have baked a cake," the elder Weidenseld joked, approaching the window of the patrol vehicle as it slid into the doorframe. "I didn't know this was a party, Ezekiel. Is something wrong?"

Ez scanned the passengers of his car and wetted his lips. "A little. Well, yeah. Um…"

"I've got something of a timely nature I need to attend to," Esau said. "Can it wait?"

Sergio noticed the knuckles of Ez's hand turning a touch white as he clenched it with his right hand.

"Not really," Ez said.

Esau cast a brief look at the folder in his hand, then took in the strained expression on Ez's face. "I… I don't suppose we could all take the squad car to—"

Not wanting to give the man a chance to change his mind, Sergio opened the door and hastened out of the passenger side, motioning to Ez's father to take the shotgun seat. "You can sit here. I'll sit in the back with Wade. And Derek." He shot Derek a wink, which Derek returned with an exaggerated blink of both eyes.

"Oh, um… alright." The elder Weidenseld said. He strode to the opposite side of the Explorer and hoisted his short body into the SUV.

"Dad, this is Sergio, Wade, and Derek. Guys, this is my dad, Esau Weidenseld."

"Family, huh?" Esau said as he took in the similarities between the passengers in the rear seat. "Well, family's important." He patted his son on the shoulder as Ez backed out of the drive. "I wish I could have you in for a cup of coffee or a beer, but my friend Rebecca has just uncovered a marvelous discovery that just won't wait."

"What's the marvelous discovery?" Derek inquired as Wade struggled to buckle his son into the slim center seat between him and Sergio.

With sparkling eyes, Esau waggled his bushy white eyebrows and said, "She thinks she's found a ghost."

❣

Minnie, still anchored to the floor by fatigue, regarded every move Luke made with an intensity born of curiosity and something akin to envy. With careful reverence, he turned each page, his fingers delicately navigating the time-worn sheets. He seemed acutely aware of their fragility, his muscular hands taking every precaution to prevent the aged documents from falling apart. In this quiet moment, with dust motes dancing in the slanting light, Minnie appreciated the man's simple, respectful act.

"This is wild," he said. "It looks like this guy," he flipped to the front of the portfolio, and the letters embossed on the leather, "Frank Wenke was an architect. The architect of this house, at least. You saw the illustration of the outside, and the layout here looks like this first floor. There are a lot of hand-drawn pictures of carvings in here—things he created for stair rails and fireplaces and so forth. Do any of them look familiar to you?"

August reached across Luke and pointed to some of the sketches. "I've seen that in the wood carvings surrounding the fireplace in the room over there." He indicated the direction with a tilt of his head. "What do the notes say?"

Luke skimmed the text with a thick finger. "The symbols are tied in with Saturn. Let's go look and see if they match."

The four of them relocated to the parlor, where they compared the sketches to those of the mantel and surrounding area. Minnie mustered the energy to trail behind them to listen in, and Clark and Leah took the rear of their odd procession.

"A king with a beard riding a dragon," Luke said.

"Right here," August said, indicating a crowned man with a flowing beard on the back of a wide-winged European-style dragon carved into the mantel. "I remember because it was so unusual."

"An old woman leaning on a staff."

"Here," Ida said, caressing the hooded, bent old woman in her long shawl.

Luke moved his hand down the line. "An owl."

"Yep, next to the old woman. Near her shoulder here."

"And a juniper tree."

"Here," LaDonna said, touching the pointed "leaves" of the wooden tree.

"It looks like he has lists for other planets, too."

"Let's see if the other fireplaces are planet-based, too!" Ida exclaimed, thrilled to uncover the secrets of the abandoned old house on their property.

The group proceeded to the dining room, where they investigated the carved forms of the mantel and surround.

"This one has another king," August said, "But he's riding on a—what do you call them? The deer with antlers?"

"A stag," LaDonna offered.

"And a lady with a flower crown," Ida added.

"And a bull."

"This one must be Jupiter," Luke said, consulting the pages before him.

"Oh, look, a peacock!" Ida pointed out. "And a little topiary tree!"

"That must be what it means by box-tree," Luke said.

"I wonder what the others are?" Ida asked.

"Shall we look?" LaDonna offered. Together, everyone, living and dead, journeyed upstairs to the first room they reached, a bedroom with high ceilings and fading wallpaper.

"Another king," August observed. "On a wolf this time."

"And a woman with a shield," Ida said. "And a goat. A horse." She pointed to each as she went.

"Sounds like this one's Mars, then," said Luke.

Ida hopped to Luke's side to peer over his shoulder again, her eyes sparkling. Luke gently turned a page to reveal an illustration of four five-pointed stars set around a ring with four more six-pointed stars in the center. Regardless of its points, each star was meticulously inscribed with curious, wiggly letters that seemed to dance across their surfaces. The ring itself was a double circle, one nestled within the other, adorned with the same unusual script. In the center of the ring was a box with a cross extending outward from each of the four lines that made up its perimeter.

"I've seen this!" Ida exclaimed. "It's upstairs in that circular room. Remember, Augie?"

August nodded, but Ida was already darting up the third-floor stairs to the sweltering tower room. In the clear light of day, the room took on a markedly less ominous quality, but Minnie hated the room regardless of the time of day. The space echoed with an eerie, lingering presence despite Frank's passing.

It didn't help that this was where she had died. And Clark. And Leah.

After consulting Frank's work again, Luke said, "That's the Magic Circle, or the Lesser Key of Solomon, according to this. It's used… it's used to protect the space of a magician during rituals, to keep them safe from harm by spirits that are summoned."

Ida's jaw fell, the smile fading from her lips. "Spirits… summoned?"

Luke moved to the double doors, frozen in place by rust and disuse. His focus flicked from another handwritten page to the forms engraved on the wooden doors. He murmured words almost more to himself than to the room.

"Seraphis… to preserve against evils brought about by earth. Canopus, to protect from water. A hawk to guard against evil coming by air… and an asp to protect against evil arriving by fire."

Putting the pieces together, LaDonna covered her mouth with a shaky hand. Her impossibly large forest-green eyes bulged. "Luke…"

"Yeah," he said gruffly. "I know."

"Know what?" August asked. "What is it? Is it, you know, witchy, like you all?"

Luke shook his head somberly. "I'm afraid not, August. Whoever built this house imbued it with occult magic."

"Occult?" August asked, his eyebrows shooting up, "What is that, exactly? It must be different from the magic y'all practice based on how y'all are acting."

"People who study occult practices tend to be curious folks," Luke said. "They are the sort of people who seek secrets to the world using supernatural means. Like witches, they believe the world holds supernatural power, but they often want to… influence the world in ways to benefit themselves."

"Isn't that what witchcraft does?"

"Rarely at the expense of others," LaDonna interjected. "The Craft is about influencing the world and the forces behind its power, yes. Occultism is about finding secrets, sometimes dark ones, and ways to make those secrets work for you. Sometimes, that means using not just the power within the world itself, but using spirits to assist you. And not all the spirits are good ones."

"Hence the need for all the protection," Luke said, pointing at the stars in the ceiling above them and then the doors. "Based on what this room tells me, Frank was working with entities he knew put him at risk and was doing what he felt he could to protect himself from them."

Ida's joy gone, she now stood with her arms wrapped around her protectively. "Is it—still here? The spirit, or whatever, that he conjured? Is that what grabbed a hold of August?"

Luke rifled through the pages in Frank's portfolio. "I have no way of knowing, but Clark didn't say anything about a lingering spirit." He turned to LaDonna. "Your friend would have warned us, don't you think?"

"Surely," LaDonna agreed. "That is far too important for him to leave out."

"What was Frank's deal, then?" August asked. "Can you tell from what's in there?"

Luke skimmed page after page, digesting the overall contents of the paragraphs before him. "Frank's intention with this house was to build a place that was not only a place to live, but a place where he could," he paused, "'make a connection between the world as a physical composition and the building I dwell within,' and to 'imbue the facets of universal power within the facets and ornaments of architecture, making them both biophilic and functional.'"

"What the fuck does that mean?" August asked.

"He believed he could imbue his house with universal energy," LaDonna translated.

Luke nodded and continued skimming. "Old Frank thought he could use mathematics, talismans, and magic to make his house a focal point for universal power and protect himself from some of the darker entities he planned to work with. And he planned to use whatever he could harness to work for his benefit."

"Math? Are you serious?"

Luke shrugged. "There are some rather magical things about math. The Pythagorean Theorem, the Golden Radio, patterns, and symmetry are all quite amazing, and they all go back to math." Luke pointed to the page before him. "Frank Wenke also seemed to think the magical symbolism he built into his house would have a 'generative force within the subconsciousness of the observer.'"

"He wanted his house to affect his visitors, too? Like, their minds?" Ida ventured.

"Sounds like it. From what I'm gathering here, Frank planned to turn this house into a home base for a new belief system."

"A cult," August said. "The guy who built this house wanted to start a cult."

"I wonder if he succeeded?" Ida asked.

Minnie, whom no one saw or heard, whispered, "He came close."

☙ ❧

Esau provided Ez with an address and then loosened his seatbelt to better turn in his seat to observe the three passengers behind him.

"There is a home on the edge of Gryphon called the Wenke House."

"Winky House?" Derek said with an incredulous wrinkle of his nose.

Esau chuckled. "No, no. *Wenke*. It's a last name."

"It would be like if one day our house was known as the Beringer house because the Beringer family — our family — lived there," Wade explained to his son. Derek nodded solemnly.

If we ever get back to the Beringer House, that is.

"Correct," Esau said. "Frank Wenke, a German immigrant, built the house with his wife, Hermina, in 1872. Mr. Wenke was an unusual man. Very brilliant, but also very eccentric. Historians of the town say he had an unnatural fear of death. Others, particularly those involved in constructing the Wenke House, say he was an avant-garde genius and deeply spiritual. I don't see why he couldn't be both, and I believe he was. He studied mathematics, astronomy, astrology, semiotics, and religions. And I think he added facets of all of these, and his spiritual practices, to the house."

"Semi-octopus?" Derek asked.

"Semiotics," Esau replied with amusement, "is the study of signs and symbols."

"Like stop signs?"

"Something like that, yes. Some signs are linguistic, using words. Some are cultural, like your dad wearing a wedding ring to symbolize his marriage."

"How did he use signs?" Derek wanted to know.

"He used the signs and all those other things I mentioned to weave all his studies together to make his own religion. And his home, I believe, was a large part of that. He hid talismans and magical symbolism around each room. Because of his home's uniqueness, many artisans involved in its construction discussed some of the unusual requests with others in their community — even though Mr. Wenke had urged them to secrecy."

"He made a religion?" Derek asked. He turned to his father. "Can people do that?"

"They can indeed," Esau assured him. "Although, in Mr. Wenke's case, it's probably more accurate to call it a… how can I say this? A secret society. And not a nice one."

The man started a cult, Wade thought, grateful that Esau used a more euphemistic expression.

"Why were they not nice?" Impressed that his son's curiosity outweighed his fear, Wade did nothing to dissuade Esau from continuing.

"Mr. Wenke was afraid of… of the afterlife, I guess you might say. One story I've read said the man wanted to live forever and thought he could build a house that allowed him to do that. This writer said that Mr. Wenke believed that if he could convince enough people that the house was capable of magical things, it would, in fact, become a reservoir of magical power."

"What does that mean?"

"It means that Mr. Wenke believed that the human mind was creating its own magic, and that if constructed correctly, his house could hold on to and use that magic when Wenke died."

Derek chewed thoughtfully on the corner of his lower lip. "Is it Mr. Wenke's ghost in the house?"

"Maybe, maybe. We don't know, do we? But my friend Rebecca believes she has found something there, and we will go see if she has."

愉   扤

No one said a word for several minutes, so immersed were they in the revelation about the Victorian home's dark history. August searched the faces around him for a hint of what they were contemplating, but no one met his gaze. Luke closed the portfolio with a quiet brush of paper against paper and rested the portfolio against his side.

"Well," LaDonna sighed, "I suppose our plan for training you on using the herb today may need to wait."

August scoffed. "No. No, it doesn't. This place is on my property, dammit, and if it's a beacon for spirits — especially dark ones — then I need to figure out how to deal with it. I don't even know if it's safe to tear this house down!"

"Your friend Clark lived here, right?" Ida said.

"Yes, he did," LaDonna said. "And he died here."

"Did he say anything to you about it being weird, then? Any strange experiences like what happened to August earlier?"

"If he did, I don't recall. And that seems like the type of story to stand out."

"How old was he when he… you know… killed himself?"

"Oh, around thirty, I guess."

"That's young. Was it really bad?"

LaDonna wet her lips. "He hung himself."

Ida let out a soft gasp. "Oh my God! That's so terrible! Do you… is that why you said some of the things you said downstairs about him being in pain?"

"Yes. Clark was a priest and fell in love with one of his parishioners. A young woman named Judith. She loved him, too, and they had a secret relationship. She became pregnant and…" LaDonna gave a slight shrug. "She ran off to a relative's house — an aunt, I think — to have the baby. Well, babies, as it turned out. The whole church wound up finding out. Judith confided in her mother, who then told everyone. Clark was mortified, and he… he hung himself. In this room, in fact."

"LaDonna was the one who found him," Luke added.

"Shiiit," Ida breathed. "Oh, LaDonna, I'm so sorry. That had to be awful. Let's head downstairs. It's too fucking hot up here, anyway."

What had started as an adventure now weighed on August heavily. LaDonna's friend had lost a loved one because of a clandestine love affair that resulted in pregnancy. He had almost lost Ida because her parents forced her to get that godforsaken abortion. Luke and LaDonna had said nothing thus far about having their own children. Was their childlessness a choice? Or did they have a tragic story as well? He'd never ask, but he wondered.

෬   ෭

Finally, some movement from inside the house. Harper, who had been taking time to focus on trees of varying distances to reduce the strain on her eyes, lifted the Winchester once more and positioned her elbow on the log, the butt at her shoulder, and the scope at her eye.

However, the muted forms faded, the bodies having moved to a rearward room. Harper lifted her gaze again, pausing and blinking to clear her vision before changing to her binoculars to continue her surveillance. A gentle breeze blew, and a chill swept over her sweaty body, though little skin was exposed. She flexed her scapula muscles to ease the tension gathered there. She alternated hands, flexing and curling her palms to keep them nimble.

She didn't have to wait long. As the vague shapes reappeared, her exhilaration surged.

Calm down. Breathe. Can't let a little excitement ruin a perfect opportunity if it presents itself.

Harper swapped the field glasses for her rifle and scope and assumed the familiar prone position behind the log, eye on the crosshairs, finger on the trigger. She leveled her breathing, holding on to the exhale for a long moment before taking another breath and willing her heart rate to slow back down.

Whatever was going on in there had the group moving around oddly. Harper caught a brief glimpse of August's purple shirt, and her finger twitched on the trigger, but then the older lady got in the way. The only way Harper could tell it was the woman was from the way her skirts shifted as she walked. Harper held her exhales until her lungs felt ready to burst in case the woman moved again and her shot cleared. No luck. The motion inside had the restlessness of a kicked anthill. A mosquito landed on the back of her hand, and she had to ignore the little bugger pulling her blood out with its annoying little proboscis so that it might create more annoying little buggers.

Bug spray must be wearing off. Fuck.

Was that an arm? It looked as though there was quite a fuss going on. Lots of movement. Harper caught a fleeting glance of the young woman's blond curls and then the burly man's dark shirt—or maybe it was his hair. They were about the same color. *Come on, give me a shot. Give me a shot. Just one little second is all I need, and I can get out of this hellhole and onto a beach far away from here. Just one glimpse of that sandy head or purple shirt of yours, and this will all be over.*

Chapter Eighteen

The temperature was several degrees cooler on the first floor, but far from comfortable. Luke tried a few windows to see if he could open one and managed to open two with a grunt and considerable effort. Given the amount of foliage blocking the view, there wasn't much improvement other than slightly freshening the stale air.

LaDonna led the way to the sitting room across from the library and motioned for August to sit on the couch. She and Luke moved a heavy wingback chair closer to August, and Ida sat at August's side. LaDonna extended a palm in August's direction, and he tugged the plastic bag of the magical herb from his pocket. LaDonna accepted the bag, extracted a small glass pipe from her purse, and packed the bowl with the herb.

"You smoke it?" he asked, surprised but not sure why.

"It's the quickest way for the effects to kick in and has the shortest-lived effects in the event things don't go well," LaDonna explained. Bowl packed, she extracted a lighter from the side pocket of her purse. "Do you know how to use it?" she asked.

August laughed, but the sound came out in a short snort. "It's been a while, but I think I do," he said. "I'm not much of a smoker."

LaDonna shrugged. "Us either, believe it or not. I keep the herb handy, though. You never know."

He reached for the tools, but LaDonna withheld them, ensuring she had his full attention before continuing.

"This could take effect instantly, or it might take a few minutes. Regardless, I want you to be prepared for what will happen. You might get light-headed, or your perception may become distorted. Sounds might change, and you might see things that weren't there before. Those things might be real, and they might not. Some people go into a trance. It's different for everyone who takes it."

"Distorted perception?"

"Your sense of spatial awareness might change."

"Ah."

"Listen, August, I'm here to help walk you through this experience. You'll need to talk me through what you're experiencing unless you are one of those who falls into a trance, in which case I hope you can recall what you see so I can help you sort out your visions."

The weight of what he was about to do hit him hard. This wasn't just a fun "trip" or knocking back a few shots of moonshine and waiting for the buzz to kick in. He was about to mess with his mind using an unfamiliar drug. Was it curiosity about the house pushing him to do this, or fear of what might happen if he didn't?

With a clench of his fists, he braced himself. "OK. I'm ready."

Satisfied that August grasped the seriousness of what he was about to do, LaDonna passed the pipe and lighter to August. The leaves in the bowl looked harmless enough, so plain that he struggled to believe they could really mess with his head the way she claimed. What made this any different from smoking a little weed? But deep down, he knew she was telling the truth. Maybe that was part of the intuition they said he had.

His first go at lighting the herb fizzled out, just a quick flicker of orange before it vanished. Frustrated but determined, August thought back to his limited experiences with weed. On his second try, he held the lighter steady, letting the flame linger over the plant until it finally caught. He drew a deep, smoky breath, feeling it settle in his lungs. He heaved a raspy cough that made his stomach tumble.

"Give him some space," LaDonna said to Ida. "I don't know if there is such a thing as a contact high with this."

Ida moved to the side, and within moments, August grew acutely aware of the soft weave in the couch's fabric brushing against the denim of her shorts. His body felt heavy, and yet his head grew detached from his body and floated away from his neck, held only by a lightweight string.

"Whoa," he said. The word plumed from his mouth, and he smiled. *I'm a dragon.*

"August, are you with us?" LaDonna's voice echoed, vibrating in his ears, tickling them. He chuckled and rubbed them to stop the tickle, careful not to spill the pipe. How had his arms gotten so long?

"Yeah. Yeah, I'm here."

"Do you see anything unusual?"

The question struck him as ridiculous. *Everything* was unusual. The feel of the couch fabric under his fingers. The way the four of them sounded when they were breathing. The smell of the dust and wallpaper, plaster, and old wood.

He tilted his head, glancing over the back of the couch toward the archway leading into the sitting room. What he saw stopped him cold. In the shadowy hallway were figures made of smoke and swirling, capering shadows. Gossamer figures as transient as thought. Some glided gracefully, their ghostly shapes more solid and vivid than anything he'd ever thought a spirit could be. Others clawed desperately, their hands curling around a shimmering surface like they were pulling themselves across a world not meant for them, a place that flickered in and out of existence.

"Yyeaaahhh… Everything's a little unusual right now," he drawled. Why did his words have a texture? He moved his mouth to see if any of the texture lingered there, but it was gone.

He stood and walked toward the specters, the feel of his footsteps vibrating up his legs and the sound of his steps grating on his nerves like steel wool against his skin. LaDonna and Ida stood to follow him, adding more scraping footfalls on the wooden floor, and he shuddered.

"Heeey," he said to the smoky ghosts. "Heeey, where ya goin'?"

"Do you see something, August?"

"He-yeah. There are smoky ghosts. And they're moooving." He swooped his hands toward the moving spirits. "*That* way."

"How many are there?"

"Um… two. Oh, three now. One's coming through the waalll." His mouth liked how the words tasted, but his lips and tongue did not want to cooperate as he talked, which was weird. He knew how to speak, didn't he?

Now, when he tilted his head just so, there was a mirage on the wall. He was supposed to tell LaDonna everything, so he blew out a puff of what he would have sworn was purple air and forced his mouth to form sounds. "SSzzhhiiny spot."

"Shiny spot?" Ida asked. "Where?"

"There." August pointed. He didn't have to tilt his head anymore. It was a big shiny spot, probably a head taller than he was and a foot wider. The silvery reflective surface reminded him of the mercury in the glass thermometer his mother had broken when he was a child. She had insisted he not touch it, but he was dying to know then what the rounded beads of quicksilver felt like to the touch.

This isn't mercury, though. Is it?

No, if it was mercury, they'd all see it. He could because he was in whatever state he was in now. And mercury didn't stick to walls. Of that, he was sure. As sure as he could be right now, anyway.

One of the ghosts slipped through the shiny spot and vanished.

Huh. That's weird. Wonder where it went?

Only one way to find out. August stepped to the wall and followed it.

☃ ☄

Esau adjusted his glasses, his eyes reflecting a blend of mischief and curiosity as he turned to Marina, who was intrigued by the purpose behind Esau's roadside meeting with Rebecca. Zeke stood behind her, having seen much of his father's excursions in the field before and wanting to allow Marina to engage his father and Rebecca with questions, should she have any. The sunlight beat on them without mercy, but Rebecca seemed too engrossed with measurements on a second device pulled from the pocket of her hiking shorts to mind.

"Marina," Esau began, his voice that of a professor at the start of a lecture, "my work in physics, particularly in theoretical physics, often skirts the edges of what many consider the realm of what is observable and understandable. It's not just about equations and experiments; it's about exploring possibilities, the 'what-ifs' of the universe."

Marina nodded, her arms crossed as she listened, grateful for the cool breeze playing with strands of her hair.

Rebecca, pacing nearby with her instrument in hand, seemed to be in her own world, but Esau's explanation drew her back in. She interjected, "That's why I think Esau can help. His open-mindedness in physics is the sort of technique I may need here. This," she waved the device, "is a turbo-charged Gaussmeter. It indicates electromagnetic activity, which could be natural... or not."

Esau chuckled softly, recognizing Rebecca's enthusiasm. "Indeed. While I don't chase ghosts in my day job, the principles of physics apply universally. Anomalies in electromagnetic fields, for instance, can be fascinating. Conventional means might explain them, or they might hint at something more, let's say, 'unconventional.'"

Marina looked between Esau and Rebecca. "Do you mean that your theoretical physics experience might give us a scientific basis for exploring... ghosts?"

"In a manner of speaking, yes," Esau replied, his shoulders rising and falling in a shrug. "Though I prefer to think of it as exploring unexplained phenomena. The universe is full of mysteries, and science has been our way of making sense of it for centuries. If there's a scientific explanation for what Rebecca is detecting, I'm all for exploring it. And if it's something beyond our current understanding... well, that's what makes science so exciting. Moreover, the anomalies we're investigating might be the key to understanding how to navigate between dimensions, potentially offering a solution to bring your husband, Wade, back from the dimension he's trapped in."

Rebecca's head perked up at Esau's comment, but she did not inquire. Marina wondered at the woman's lack of curiosity. She would have never let a topic that curious go without question.

Zeke, who had been quietly observing, finally spoke up, a smile playing at the corners of his mouth. "So, we're ghost hunters now, Dad?"

Esau laughed, a genial, rich sound that warmed Marina's heart and left no doubt about the source of Zeke's good humor. "Not exactly, son. But let's say we're on an adventure to explore the unknown, guided by curiosity and a healthy dose of skepticism. After all, science isn't just about answers; it's about asking the right questions."

Rebecca smiled, visibly pleased with Esau's statement. "Exactly. And with Esau's insight and his natural skepticism, we can approach this investigation with a healthy balance of science and acceptance of the possibility of the paranormal."

Marina, now with a newfound glimmer of hope, stepped closer to Rebecca and her tools. "Well, let's see what mysteries this house holds. It'd be wonderful if this helps us find a way to bring Wade back."

As the group moved down the driveway towards the house, the conversation shifted from speculative physics to the immediate task. Rebecca was filled in on the strange occurrences of the past forty-eight hours, and Esau added more questions to those he'd asked earlier. Rebecca's acceptance of Wade's disappearance into a "shiny spot" astounded Marina.

Rebecca, her attention primarily focused on her Gaussmeter but still not tripping over a single tree root or rock, turned to Esau and Marina with excitement and solemnity. "A vertical 'shiny spot' that acted as a quantum portal? Esau, this sounds like what you've suspected about spatial anomalies."

Esau nodded, his expression thoughtful. "If we're considering the quantum mechanics, we're talking about a potential breach in space-time; a particular condition or event created a bridge between different points, and Wade somehow slipped through."

"That's amazing," Rebecca said with giddy excitement, as if Esau had helped her find a treasure in plain sight.

Marina, her eyes wide with a blend of hope and uncertainty, looked from Rebecca to Esau, but she remained silent, not wanting to interrupt the flow of conversation. Who knew what might bring about a eureka moment?

"It's only a possibility," Esau replied gently with another one of his shrugs. "And the quantum portal would probably be incredibly unstable and transient. Most likely, it was a localized disruption in the fabric of reality. If Wade encountered one, it could explain his and Derek's disappearance, but we still need to find a way to recreate a similar portal, locate them, and for both of them to cross that bridge again."

Rebecca added, "With the electromagnetic anomalies I'm detecting, we may be looking at the residual effects of a second portal's opening. It's faint, unlike any typical ghostly activity I've tracked before. This could be a physical trace left behind by a portal. Maybe there's a... what do you call them, Esau?"

Brushing at a cloud of gnats, Esau said, "A quantum flux anomaly. If so, we'll need to search for as much data as possible with the limited tools we have on hand to study the portal's characteristics. And I highly doubt that one instance will provide us with enough information. That we might encounter another portal so soon after the last is incredibly unusual—if that is what Rebecca is picking up on. We'll do our best to learn what we can, though. Don't worry, Marina. We'll do what we can."

Marina took a deep breath, extremely appreciative of the kindhearted scientists willing to help her husband find his way home.

Chapter Nineteen

August's skin felt like it was being pulled tight, stretching from his forehead past his chin and across his whole body as he slipped through the shimmering silver passage. It felt like he was stretched out, long and thin, like taffy pulled too far. The moment he made it through, the mirror-like doorway snapped shut behind him, and everything around him shifted—blurring, growing bright and watery, all in shades of beige. His vision wavered as the new surroundings came into focus, sunlight bathing the space. The air was chillier, a relief from the sticky humidity he'd left behind. But with the lower temperature, the sweat on his skin turned cold, leaving him clammy and unsettled in this weird, sunlit world.

What in the—? Is this part of the trip? LaDonna said I might see some weird shit. Hell, I could be back at the house hallucinating, for all I know.

He blinked, and the watery tears in his eyes broke free and slipped down his cheeks, clearing his vision somewhat. His skin no longer felt stretched to the point of peeling from his body; now gooseflesh broke out where the sweat had cooled.

Maybe it's a ghost thing? A magic thing? Both?

As his vision cleared, August took in the surrounding room. It was the same size and shape as the dining room of the old Victorian house he'd just left, but everything looked and felt different. The air was perfectly climate-controlled, a far cry from the stuffy heat he'd gotten used to. The walls here were smooth and freshly painted, with no sign of the fading old wallpaper from before. The wainscoting was simple, clean white rectangles, none of that strange, fancy carving like in the Wenke house. Everything felt… normal. Almost unsettlingly so.

The high he'd gotten from the smoke was still there, but his body was more under his control now. Woozy, yes, and off-center, but his thoughts weren't jumping around, and his sense of touch wasn't so disturbing. Maybe he was getting used to the feeling.

A soft clicking came from the distance and slowly grew louder. August turned toward the sound just in time to see a skinny gray pit bull slip into the room, her claws ticking on the wooden floor. She stopped dead in her tracks when she spotted him, head tilting in that curious way dogs do. She didn't seem scared of him—if anything, she just looked tired. Her coat was dirty, her ribs sticking out like she hadn't seen a good meal in a long time. August figured it had been a while since anyone had looked after her.

"Hey, girl," August crooned softly. "Hey. How are you?"

Seeing that August was a fan of critters of the canine persuasion, the dog approached him cautiously with a tucked but wagging tail and allowed him to give her pets. Her worn collar jangled with tags, and he noted the pooch's name engraved on a golden bone around her neck. No phone number, though.

"Misty? Are you Misty?"

Misty's ears perked up at the sound of her name, her tongue lolling out in a display of canine happiness as she panted happily.

"Misty, are your parents home?"

Misty offered a headshake, but August interpreted it as an attempt to adjust the snug collar around her neck rather than an answer. He supposed it had been quite a while since she'd seen her human caregivers.

"Cool. I'm August. Wonder why you're here. Did you used to live here, huh? Was this your house? Maybe you moved to a new place, didn't like it, and thought you'd come back?" *Or maybe her last owners were assholes and left her here. Some folks are heartless. Poor pup.*

The sudden creak of a door yanked him from his daydream, reminding him of the fact that he was, in fact, trespassing in a house he did not belong in.

Shit. Time to bail. The others are probably worried about me.

He debated the idea of leading Misty back with him, but quickly dismissed it as the dog trotted off to investigate the arrivals. Besides, what if traveling with him did something weird to her? Maybe people have to be on that weird herb of LaDonna's to pass through the —

Wait, two doors? Were there always two?

Thinking back, he realized he hadn't paid attention; his entire focus had been on Misty. He'd never looked behind himself until now. There was not one shimmering door but two to choose from.

Which door do I go through?

Voices and soft steps approached quickly, and Misty cocked her head at the sound of the approaching people. His adrenaline spiked with every footfall.

"The readings are like nothing I've ever seen before. Esau, look!"

"That is remarkable. Would you like me to document your data so you can have your eyes and hands free to observe the meter?"

"That would be very helpful, thank you."

"Of course. It will be my pleasure to assist."

Who talks like that? They sound characters from Star Trek.

Cornered by the need for a believable excuse for his intrusion, August narrowed his options. It didn't look abandoned, so trying to explain his presence as exploring was too farfetched. Could he tell them he was a realtor? That might work, but what if they were realtors, too? They might expect to know the same people.

Think! Think!

As if cued by his desperation, the effects of LaDonna's herb intensified. The beige walls drew nearer, inching closer in a silent, suffocating advance. He flashed back to a scene from Star Wars and blinked as the sensation of dust motes in his eyes grew irritating. A sudden dampness on his right hand startled him, and he flinched, thinking crazily that it was blood, until he realized Misty was soothing him with gentle licks.

Does she see the walls closing in? Or is that just me?

Time warped, stretching moments into eternity, but the people he heard had not come into view yet. How long had he stood there?

Just pick a fucking door!

With a rush of determination, August made his choice, diving through the shining silver door on the right into the unknown.

ை ۞

What bright hell is this?

A crew of newcomers drew near, not bothering to hide their

approach as they trekked up the gravel driveway. Twin husky, dark-haired men, an elfish dark-haired boy, an older man with fading red hair, a fit adult man with bright red hair, and a brown-haired woman in a chambray shirt and shorts. The woman held a device that consumed her attention, though she occasionally traded words with the older man, drawing in the others as they trailed behind. The red-haired man, Harper noted, had a gun.

Harper couldn't make out most of their discussion, but she picked out the words energy, house, and spirit.

Are they here for a fucking séance? What in the hell is going on?

Harper knew how to blend into her surroundings; the odds of them spotting her dark clothing among the shadows and the foliage were low as long as she remained motionless. Still, she remained as motionless as possible, hoping they were using the driveway as a starting point for a nature walk. No such luck. They reached the front steps of the large house, pausing while the woman with the device waved it around, chattering excitedly.

The dark-haired man, who moved like he had military training, raised a hand, signaling the group to stop. They quit talking and watched him with wrinkled brows. He pointed to the leaves and debris scattered near the entrance and the cleared doorway, his expression sharp, his speech hushed. A quick exchange followed, and it was agreed that the good-looking redhead would enter the home first, with one of the dark-haired men following close behind. The man in the lead drew his weapon from a side holster.

The two men at the lead opened the door cautiously, sweeping the room with trained eyes. Once the all-clear was given, the rest of the group crept inside.

Not soldiers, then, I bet. Cops. Fuck. As if her day couldn't get any worse. She wasn't ready to pack it up and leave, but the odds of her getting the shot she needed had just nosedived. *Dammit. Dammit, dammit, dammit.*

Harper let out a slow breath, propping herself on her elbows to stretch her back. She settled back into position, brought the rifle's sight to her eye, and resumed her vigil. Her patience and confidence in the success of this mission had nearly evaporated, but for the money the Kightlingers were offering her, she was willing to take a few risks. Besides, today was supposed to be a scouting mission, anyway. Getting her mark early would have been nice, but she had time.

ଓ   ଞ

"Where. The fuck. Did he get to?" Ida's voice, sharp and incredulous, pierced the air. Her eyes threatened to bug from her skull as she ran to the peculiar section of the wall through which August had passed, as effortlessly as if stepping through a curtain of mist. She ran her trembling hands over the fat, winding flowers on the wallpaper, pressed frantically on the unyielding surface as if half expecting a hidden passageway. *Where did he go?*

"He must have found a supernatural door," LaDonna mused.

"A *what* now?" Ida's skepticism hung in the heavy air.

"The herb allowed August to see into realms our eyes can't see, and he followed a door only he saw into another realm." LaDonna's voice was like a calm stream, and while Ida appreciated the woman's equanimity, she also had a slight urge to wring her neck for remaining so composed.

"That's insane," Ida said, sounding less sure than she liked.

LaDonna shrugged. "Can you think of another explanation? We just watched August pass through a solid surface as easily as strolling through fog."

"But he'll return, won't he?" Ida's voice quivered, her gaze flitting between the two witches for reassurance.

"I'm sure he will," Luke said.

The sound of a door creaking open at the front of the house sliced through the tension. "August!" Ida's relief was palpable as she bolted from the sitting room.

But it wasn't August who greeted Ida. Instead, she was met by six strangers, each as taken aback by her sudden appearance as she was by theirs. Twin men stood beside an older man with fading red hair, a tall, muscular man who also had red hair, and a woman who looked like a scientist about to embark on a safari. A young boy who looked like a sprightly miniature of the husky twins rounded out the group.

"Who are you?" Ida barked.

The six of them exchanged quick glances and wordlessly determined the eldest would handle the introductions.

"I am Esau Weidenseld. This is my son Zeke, my associate

Rebecca, and our new friends Sergio, Wade, and Derek."

"Hi!" Derek piped up with a wave.

Ida, despite the gravity of the situation, smiled. "Pleasure, Derek. I'm Ida."

"Like the potatoes?"

She let out a snort, and some of the tension binding her chest loosened. "I've never heard that one before."

Rebecca nudged Esau, hinting. "It's saying this way."

Esau hesitated, then admitted with a mix of caution and intrigue, "We're, um... We're ghost hunting."

"You're in the right place," Ida said somewhat caustically. Five faces displayed surprise at her simple acceptance of their task. Rebecca, on the other hand, beamed. "Come on," Ida said with a beckoning arm. "Since you're going that way, I'll introduce you to Luke and LaDonna. And hopefully, my boyfriend, if he comes back from whatever world he's strolled off into."

"Come again?" Wade said, but Ida was already walking into the next room where her magical friends awaited her.

⚜ ❧

The moment August's feet touched the unfamiliar ground, he knew he had made the wrong choice. The Victorian house he expected to enter had dissolved into nothingness. It left behind a desolate tableau of scorched earth and skeletal trees, their branches like thin charcoal lines on a winter canvas. The drug LaDonna had given him still had a faint hold of him, making the bond he had felt with his environment horrific, like he'd joined a post-apocalyptic universe that mourned for the hot, colorful Alabama summer he'd left behind. It was winter here, a stark contrast to the sweltering heat of the South he had just fled. The temperature in this world was easily twenty degrees colder, but not air-conditioned cold. No, this was the end-of-the-universe variety of cold.

The sun barely pushed through the thick, gray clouds, nothing more than a pale silver disc hanging in the dull, slate-gray sky. It was muted, almost lost in the haze. He coughed, his lungs burning in protest against the foul air around him. Every breath he took felt like standing too close to a fire pit, the smoke biting at his throat and clawing its way into his chest.

A stark epiphany struck him: he had stumbled into the aftermath of a nuclear apocalypse. *It's a nuclear winter. I've come to a world ruined by nuclear war!*

August turned, and despite the lack of a wall to hang from, the portal he had passed through lingered, suspended in an atmosphere packed with solid particulates. He had half-expected it to have vanished like the house, given that the effects of the herb he had smoked were wearing off with frightening speed. The air around the portal shimmered with a haze of radioactive particles.

August flinched. Was he at risk for radiation poisoning? Dread tightened his gut, but so did a thread of determination. He weighed his choices; none of them were good. The thought of confronting whatever lay in wait back in the previous house suddenly seemed a lesser evil compared to what might wait for him in this dismal landscape. And he needed to get moving before the herb that made him able to see the portals left his system. But he also needed a plan.

Strangely, his mind first went to the neglected dog, Misty. She didn't belong in the house—that he knew. The notion that the newcomers stumbling through its doors might look after her was a gamble at best. From snippets of conversation he had overheard, they were also exploring the house for the first time. People living in a place don't discuss readings and data collection. That sounded like something a scientist or someone on one of those exploratory missions would say. Regardless, he wasn't going to leave the dog to the mercy of people who may or may not help it.

I'll jump in, grab the dog, and bounce back to my world. If the door is still there. If she can come with me. The world August stood in was becoming more focused as the drug faded, his vision less full of unusual patterns at its perimeters. He was running out of time.

He suppressed the instinct to draw a deep breath of the tainted air to steel his nerves. Without allowing himself another moment of hesitation, he lunged towards the shimmering portal.

Chapter Twenty

As Wade gently rested his hand on the back of his son's head, nudging him to follow Ida into the next room, Sergio couldn't shake a pang of regret about the course his life had taken. Here stood Wade, a man acquainted with this peculiar realm for only two days, and the man moved with more confidence than Sergio ever imagined having.

Maybe it's just bravado. It works for you, doesn't it?

Even as the words crossed his mind, Sergio knew it wasn't true. It had taken an extreme amount of convincing for Wade to accept the reality of his movement into another dimension. Still, now that he had wrapped his mind around that concept, Wade approached the situation with the instincts of the seasoned detective he was. He searched for answers, investigated theories, and moved with determination toward a solution to his problem.

The way Wade instantly fell into a rhythm with Ez was odd, too. Ez seemed unfazed by Wade's nonchalant acceptance of him as an otherworldly echo of his partner and best friend. Instead, he took it in stride as if they were kindergarten pals reuniting after a summer apart.

Rebecca, the woman with the peculiar meter, aimed her device at Ida's back as if Ida herself emitted the crucial readings she sought. "It's the highest I've ever seen, Esau," she gushed. "This is incredible."

Ida pivoted, patting the wall to her right. "This is where he disappeared," she explained.

"The wall?" Derek asked uncertainly. He turned to Wade. "That's weird. It's not shiny, Dad."

Ida nodded. "He walked right through the wall like it wasn't even there. Oh, hey. Luke, LaDonna, this is… um…"

A middle-aged couple stood behind Ida, concern etched on

their faces as she readily divulged the strange circumstances surrounding her boyfriend's disappearance.

"They're ghost hunters," Ida offered as an explanation.

"Sort of," Sergio added. He pointed at Rebecca. "They are. Well, she is. He's a scientist. And we're…" his voice trailed off as he pondered how to clarify what he, Wade, and Derek were to one another.

Amidst Rebecca's muted readings and Esau's diligent note-taking, Wade voiced their collective curiosity. "We're wondering where your boyfriend went off to," Wade said. "Especially me, because he may have found a way for Derek and me to return home."

Ↄ ⁊

The house Marina and her group approached was old but well-loved. Its weathered facade boasted three stories of pale yellow siding and stood crowned with a green tile roof that blended with the surrounding foliage. Green gingerbread curlicues decorated the eaves, along with fat Boston ferns, their leaves cascading from large hanging planters. A soft breeze stirred the air, causing the ferns to sway gently, as if stirred by ghostly hands.

To the left of the porch, a swing with faded cushions hung motionless, its wicker frame creaking softly in the silence. The interior lights were off, and no cars waited in the driveway. Despite the rocking ferns, the house felt eerie, deserted. Marina couldn't shake the feeling that there was more to this place than met the eye.

"Is it occupied?" Marina asked.

"It's about to go on the market," Rebecca said. "I have a friend working with the realtor, and finagled a key from her before the listing went live."

"They know you're here?"

Rebecca nodded, her gaze flickering towards the darkened windows of the house. "I'm curious but not a criminal. I got authorization for this venture."

Esau's red cheeks fattened as his lips curved up in a smile. "When will the listing be available?"

"Why do you ask?"

"We may need to come back with more equipment for further investigation if we discover something here today."

Rebecca cocked her head to the side in thought. "That's a good point. I'll find out when I speak to my friend about returning the key."

"Do the homeowners know you're doing this?" Marina asked, her eyes scanning the vicinity for any signs of activity.

"Yes," Rebecca said, her attention again on her meter. "They've believed for some time that the house channeled something unusual. My friend wouldn't go into details, though."

Rebecca and Esau returned to a hushed conversation about readings. Marina couldn't help but notice Zeke's stoic demeanor. He caught her eye, gave her a patient eyebrow raise, and his eyes crinkled with amusement. Clearly, he was used to his father's unusual voyages into scientific discovery.

As they stood mere feet from the steps leading up to the porch, Marina's gaze lingered on the Victorian-style screen door and its intricate scrollwork and well-worn, flaking white paint on the concrete steps. Did the secret to Derek and Wade's return lie waiting for them on the other side?

"Ready?" Esau's voice broke through her reverie, his hand resting lightly on her elbow.

"Very," Marina replied with a determined nod, steeling herself.

"Well, let's go," Rebecca said, her voice tinged with anticipation as she produced a set of jingling, old-fashioned-looking house keys. She swooped them into the hand not holding her meter, ascended the steps, and pulled back the screen door on creaking springs, tucking the meter under one arm as she did to free her hands to work the lock. The lock was stiff, and Marina wondered if this was from disuse, the humid air, or perhaps a combination of both.

With a few seconds of wriggling and twisting, the doorknob twisted in Rebecca's hand. She pushed it open, and the four caught a breath of somewhat stale but much colder air.

"They left the a/c on," Marina noted.

"Hmm," Rebecca responded, her attention already back onto her gauge as she slid the house keys into a pocket. Marina took a moment to peek over the other woman's shoulder at the readings, but the ever-changing numbers on the screen meant nothing to her.

Zeke held the screen door back for them to enter, the creaking hinges singing a welcome as they moved inside. Right away, the home took Marina's breath away. The decorative hand-carved wood in so many areas gave the home unique touches that reflected the soul of its creator. She yearned to pause and study them more closely, but an odd sound caught her attention.

An "Oh!" of surprise escaped Marina's lips when a gray pit bull trotted into the room. The shy girl approached them reluctantly, her tail between her legs, her head low, but eyes hopeful. She chose Zeke to approach first, and he held out a freckled arm, letting her sniff his hand before scratching the top of her head.

"I thought you said this place was going up for sale," Zeke observed, his voice echoing slightly in the empty, high-ceilinged space. He paused in his affection, and the pup nuzzled his hand. Zeke gave her chin a scratch. The tags on her collar jingled, and Zeke read them.

"It is," Rebecca replied, her voice carrying a note of uncertainty. "They must have a flap for a dog door on the rear entrance or something. That's not good. I'll make sure to tell my friend about her."

"From her license, she's not current on her shots. Her name is on the tag, but not a phone number. Do you think they left their dog, Misty, here, behind?"

"Either that, or maybe the dog found its way back to its old home. You know how homesick animals do that sometimes."

Zeke regarded Misty with a knit brow, and Marina had a feeling the pup would be joining her and Derek in Zeke's backseat on the way back to town.

A heavy pressure developed in her ears, and for a moment, Marina felt uncomfortable, as if the very air of the house was as thick as the deep sea. A moment later, the pit bull's ears perked up, and she trotted from the room, having picked up a cue with her canine senses the others did not.

"Is Misty leading us in the direction we wish to proceed?" Esau asked.

"She is," Rebecca confirmed.

The group followed the sound of clicking animal claws on wooden floors, Marina walking alongside Rebecca, while Zeke and Esau trailed close behind them.

Rebecca's eyes grew in amazement, and she turned and thrust the meter at Esau. "The readings are like nothing I've ever seen before.

Esau, look!"

"That is remarkable. Would you like me to document your data so you can have your eyes and hands free to observe the meter?"

"That would be very helpful, thank you."

"Of course. It will be my pleasure to assist."

They continued their conversation softly as they turned toward the back of the house. Marina caught a flash of movement near the end of the hall and expected to see Misty there—but no, Misty was near the stairs, an expression of doggy bliss on her sweet face. She stretched and moved to the other room, uninterested in the people who had invaded her space.

Did I see another animal? Marina turned and discreetly peered around, checking up the stairs while Rebecca and Esau were engaged in their scientific conversation, but no other animals waited there.

"Looking for something?" Zeke asked.

"I... I thought I saw movement. Another animal, maybe. But there's nothing there."

"Maybe it was the ghost they're looking for," he said, only half kidding.

A chill settled over her. The home, which had seemed so beautiful only moments before, now felt filled with ghostly conservators watching and listening, studying them in return as they studied it.

A murmur from the next room caught her attention, followed by the clicking of dog claws on wood as Misty meandered to the far room, panting contentedly.

"Did you hear that?"

"Probably the dog," Zeke offered.

"Dogs don't whisper," Marina countered.

She set off with a purpose to the room in the back of the house where Misty had wandered. Her company followed her, curious about what she might find. Marina doubted it would be the ghosts Rebecca hoped for, but that might be preferable to what they might find in what should be an empty home.

Pivoting into the dining room, she came face-to-face with a ruggedly handsome man in his twenties wearing jeans and a sleeveless shirt. His mouth hung agape and flapped a couple of times as if he were trying to talk, but the words were tangled in his mind. He shook his bangs from his eyes and eyed them all in turn, blinking his red, dilated eyes.

"Are you… the homeowner?" Rebecca asked.

The man said nothing to them, just reached down for Misty's collar, the muscles in his forearms flexing powerfully as he bent down and whispered inaudibly into the dog's ear. The canine heard him, though; her tail wagged happily, and every muscle looked ready to take off running.

Where does he think he's going to run to? They're facing the wall!

"Sir?" Rebecca asked, her voice more demanding.

Maybe it should have occurred to Marina, after the events of the past few hours, what the man planned to do, but it did not.

"Come on, girl," he said. His body tensed, and he appeared to be gathering his courage as he stared fixedly at the wall. Then he plunged through as if it was no more solid than a beaded curtain, taking the dog with him into nothingness.

Chapter Twenty-one

Thank God he only had to choose from one door this time. August burst into the freshly painted, wainscoted dining room he'd left moments before, praying he'd left any traces of nuclear winter behind. Misty trotted into the room with a smile, glad he'd returned.

We don't deserve dogs.

Conversation quickly approached. Whoever these explorers were, they were about to turn the corner and discover him in a house where he had no business.

"Come here, Misty," he whispered, motioning. Misty, tongue lolling, moved to his side without question, but it wasn't fast enough.

Four people turned the corner, each so different in appearance, clothing style, and carriage that August had no idea how they could be connected. Two of them had reddish hair, though. Father and son, maybe? Their builds were very different.

Everyone stood in place, flabbergasted. No one spoke. August blinked to shake the trance. The world was nearly in clear focus now, the shimmering oval on the wall fading to what he otherwise might have mistaken for a gray faded patch on the wall if he hadn't known its purpose.

"Are you… the homeowner?" the long-haired woman in cargo shorts asked. A tool in her hand displayed wildly rising and falling numbers.

August didn't reply. If this worked, he wouldn't need to. *Please let this work. Please let this work.*

He leaned to the dog and crooked a finger into the loop of her collar. If it took more effort than that to lure her along, he would have to leave her behind. "We're gonna go bye-bye," he crooned to her softly. "Want to go bye-bye?"

Her ears perked up, and he pulled on her collar, praying it was enough. She stood.

Four sets of eyes with confused expressions watched him.

"Sir?" the woman asked.

"Come on, girl," he bade Misty. And they darted together through the portal.

૭   ૪

Ida rushed into August's arms the moment he was fully formed in her world, but something was off. His embrace was sluggish, one arm hanging by his side as though something heavy was pulling it down. With his arm slung around her back, August advanced them a pace with a stumble and made a funny motion with his arm before hugging her loosely with both hands. His grip was weak, almost hesitant, when he finally brought both arms around her. An odd, wet sensation emerged on her leg, followed by an odd thumping sound on the wall behind August.

What in the – ?

Then she heard the panting, looked down, and saw the dog. A smallish pit bull, she believed, with gray fur and bright eyes. The poor thing looked half-starved, but her mouth was open in a smile as her tongue lolled from her mouth as if mocking the gravity of her passing into a new world with a stranger.

"You… have a dog."

"I do," August said, bending stiffly to pat the canine on the head. His fuzzy friend regarded him with reverence. "Ida, meet Misty. Misty, Ida."

"How do you disappear into a wall and come back with a *dog*?"

"Can we sit down? I'm exhausted, and I have a lot to tell you about. I went to a couple of places, and—" August cut himself off as his eyes landed on the newcomers. His eyes bugged, and he froze in place, his mouth agape. Clearly, he had not expected five additional faces watching him, one of them inching closer to the wall he'd just emerged from, holding some strange contraption that buzzed faintly, an eager expression on her face.

Ida offered a tentative smile, trying to keep the mood light.

"August, these are… help me out here. Wade?" One of the big men nodded. "Sergio?" The other did the same. Ida continued, pointing her finger at each person as she went. "Um… Ez. Esau. Re-bec-ca? And… Eric?"

"Derek," the boy corrected her, smiling. "And you're Ida potatoes!"

Ida's eyes lit up with amusement. "And I'm Ida Potatoes."

August's exhausted countenance regarded her urgently. "Can I—did they?—"

"See you walk through the wall from out of nowhere? Yes."

"And they're?—"

"Not freaked out? Not a bit. They've got a story, too, apparently. Rebecca is a ghost hunter, and we were all waiting to hear another story about Wade and Sergio when you came back."

In a few minutes, everyone settled down, finding seats on chairs, the window seat, or the floor. Ez leaned against the wall, his arms crossed, observing August intently. Misty sprawled contentedly with her head resting in August's lap, her eyes half-closed but alert. Wade and Sergio took turns narrating their tale. For all their different style of speaking, the two men finished each other's sentences and gesticulated like family would after years of living together. It was hard to believe they'd only met mere hours before. Sergio had a roughness that reminded her of August, a cunning, quick-witted self-assurance that spoke of years of hardship overcome by stubbornness and taking chances. Wade was also intelligent, but he spoke with a heavy heart and a mirthless demeanor that suggested he believed the world he left had forsaken him. Ida suspected the only thing keeping him together was the mask he wore to hide his gloomy heart from his son.

Derek chipped in on parts involving the shiny spot in the warehouse that allowed him to follow his father. August, who had seemed half-asleep moments ago, snapped to attention.

"Did you say shiny spot?" he asked, his voice tight with curiosity.

Derek paused. "Yeah, why?"

Wonder crossed August's face. "I saw a shiny spot, too. Right there." He pointed to the hall. "I can't see it now, though. It was only visible when—" He stopped when he realized Derek's father might not be too keen on his son learning about recreational drug use in such a casual way. "When LaDonna gave me something that helped me."

"What was it?" Wade asked, eyes bright with desperation. He came off the window seat and loomed over August, where he sat on the floor. Misty let out a low growl, her lips pulled back slightly, and the hairs on her back bristled. August soothed her with a hand. She stopped growling, but eyed Wade distrustfully.

"An herb," August replied to the detective, cautiously side-stepping specifics. "Not the one you might think, though. This one has really weird side effects."

"Did it make you dizzy?" Derek inquired.

August chuckled. "A little bit, yeah. For a moment. And then really tired."

Derek grimaced. "Ew. I don't like feeling dizzy."

"Yeah, this stuff was rough," August said.

"Do you think if I took some, it might allow me to see the portal, too?" Wade asked, hope plain on his face.

LaDonna and Luke exchanged a glance, a silent conversation passing between them. LaDonna sat up, and Luke put a supportive hand on her back.

"August is… unusual," LaDonna said, her words deliberately vague. "Not everyone has the same experience from taking it. I've seen some who weren't affected, but most have only minor side effects unless they are… inclined. And even if he could, I didn't bring enough for more than one test. I'd have to get more from my garden, dry it, and… do my preparations to it." She shot Ida and August a look that told them she was unwilling to admit to the newcomers that she was a witch. "I could do that today if August is willing to try again tomorrow."

"I don't suppose alcohol would do the same thing," August said with a laugh. "That stuff was rough. I am seriously wiped out."

"It could, but it would take longer. I'd have to infuse the liquid with the herb and —"

"Whatever's quickest," Wade implored. He turned to August, his weary voice pleading. "Please, August."

"I would like to go home," Derek added, looking sad for the first time since he'd arrived. Ida's heart broke for him. *I wonder if he's ever been away from his mother for long before?*

Ez stepped forward, his calm voice cutting through the tension. "If this herb is what makes the portal visible, then August should rest before he takes it again. We don't know what will happen if he pushed himself too hard."

August pulled in a deep breath and let it out slowly. The entire time Wade and Sergio shared their story, he watched their group curiously. Misty shifted in his lap, her head nuzzling against him as if to reassure him.

Ida crossed her arms in front of her. *Why is he looking at them all so strangely? He's usually way better at meeting people than I am. Something's got to be up, and it must have to do with wherever he traveled when he went through that wall.*

Misty twisted her neck to peer into August's face, and he addressed the pooch playfully. "What do you think, Mist? Tomorrow should work, right? After a good night's sleep, and LaDonna gets more of the stuff ready?" The dog huffed in agreement and rolled her head back into his lap, and he laughed.

"Yeah, we can try tomorrow. She stays here, though." He motioned to the dog. "It looked like she was left behind in her world."

"Did we just adopt a dog?" Ida asked.

"I think we just adopted a dog," he agreed. "Welcome to your new world, little girl. Let's hope it's better than the last one."

And in the silence that followed, Ida couldn't shake the feeling that the mystery was only beginning.

Chapter Twenty-two

Marina suspected her face mirrored that of the startled young man she'd just encountered, her mouth flapping as she fought to find the right words to express her disbelief at what she had just witnessed.

"He—he—"

"Walked through the wall," Zeke confirmed. His voice was too calm for the storm brewing in Marina's mind. Marina knew that police officers were used to maintaining a façade of serenity in extreme situations, but this was beyond extreme—it was impossible.

And Wade walked into nothing and disappeared. This can't be a coincidence.

"Was he a ghost?" Marina asked Rebecca.

"I don't think so," Rebecca said, but her voice wavered. "He looked far too corporeal to be otherworldly."

Rebecca then paced with her meter from one side of the wall to the other, barking numbers at Esau excitedly. Esau, meanwhile, was doing his best to keep up with his friend's dictation, jotting notes down hastily, the scratching of his pen and Rebecca's eager voice the only sounds breaking the suffocating stillness. They tossed around words like "spatial anomalies," "portals," and other subjects beyond her understanding. She resolved to look into what the word "milligauss" meant later.

"What I want to know," Marina interjected, "is if he walked into wherever Wade is."

Rebecca stopped mid-step, blinking like she'd snapped out of a trance. "Well, I—it's possible. But it's not likely, though."

"It's not?" Marina's heart sank, the hope draining from her, leaving her cold.

Rebecca shook her head slowly, almost as if she didn't want to admit it. "It's more likely a second portal. There's nothing specifically linking the two instances to the same location. There could potentially be an abundance of alternate universes."

"This can't be a coincidence," Marina murmured, using her mantra to fight off the despair that threatened to overwhelm her. "It can't be." *An abundance of alternate universes? How many would that be? Ten? A thousand? A million? More?* How would she ever find Wade if the portal he'd slipped through was gone, and now her son, the only person who could see it, had vanished too?

Satisfied that she had tracked readings from every square inch of the dining room wall, Rebecca moved on, her neck craning over the meter as she searched for spikes in electromagnetic activity or other indications of supernatural presence.

"Esau, the levels are going up in this direction. I may have found another hot spot. It's shot from five to six in just a few paces. This place is astounding. My meter hasn't dropped below five since we walked in the door."

The library's dim light flickered overhead as if the house agreed with Rebecca. Rebecca used the device in her hand more than her eyes to lead her through the library.

"Up to seven now." She glanced around the room, her brow furrowed. "I don't see an extraordinary amount of wiring in here. There are no computers. Nothing that might cause a spike. Unless I'm missing something?"

Heads shook around the room.

"The temperature's gone down a little, too," Rebecca observed, her voice softer now. "Which is odd. This is the east side of the house, and there's a window over there letting in plenty of sunlight."

Marina, Esau, and Zeke watched, transfixed, as Rebecca swept the meter from side to side. The library was not large, and it took little time for her to narrow her search to a bookshelf. The woman pulled her head back in surprise as her search targeted a single, weathered volume.

"It's this," she said, pulling a leather-bound book from the shelf, the aged pages crackling like dried leaves.

"A book?" Marina asked.

Rebecca shook her head. "No, it looks like a collection of documents." She set her device on the shelf to free her hands to inspect her discovery. "Whoa," she breathed. "This is information on the house. On the builder."

"How interesting." Esau made his way to her side to view the contents. "Stars above, Rebecca. This is Frank Wenke's personal portfolio. This is where he kept his records on the house."

"Esau, this is incredible," she breathed, her finger tracing down a page. "He studied John Dee, Paracelsus. He planned this entire house to be a focus of power. To trap energy here. Look here. He planned to use psychogeographical forces and those around him as human batteries. And listen to this: 'I propose that when a devotee crafts a talisman, the conveyance of this arcane energy is tangible; the talisman is imbued with power because of the reflective influence of the creator's own psyche.'"

"Was that English?" Zeke joked, his voice thin in the growing tension.

"Not that old," Esau said. "Written probably around the 1870s."

Marina stepped forward, her throat dry. "Did I understand that correctly? He believed that if someone created a talisman, it held energy because the creator wanted it to?"

"Correct," Esau said, though his gaze lingered on the pages.

"And if what I'm reading here is correct," Rebecca said, her voice barely above a whisper, "this entire house was designed to be one enormous talisman holding energy for Frank Wenke."

૭૪ ૪૭

With Sergio and Wade's adventures fully explained to August's group, it was finally his turn to share what happened when he crossed through the wall into another realm. He wished he'd picked a chair instead of sitting on the floor. Sure, it was nice having Misty's head in his lap and Ida there beside him, but the way those two big men loomed over him made him feel like a kid about to fess up to something he shouldn't have done. They seemed friendly enough, but you never could tell how people might react when you started talking.

"So, um." He cleared his throat and shifted uncomfortably. "I guess I should tell y'all about where I went when I stepped through..." He nodded toward the hallway where the portal had been. "It was… well, it was strange. And it got even stranger when I came back."

Baffled expressions crossed their faces, but no one interrupted. August took a breath.

"Let me start from the beginning."

He explained it all, starting with how he crossed into a strange mirror version of the house they were in—a more modern version—and how he had two identical portals on the wall to choose from. He described the bleak, almost suffocating landscape of the world he'd stepped into. But no matter how he explained it, the words didn't do justice to the heavy sense of desolation that had hung over everything.

"Sounds like a nuclear winter," Sergio said, raising an eyebrow. "From what I've read, anyway."

"It felt like hell," August replied, his voice somber. "I never want to set foot in a place like that again."

"At least you know now not to go through that door again," Ida offered.

"True," he said with a sigh. "But here's where it gets weirder."

"Weirder than the scary world?" Derek asked, wrinkling his nose in disbelief.

August nodded, his face solemn. "Even weirder. When I came back to the version of the house we're in—the one that looks lived in—I saw…." He trailed off, steeling himself before plunging forward. "I saw you." He pointed to Rebecca, Zeke, and Esau, feeling a little like Dorothy from *The Wizard of Oz*, telling her friends they'd all been there with her. "All three of you. And a blond woman."

"The woman," Wade said, reaching into his back pocket for his phone, "did she look like this?" He pulled up a picture of a woman with deep green eyes, fair skin, and hair as golden as cornsilk.

"That's her!" August exclaimed. "Who is she?"

"My wife," Wade said, his voice tight.

Derek's face lit up. "You saw Mommy?"

August sat up straighter, relief washing over him. *Finally, something that might actually help.* "Apparently."

"And she was with Zeke, Esau, and Rebecca," Wade said, shaking his head in wonder. "What are the odds of that?"

Esau gave a slow nod, like he was chewing on a puzzle. "The odds against parallel phenomena happening in two separate worlds are tricky to pin down," he said, rubbing his chin. "But it sounds like maybe creating another mirror event that draws you back home isn't as far-fetched as we first thought."

"Well," August said, glancing around the room, "that's something, I guess." He looked around the room at the faces slowly shifting from skepticism to hope. He had the feeling that whatever happened next, they were all in it together—whether they liked it or not.

☙ ❧

The sun had climbed higher in the sky, turning the morning heat into a suffocating blanket. Harper wagered the temperature had risen by at least ten miserable degrees. Her moisture-wicking clothes were useless now, clinging to her like a second skin. This place was a pathetic, poorly educated, redneck, bug-infested nightmare. Why would anyone live where it was hot without a body of water nearby? These people were idiots.

They had a good football team, though. She'd give them that.

She pulled a cotton cloth from her pocket, wiping her hands dry in one deft motion, then tucked it back where she could grab it quickly. So far, the fabric had kept her hands dry sufficiently. The rosin powder was a last resort—too risky with cops sniffing around. If she managed to get her shot off, she'd have to bolt to the car with no time to cover her tracks. A sprinkle of powder where she lay could blow her cover if it ended up on the grass or, worse, the rental car's door handle or steering wheel.

Harper's hiding spot was closer to the house than she'd have liked, but it was the best she could do. A fallen log hid her from view reasonably well, at least. The trees, still thick with leaves, didn't provide a better hiding spot at a safer distance. It was far enough that she'd vanish into the forest before anyone in the house was aware of any danger. That was all that mattered.

Harper sighed and worked on her eye-adjusting exercises again. How long had they holed up in there? An hour? At least an hour. Probably more. Why in the hell were all of those people crammed into that run-down place, anyway? It wasn't exactly the sort of house where normal people congregated. Something was up. Something weird. Devil worship? Drug deals? Hidden sex cult? Probably not a sex cult. Not with the kid there. What the hell kind of bizarre shit were they up to with the kid in there?

Let it go. It doesn't matter. Nothing matters but getting this job done and getting the hell out of here.

She'd about given up on getting her shot today, but wasn't ready to give up yet. On the off chance August headed out alone, she'd have enough time to tag him, throw her rifle over her shoulder, and vanish into the woods before anyone realized what had happened. She'd be out of sight before he drew his last breath.

One shot. A quick sprint. Then she'd be gone.

The door creaked open. Harper tensed and assumed a perfect firing position, not daring to take a breath. But August wasn't alone. The entire group spilled out together, an entourage chatting in clusters, strolling in the direction where August, Dahlia, and that hippie couple had come from. A dog danced at August's heels. Harper blinked furiously.

Where did the fucking dog come from? I never saw a dog go in. What the hell? This is un-fucking-real. She made a mental note that there might be a dog to contend with on this job now. Dogs could make things more difficult.

No shot today, then. So much for an easy in-and-out. Harper let out a slow breath, loosening her grip on the rifle and flexing her cramped hands. Fine. Tonight, she'd kick back in her suite, order room service, and stretch out her tense muscles. Maybe take a bubble bath.

Tomorrow, though... tomorrow might bring better luck.

Chapter Twenty-three

Rebecca shut the portfolio pages with a whisper of old paper, her eyes alight with an almost manic gleam.

"This is it!" she exclaimed. "This explains what has been triggering the odd energies in the house. It's the construction of the house itself!"

"You mean because the house is harnessing energy the way Wenke had planned, that's what let that man and his dog walk straight through the wall?" Marina asked.

"I'd say it's a possibility," Rebecca replied, her smile widening, happy to give Marina a sliver of hope.

Marina gripped Zeke's forearm, her fingers digging in as if he might vanish as well if she let go. A wave of light-headedness washed over her, and Zeke, ever steady, placed his hand gently over hers as he searched her face to make sure she wasn't about to fall to the floor. Was it too much to hope that the answers to her family's disappearance lay hidden in the pages of that old leather-bound file?

Esau cleared his throat, breaking the spell. "Considering the elevated energy readings Rebecca's been picking up — plus the fact we saw a man and his dog literally walk through a wall — I'd say Frank Wenke might have succeeded in creating a house capable of doing things most people would call impossible. However, please keep in mind that there are likely a multitude of alternate universes."

Rebecca grabbed her Gaussmeter from the shelf and shoved it into her back pocket, her need to measure the atmosphere diminished by her discovery of Wenke's strange architectural plans.

"Esau, I'm going to take this with me," she said. "I'll smooth it over with my realtor friend later. I know it's unorthodox, to say the least, but…" Her hands caressed the leather cover, "I wonder if the owner even knows what they've got here—or if they just think it's a neat piece of their home's history?"

"Why don't the people living here have a clue what the house can do?" Marina asked. "You'd think they'd have noticed the house had weird power."

"That's a good question," Rebecca said, her fingers drumming on the book's cover. "I hope I'll find the answer when I read more of this." She gave the book a gentle pat.

"I want to come with you," Marina said. It was a request, but her tone told Rebecca there was no turning her down.

"Count me in, too," Zeke said, equally fervent. "If there's even a slim chance I can help bring Wade and Derek home, I want to be there."

"It might take a while, you two," Rebecca warned. "I don't know how long it will take to unravel this thing. It could be incredibly complex."

Marina shook her head, her jaw set. "I don't care."

Esau drew near and rested a hand on Marina's free arm, his touch warm and grounding. "You look like you're running on fumes, Marina. Are you sure you wouldn't rather go home?"

Marina gave a curt, defiant nod. Her eyes burned, but she refused to shed tears.

Esau's features softened. "I'll tell you what. Why don't we all go back to my place? Rebecca, do you need anything to conduct your study?"

The scientist thought for a minute, then gave a curt nod. "I'd like to retrieve a couple of books from my apartment. I should be able to access most of what I need through the university library website, though."

"Excellent," Esau said, a hint of relief in his smile. "Would you mind if we all met back at my house? Marina, you can sleep in the guest room. Zeke, you know your old room's still there if you need to get some rest. That way, we'll all be gathered under one roof if Rebecca finds a potential answer to our dilemma. Does that sound good?"

The group exchanged glances, a silent agreement passing between them. They left the Victorian, Marina hoping against hope they'd soon have the answers to her family's return.

❧

LaDonna set a pitcher of sweet tea on her dining room table, filling glasses for everyone as the two couples gathered around the old dining room table. Everyone poured over the dusty file that Luke had uncovered with the help of the ghost in the Victorian home. The sheets were loose within the leather cover, and each took different portions of the file to pore over in search of clues. Ida and August sat across from one another, heads bent low, and LaDonna and Luke took the opposite chairs. Sergio, Wade, Esau, Ez, Derek, and Rebecca sat in the nearby living room to relax and contemplate their next move.

"Good thing his handwriting is legible," August said, squinting at the faded ink. "This English is so old I'm not sure I understand it correctly. But check this out. Wenke said he thought his house could, 'manifest a palpable influence upon the observer and, indeed, the entire society in its environs.'"

"He had some interesting ideas," Luke agreed. "Here he writes that he's 'exploring the bond between the grand design of the universe and the craft of constructing edifices."

"Y'all, that's not even the craziest of it," Ida breathed. She ran a finger down the page in her opposite hand. "In this part, he's rambling about his experiments contacting various… well, he calls them 'angelic spirits,' but y'all… these things don't sound angelic at all. Here, he says, 'I have exercised the utmost caution in contriving a passage within the uppermost chamber of my abode, which permits the entry of these celestial spirits solely at my bidding. Once summoned, they are bound to depart at my very word, and I have labored with care to construct this portal in such a manner that its access is granted only by my express invitation, ensuring that my dismissal is met without question. Yet, there is one among these spirits, whom I shall call Brightness, for he surpasses all in radiance. His obstinate disposition nigh unto strains my wits to their utmost limit. He doth weary me greatly, and I fear that, in due course, he may become more than I am able to command.'"

"That's… formal," August said slowly.

"That's flat-out terrifying," Ida corrected him, eyes wide. "The man had a spirit that wouldn't obey him. I wonder if it ever got loose? What if it's still there? August, what if Brightness is the thing that possessed you that Clark had to help you get rid of?"

"That's only if he actually contacted any spirits in real life and wasn't going crazy," August countered. "He could have been bananas and just imagining things."

"August, we watched someone walk through a wall in that house," LaDonna reminded him, deadpan. "I think it's safe to say he knew what he was doing."

Rebecca, on her way through the room to return her glass to the kitchen sink, paused when she caught sight of the group poring over Frank Wenke's many notes. Her eyes narrowed, zeroing in on a page filled with symbols.

"What have you got there?" she asked, her curiosity piqued.

"It's a file we came across in the home where we met you. We might need your input," LaDonna said. "You study this sort of thing, I imagine, being a ghost hunter. How familiar are you with Frank Wenke?"

"The architect of the house?" Rebecca motioned to the path they'd walked from the Victorian. "I've read bits and pieces. If I remember correctly, he was trying to start a local congregation, the Universal Temple of Celestial Harmonies."

"He kept a record of all his plans for the house," Ida said, "every symbol he used, all the—"

"Are you serious?" Rebecca interrupted, excitement lighting up her face. "Let me see."

She dropped to a crouch between LaDonna and Ida, pulling the pages of symbols toward her, her eyes scanning them with fascination and intense concentration.

"This guy was all *over* the place," Rebecca said. She pulled the image of a fancy cross with a rose at the center and held it up. "This is a Rose Cross, linked with Rosicrucianism. This group has some pretty interesting beliefs. Its members thought—think? I think they're still around—that they have esoteric wisdom that has been passed down for centuries. And this," she held up a picture of a man with a long beard over his ruff collar, "Is John Dee. He thought he could speak to angels."

Ida raised her eyebrows at August, who matched her

expression. Rebecca went on fervently.

"And *this*," she held up a black-and-white photograph of a woman with a soft face and wide eyes, "Is Helena Blavatsky, philosopher, occultist, and the co-founder of the Theosophical Society. I don't know that anything Helena wrote was necessarily good or evil—her teachings blended a lot of theologies and religions into what she called 'theosophy.'"

"That sounds a lot like Wenke," Ida noted.

"That might explain this," Luke said. He pulled another photograph from the file, one that held a picture of a stern man in a suit and hat standing next to two women. One, a woman who looked very much like Helena Blavatsky. The other, a beautiful woman in a Victorian dress, her hair pulled under an elaborate hat. On the back of the image, in Wenke's handwriting, were the words *Helena Blavatsky and Hermina and Frank Wenke, New York, 1876.*

Rebecca went on. "Helena's penchant for pulling her belief system from whatever resonated with her probably sat well with Frank. Based on what I'm seeing here, he's got images and notes from… Hermeticism, Freemasonry, sacred geometry, Kabbalah…"

"Are these bad?" Ida asked.

"Not bad in and of themselves," LaDonna said. "But it shows he desperately needed understanding and power."

"And he was ahead of his time in many ways," Rebecca added. "Wenke, like many nineteenth-century esoteric practitioners of things like Hermeticism and Theosophy, believed in a 'universal consciousness' or the interconnectedness of all life. Very similar concepts to modern-day quantum physics. Traditions like Rosicrucianism, Theosophy, and alchemy were all about the idea that your thoughts and intentions have genuine power. They believed that the mind could shape reality, almost like a tool you could use to physically and spiritually influence the world around you. So, when they practiced rituals, meditation, or even magic, it was about focusing their thoughts and willpower to make things happen in the world."

"What if Wenke was right?" Ida said, her voice laced with a hint of excitement. "What if… what if *we* could use the power in the house for our own purposes? If we could choose, out of all the alternate universes, to send Wade and Derek back to their version of the world? Do you think anything in these notes can show us how?"

Wade's voice carried in from the next room. "Did you call me?" The sound of creaking couch springs followed as Wade hauled himself up.

"We were just talking about you," Ida replied. Wade lumbered into the doorway, his broad frame nearly filling the space between the rooms. "Rebecca thinks that the architect of that house was an occultist who put some wacky stuff into the building of the house."

"Oh yeah," Wade said with a nod. "Esau was telling us about that on the way over. Hey Esau, you want to tell them what you told me?"

Luke, noting the growing crowd in the cramped dining area, gestured toward the living room. "Why don't we move in there? More space to spread out." Luke and LaDonna had bought their home to have ample living space to accommodate coven meetings when thirteen witches gathered to celebrate holidays, perform rituals, and enjoy one another's company in comfort with plenty of space to spare.

After giving Misty a quick trip outside, August and Ida joined the rest of the crowd in the living room. Talk turned to Frank Wenke's mysterious house and the possibility that it held the key to getting the Beringers home.

Chapter Twenty-four

"Did you know that book was there the whole time?" Leah asked pointedly. Thunder loomed in the heavy storm clouds behind her eyes.

"Of course," Minnie responded curtly. She gathered her skirts in hand and made as if she intended to retire to the parlor, but Leah, ever the obstinate one, jumped into her path.

"You *knew* that was there the whole time? All the information about this house? And you never *told* us?"

"What good would it have done?" Minnie snapped with a soft stomp of her foot, her ordinarily soft voice fierce with anger. "This house is a prison!"

"Oh, I don't know." Leah rolled her eyes before leaning forward and pointing to where Clark stood nearby. "We might have discovered something. At the very least, you could have pointed it out to the guy who *lives* here with us who spent years *studying religion for his career.*"

Minnie's demeanor eased as she realized the futility of trying to argue, but the grim twist of her mouth remained. She chose her following words carefully.

"Leah, my power is very limited. Moving things in the mortal realm exhausts me. What you saw me do just then drained me. You saw how I couldn't stand up. I—"

"Minnie, we have fucking eternity. Eternity! If you'd dragged that damned book out, dropped it on the floor, and we only turned a page a day, we might have figured something out! We might be *gone* by now!"

Minnie blanched at Leah's use of profanity, but she refused to give. "Leah, there are many, *many* things in that book that have scared me near to death."

"You're already dead," Leah deadpanned humorlessly.

"Child, you *know* what I mean." Leah rolled her eyes at Minnie's use of the word 'child,' but Minnie continued. "We already have to share this house with those—those *travelers*. And we don't know what they are, just that they're always passing through."

"And touching them feels horrible," Clark added from where he was staring out the sitting-room window. Leah shuddered at the thought, but said nothing. The fingers on her crossed arm drummed against her biceps impatiently.

Minnie pressed on, her voice quieter, more somber. "There are things in that book that have terrified me."

"We're already *dead!*" Leah exclaimed, arms windmilling in frustration.

"Yes, but it's not the dying that scares me. It's what might come after." Minnie's gaze drifted, her fingers fidgeting with the lace hem of her skirt. "Frank poured his whole being into this house, into that book. The power in this place… it doesn't come from the walls or the rooms. It's something else, something that grows, Leah. I've seen it in the way the house pulled on people when they entered. The way it… changed people. That book doesn't just tell you how this place works—it tells you what it wants."

"Wants?" Leah scoffed, though her voice was quieter now, cautious. "It's a house, Minnie. It doesn't 'want' anything."

"That's what I used to think. But I've felt it. Since Frank first laid that foundation, I've felt this… pull. Something dark is rooted here, and it's grown stronger, feeding off of—off the people who visit here, off those who had lived here." Her eyes, usually so calm, flickered with terror. "What if the book isn't the key to escape? What if it's a way to… feed it more?"

"So, you didn't tell us because you're scared of what we might unleash." A hint of forgiveness crossed Leah's face.

"I didn't tell you because I'm scared we might release something worse than being trapped here." Minnie's eyes met Leah's, and for the first time, Leah saw not just the prim, proper housewife but a woman haunted by the possibility of an existence far worse than her death. "But like you said, it's been a hundred and fifty years. Maybe it's time to finally find out."

Silence hung between them, the tension easing but not entirely gone.

"We may get out of here," Leah said hopefully. "Maybe the book can help with that."

Clark tore himself from studying the woods beyond the window now that the argument had lost its steam. "If the book reveals how this house is built and how it can be controlled, LaDonna will most certainly help. She's quite a powerful witch in her own right, and her foster daughter is even more powerful."

"What if we get out of here," Leah said to Minnie, "and you come face to face with Frank in the afterlife? What would you say to him?"

Minnie's gaze dropped as she pressed her palms together like a woman in prayer.

"I'd ask him… why."

كظظظظظ

Harper knew she'd have no problems with mornings if they weren't so bright. Well, she was almost certain. Pretty sure, anyway.

She rolled to the edge of the bed, scowling. The wine had gone down well enough, but she could do without the residual effects on her breath in the morning. Even drinking water sounded disgusting. Only a toothbrush would solve this nastiness.

Tottering on unstable legs toward the bathroom, she wondered if thirty-two was too young to suffer a headache this bad after half a bottle of wine. While brushing her teeth, she decided it must be a side effect of dehydration from lying in the woods for a good part of the afternoon the day before.

Her mouth full of toothpaste, Harper swore when her burner phone rang on the nightstand. She finished a perfunctory brushing, spat, rinsed, and padded to the phone, taking a second to ensure the voice modulator was primed before answering.

"This is Stone."

"Mr. Stone, this is Fletcher Kightlinger. I apologize for calling so early, and I know you've probably only just arrived in… where you are and haven't had time to settle in yet. But I wanted to talk."

Thankful she had deposited her retainer, which more than

covered her expenses so far, Harper said, "Is there a problem?"

"Problem? No… well, not exactly. I um…." Kightlinger trailed off, and Harper delighted in doing nothing to put the pompous ass at ease. "I was wondering if you had an idea of a timeline yet."

"A timeline?"

"Yes, I, um…. My wife is concerned. It's been several months since Dahlia's been seen with us, and… people are talking. My wife is running out of things to tell her friends, and I find myself struggling to make excuses as well."

"So you want me to speed things up." Harper added as much disdain in those words as humanely possible.

"Not at the expense of the job, of course, or… well, Mr. Stone, I'd never assume to tell you how to do your job. I can't imagine…" Kightlinger's words stumbled over each other. "Would adding an incentive be out of the ordinary? Say, double the fee if you finish in the next forty-eight hours?"

Harper's heart skipped a beat. *Double the fee? Holy fucking shit. I'd never have to work again.* Dreams of life as an expatriate danced behind her eyes.

"Mr. Stone, I'm sorry. Is that not acceptable?" Fletcher stammered. "I don't mean to offend you. I've—I've never done anything like—"

"I can't promise anything."

"Of course not," Fletcher said. A hint of the old business tycoon crept back into his voice, although whether it was out of habit or an attempt to save face, Harper couldn't say.

"I'll do my best. And Fletcher?"

"Yes?"

"Don't fucking call me again."

She hung up.

☙ ❧

Rebecca sat cross-legged on the floor of Esau's study, her brow wrinkled in study as she stared at the pages of the old book scattered in the space between her and Marina. The room was brightly lit, but the setting sun through the window cast long, twisting shadows on the walls.

"This doesn't make sense," Marina muttered, tracing a finger along an intricate diagram in the book. It looked like a blueprint of the house but twisted and layered with symbols Rebecca said she couldn't recognize. "Huh. It's like you said, though. Frank Wenke didn't just design this place—he built his home with an ulterior motive. This is unbelievable."

Rebecca sighed, leaning back against the cold stone hearth, trying to make sense of the swirling thoughts in her head. Strange architectural details framed the room she'd been examining: arches with words carved into the leaf work promising a bond between humans and nature. Staircases with elaborate banisters engraved with chants promising ascension to a heavenly layer. Even the floor had odd geometric inlays, shapes that felt more like puzzle pieces than simple decorations.

"Why would he go through all this trouble?" Marina continued, squinting at the writing. "He had to know something. Listen to what he says: 'The walls of this house are no mere timber and stone. They draw upon the force of those who enter, ensnaring their vitality, as a spider spins its web to catch life itself. Be it power or the soul, once within these walls, nothing leaves untouched.'"

Rebecca's eyes drifted toward the window, where the wind howled outside. At the nearby desk, Zeke pondered pages of his own while eying the weather radar. A storm was brewing to the south and west, and though it looked like the worst of it might miss them, the much-needed rain would be welcome.

"Wait," Rebecca said slowly, her thoughts clicking into place. "What if... we've been thinking too small? Wenke didn't just use the house to drain his guests like batteries, but..." Her heart pounded as the realization hit. "He said *to catch life itself.*'"

Marina looked up from the book, frowning. "So... it was a ghost? Do you think it might have led us to the book? Or maybe it was the house. After reading all this, I wondered if the house was communicating with us."

Rebecca nodded, feeling the weight of it all press against her chest. "Think about it. All this weird architecture—what if it's trapping the previous people who lived in the house? What if they know how it all works? The dimensions, the portal, everything?"

Marina's eyes widened. "Could we talk to them? The ghost, or ghosts, or whatever they are?"

Rebecca's eyes shone with an almost manic grin. "Marina, I'm a ghost hunter. I've been waiting for this moment my entire damned life."

☘ ☙

"Wait a minute, wait a minute, wait a minute," Rebecca said, hands up, her long hair swaying back and forth as she shook her head, trying to wrap her mind around what August told her. "You had a *ghost talking through you*? As in, using your body, your mouth, and everything? Are you serious?"

"As a heart attack," August said, now able to smile about the experience.

"Esau, are you hearing this?" Rebecca cried.

"I heard it," the older man replied. "It's been a rather remarkable day."

Rebecca blinked, then rubbed her temples with her fingertips, clearly working through the implications. "I don't... I don't...." Her expression cycled through confusion, disbelief, finally landing on pure joy. "I've spent my whole life searching for proof of supernatural phenomena, and today—just today—I've learned that ghosts do, in fact, exist, they're in a nearby house filled with occult architecture, and that house also acts as a portal to other dimensions."

"Too much?" Ida asked, arching an eyebrow.

"Are you freaking kidding me?" Rebecca's voice burst with excitement. "This is the *best day* ever."

Esau, from his corner of the room, offered a fatherly smile. "Rebecca, I don't think I've seen you this excited in all the years we've worked together."

"I've never been this thrilled in my life!" Rebecca beamed, turning back to August. "Do you think you could do it again? Let Clark speak through you? I mean, I imagine you could. Would you be willing to? LaDonna, could you ask Clark to—"

A bright spear of lightning flashed outside the window, followed by a long, low rumble of summer thunder.

"Ooh," LaDonna breathed, momentarily distracted. "My plants will be very happy."

"LaDonna?" Rebecca urged, "Do you think Clark would be willing to help?"

"It's very likely. If Clark knows the answers you're looking for, he'll happily share them. He's always been very kind."

Rebecca took a deep breath and let it out in a controlled *whoosh*. She looked like she was trying to steady her heart, calm it down a notch. Once composed, she gave her attention to LaDonna.

"I know you said you had to prepare more herbs before August can walk through walls into whatever dimension he went to," Rebecca began. She shifted her gaze to August. "August, do you need anything to see the ghosts?"

"I don't rightly see them," August replied, running a hand through his hair as if the memory alone gave him a chill. He winced, recalling the sensation of the thing that had shared his body before Clark came to the rescue. "When the first thing, the creepy, cold thing Clark called a Passerby, came in, I didn't see that, either."

"None of us did," Ida chimed in, shaking her head.

"It felt like cold...." August trailed off as he searched for the right words to describe the eerie sensation.

"Like cold clay, maybe?" Rebecca ventured, "If the clay were pliant? Melted?"

"Yeah!" August agreed. "And then the clay solidified around me. Trapped me. Until Clark helped."

Rebecca's eyes narrowed thoughtfully. "How did they feel different?" she asked.

August pondered the question for a moment, his hands tapping a muffled staccato beat on the leg of his pants. "The first one didn't speak. But it was... thinking, I could feel that. Like it wanted something. Wanted *me*. To take me over." Ida shuddered at his side, and he put a comforting hand on her leg.

"And Clark? He did control you. How was that different?"

"For one, Clark asked," Ida cut in. "Right?"

"Yeah," August agreed. "He did ask. He offered to help evict the first thing, the Passerby, and then he asked if it was OK if he borrowed my body for a minute to talk to LaDonna. After what he did, I wasn't about to say no."

"Clark didn't have to enter you to help you evict the Passerby?"

"He did, but the feeling was completely different. It was like someone handing me a warm blanket after being dunked in ice water."

Rebecca nodded as if this made perfect sense. Maybe to her, it did. "Would you be willing to talk to him again tonight?"

The soft patter of raindrops tapping on the glass drew everyone's attention to the long-awaited summer storm.

"I don't know," August hedged, shooting Luke and LaDonna a questioning look. "It's getting late, and now it's raining. And LaDonna has to do her herb thing…"

"LaDonna and Luke don't have to come if they don't want to," Rebecca said. She shot the two of them an apologetic look. "I mean, you can if you want to, of course."

"I kind of need them there," August said, not willing to offer further explanation.

"You do?" Rebecca said, puzzled.

A pause ensued, during which Luke and LaDonna shared one of their wordless conversations. For a moment, LaDonna hesitated, her fingers playing with the hem of her billowy shirt collar, and August caught a brief flicker of uncertainty in her eyes. He wondered if she was wishing Luke were there for support.

"We're witches," Luke explained. "And LaDonna and I suspect August might be one, too. One with the gift of clairvoyance, spiritual sight. Specifically, the gift of seeing ghosts."

August fought the urge to tilt his head like a curious dog as he studied Rebecca, Wade, and Sergio's reactions. The way they reacted was a study in contrasts. Sergio nodded as if this made perfect sense, while Wade's gaze narrowed as he considered the plausibility of LaDonna's claim. August could almost see Wade realizing that witches weren't much of a stretch after everything they'd seen over the past couple of days. Rebecca's mouth dropped open, hand flying up to cover it. "What gifts do *you* have?" she asked.

"I'm a green witch," LaDonna said. "I can weave magic into plants. For instance, I can use them to heal, or, in August's case, use them to enhance his ability to tap into realms beyond our visible one."

"She also has a way with animals that would blow your mind," Luke added, pride in his voice.

"What about you?" Rebecca asked Luke.

"I see the future," he said casually. "With the right tools, of course."

"Have you done it before?"

"Oh, yes. All the time. I knew August and Ida were coming before they moved in next door."

"You did?" Ida said, her hand flying to her chest in surprise.

Luke smiled and nodded. "I did."

Rebecca shook her head in disbelief. "Well, I'll be damned," she muttered. "Ghosts, and portals, and witches. Oh, my."

Chapter Twenty-five

Sergio handed Wade a bottle of cold Medalla Light and sank into the chair beside the couch. After a long day of trying to be as grown-up as he knew how, Derek was asleep in Sergio's guest room, giving the two of them their first chance to really talk since Wade's son had arrived.

"What you thinking, man?"

"A lot," Wade admitted, running a hand through his hair the way Sergio himself often did when frustrated. "Hell, I can't *stop* thinking."

Sergio gave a low chuckle. "I can imagine. Our whole lives have turned upside down, huh?"

"A bit," Wade said, his tone dry. "First, I drop like a brick into some parallel dimension. Then, just as I'm wrapping my head around that, my son shows up, thinking it's a good idea to follow me. Then we're following my parallel world partner's dad to a haunted house to figure out—surprise!—not only does it have ghosts, but it's got doors to even *more* dimensions. Oh, and we watched a guy stroll right through a wall back into this world."

"But he can only do that when he's high," Sergio added with a pointed motion of the bottleneck.

"Yeah, on some mystery herb," Wade muttered before taking a long pull of his beer. "What's your take on that, by the way? The herb part?"

Sergio shrugged. "Could be just regular weed."

"He said he saw odd things, though. Walls moving, that sort of thing."

"Maybe he got some really good shit," Sergio laughed with a waggle of his eyebrows.

"Maybe," Wade said, dubious. "But if it was just weed,

wouldn't he have come back still high?"

Sergio tilted his head, considering. "Maybe. Or maybe it wore off while he was…over there."

Wade thought about that for a moment. "Ida said he was only gone a few minutes."

"Time could pass differently in the other worlds he was in," Sergio suggested.

Wade blinked. "Do you think that could be a thing?"

"It is in the books I've read."

"And LaDonna said he was predisposed to such behavior. What do you think she meant by that?"

Sergio snorted. "It doesn't mean he's predisposed to picking the right world to walk into. Otherwise, he never would have taken a wrong turn into that nuclear winter world."

"Which means that he can walk through walls but won't necessarily pick the right door." Wade paused, mentally digesting the idea. "At least he saw Marina, so I know I can go home if he picks the same door."

"Maybe, maybe not," Sergio said, taking a sip of beer.

Wade narrowed his eyes. "What do you mean?"

"What if the Marina August saw is to your Marina like I am to you?"

Wade opened his mouth but snapped it shut as he processed the bizarre statement, and the implications of Sergio's words hit him. "Crap. What if she *is* another Marina?" He paused. "That can't be it, can it? She has to be my Marina. There's no way all of this could be coincidence."

"They're called parallel dimensions for a reason, bro," Sergio countered.

"Well, shit," Wade breathed. "How will I know if I'm back in the right world?"

"Keep your phone charged," Sergio suggested nonchalantly. "If you're back in your own world, it should work again."

Wade thought of the phone, which sat in the pocket of his borrowed pants like a useless lump of glass, plastic, and electronics. "That's a damn good idea. I bet you'd make a hell of a detective."

Sergio chuckled. "I know."

Wade sank back into the chair with a huff. "I'm going to need to borrow a charger."

ଔ   ଓ

Marina thought the morning would never come. The house felt hollow without Derek and Wade in its walls, their absence leaving an uncomfortable, aching silence. She'd tossed and turned for hours, catching only brief, fitful sleep before dawn's first magenta and gold light filtered through the blinds, painting stripes across her lightweight flannel blankets. The cool air conditioning chilled her as she kicked the blankets away, her body yearning for more sleep, but her mind was far too restless to try.

Rebecca had headed to her place after leaving Esau's the night before to gather some of her "best equipment," as she'd called it. She had mentioned repairing a few pieces of equipment that might be useful and ensuring everything was ready. "If there's anything to detect, we'll find it," she'd said, her voice confident. Marina hoped she was right.

After performing a perfunctory morning hygiene ritual, Marina grabbed her keys and drove to the Victorian home, her mind in a fog. Miles passed under her tires unnoticed as she drove the familiar roads. She almost missed the turnoff to the narrow driveway but managed to hit the brakes with a jerk and pull into the path, the crunch of gravel underfoot loud in the stillness,

Rebecca was a vision of organized chaos, her pink denim top and tan shorts clashing slightly with the headband barely containing her thick hair. She waved Marina over with a grin and immediately handed her an armload of equipment. One of the more oversized items looked like a miniature satellite dish.

"We're going to use these to try to capture EVP," Rebecca said. "Electronic Voice Phenomena. What you have is a parabolic microphone. It's used to amplify sounds we might miss. And this," she pulled out an outlandish box composed of wires, gages, crystals, what looked like a couple of guitar pedals, LED lights, a speaker, an old microcassette recorder, and what Marina believed was a Tesla coil strapped to it. "This is what I call my Spectrosonic Resonator."

"Spectro-what now?" Marina asked, raising an eyebrow.

"It amplifies the sounds of specters," she said with a grin. With a tilt of her head, she added, "Come on, this is going to be fun."

The morning air was thick with the scent of dew and earth as Marina followed Rebecca inside the house, its once-grand Victorian rooms now stripped bare. The floorboards creaked underfoot, their echoes unnervingly loud in the largely empty space. Clueless as to the purpose or function of the tools Rebecca was setting up (except for the small power generator), Marina worked in silence, following Rebecca's instructions to set up microphones, video equipment, and anything else Rebecca had reason to believe might serve as a ghostly conduit.

Zeke showed up halfway through preparations with a large bag of warm bagel sandwiches and coffees. Rebecca barely broke her stride as she munched her breakfast and finished setting up.

As she slung a set of headphones around her neck, Rebecca said, "Now, we're going to have to be cautious of audio pareidolia—how our brains tend to want to make familiar sounds out of random ones. Ever watch a ghost hunting show where they think they hear a voice, but you're like, 'What? I didn't hear that?'"

"I never hear what they do," Zeke laughed, washing down the last of his breakfast with a swig of coffee.

"I don't, either," Marina admitted.

"Well, today's not a good day to start," Rebecca said. "Would either or both of you like to have a headset as well? It might be helpful in the event a sound pops up." They both agreed, and Rebecca helped them connect their equipment. The soft leather of the headset blocked out almost all the ambient sounds. When Rebecca strolled to the center of the room, every footfall sounded like a giant stomping on the wooden floorboards.

"Now, try to be as quiet as possible while I speak," she whispered. Her voice sounded like a stage whisper through the headset. "I don't want the machines to get any more false readings than they have to." She pressed Record on one of her devices, crossed the parlor, started the camera on another, and then headed to the library where she'd set up her Spectrosonic resonator—clearly the star of the show.

"Hello?" she said to the room at large. "My name is Rebecca. I'm a paranormal researcher. Please don't be afraid of the equipment you see. I don't know if any of it looks strange to you, but it is there to help us talk. Is anyone there?"

The thick quiet that followed was broken only by the faint noises of the wind causing branches to scrape against a nearby window.

Marina's heartbeat thundered in her chest, loud enough that she worried it might drown out any ghostly voices they were trying to catch. Then, a faint creak echoed from deep in the house, making the hairs on the back of her neck stand on end. Was something—or someone—listening?

Less than thirty seconds after Rebecca had addressed the room, it came.

"He—llo? I... Cla—rk."

The voice crackled through the static, broken but unmistakable. Marina's breath caught.

"Clark? Did you say Clark?" Rebecca's eyes revealed her excitement, but her voice remained steady. Marina had to give the woman credit. She was about ready to faint. Zeke shot her a smiling side-eye, and she tried to focus.

"Yes. He—llo."

"Do you live here alone, Clark?"

Good question, Marina thought. She hadn't considered that there'd be more than one.

"No."

"How many others live here, Clark?"

"T—wo oth—ers... But... th—ere are m—ore."

Two others, but there were more? What did this ghost mean? Just how many ghosts were they dealing with?

಄　ಀ

Forty-eight hours. Harper had two days to get the shot of her life. One that would allow her to never have to work again. No more stress. No more fear of leaving behind a trace. No more running. She could almost taste the salt in the air, feel the sun on her skin, and hear the gentle lapping of waves while she sipped something fruity and cold. The image was intoxicating—sandy beaches, shirtless guys at her beck and call, and nothing but time.

I could get used to that, she thought, a smirk tugging at her lips

Sure, she'd have to find new ways to get her adrenaline fix. Bungee jumping, skydiving—hell, maybe even lion taming. When she got older, maybe she'd open an alligator farm or, for kicks, run a sex club. *Something wild and completely legal.* But first, she had to get through this.

Failure wasn't an option. Harper wasn't about to lose her biggest chance at freedom.

Before dawn, she carefully prepped her gear, laying everything out like it was her personal altar. The extra water bottles she'd bought the night before from the sporting goods store sat next to another piece of equipment, one she hoped to avoid using—a six-inch survival knife, its newly sharpened blade gleaming under the hotel room light. She'd ditched the cheap accessories that came with the knife's package the second she left the shop, leaving them in a trash bin in the parking lot. She didn't need the cheap compass or useless fishing line and hooks. All she needed was a manageable handle with some sharp steel at the end.

A sharpening stone had been her last purchase. By the time she was done with it last night, the knife could easily slice through the proverbial ripe tomato. *And if it can do that...* Harper ran her thumb along the blade, just enough to feel its lethal sharpness without drawing blood. Satisfied, she slid it back into its sheath and placed it alongside her change of clothes, a disposable lighter, and a small can of lighter fluid. *Just in case.* Bloody clothes had to disappear fast, any DNA destroyed, and she wasn't taking any chances.

After loading everything into a duffel bag, she headed to the hotel parking lot. The rental car gave her pause. She'd tossed the rental agency's frame into the trunk at her first pit stop, but the license plates... *That's a problem.* Her gaze darkened. She hated loose ends, and leaving a rental at a scenic overlook in the middle of butt-fuck Alabama felt like waving a flag for nosy neighbors or curious cops. She tossed the duffel into the trunk, grabbed a screwdriver from her small tool kit, and deftly removed the license plate.

A quick stroll to the nearby parking garage was all it took to spot a car identical to hers—same make, model, year, and color. *It is so convenient how rental agencies love using bland, forgettable cars.* In less than two minutes, she'd swapped the plates. In less than ten, she was back on the road with someone else's tags on her car.

As she drove, Harper mentally ran through the details. Yesterday's trek through the woods had given her a solid lay of the land—seven, maybe eight acres between her target's mobile home and that odd Victorian house. *Why a Victorian, of all things?* She shook her head. It didn't matter. The house was far enough back in the woods to provide decent cover, and her base would be triangulated between the mobile home, the Victorian, and the hippie couple's place. She'd have everything she needed close at hand.

She pulled into the overlook and backed the car into a spot. *Nosy cops love running plates,* she mused. Sure, she'd swapped the tags, and the actual owner probably wouldn't notice for a while, but why tempt fate when backing in was an easy extra precaution? If she couldn't wrap things up today, she'd swap the car out for another one, telling the rental company this one had a problem. *A disconnected air conditioner should do the trick in this heat.*

Harper pulled her hair back, tucking the last few strands beneath her cap, and stared at the dimly lit horizon. Forty-eight hours. The clock was ticking.

I'm not leaving this one to chance.

Chapter Twenty-six

The previous night's storm had cooled the air, but now it was muggy on top of hot. August peeled the clinging bedsheets from his skin in the morning with a grimace. The droning fan near their bed barely stirred the hot, muggy air in the room. Mostly, it was white noise that helped them sleep.

Alert to August's movement, Misty picked her head up from the end of the couch and startled him. Her excited panting sounded loud in the quiet morning.

Oh yeah. We have a dog. August smiled at her and shushed, hoping she understood what he meant. She seemed to. Her mouth snapped shut, and she cocked her head at him.

He crept across the creaky couch, not wanting to disturb Ida, who had slept fitfully through the storm. He let Misty out for her morning potty before dragging himself into the shower, the cool water a welcome contrast against his overheated body. Shower thoughts tumbled through his mind as he stood under the cool spray. This might be his only moment of quiet today. Soon, he and Ida would head out to meet everyone back at the Victorian house again.

The Wenke house, he thought as he toweled off. *And unless we get rid of all of those freaky cult symbols in there, it's going to stay his. I will not move in with it like that. Hell, maybe I'll have it knocked down.*

The scent of fresh coffee filled the small living space as he brewed a pot. He and Ida both drank coffee every morning, heat be damned. He poured a cup for her, adding the sugary creamer she couldn't go without, and carried it over to wake her. Her tangled curls fell over one eye as she stirred at his footsteps.

"Morning already?" Her voice was thick with sleep.

"Yep. And I let you sleep as late as I could. We need to meet everyone in about half an hour."

"So you can try to speak to ghosts." She sat up, took the cup, and slipped the hot brew carefully. "You think you'll be able to?"

He sat on the edge of the pull-out couch, his half-full coffee mug curled in both hands. "I hope so. And I hope they have answers. I know you want to live there, Ida—"

"Not the way it is now, I don't," she interrupted softly, her eyes darkening. "I love how the house looks, but if we can't get the creepy cult stuff out…" She didn't finish, but he didn't need her to. They both knew the house was stunning, but the occult power Frank Wenke had built into it overshadowed its unique beauty.

"It's no wonder no one has lived there in so long," Ida said. "I wonder if anything bad has happened to anyone other than Clark and Wenke? I mean, they both hanged themselves in the same room, right? What are the odds of that?"

"Pretty slim," he admitted. The thought sent a shiver down his spine despite the heat, and he stifled a shudder. "At least, I imagine so."

Ida pulled in another sip of coffee before handing the mug to August so she could pull back the sheets and swing her bare legs over the side. "I need to shower so we can head out."

ۈ ۊ

Within thirty minutes, he and Ida arrived at the door to the Wenke house, where an unfamiliar car was parked at the head of the driveway. The air inside had that musty, old-house scent, and the faint squeak of the weathered wooden boards announced their presence before they even reached the parlor.

They found Sergio and Wade, who had arrived with Wade's son. Derek was telling Sergio all about his mother, and it was clear by the way he spoke so animatedly that she meant the world to him. From the sparkle in Wade's eye as he watched his son, August gathered that Derek and his mother were everything to him.

August opened his mouth when Derek paused in his monologue to say hello to the men, but the closing door behind him interrupted his greeting. LaDonna had arrived as well, this time without her husband.

"No Luke today?" August asked.

"Not today," LaDonna replied, pulling a crinkled paper bag from her purse that August was sure held the supplies he'd need to "travel" today. "He had to work. But I found another friend on the way in."

Behind her stood Rebecca, who offered them all a wave. "Hey, y'all."

Eying the paper sack, August said, "Do you think we could try to do things… naturally first?"

"Of course," LaDonna said, giving him a knowing smile as she placed the bag and her purse on the dusty side table. "I had thought we'd try that first. We still haven't seen how far your natural gift extends."

Sergio sauntered over. "How exactly does listening for ghosts work? Is it like ESP or something?" He folded his arms, curious.

LaDonna bobbed her head back and forth, suggesting a so-so agreement. "Sort of. ESP is the ability to perceive things beyond the five senses — telepathy or precognition like Luke has. I suspect August's skills are more along the lines of… the ability to perceive ghosts."

"Huh. Do you really think you can help him?"

LaDonna set her shoulders back and said, "I'm certainly going to try."

"Ok," Wade said. "August, are you ready to see what you can do?"

August gave what he hoped looked to be a good-natured shrug. "As ready as I'll ever be."

LaDonna gave them all a motherly smile, despite likely being close to Sergio and Wade's age. She had a way about her, like she'd seen enough of the world to know exactly how much of it was real and how much was smoke, and August liked and respected it.

"Let's get started, then."

August swallowed a lump of what he was sure was anxiety and drew closer to LaDonna.

"What—what do I do?" His voice came out rough, revealing his tension, and he hated it.

"Why don't we sit down?" LaDonna suggested. "You need to relax some, or this won't work."

Embarrassed that his tension was so apparent, he trailed her to the couch. He, Ida, and LaDonna assumed the same seats they had yesterday. The memory of the herb he'd smoked lingered on his tongue — unpleasant, bitter. Except this time, Rebecca, Sergio, Wade, and Derek hovered in the background like a murder of crows, watching the whole thing unfold.

LaDonna regarded the group over her shoulder. "Depending on how well August does, I may need you to step into the other room. He needs to focus."

Not feeling like I'm on display would help, August thought wryly.

Sergio nodded, calm as ever, while Wade's expression screamed his displeasure. The guy hated being excluded, especially when the events here were the key to his trip home.

"All right, August." LaDonna's gaze fixed on him now, calm and intense. "I need you to focus for me, okay?"

His eyes flicked to Ida. She caught his glance and gave a quick nod, and his heart rate slowed a little.

"Close your eyes, August," LaDonna said, her voice low and soothing. "I need you to let go of what you see in front of you. You need to pay attention to the things you can't see."

He sighed and followed her direction. With his eyes closed, the room felt too big, like the walls had taken a step back. He forced on the sensation of the sofa under his backside to keep him grounded. "I'm not feeling anything," August muttered.

Ida let out a small laugh. "Maybe they're scared of you, August. Not the other way around."

He opened one eye and gave her a dry look. "I doubt that."

"Close your eyes, August," LaDonna admonished. "You need to block out any distractions. What we're looking for isn't on this side of things."

He heard Ida whisper "I'm sorry" to LaDonna, and he forced himself to focus on internal things. His heartbeat. His breathing. It wasn't much, but it was enough to tether him to the moment.

That's better.

"Focus on your breathing. In… out…" LaDonna's voice was soft but commanding, and August was pleased to know he'd had the right idea. He followed her voice as easily as a clear-cut trail in the woods, her words making him confident that this would be a happy journey, not a frightening discovery.

Gradually, with each breath, the edges of his awareness blurred. The room felt even more distant, almost like it was slipping away from him. The sounds—footsteps, creaking floors, the scraping of shrubbery on the window glass—faded until it was just him and LaDonna's voice.

"Good," she whispered, like she could sense the shift. "Now, don't force anything. Don't try to control it—just let yourself *see*."

His pulse quickened, but not with fear. Anticipation hummed through his veins. His jaw clenched as he fought to calm the thrum of energy building inside him. For a moment, nothing happened. Then, slowly, like a veil lifting, the air shifted around him. It wasn't dramatic like he'd expected—no sudden gusts of wind or dazzling insights—but it was there. The atmosphere felt electric, like the room had grown smaller, more intimate. He wasn't sure what he had been expecting, but it wasn't the way he noticed all the energy in the room thrumming like neon.

And he could hear it.

A fluttering sound emerged from just behind his left ear. A shadow grew in his mind's eye, the presence of someone he almost knew. It passed through a corner of his consciousness and moved—glided—before him. He had the urge to try something and went with it.

He opened his eyes.

And there, standing beyond LaDonna's shoulder, but before the doppelgangers, stood a man. He wasn't entirely there, but August had eased into his altered state enough to discern the newcomer's details. A leonine face. Thick eyebrows, thick lips. Wavy hair that August guessed was brown, but it was hard to tell because of the being's translucence. Eyes that were likely a striking shade of blue when he'd been alive.

"Are you Clark?" he ventured. The man met his eyes, and the corners of his lips rose in a smile.

"I am. Nice to meet you, August." Clark's voice was a whisper of the baritone it had once been, but it was audible. To him, at least. Though others looked around, no one else's eyes landed on the ghost he saw and heard.

Holy shit.

☙ ❧

"Clark, can you tell me about the others?" Rebecca asked. She spun around in a slow circle, the sound of her boots scraping against the dusty wooden floor as she spoke, almost as if expecting to pick up on where Clark stood if she tried hard enough. Dust danced in the thin beams of light filtering through the room.

Clark's response sounded like a poorly tuned radio. "Th-ere's Le-ah Mad-son. She's—teen. And Mi-nnie. Mi-nn-e Wen-ke."

Wenke? As in Frank Wenke?

Marina's mind jumped to the yellowed photo she'd seen tucked among the documents in the portfolio—a stern-looking Frank Wenke standing beside a woman with dark, intense eyes. Hermina. She glanced at Zeke, who stood in the corner, leaning against the peeling wallpaper. His eyes narrowed as if by will alone he could see through the veil between realms. When their eyes met, he raised an eyebrow in a silent question but said nothing.

"Is Minnie's full name Hermina?" Marina hated the tentative tone in her voice, but the idea of speaking to beings in another realm was more than a little terrifying.

The answer came not from Clark but from another voice that had none of Clark's broken connection.

"I am Hermina," the feminine voice said, the faintest hint of a German accent in her delivery. If Marina's own family had not been German, she might have missed it. "Who is this? How are you speaking to us?"

Zeke shifted his weight, arms crossed, his gaze flitting between the resonator, Rebecca, and Marina. Marina knew he was absorbing every word, every detail, just like a good cop would—trying to deduce the answers they sought from any clues that might emerge from the conversation.

"I am Rebecca," the scientist said, "and my friend is Marina. We would love to speak to you, if that's alright. We are speaking to you through machinery I developed to speak to beings on a plane other than mine."

"No sorcery?" Minnie asked, her voice edged with suspicion.

"I wouldn't know the first thing about sorcery," Rebecca assured her.

"This is all science. I could walk you through it if you like, but I suspect the specifics might sound… foreign." She adjusted a dial on the Resonator, and the hum coming through the headset grew louder. Zeke stepped closer, and while he didn't say a word, his expression said he wasn't about to let anything get past him.

"I would," Minnie said, her voice stronger now. "But please, I… I am not familiar with modern machinery."

"May I ask when you passed?" Rebecca inquired.

"I died in 1875."

Holy hell.

"I can try to make it very basic," Rebecca offered.

"Please. I would appreciate that greatly."

With that, Rebecca took Minnie, and, by proxy, Marina and Zeke, through the functions of each part of the Spectrosonic Resonator. Zeke unfolded his arms, stepping closer to get a better look at the device Rebecca was only too proud to explain. Marina thought she did an excellent job touching on the functions of each part of the machine without making it sound as if she was dumbing-down the description. Hermina's voice made no interruptions during Rebecca's explanation, and when the scientist asked in conclusion if Minnie had questions, the spirit simply stated, "No. That is sufficient. And thank you for understanding my concern."

Rebecca paused before asking, "Was Frank Wenke your husband?"

A pause of equal measure lingered before Minnie answered. "He was. I take it you reviewed the contents of the compendium?"

"We have," Rebecca admitted. "But there is a lot we don't understand."

Another long silence. Marina was about to speak but then realized an agitated conversation was coming through the headphones—a quiet one. A third being was talking now, a young woman who finished her portion of the conversation by adamantly stating, "You have to tell them!"

"Minnie, are you there?" Rebecca asked.

"I am," Minnie replied.

"And Clark?"

"I'm here, too," the young woman who'd been in the background stated. It occurred to Marina that the static present as Clark spoke was conspicuously absent now. "My name's Leah. I'm forever sixteen, un-fucking-fortunately. And I died in nineteen fifty-nine."

"Did you die in the house as well?"

"We all did," Leah said. "That's why we're freaking stuck here. Minnie's husband made this place an energy trap—an eternal trap if you're dead."

"Is Frank—"

A sound like a Tesla coil machine broke through the headset, followed by a pounding sound so loud it felt inside her skull. Marina belatedly realized the sound was footsteps raised to a thunderously loud volume by the resonator. She ripped the headset off with a wince and turned to find herself face to face with the man who'd walked through the wall yesterday, trailed by the last person she expected to see.

Chapter Twenty-seven

"Hi, Clark," August said, sounding more like a breathy fangirl than he would have liked as he took in the specter's less-than-opaque aspects—like his pleated slacks and oxford shirt with the sleeves rolled to his elbows, his dated haircut, his lopsided grin. "Um… nice to meet you. Officially, I mean."

Clark smiled, his ghostly eyes bright, removing any apprehension August may have felt that the man was anything but genuinely friendly. Clark had that kind of easy warmth that made you forget you were talking to a dead guy.

"He's here?" LaDonna asked, joy brightening her face.

"He is," August replied. "He's, um… about thirty, like you said. Wavy hair. Blue eyes. A friendly face."

Ida reached over and slipped her fingers through his, gently squeezing his hand. He clasped hers tightly, allowing her presence to anchor him in this surreal moment.

"That's him," LaDonna said, her eyes glassy with unshed tears. August couldn't tell now if they were for joy or sadness. Perhaps it was both.

"It's nice to meet you as well," Clark said. "I'm sorry our last meeting was under such horrible circumstances."

"Yeah, no kidding," August mumbled.

Clark started to speak but was cut short. August didn't have time to blink before Sergio strode through Clark to be closer to August during the seemingly one-sided conversation. Wade followed close behind Sergio. Clark shuddered and let out a sound between a wail and a howl.

The spirit quaked and twitched his arms as if trying to shake off water for several seconds. August winced in sympathy. He had no idea what the ghost was experiencing, but from the look of it, he didn't care to find out. He waited until he was sure Clark would be alright before starting again. "That bad?"

"What happened?" Ida asked, eyes wide.

August snorted. "Sergio and Wade just walked through him," August said, barely holding back a laugh.

Sergio's eyebrows shot up, his mouth dropped, and he threw his hands up in a mea culpa gesture. "My bad, dog. I'm sorry."

With an identical expression of horror on Wade's face, he croaked, "I'm sorry! I didn't know."

Clark, now steady again, gave a tired smile. "I'll live—well, figuratively speaking. Please tell them I'm fine."

"He's OK," August communicated to the others. His curiosity piqued, he asked, "What does that feel like?"

Clark scoffed. "Ever have a relative say someone was going to have a come-apart?"

"Yeah, my grandma used to say that when someone was losing their mind over nothing," August laughed.

"It feels like a literal come-apart," Clark said. "Like my body falls apart into about a billion or so atoms for a moment and then snaps back together."

August blinked. "Whoa."

"Yeah," Clark agreed. "Not something I'd recommend. Thankfully, it's usually avoidable. But anyway, about your question. The thing that forced its way into you? We call things like that a Passerby. This house is… what is that word?"

August opened his mouth to say he didn't know when a woman entered the scene. This ghost had delicate features, a small upturned nose, and her hair was gathered at the back of her head in what he believed Ida had called a French twist. Her direct gaze hinted at a sharp intellect beneath her refined exterior. She wore a dress with a high, fitted collar that reminded August of dresses from the nineteenth century.

"It's a gateway," she said. "Multiple gateways, to be precise. Frank intended it to allow spirits to enter easily when he called. Regrettably, when he died, he… left the door open, so to speak."

"That's amazing," August breathed. "Another ghost."

Rebecca's eyes lit up, her gaze fixed on August with barely contained awe. "You're really talking to him. And he's answering. That's incredible," she murmured, half to herself. "I never thought I'd actually see anything like this."

"My apologies, sir," the woman said. "My name is Minnie Wenke. My husband built this house."

"Hell-hole, you mean," came a third voice. A young woman entered the room. Another spirit, one with a heart-shaped face, full lips, and bold, expressive eyes. Everything about her screamed "late-fifties rebel," from her crop-sleeved T-shirt to her high-waisted denim shorts and how she bore herself with feminine confidence and defiance.

"This is Leah," Minnie said, her tone apologetic, like a mom introducing her wayward daughter.

"A third ghost," August said by way of explanation to the living beings in the room. "Minnie and Leah."

"God bless," Ida muttered. "How many people have died in this house?"

"Five," Minnie said. "My husband Frank, me, Leah, Clark… and one other. What was his name?" She turned her attention to Clark, then Leah.

"Jeffrey," Leah mumbled. "Jeffrey Brown. Died in the seventies. You weren't around yet," she added, looking at Clark.

Clark placed a reassuring hand on Leah's arm, and August marveled at how their colors strengthened where they came into contact with one another. "You've mentioned him before."

"He got out," Leah said, her eyes closed as her jaw trembled slightly. "How'd he get out?"

"He died of a heart attack," Minnie explained. "His death was not… self-inflicted."

"Neither was yours!" Leah argued. The conversation had the tones of one that had played out many times before.

"No, but I… am part of the home," Minnie explained. "I think Frank's plan to live forever bound me here. He wanted to keep me with him."

"And yet, Frank got out," Leah added bitterly as she crossed her arms. Clark and Minnie had no reply to that. August relayed the conversation to the others.

"I thought Frank didn't want to die," Rebecca observed. "But his death was self-inflicted?"

Minnie paused, her countenance grave. Her hands fidgeted at her sides for a moment. "Frank was… a very troubled man."

Once again, August passed on what he heard. Then he asked the ghosts, "You've never tried the portals — uh, gateways?"

Leah snorted. "They weren't meant for us," she said. "Just for the dead who need a place to pass through."

"So, they don't stay? And you don't know where they go?"

"No," Clark admitted.

"Can you see the gateways all the time?"

"Only when the Passersby are moving through," Clark said. "And I saw them when you were about to walk through one, and again just before you returned."

August relayed this to the others in the room.

"It sounds to me that you are an indigo witch with an extra gift," LaDonna said. "That's a blessing. Not many have that."

"How many witches do you know who do?" Ida inquired.

"I know one witch who is both red and brown, and one who is… let's say extra colorful," LaDonna replied with a sly smile.

"Do you think my ability to travel to other dimensions is tied to the weirdness of the house?" August asked. "Like, am I limited to passing through walls in this place?"

LaDonna pursed her lips in thought. "I doubt it. It's something we can look into, though."

"Another time, though," August said. "Today, we'll try to get Wade and Derek back home."

m €

August hated the effects of that god-forsaken herb LaDonna had him smoking. He really, *really* hated it. He'd much rather sit back with a short glass of some shine, maybe something infused with tasty herbs like rosemary or juniper berries. But what he hated even more was the idea of that little boy of Wade's spending the rest of his life away from his mother. August knew something about how that felt; he wouldn't wish it on anyone.

So, when LaDonna picked up her brown paper bag from the side table, he braced himself for another trippy experience on a mental carnival ride. He watched as she packed the pipe, Wade peering over her shoulder like a curious kid. Once Wade seemed convinced the herb wasn't illegal, his posture relaxed, and he moved a few steps away to lean against the wall. August noticed how LaDonna moved her lips as she pressed the herbs into place.

Casting a spell, probably. It didn't matter. August trusted her at this point.

Herbs packed, LaDonna paused a moment with the pipe clasped in her weathered hands, which were settled in the folds of her skirt. With closed eyes, she took a few deep, even breaths. The calm that settled over her reached beyond her. The very air around LaDonna took on a serene quality he couldn't define, but watching her engaged in her practice calmed him. Without being aware of it, his breaths slowed until they matched hers. The reluctance he'd felt moments ago evaporated in LaDonna's calming presence. August wondered if her power had him spellbound to the point he shared in her serenity. It didn't matter—if she had, he was grateful.

Rebecca sat nearby, her notebook open on her lap, pen poised as she scribbled notes furiously. Despite her reserved demeanor, her gaze darted between August, LaDonna, and the pipe with a mixture of fascination and scientific curiosity. "I can't believe this works for you," she said softly, half to herself. "I mean, herbs influencing dimensional perception… it's incredible. But also terrifying."

"Terrifying's about right," August muttered, glancing at her. "But, hey, if it gets the job done…"

She gave a small, wry smile, but her eyes lingered on the pipe with that same curiosity.

LaDonna passed the pipe and a lighter to August. Everyone's eyes were on him, and he grew a tad self-conscious.

"Ok, so here's the plan," August said. "Wade, you're going to give me your cell phone. I'm going to smoke this," he held up the pipe, "and I'm going to see if I can't make my way back to that house I saw before. I'll turn on the phone. If it works, I'll come back and take Derek over. I know I can at least do that. He can't weigh any more than Misty did."

Heads nodded all around the room, and his confidence grew.

"Then I'm going to come back and see how I feel. I might need more… stuff." August motioned to the paper sack of herbs. "I don't know how long it lasts, but I'll take more if I do. Then, hopefully, I'll take Wade across and come home. Sound good?"

"Sounds amazing," Wade let out a huge exhale.

Rebecca scribbled something else in her notebook, paused, and put the end of her pen near her lips, tapping them thoughtfully. "I wonder," she murmured. "What exactly triggers the portal? Is it always open? Do they move?"

August shrugged. "Beats me." He took a deep breath, let it out in a sigh, and lit the pipe. He inhaled the magical herb filling his lungs with bitter smoke, held it in for a moment, and let it out in a relaxed *whoosh*.

The herb hit fast this time. Perhaps he had some residual drug in his system from his previous experience. His vision grew watery, then oddly pixelated. Someone spoke, but he couldn't process the words; they echoed over and over like wavy, distorted movie dialogue. Colors shifted—dark ones deepened into black, bright ones melted into autumnal oranges, yellows, and red as if they were crayons in the summer sun.

"Whoa," he murmured.

The room turned into a kaleidoscope of swirling hues, and he stood carefully, not trusting his eyes or legs. The room itself rocked side to side like a rowboat on choppy water.

"Phone," he gasped, holding out his hand. At least, he thought he did. It felt like Wade had dropped something into his palm. He curled his fingers around an object that felt vaguely like a plastic brick and stumbled toward the hallway, the shiny silver door beckoning and shimmering. Nobody stopped him, so he figured he was doing something right.

Not that he could tell, anyway.

Rebecca's voice came through the fog just before he reached the door. "August, wait. How does it feel to… you know, move between dimensions?"

"I don't know. Like being on a rollercoaster in the dark, maybe?" he said, his voice slurred. He blinked at her before lifting an index finger and muttering, "I'll let you know when I get back."

He paused before the portal, wavering as he stood, blinked as if it'd help clear his vision of the wild images before him, and stepped through the gateway. Gateway, portal, door, passage…

and into the dining room of the restored version of the Victorian house in the other dimension.

It looked like the right house. And the trip into the new world had dulled the worst of his mind fog.

He took Wade's phone and turned it on. It buzzed to life as messages poured in.

Holy shit. This is the right dimension. Holy shit! He paused and lifted his head as a faint conversation caught his attention. He walked as quietly as possible, keeping himself distant so he didn't draw attention to his presence, but close enough to hear the conversation.

"I would. But please, I... I am not familiar with modern machinery."

That's Minnie!

"May I ask when you passed?"

And Rebecca!

"I died in 1875."

Holy hell.

He couldn't stop himself from risking a quick peek around the corner. Not only was Rebecca there, but Wade's wife and—holy crap, was that Ez?

Not Ez. Zeke. Damn, this is weird.

The drug made the walls wavy, and he caught himself on a threshold as he swooned, his fingertips turning white with the pressure of his grip. He let out a soft breath, found his balance, tiptoed his way back to the portal, and slipped back through.

August stumbled into the hall, the vibrant colors of the other house fading into the faded surroundings of the dilapidated Victorian in his timeline. He blinked a few times, trying to shake off the kaleidoscope of images dancing before him. Everyone was watching him like he'd just stepped off a spaceship. A ghost drifted by on his left, and he jumped as if he'd been goosed.

He waved the phone in the air, the buzzing now gone with the return to his world. "OK. So... good news." His words slurred slightly, so he paused, straightened his tongue out, and pushed through. "Wade, your wife... Derek's mom? She's there. Like now. She's in the house over there. Now."

"What?" Wade nearly flew off the couch. "You're serious?"

"As a heart attack," August muttered, rubbing his eyes. "Sorry, Leah. I forgot about your friend Jeff. Anyway, I heard her talking to Rebecca and Minnie. Over there. She sounds the same. All three of them sound the same. So… yeah, right dimension. I don't know what your wife sounds like in your world, but she sounds the same as the lady I ran into the last time I was over in that world, so… Yeah, definitely."

Rebecca said nothing, her hand hovering near her notebook. It was clear she was itching to ask questions, to hold August to his promise to tell her what it felt like to slip between worlds, but she held back, letting August focus.

LaDonna cocked her head. "You sure, August? You're lookin' a little… wobbly."

August nodded, still trying to find his balance. "Trust me, I wouldn't mess this up. I swear."

Wade stood up. "Derek?"

"Right here." Derek's voice piped up from his father's side. The boy was practically bouncing on his heels. "I'm ready!"

August turned to him, blinking a few times to clear his vision. "You said you saw the shiny spot, right? The one on the wall?"

Derek nodded, pointing at the silver door that hung in the hallway. "Yeah. I can see it clear as day. Not always, though. It kinda showed up today when LaDonna got here."

"Figures, August muttered, shaking his head. "No herb for you, kiddo. Guess you've got natural talent."

LaDonna chuckled softly. "Looks like we've got ourselves another gifted one."

Rebecca finally spoke up. "So, the portal responds to Derek, but not consistently? Could it be tied to something environmental — or emotional?"

August blinked at her, his brain still sluggish. "Good question. Add it to the list," he said with a faint smirk before turning back to the group.

August gave Derek a half-smile, then turned back to the group. "OK, this is what I'm thinking. I'll take Derek through first, like we talked about. If everything works like we hope it should, I'll come back for Wade." His brain felt like it was swimming in molasses, but he swallowed, got a grip on his nerve, and held out his hand for Derek.

The kid leaped forward and took his hand, looking more eager than anyone should be to step into another dimension. "Let's do this."

"Alright, kid," August said, straightening up and feeling himself waver. His stomach rolled, but he fought it down. "Stick close to me. Don't wander off. If you see something weird… well, just ignore it for now."

Derek grinned and gave him an enthusiastic head bob. "Got it."

With one last look around the room — and a slightly wobbly thumbs-up to Wade — August led Derek toward the shimmering portal. The kid didn't hesitate as they stepped through the silver doorway together. The now familiar, surreal sensation washed over August as they crossed dimensions, but Derek didn't seem phased. In less time than it took to take a full breath, they stood in the dining room of the restored Victorian home. The smell of air freshener floated in the air. It smelled like cookies.

August glanced down at Derek, still trying to wrap his head around the fact that Derek could see all of this without the herb.

"What did you feel when we walked through the portal?"

"Um," Derek said, eyes gleaming. "It's like… I felt a little wavy. And kinda… I don't know, it hums."

August raised an eyebrow. "Hums?"

"Yeah. Like it's… alive." Derek shrugged, like it was the most normal thing in the world.

"Of course it does," August muttered. "Of course it does."

Chapter Twenty-eight

Derek's father's phone appeared enormous in the kid's little birdlike hand. The dreaded words NO SERVICE disappeared as August watched, replaced with a full line of signal bars. Derek beamed, bit his lower lip excitedly, and then peered up at August for guidance.

Well, August thought, *we're either back in Wade's dimension, I'm still hallucinating, or his service plan covers alternate realities.*

The world wobbled a little, but the worst of the drug was wearing off, thankfully. August needed to get Derek to Marina before the effects completely vanished. And preferably before they decided August was a prowler. He wasn't sure if the women in the other room were armed—this was Alabama, after all, and they were technically trespassing. He wasn't about to gamble with the possibility of someone packing heat and being a fan of the "shoot first, ask questions later" philosophy. Once they saw Derek, all would be forgiven.

Way to go, August. Even high, you're still a problem-solver!

He tugged on Derek's hand and led him to the other room where Rebecca—the "other world" version of Rebecca—stood near a funny-looking device. Marina and Ez—Not Ez, Zeke—were there too. All three had headphones in their hands and a baffled expression on their faces. Each looked at their headset as if it had just tried to bite them.

Marina was the first to notice their presence. Her eyes lit up with recognition at seeing August. Then her gaze landed on Derek. The flood of emotions on her face—relief, disbelief, pure joy—hit August like a punch to the chest.

"Derek!"

She dropped to a crouch. Derek needed no more encouragement. He practically threw Wade's phone to August and bolted into her arms. Marina scooped him up, holding him so tight August wondered how the kid could breathe. One hand cradled his head, pressing it to her shoulder, while the other wrapped around his slight frame, clutching him like she'd never let him go.

"You're home!" she whispered, her voice thick with emotion. "Oh, baby, you're home! Oh, thank the Lord. Thank you, Lord."

August hovered awkwardly in the background, shifting his weight from heel to toe, trying not to intrude on the moment. It was like he was witnessing a miracle, and for a brief second, he felt like a hero. He hoped the cop looming in the background agreed.

After a prolonged embrace, Marina held Derek at arm's length.

"Where's your father, sweetheart?" she asked softly.

"He's in August's world!" Derek said excitedly, pointing back at his companion.

August cleared his throat and hooked a thumb toward his chest. "Uh, I'm... I'm August."

Marina's brows met toward the middle of her brow. "August's world? How did you get here?"

That she was willing to accept they'd crossed dimensions to come home told August a great deal about how Marina must have spent the last couple of days.

"I can walk through dimensional portals," he explained. "But not all the time. I have to use... something. It's a long story. Anyway, I knew I could bring Derek back because the last time I crossed through a portal, I brought a dog back with me. And Derek here is little, so I figured I could bring him home without a problem."

Marina's grateful expression made August's heart swell with pride. "Thank you." She breathed. "Will you bring Wade across as well?"

August rubbed the back of his neck as a half-smile crept across his face. "That's the plan," he said with a half-smile. "But I gotta move quick. This... stuff I'm using doesn't last long. If I don't return soon, I might be stuck here, and I don't know if I can find the same thing in this world."

Baffled, Marina stood, but not before she had Derek's hand clasped in hers. "Alright. Be careful, August. And hopefully, I'll see you soon."

With one last look at the two of them—their small reunion scene still tugging at his heart—he turned and hurried back toward the portal. He'd gotten Derek home. Now, it was Wade's turn.

ᛒ ᛒ

The lingering traces of the herb burned out of August's system as he crossed the silvery threshold back into the familiar, musty, worn-down Victorian. He inhaled a deep breath of it, grateful to have returned. The glow of Marina's joy still lifted his spirits.

Wade raced to his side faster than he would have guessed he could.

Guess all those donuts don't weigh him down much, he thought. *Cop life must keep him fit.*

"Derek?" Wade's voice held a sharp edge of hope.

"With Marina," August said with a grin. "She was so relieved. Oh, here." He threw Wade's phone at him. The big man easily caught it, a grin splitting his face.

"Thank you," Wade said, his voice gruff with gratitude. August could tell he was debating between a handshake and a bear hug. Fortunately, he stuck with a nod.

Rebecca appeared at August's side, her brow furrowed with concern. "You look like you've been through a wringer," she said softly, her tone tinged with humor but underpinned by worry. "Are you okay? Do you need anything before you do this again?"

August gave her a small, tired smile. "I'm good. Just need more of LaDonna's magic herbs and spices, and I'll be ready."

Rebecca's lips twitched into a smile, though her eyes retained their watchful edge. "If you're sure. Just… be careful, okay?" Her voice dropped to a murmur. "We're all counting on you."

Turning to LaDonna, August held out a hand. "Got any more of that magic herb?" he asked, a smirk tugging at his mouth. "I'm gonna need it. My last dose is long gone."

LaDonna reached into her paper sack and showed him she'd packed extra herb. She extended it and the pipe toward him and pressed them into August's hands.

Rebecca hovered nearby, still observing him. "You're taking a lot in pretty close succession," she said quietly, her voice for his ears only. "It's okay to take a moment if you need it. I'm sure Wade will understand if it means it keeps you safe."

August shot her a lopsided grin. "You're gonna make me feel like I'm going into battle. It's just a door."

"A door that bends reality," Rebecca quipped, a dry note of humor creeping in. "No pressure, though."

August slipped around the couch to sit by Ida again, realizing that Ez had arrived in the short time he'd been gone. It was a little surreal, seeing two versions of the same guy in one room, but existing in two different worlds.

He took the pipe and lighter from LaDonna and paused. Was the atmosphere in the room tenser than it had been? It seemed to August that something more significant than the trip through a dimensional portal was about to take place. Everyone's eyes rested on him.

August's heart raced. This was it. He had to come to grips with what frightened him. It was time to bring a man who probably outweighed him by ninety pounds through a door that was only there sometimes back into his own dimension. Bringing Misty and Derek hadn't seemed as substantial and accomplishment, but Wade… With everything he had, he hoped that weight wasn't an issue when it came to trans-dimensional travel.

Don't be stupid. You're paranoid because everyone is staring at you.

August lit the herb and breathed in, held, and released. He took in Wade's height and girth and decided that another half-hit might not be a bad idea. He pulled in another small toke, the smoke prickling his lung like tiny cactus spines, held it a heartbeat, and breathed out a plume of smoke that coiled and unfurled, traveling like the stars in a work of Van Gogh.

"Heere I go again," August slurred, feeling the world around him ripple and distort. The wall across from him became inverted, then righted itself, but the world remained wavy and unstable. Everyone's faces looked a little like a horror-movie ghost mask in varying flesh tones. The flowers in LaDonna's blouse began dancing, as did the fringe on Ida's denim shorts. He snorted.

"Wavy gravy," he joked.

He looked toward the two identical men. "Wade," he said to one with a pointed finger, furrowed his brow, and pointed the finger at the second man. "Wade."

The first man laughed. Gone was the despondence he once displayed now that the return to his world was imminent. "Should have stuck with your first guess, my friend." He slung an arm around August's shoulders and gave him a solid, friendly thump. "Come on. Show me where the door home is."

With a dazed grin, August nodded, doing his best to focus. "Alright, big guy," he said. "Let's go find that shiny door."

Rebecca's voice followed him as he steadied himself. "Be careful, August. And come back in one piece."

He glanced back at her, giving her a mock salute. "Yes, ma'am."

ဆ ဆ

Harper slapped another mosquito from the back of her leg, muttering a curse under her breath before turning her attention back to the rifle scope. So much for insect repellent. She'd practically bathed in the stuff, but the bugs kept coming. Alabama mosquitoes must drink this crap like it's a mojito special. She smirked — mosquito mojitos. She chuffed at the thought.

Unlike her seemingly unlimited supply of "mosquito mojitos," Harper's patience had just about run dry. Normally, stoicism and perseverance were more characteristic of her. It was why she'd made a lucrative career as an assassin. Recklessness and disregard for laws and morals did not blend well if one wanted a long career.

Ten years in, though, and she was ready to move on to a more relaxing life. It was time for a house of her own, along with a beach somewhere warm, a fruity drink in hand — and mojitos with no fucking mosquitoes.

Her gaze drifted back to the derelict house, shadowed and strangely ominous. She still hadn't pieced together what they were doing in there. It sure wasn't a renovation team; nobody had come in with so much as a hammer. And they didn't look like house hunters, either — too mismatched, too tense around each other. So, what was it?

It didn't matter. What mattered was the absolutely obscene amount of money the Kightlinger couple was going to send her for the small favor of pulling a trigger. That was what mattered.

She eased a pistol out of her kit, twisted on the silencer, and set the weapon on the ground beside her. Next, she pulled out a pair of rubber gloves and a cleaning kit, setting about the meticulous task of wiping down her rifle. No fingerprints. No DNA. Nothing to show she'd ever been there. That done, she buried the Winchester in her shallow trench and brushed leaves over it to hide the dislodged dirt. Gloves off and tucked into her back pocket, she stood slowly, stretching out her legs as she surveyed the house for movement.

She'd had enough of waiting around, hoping she might have a chance at the perfect opportunity to get her shot off without a witness's detection. For the amount the Kightlighters were paying her, a couple of bodies in collateral damage was worth the extra effort. If it meant more than one person had to die for her to retire in comfort, so be it. It was time to get her hands dirty.

Chapter Twenty-nine

August weaved on wobbling legs to the gleaming portal that had appeared on the wall shortly after his second pull on La-Donna's magical herb. During his trip with Derek, he hadn't noticed any Passersby in the house, but now several loomed nearby. Had their observation always been so furtive, their presence so dark and unnerving? He couldn't recall them actively watching him before, their gazes probing, their ghostly bodies swimming like eager, hungry, circling sharks.

Then again, maybe it was the drugs that made the dim morning shadows swirl and coil like they were ready to pounce.

With every step nearer to the door, the air in the room grew heavier and thicker. The Passersby, which had appeared predatory and excited before, now swarned around Wade and him like sharks in a pool of chum.

It's the drugs. It's gotta be the drugs. I'm having a bad trip, that's all.

But Wade's grip on his shoulder had grown tense and claw-like, his body rigid. Even though Wade was a brick wall of a man, he'd sensed the unseen forces, and it had the man on edge.

Ida's voice came from behind him, soft and anxious. "Do y'all feel that?"

The remaining walk was less than ten steps away. Ten steps, and he'd have Wade back in his world. So why did he feel like a stowaway on a pirate ship being forced to walk the plank to his death?

Passersby floated frantically around them now. August squinted, trying to keep his direction steady, but the shadows combined with the herb's effects blurred his vision, grays and blues melding into dazzling silver specters. Only Wade, who saw no distractions, kept August from losing his footing in the swirl of grays, blues, and brilliant, ghostly silvers.

"You holding up?" Wade asked, his tone more serious than curious. The voice of a cop dealing with a tense situation.

"Yeah, I, uh… a lot is going on." August's attention darted from ghost to ghost, from dancing shadow to new beings emerging from the walls and ceilings like virtual ectoplasmic waterfalls. All of them aggravated. Every single one focused on Wade and August.

"It's not the drugs, is it?" Wade asked, but it wasn't a question. His cop instinct must have clued him to the activity behind the spiritual veil.

"No. Not entirely," August admitted. "The Passersby, the other ghosts, they're agitated. I'm kinda new at this. I don't know if it's normal or —"

"It's not," a troubled voice cut through his haze, unmistakably Clark's.

"The temperature's dropped about ten degrees between the couch and where we're standing," Wade observed.

"Something bizarre is going on," Leah murmured, her gaze darting as she traced the movement of the agitated spirits. "I've never seen them act like this."

"They have never acted like this before," Minnie interjected. "And I have a feeling I know why."

August and Wade had advanced only two steps before a path cleared between them and the portal. Fluttering in a nervous flurry, Passersby hastily assembled on either side like soldiers parting for a figure they recognized — or feared. When the swirling energies and creeping shadows subsided, a being stood. Not a Passerby. Not a ghost. Not a man, either. An entity that was part of all of those, and yet none of those — wholly *unearthly*.

Without being told, August discerned that this was an entity woven from the fabric of the house itself. His wavy brown hair framed piercing gray eyes, and a thick, meticulously groomed beard traced his jaw and chin with a prominent mustache. His clothes were sharply tailored, a high-collared shirt with a black cravat pinned in place, the immaculate lines of his Victorian jacket and waistcoat standing in stark contrast to the faded decay around him.

August had seen this face before, in an old photograph, this same man standing alongside Hermina and Helena Blavatsky.

This was Frank Wenke himself, the house's architect and, possibly, its very soul.

⌇ ⌈

Wenke's gaze swept over them, intense and unreadable, his form both present and somehow not, as if he were both a ripple in reality and simultaneously profoundly ingrained within the fabric of the house—the very thing that made it *alive*. The sight and sensation made August's thoughts tumble in confusion that went beyond the sickening sensations he already suffered in his altered state of mind.

If there was any doubt about who it was, it disappeared when he heard Minnie breathe, "Frank!" Her voice trembled with recognition and fear.

From the corner of his eye, August watched as Leah stepped to Minnie's side, taking her hand. Clark drew close as well, and together, the three stood, silent and watchful, as Frank and August faced off.

August was about to explain what was transpiring to those without spiritual sight, but then he heard Sergio speak from the neighboring room.

"Mary, mother of God." The room remained silent, punctuated only by the brief sound of Sergio crossing himself.

"You see it, too?" Ez's voice was filled with awe.

"I think we all do," Ida said. "Holy crap. There are so *many* of them!"

Rebecca stood near the back of the room, her wide eyes darting from Frank to August. She didn't say a word, but the tension in her posture spoke volumes.

Wenke's presence must make it possible for the others to see everything. But then he recalled the conversation with the ghosts earlier. *I thought Frank didn't want to die. But his death was self-inflicted?*

Bits of conversation from the past day started clicking into place like bits of a puzzle. Frank's obsession with staying alive. The way he'd dedicated his life obsessing over every inch of the house, studying occult lore, honing every inch of its designs until even the most minute detail channeled something beyond its architecture, and the structure became more than walls and timber.

Wenke's close relationship with the spirit he called Brightness, who was undoubtedly anything but holy. The way the house drew spirits from unknown realms and allowed them to use the house to pass through. The house, hidden and abandoned for years, remained untouched by time or decay. Dust had settled, colors faded, yet the wood held firm, and the foundations never faltered. A timeless prison that trapped souls that perished within its walls, where spirits wandered, unable to escape, and yet— Frank himself had never been seen.

Frank hasn't died. Frank is the house. He became the house!

Were the Passersby tied to Wenke? Did they bend to his will, hoping he'd grant them passage to their final realm? Or did they have another reason they moved in seamless unison, as if choreographed? Clearly, they kowtowed to him. How much power did the man have over them? And if Wenke wished them to harm Wade or him, would they become corporeal enough to inflict actual damage? He thought of the book that had appeared to nudge itself from the shelf enough to be noticed.

They can affect the physical realm if they want to. But how much? August's mouth grew dry, and he desperately wished the drug's effects would fade faster. Wenke now wavered before him like a stubbornly persistent mirage.

"Where do you think you're going, son?" Wenke asked sharply. His voice had the same faint hint of a German accent as his wife.

Keeping his gaze steady, August motioned to the man on his arm with a tilt of his head. "Taking him home."

Wenke shook his head, his eyes gray ice. "I think not." There was nothing but confidence in the man's delivery and the iron-clad confidence of a man who held all the cards. Nothing but surety in his stance. August was taller than the man by half a head, and he guessed they were of about the same stature—if ghosts could be said to have stature—but Frank Wenke met him eye to eye, his expression fixed and stony.

"You let me take the boy," August pointed out.

Was that the hint of a smile under the beard? "Your travels through this house are done."

"Why does it matter?" August asked.

"You cannot continue to travel through the portals." Frank's voice grew more clipped and severe with every word.

"Why not?" Wade asked.

Frank's jaw jutted slightly, and his expression darkened. "To do so will corrupt their very structure. Humans—living humans—were never meant to pass through them."

Corrupt the portals' structure? Or the house's?

"You've let me cross four times already—more if you count your house in the parallel world."

"Exactly. Each time you cross through, you weaken the very foundation I have lain, fraying what binds me here," Frank said, his voice cold and measured.

"Two more trips," August pleaded. "One for me to take Wade across," he motioned to the main with a slight lift of their intertwined arms, "And one back. Then I'll leave your precious portals alone."

"I'll not stand by and let you strip away all the power I spent over a century building!" Frank spat, the edge of all-consuming rage creeping into his eyes. His hands clenched into fists, and August couldn't help but wonder—what would a ghost's punch feel like?

"Frank, let him through," Minnie pleaded. "His wife and son are on the other side."

"Hold your tongue, woman!" Frank ordered, not bothering to look at the woman to whom he spoke. "As for you, August Webb, if you and your friend take so much as one more step toward that passage, you will see what a hundred and fifty years of mastering the knowledge of earth and sky makes one capable of wielding."

୭ ୬

Marina pulled her phone from her back pocket and looked at the screen for what was probably the tenth time. Five minutes had passed since the man—the one Derek had referred to as August—had vanished into the wall once more. Five very, very long minutes that were fraying her already frazzled nerves to shreds.

Her voice was steady, but barely. "It's been five minutes," she told Rebecca.

Derek's face remained calm, as though five minutes were nothing. "Don't worry, Mom. August will be back. He said he would, and he will."

Marina forced a smile, but worry etched into her features. She shot Rebecca a look that screamed a thousand concerns without a single word. She refused to share any more of her fear with Derek. She had to be strong.

The other woman shrugged. "It's possible Wade had some good-byes to say. And maybe time moves differently through the portal. Derek said they walked right through, but we don't know for sure, do we?"

"He's probably saying goodbye to Sergio," Derek said matter-of-factly, his innocent conviction oddly comforting.

Marina's head tilted. "Who's Sergio?"

Derek grinned. "Dad can tell you. It's... um... complicated." The young boy stood straight, proud of using the new, important word.

Before she could question him further, a shimmering at the wall caught their attention, pulling every gaze to the spot where August had vanished. Marina's heart raced, and her fingers closed tightly over her phone.

The portal re-opened, spilling silvery light that danced across the room, giving them a clear, if narrow, view into the other world. But the scene was not what Marina expected at all. A strange man in Victorian clothes stood between her, Wade, and August. An assembly of ghosts stood on either side of the opening.

Marina's eyes flicked to the rest of the room, and her breath caught.

They were no longer alone in the room. They shared the space with three others. They had to be ghosts. One was a woman in clothes from the 19th century. Another was a young lady in a style that Marina guessed was the late 1950s or early 1960s. And a man with a worn denim jacket, dressed like he'd probably graduated high school around the time Marina's mother had.

My God! It must be Clark, Minnie, and Leah.

From the other side of the dimensional breech before her, Wade mouthed her name, and it was like a siren song pulling her, arm out-stretched, to the rift between them.

"Wait," Clark said. And she froze.

☙ ❧

It was only the slightest of glances shared from the corner of their eyes, but that was all it took. Wade and August moved as one, advancing toward Frank Wenke and the portal, heedless of the potential consequences in their determination to get Wade home. Come apart or not, August was getting Wade through that gateway and then back to his plane and Ida before LaDonna's herb wore off.

Wenke didn't move against them. Neither did his ghostly foot soldiers. He didn't have to.

The house moved instead.

Floor planks peeled up like flat, wide snakes, groaning and cracking as they unfurled and their nails snapped free. Old, roughly hewn wood boards crept against their legs and ankles, impeding their progress, and August shuddered as splinters snagged his socks and scraped his legs raw. The wall before them trembled, shaken by a violent unseen force. August blinked repeatedly, hoping to clear the illusion from before him, but nothing changed save for the sly smile on Wenke's smug, psychopathic mouth.

August wasn't sure how much of what was before him was real and how much was herb, but when Wade jerked his arm from around August's shoulder and staggered, cursing as he struggled to yank his legs out from the grip of the tangling floorboards, August acted as well. He yanked and pulled at his legs with all his strength, but it didn't make a damn difference. The wood may as well have been made of iron.

"LaDonna!" Ida's voice was shrill, strained. "Can't you do something about this damn wood? Don't you have power over nature?"

LaDonna shook her head, her expression pained. "Living wood, yes." Her voice was tinged with sorrow and frustration. "This wood's been dead for at least a century. It's not within my power."

Desperation shot through the group. Zeke and Sergio lunged forward to help, only to find themselves also snared in the grip of the thick, snaking, twisted floorboards. Ida yelped and yanked her legs back from the planks at her feet as she, Rebecca, and

LaDonna leaped on the cushions of their chairs. Rebecca, clutching the back of her chair for balance, danced to avoid the predatory planks as she tried to stay out of the fray.

"Shit! How do we fight these fucking things?" Ida exclaimed.

The helplessness in her voice twisted August's gut. He needed to help Wade. But he longed to save Ida. And the house—Wenke's godforsaken house—seemed determined to keep them all on the defense, clawing for each step.

Crack.

Wade, determined not to let anything stop him, had somehow found the strength to snap the boards tangling first one foot. Then another. Now that he knew what to expect from the living floor, he moved deftly before August.

Wade slapped a hand on August's shoulder, and August paused in his battle with the floorboards.

"Brace yourself."

August, stunned but willing to trust, simply nodded, wide-eyed.

The big man must have studied martial arts because his foot struck at the boards holding August's legs with calculated force, breaking August free. And while it hurt like hell, it didn't incapacitate August. He'd have some hellacious bruises for a while, though. But he could move again as long as he managed to dance away from the twisting planks determined to seize hold of him.

Frank Wenke stepped to the side of the portal, and August couldn't believe their luck. A flicker of hope shot through him—had the man decided to let them go?

He hadn't. Of course he hadn't. Wenke made a slick motion with his hand toward Wade and August, and the ghosts standing sentinel on either side of them surged to life. August half expected to hear Wenke cry, "Seize them!" like a deranged villain, but the man didn't have to speak. His ghostly attendants swooped into the intervening space between August and the portal Wade so desperately needed.

As their spectral forms coalesced near the silvery gateway, the cosmic doorway rippled and brightened, affected by whatever force they inhabited. Through the portal's glow, August saw the other Wenke house, the restored one from the parallel plane—and who stood waiting beyond it.

"Marina," Wade breathed, his voice thick with emotion. The sight of her broke something within Wade, and he fought like a cornered wolverine, but to no avail. Their ghostly adversaries held him fast.

August, however, was conscious of more than the presence of Marina Barringer. Three ghostly souls stood in the opening, staring fixedly over August's shoulder.

"Holy crap," Leah said. The Leah in his world. "It's us!"

C3   & ᔡ

What the fuck are they doing in there?

Harper sidled up to the house, pistol in hand, intending to peer through the least obstructed window she could find on the side of the house where the ruckus was taking place. Once she reached within a few feet of the pane, however, she saw the flaw in her plan. Vines laced through the branches in front of the dusty windows, making her proximity not the advantage she'd hoped for. She cursed under her breath.

Sounds of destruction came from within the house. Ripping wood. Popping nails. Excited voices told her that a great deal of activity was happening within the house. Lots of wood being moved about. *Guess I was wrong. They must be demoing the house.* Either that or a hell of a fight had broken loose.

With luck, it was the sort of activity that would lend itself to a little clandestine work. The place already sounded like a war zone—a single silenced shot would barely raise an eyebrow. It might be possible for Harper to take her target out without anyone noticing. All she needed was luck. If August was on the side of the house nearest the single cleared doorway, she could enter, pop him, and sneak out before anyone noticed she was there.

It was a big if, but she'd taken riskier shots. At least with all this noise, she might not have to knock off as many people. The less mess, the better. She didn't mind bodies stacking up, but slipping out without a trail? Now, that was a fine art. It meant there was a better chance she'd escape without friction.

Harper crept to the front door, her finger slipping toward the trigger.

❧   ☙

Marina stood at the edge of the room, her hand hovering, fingertips inches away from the shimmering edge of the dimensional vortex. Though the ghostly man in old-fashioned clothes had stepped aside, she could hardly make sense of the commotion before her. For a moment, she thought she was seeing things—wooden floorboards splitting and rising, slithering like living creatures, snaking up Wade and August's legs, while the walls themselves pulsed and shuddered with bizarre spasms. The entire room shook like it was on the verge of ripping itself apart. But that couldn't be right.

Could it?

"Clark, why am I waiting?" Marina's voice came out sharper than she intended. "Something crazy is happening over there, and they need help. Wade is *almost home.*"

Clark's gaze remained fixed on the portal, his expression as composed as his tone. "I agree," he said with exaggerated calm. He sounded like he was trying to coax a panicked canine into allowing him to approach without getting bitten. "But I'm afraid you may do more harm than good."

Marina's jaw clenched as Wade struggled to free himself from the wooden bonds. "How?"

Rebecca glanced at Clark, tension tightening her mouth, but she didn't speak.

"Under the—weight, for lack of a better way to explain it—of another human passing through, the portal may collapse," Clark said. "It's not designed for corporeal passage."

Marina felt her whole body deflate in frustration. She clenched her fists, resisting the urge to scream.

"What can I do?"

Clark hesitated, but before he could answer, Leah's voice broke in, defiant and strong.

"You can't do anything," she said. "But *we* can try."

❧   ☙

Harper found the doorknob to the old house broken. She pushed the heavy door open, heedless of the squeaking hinges. The commotion from indoors more than masked any sound the door might make. A set of stairs to her right scaled to a gorgeous landing with stained-glass windows, and to the left—

What. The fuck?

The floors before her shifted, rippling and writhing, bending and buckling in undulating waves. August and another man—broad, dark-haired, and determined—struggled with the planks as they twined around their legs. That was bizarre enough, but more than that were the odd shapes floating around the room almost as if they were… capering. Was it smoke? No, whatever this was moved with intention. And its intention was to keep August and the man beside him from reaching some weird, warped, mirror-looking thing on the wall.

It wasn't a mirror, though. There was another room inside the glossy mirror-thing. So why did the edges sparkle like the light had turned into liquid and writhed around its edges?

Harper shook her head. A surge of unease twisted in her gut, her instinct screaming at her to run. Maybe these people *were* doing drugs in here, and she'd just become exposed to them. Some kind of hallucinogen in the air, potent enough to give her a contact high within a few shallow breaths. That would explain why they came out to this hidden old place. Who'd want this to be in the air where they *lived*? She'd have laughed if her nerves weren't strung so tight. Great. Just what she needed. A high fucking with her sense of reality as she closed in on her mark.

The heavy weight of the gun in her grip reminded her of why she was there. It was the only thing real in this madhouse.

Okay. Enough. The floor isn't moving. The walls aren't shimmering. The whole thing is bullshit.

Resolving to let go of trying to process the impossible, Harper braced herself. The floor wasn't moving. The wall wasn't shining. And there weren't any transparent—*things*—in the air. But since the world looked absolutely insane, she couldn't risk trying to take the hit from a distance and leaving. She had to be close. She had to ensure August was one hundred percent dead before she fled to guarantee her payout.

A trickle of doubt wormed its way into her thoughts. This entire scenario was wildly unusual. Even if she shot her target, could she trust herself to believe what she saw? Was she really going to take a shot in the middle of a drug-induced fog? But she had to.

I'll have to take a picture to look at once all of this shit wears off. It was a risk, even with a burner, but one she had to take. Just this once.

Gun clenched in her hand with a vice-like grip, Harper advanced toward the inexplicable chaos. One step. Two. The floor shuddered under her feet, and she faltered, then found her stance. Three. Four. She refused to believe in the way the floor quaked under her feet. It wasn't real. None of this was real.

Nothing mattered but reaching a distance that guaranteed a headshot, even in this insanity.

She fixated on August, who still writhed in the grasp of the wooden serpents. He looked desperate, exhausted, determined, but also terrified. It was almost satisfying to watch him like this. Almost.

She raised the gun, took a deep breath, and sighted down the barrel. The chaotic noises, weird shadows, and the unholy hum coming off the mirror all faded into the background. All that mattered was the gun, her aim, her breath, and her target.

Her finger poised on the trigger, she drew a steadying breath, exhaled, and froze just as one of those sentient smoke-shadow things dove in front of her and threw off her shot. Harper staggered back, barely keeping her grip on the gun.

Fuck!

Another step forward. Harper adjusted her aim again, determined to ignore the phantoms and apparitions. Bullets flew through smoke just fine. And if it was a ghost, she couldn't kill the bastard twice, could she?

It's not a ghost. It's a fucking hallucination. And hallucinations don't stop bullets.

The floor buckled again, roiling beneath her, a sickening motion that made her stomach churn. She caught herself by throwing her free hand against the shuddering wall as she fought for balance.

Damn it. If Harper didn't take her shot soon, she might not get another chance — these drugs might make her lose her mind. She took another breath, let go of the wall, and prepared to aim.

"August!" the bigger man shouted, his voice cutting through the noise. "Move!

Chapter Thirty

As one, the versions of Clark, Leah, and Minnie on either side of the quantum corridor moved to the gate. The ghosts at Wenke's command fought with Wade and August, who had only made slight progress to the portal because of the spectral tendrils that clawed and stretched toward them, wood splintering and twisting, striving to bind them once more. The living wood snaked around Wade and August, desperate to halt their progress, but the ghosts—Minnie, Clark, Leah—remained untouched.

As the six of them approached the passage to Wade's world, Minnie realized a critical truth.

They were part of the house, too.

Just as surely as Frank's death bound him in spirit to the house, her death, and those of Clark and Leah, had bound them to it as well. The three of them were also part of what made the house *alive.* And if it was Frank's will that made the house the nightmarish form their friends fought against now, *their* thoughts could save them.

"We are part of it, too!" Minnie exclaimed. As she said the words, she noted her spiritual equivalent on the other side echoing her thoughts to the duplicate version of Clark and Leah.

"What?" Leah asked.

"Frank's will—it's what has made the house this horrible thing we see now; but the three of us died here, too. We are also what makes this house alive. We're as much a part of what holds this place together as he is. And we can use that. We can fight it!"

"How?" Clark asked.

"We form a bridge around August and Wade and will it to stay open; that way, we anchor the gate to stabilize it. If we feed our energy into it, use the power of our presence to deny the house's ability to let anything happen to them, we may weaken

Frank's grip, protect them from the ghosts, and give them a chance to escape."

It was surreal watching the other world's version of her narrate the same revelation to her twin friends. Their counterparts in the parallel dimension mirrored every movement, simultaneously moving to the struggling humans' side, then stretching their spectral arms forward until the six of them surrounded August and Wade, forming a spiritual barrier to keep Frank's malevolent ghosts away and the portal open. As they touched, their forms rippled with energy. They became faintly translucent, then almost skeletal, as their otherworldly power and determination fed into the portal, turning it into a bright light and stabilizing the rift between worlds. As the shimmering gateway steadied, it momentarily disabled the Passersby's ability to interact with Wade and August.

The Passersby prowling the room paused, disoriented, as if robbed of their power. They hovered on the edge of the light the six ghosts radiated, held at bay by the bridge they had created.

Clark muttered, "About time this place gave back some of what it took."

Minnie's arms shook, her concentration split between holding the portal steady and the dread creeping through her thoughts as she felt the horrible, awful power within the house, and Frank's terrible wrath pressing back against them. For a moment, Minnie caught sight of Frank's spirit, his face contorted with fury, hovering just beyond the edge of the glowing light of their barricade. His eyes, filled with venom and twisted betrayal, bored into hers. She looked away, but it didn't help. Images of demons, of the entity Frank had called Brightness of the blood Frank had shed to prolong his mortal life crept into her mind. She shuddered to clear it, wondering what went through the others' minds as they fought to maintain the gate for Wade.

The house's foundation trembled, a deep shudder shaking the walls and floors as Frank fought with all his demonic strength against their combined will. But it was too late for the house and its architect to win this war. Minnie, Clark, and Leah now understood that they were part of the web that held it together, and now they were unraveling it from within.

They had to succeed. They were Wade's last hope.

ɑ ꙅ

With Wade's arm clenched firmly in his hand, August had finally closed the last few inches toward the gate they'd fought so desperately to reach. Around them, the ghosts from either side of the temporal door had somehow protected them by surrounding Wade and him in an odd, spectral variation of ring-around-the-rosie. Now, just inches from the rift, the path was more treacherous than ever.

Frank, however, was not prepared to surrender. He'd clearly clued into the ghosts' intentions, and from the dark expression on his face, like a predator about to be denied his prey, he was prepared to fight like hell to keep them from passing.

He's only got seconds, though. What can he possibly do?

"Stay close," August said, pulling Wade forward by the front of his shirt. As he did, the world around them warped, twisting like melted glass. The distance to the portal stretched and expanded until what had been mere inches grew longer than the span of the Tennessee River. He nearly lost his footing, his balance thrown by the misshapen walls. The surrounding walls stretched into impossible angles as if the house had peeled open, showing them a nightmare reflection of itself.

Oh, shit. What the hell?

The house was Frank, was sentient, and it knew exactly how to mess with them. But if it was an illusion, it was a damn good one.

And yet—it didn't. The ghosts, their arms linked, were still in this version of the Wenke house and the other. Their bodies hadn't expanded. The six of them didn't appear distended at all. Their linked arms created a solid bridge between dimensions, while the house's shifting walls tried to push August and Wade backward using the distorted perception.

"It's an illusion!" August yelled so Wade could hear him over the clamor of the hovering, pulling, blocking ghosts who still fought to distract them from their mission.

It didn't feel like an illusion when the walls on either side, once terribly far apart, swiftly began closing in on them. Panic spiked. His body was instantly clammy with sweat, his palms slippery. August felt himself pulling in his elbows and other parts of him puckering up as well.

He tried not to think about Ez, Ida, and LaDonna, just a few feet behind them and desperately trying to come to their aid. He knew the house was still holding them fast, the wooden planks twisting around their bodies like gnarled vines. Their shouts echoed faintly through the distortion.

If we cross, this may be the trip that breaks Frank apart. Then we're all saved.

"Almost there," he said encouragingly to Wade. "Just a few inches more."

Frank, however, wasn't done with them yet.

The ghosts inched them closer, but the floor shuddered violently and turned slick with oil. August's eyes bugged. *If I fall, will the floor open up and swallow me? Can the ghosts get Wade across without me?*

ڃ   ࠉ

What is wrong with him? Why is he acting all weird? Harper's brow knit as she tilted her head from side to side, trying to see why the men quaked and hollered with fear.

August moved like he was underwater, slow and strange, as he and his companion strove to reach the thing on the wall. It had to be to another room, but that didn't explain why the edges of it looked so odd. Harper shook her head again in an attempt to dislodge the vertigo from what must be an atmosphere full of drugs. There was no other rational explanation for the sight before her eyes. It looked like two sets of identical ghosts with interlocking arms surrounded the two men. And all eight of them were moving as one to the hole in the wall. Could they all be suffering from a mass hallucination? Was that possible?

I can't risk a sloppy shot. I just can't.

She crept up to August, not wanting to distract him from where his attention was fixated on the weird mirror/not-mirror on the wall. When she reached within an arm's length, she slowly lifted her gun and took aim.

At the last possible second, August must have noticed a human-like motion among the swirling clouds of shimmering, pluming… whatever they were. *Drugs. That's what it is. Those cloud-looking things are all the drugs in the air!*

In a split-second, August twisted, eyes widening as he registered her presence and the gun in her hands. In one fluid motion, he dropped low, ducking as if he'd known she was there all along. Before she could react, he lunged, grabbing her and pulling them both to the ground. The gun fired, but the shot went wide, the bullet embedding into the wall behind him with a *puff* of flying horsehair plaster.

Dammit.

They grappled, his hands gripping her wrists, his face inches from hers. She could smell his sweat and felt the heat of this breath as she and August scrapped for the gun, his grip ironclad as he fought for control. Gritting her teeth, she twisted, wrenching herself free with a sharp tug that sent pain lancing up her arm. He yanked fervently, but Harper had chosen the weapon for a reason—it was the perfect size for her grip and nearly impossible to dislodge when she set her mind to it. She wrenched one hand free and pulled back, ready to slam the butt of her pistol in his face, but another tremor rattled the room, sending them both sprawling.

The floor shuddered like they were in the middle of a damn earthquake. The mirror on the wall flickered, its light dimming, growing erratic as the edges rippled like water. Whatever light it was emitting was slowly dimming, growing unstable. The strange, watery images of people standing in the room on the other side also darkened.

Something in the dark-haired man's face changed as he saw the mirror dimming. He lunged forward, grabbing her target, yanking him into a standing position, and half-dragging him toward the closing portal.

Shit no. No, no, no! I have to kill him! Her fingers tightened around August, her final ticket out of the game.

The mirror's light sputtered in and out, flickering like a candle caught in a storm. An Alabama earthquake—seriously? She'd have laughed if she weren't furious.

They fought, all three tangled together in a chaotic mess of limbs and determination. Harper clung to August, her grip unyielding as she fought to keep her balance. But the big guy's hold was unbreakable as well. His arms wrapped around August like a vise, dragging them closer and closer to the mirror's unstable light.

Panic clawed at her, a rare feeling, and one she hated. She'd taken on dangerous marks before, marks who fought back, but this—this was different. She knew now that this place was alive, twisting and bending with a force that defied reason. It wasn't drugs. She wasn't just fighting a man. She was fighting the house itself.

With one final, brutal lurch, the three of them toppled forward. Harper had one last, fleeting thought as they were pulled through the silver gate, a desperate, lingering hope that maybe, just maybe, she'd still get the chance to finish the job.

And then the world shattered into a blinding white, and they were gone.

⚃   ⚂

Holy crap, there's a kid here. Get the gun away from that crazy bitch!
August's mind reeled as if it, too, had been locked in a disorienting battle within a horrific funhouse. The woman with the gun—whoever she was—hadn't even seemed to realize they'd passed into an entirely different house. Well, not entirely, but close. She was relentless, wild, and only had eyes for August.

She found her feet quickly and crouched before him like an animal, ready to leap at him if the gun in her hand wasn't able to take the shot she'd planned. However, he refused to let go of her right wrist, which clutched the pistol, and she didn't appear to trust her left hand to take a swing at him effectively.

"What is *wrong* with you?" he screamed as he panted. "What do you want?"

"I... want... you... to... die!" she shouted, her words punctuated by a ferocious snarl. Her gaze darted to the wrist he held, assessing her next move. She twisted sharply, her entire body shifting as she lunged toward her ankle. August caught a glint of metal—a knife strapped in a holster.

Not happening.

Gritting his teeth, he twisted her arm and pulled her off balance. Her feet slipped on the unstable floor, and she let out a guttural growl as she stumbled. The knife was nearly within her grasp, but August wasn't going to let her use it. For a split second, she froze, eyes widening with rage and desperation. Then, with renewed fury, she clawed at his face with her free hand.

"Stop fighting me!" he shouted, though he wasn't sure if he was begging her or himself.

Drawing on every ounce of strength remaining, August yanked her toward the glowing portal. She screamed, the sound sharp and raw, and her nails raked his arm, leaving a searing red trail of pain, but he didn't let go.

With a final, desperate pull, he flung himself and the woman toward the portal. The world lurched violently around them, a phantasmagoria of color and noise. August's stomach churned as he forced the killer with him through the only open portal remaining, and together, they fell into the unknown.

03   80

In an instant, the air-conditioned world was replaced by a bone-chilling wasteland. The barren landscape stretched endlessly, a gray desert smothered in thick, choking ash that swirled in lazy, fat flakes. Their breaths plumed in gray mists, and dust settled on their clothes as he and his attacker stumbled, disoriented and coughing, kicking up clouds of ashy dust in their wake.

The sudden change of environment had finally gotten his attacker's attention, and her grip on the gun finally slipped and fell with a muted *thunk* into the dust. August hastily snatched it up and pounced to his feet, the unfamiliar feeling of the pistol warm in his grip. He carefully maneuvered himself between his attacker and the interdimensional door—a beckoning, undulating rift that only he could see.

Barely.

Each leap through the dimensional breaches had drained the herb's effects, wearing them down by degrees with every transition. Or perhaps the portal itself was collapsing. Or both.

Wild-eyed, she looked around herself furiously.

"Where are we?" she demanded. Her voice was muffled, strangely absorbed by the oppressive atmosphere.

August couldn't fight a smirk. "I'm pretty sure it's a nuclear winter," he replied.

He backed up slowly, not daring to turn his back on her until the portal was only inches away. The powdery ground crunched faintly beneath his boots, leaving faint trails behind him. He kept the gun level, his arm steady despite the adrenaline roaring.

The killer's wide eyes frantically sought whatever contrivance had brought them there, but saw nothing. Her eyes darted between him and the surrounding wasteland, her mind racing. August could see her frantic calculations, the growing realization that she was in a deadly situation and clueless about how to escape. He had the weapon. He had dropped them into this hellscape through a means only he knew, and he could vanish just as easily, leaving her stranded in this desolation to die.

He had to give her credit. She didn't beg or plead. She didn't make excuses for her behavior. The woman scrutinized every motion he made, though. She knew he was on his way out, though the means were a mystery to her.

The portal hovered inches from his ear. At this distance, without the chaos of Wenke's house to disguise it, August noticed how it droned like a hive of bees.

August tensed. He'd have to move fast—faster than her. The door was barely holding, its edges flickering like static, and she was advancing. He contemplated using the gun in his hand, but was too unfamiliar with handguns to try.

He jerked, ready to leap, but she was quicker than he'd anticipated. Her hand shot forward, fingers clawing through the air, nearly catching his ankle as he dove headfirst into the shimmering doorway.

The silver light engulfed him, and for one dizzying moment, he felt the pull of both worlds tearing at him. His ears rang like clarion bells, and his midsection burned like butane flame.

This is it. I'm stuck between two worlds. That bitch is going to split me in half!

Then he was through, landing hard on the floor of the well-preserved version of the Wenke home. Behind him, the *portal sealed with a soft, final hum, winking out like an old television and cutting off the wasteland—and her—for good.*

♋　♌

Cold gave way to warmth as August lay on the wooden floor, shedding ashy gray dust from the badlands. It wasn't home, but at least it wasn't deadly. Weak and unsteady from the jumps, he forced himself upright, brushing off his clothes in slow, clumsy motions. The polished wood planks beneath him, pristine and unscathed, gleamed like something out of a realtor's catalog. He felt disoriented, barely able to stay upright, and he was still breathless from tussling with the crazed woman who had tried to kill him.

August blinked, and grit scratched his eyes. He resisted the urge to rub them. His hands, caked with the same filth, would only make it worse.

The once-shimmering portal to the wasteland was now gone. Even if the portal hadn't collapsed, LaDonna's herb had depleted almost entirely with all the dimensional jumping he'd had to do.

The room around him felt surreal, and he wondered if he hadn't accidentally traveled into yet another unfamiliar dimension. That lasted until Wade entered the, catching August's arm with one hand while holding Derek securely in the other. Marina stood at their side. Wade, conscientious of the weapon in August's hand, gave the man a half-hug before August surrendered the weapon to the cop.

"You don't look so good, dude," Wade said, concerned.

August cast a glance back at the wall where the dimensional rift had been. There was no trace of it now, just an unremarkable stretch of freshly painted surface, and he was out of the precious herb needed to bring it back. His breathing had finally steadied, but the sight filled him with a sinking sense of loss. Ida was over there without him. Ida, the love of his life, who desperately hated being alone.

Wade followed his gaze, though August had little doubt that the other man saw nothing.

"Is it gone?"

"It's gone," he said, his voice hoarse. He coughed, and some of the grossness he'd recently inhaled became dislodged, making him grimace. "And I'm guessing Wenke's gone with it. Probably in your world and mine both. "

Wade's eyebrows drew together, and he frowned.

"What are you going to do?"

August took a deep, steadying breath. There was only one path forward, one plan that made any sense. If any of this insanity made sense.

"The only thing I can think of."

◌ ◌

The chaos ceased as abruptly as it had begun. The floor, the walls, and every once-distorted portion of the house had stilled as though nothing out of the ordinary had transpired. Ida blinked, her eyes wide, taking in the sudden serene atmosphere. The planks beneath her feet, though twisted like licorice, lay unmoving. The damage didn't look too terrible now that they'd ceased their attack.

"It was all an illusion," Ida breathed.

"I don't think so," LaDonna disagreed. "I think, however, that Frank's influence on the house is gone, and the magic that had once broken it has been destroyed. And I believe Frank is as well."

Ida lowered herself shakily onto the chair she'd been standing on. Maybe it was the calm in LaDonna's words. Perhaps it was the inexplicable way the house had come alive and now stood silent and serene in the summer afternoon, but Ida would swear the ominous presence looming within the house was now absent.

Rebecca sat nearby on the edge of another chair, her posture tense, as though braced for something else to go wrong. She exhaled slowly, her gaze shifting from the warped floorboards to the ceiling, the walls, and the windows, now cracked, the sharp shards sprinkled on the busted floor. Her scientific mind visibly struggled to reconcile what she'd just witnessed.

"Do you know who that woman was?" Ez asked.

Ida shook her head with an angry frown. "No. But I have a feeling I know who sent her."

◌ ◌

Later, August and Wade stood just beyond the threshold of the house. August talked Wade into going home with his family, but not without resistance. Wade had been reluctant to leave, his protective instincts at war with the reality that his family needed him now more than ever.

"You need to go home with your family," August said firmly, his voice low but unyielding.

Wade folded his arms, his jaw tightening. "You really think I'm going to leave you here? Alone? You don't even belong in this world."

"I don't belong here. But you do," August countered, looking over Wade's shoulder to where his family stood on the front step. "They need you, Wade. Your son needs you."

Wade hesitated, his resolve wavering. Finally, he exhaled and held out his hand. August peered at him blankly.

"Give me your phone. Let me put my number in. Just in case."

August took the phone and frowned at the screen, where the dreaded words NO SERVICE loomed. "You realize this doesn't work here, right?"

"It's not about the phone," Wade said, his tone softer. "It's about knowing there's someone on the other end if you figure it out. If you need me, you know how to find me—or go to the station. Zeke can help you. He might not be Ez, but he'll help you. Any of us can."

August handed the phone back, a weary smile tugging at his lips. "Not with this," he said, gesturing vaguely to the world around them. "But I have an idea who might be able to."

Wade stared at him for a long moment, as though he wanted to argue but knew better. With a reluctant nod, he turned back toward his family. Rebecca was already climbing into her Subaru, and Wade's family was loading into their vehicle. As the engines started, the weight of their absence settled over him.

Once they were gone, the world felt quieter. August stood there for a moment longer, gathering himself, before turning toward the now-familiar trail through the woods. The path was worn, and the crunch of his boots on the underbrush was the only sound he heard as he made his way to the Whelens' house.

August hesitated at the door, taking a steadying breath. He'd been here before, but not like this—not as a stranger. Lifting his hand, he knocked, the sound echoing dully against the wood.

For a moment, he thought no one would answer, the silence inside the house stretching unnervingly long. Then the door eased open, revealing two familiar faces—familiar to him, anyway.

"Hello," Luke said, his affable grin lighting up his face. He leaned casually against the doorframe, his sharp eyes scanning August with curiosity. "I had a feeling someone was coming over."

LaDonna appeared beside him, her warm smile as inviting as ever. "Would you like a glass of tea?" she asked, gesturing for him to come inside.

"Nah," Luke interjected before August could respond. He tilted his head, studying him for a beat longer. "This guy doesn't need tea. He needs a smoke."

The comment startled a laugh from August, the tension easing just enough for him to step inside. "I, uh... I need to tell y'all an incredible story," he said, his voice tinged with both exhaustion and a hint of hope.

Luke and LaDonna exchanged glances, their expressions a mix of intrigue and amusement. "Well," LaDonna said, closing the door behind him, "you've come to the right place."

As they led him into their home, August felt the weight of his situation starting to lighten. These people didn't know him yet—but as they did in his world, they already felt like home.

⚃ ⚂

The light was sudden, powerful, and blinding, enveloping Leah in a warmth so intense it was almost overwhelming. She couldn't see anything but knew her friends were beside her. She could feel them. Feel their love, their strong presence. Their support.

"Where are we?" she thought, or rather, the thought existed without words or sound. In this place, words were felt more than spoken, like thoughts manifesting in the purest form.

"I think we've moved beyond the house." Minnie's reply came as a pulse of knowing.

The atmosphere felt crystalline, light, unending, as though she were floating in an endless, shimmering space. She sensed herself stretching out, unbound, weightless, her essence capable of expanding or shrinking. The freedom was intoxicating, as if her consciousness could drift for days, expanding freely for eternity or the power to contract to a single atom, whatever she chose.

"This is wild," Leah thought, marveling at the sensation.

"It certainly is," Minnie replied, her amusement evident even in this inexplicable formless realm.

Another being approached them. Not seen, but felt. Happy. Patient. Caring. Its presence warmed Leah and stirred familiar feelings and joyful memories.

"Hello, Leah." The words resonated within her, pure and gentle, and the feeling behind them was familiar and full of such deep compassion it made her soul ache.

"Bu-Bobby?" Leah replied.

"Your baby's father?" Minnie asked. She didn't keep it private, for life was open and unguarded where they were. There was no need for secrets, and there was no guilt, no shame.

"Yes," Leah breathed. She sent her formless presence to the being who had drawn near, and they embraced as only eternal beings can, their bond untouched by time or regret.

Together, they shared a moment that spanned eternity, an embrace without form or boundary, two souls reunited in a timeless, endless space they now called home.

℘   ℘

"It's been a really long time," Ida said. Her attention hadn't left the wall where August left for several minutes.

"Do you think the portal's gone?" Sergio asked, hesitant. "It looked like it was getting weaker toward the end."

"Don't say that," Ida snapped. Sergio only nodded, understanding. She wasn't ready for doubt. Not yet

So, they waited. After thirty minutes, Ida's heart grew heavy. After an hour, that weight had become a cold, unmoving ache lodged in her chest. But still, she waited. And they stayed with her. She paced, noting as she did that many of the strange items once carved into the mantles and banisters were cracked and tarnished.

Not gone yet. When August came back, they'd see to removing all of that crap.

If August came back.

Rebecca finally left after an hour, making sure to give her information to everyone present so they had a means to contact her in the event something happened — or if they needed her help.

Ninety minutes into their vigil, Ez's phone rang. The sound was so unexpected that everyone in the room jumped. Ida's breath caught as Ez raised the phone to his ear.

"Hello?"

The voice at the other end was muffled, but Ida saw how Ez's face transformed, his eyes widening with surprise, his mouth growing into an almost disbelieving smile. He interrupted the speaker.

"Hold on, hold on. Just a second. I'm going to put you on speaker." He pushed the button and increased the volume so the whole room could hear.

"I said I've got a guy here named August Webb. He asked me to call y'all and let you know he was OK. That he came back at the warehouse? I'm guessing that makes sense to y'all for some reason."

A collective sigh of relief swept over the room, so powerful it felt almost physical. Ida slumped into a chair, her knees weak, feeling the overwhelming emotional flood surge through her. If she hadn't sat down, she might have melted to the floor.

"It does," Ez told the woman on the phone. "Thanks, Yolanda."

"Uh-huh," Yolanda replied, a hint of curiosity in her voice. "See you tomorrow."

They glanced at each other, hesitant smiles breaking through the lingering tension. Ida closed her eyes, letting the last of her anxiety melt away. August was home.

As they sat in the quiet, a faint creak echoed from deep within the house — a lingering reminder of the spirits who'd helped them. Ida couldn't be sure if they were still there. She wouldn't know for sure until she returned with August, but something in her heart told her the house was finally at peace.

Yes, there were new challenges to face. Soon, she'd have to confront her parents and uncover the truth behind their attempt on August's life. But tonight, none of that mattered. Tonight, they'd be together.

She felt it for the first time in as long as she could remember — an unfamiliar sense of freedom, a quiet they'd fought so hard to reclaim.

They were free.

Support

Indie

Authors

BUY

READ

REVIEW

www.ingramcontent.com/pod-product-compliance
Lightning Source LLC
Chambersburg PA
CBHW061648190726
48289CB00006B/1785